JESUS
THE SECOND ADAM

A NOVEL ABOUT JESUS AND MARY MAGDALENE

Pietro Marchitelli

To Ken with
appreciation
God bless you and
your family
Pietro Marchitelli

Published for Pietro Marchitelli by
Paragon House
1925 Oakcrest Avenue, Suite 7
St. Paul, MN 55113

Library of Congress Cataloging-in-Publication Data

Marchitelli, Pietro, 1957-
Jesus, the second Adam / by Pietro Marchitelli.
    p. cm.
Summary: "An aging Mary Magdalene tells the story of her life with Jesus and reveals secrets about his birth, his death, their life together, and the association with John the Baptist that led to Jesus' crucifixion"--Provided by publisher.
ISBN 978-0-89226-109-3 (pbk. : alk. paper)
1. Mary Magdalene, Saint--Fiction. 2. Jesus Christ--Fiction. 3. John, the Baptist, Saint--Fiction. 4. Bible. N.T. Gospels--History of Biblical events--Fiction. I. Title.
PS3613.A7347J47 2011
813'.6--dc22
                    2010053165

The paper used in this publication meets the minimum requirements of American National Standard for Information Sciences—Permanence of Paper for Printed Library Materials, ANSIZ39.48-1984.

Manufactured in the United States of America
    10 9 8 7 6 5 4 3 2 1

Book website: www.JesustheSecondAdam.com

What if Jesus had a biological father?

What if Jesus was not God, but a man who earned his perfection?

What if Jesus was married?

What if John the Baptist's uncommitted attitude cost the life of Jesus?

What if Jesus' destiny was not to die on the cross?

Would your faith fade away or would you still love him as your Messiah?

I would, as always.

PREFACE

I DIDN'T REALIZE IT THEN, but there was no other path than the one I took. I followed Jesus as he asked me to. I have no regrets.

By being constantly beside him, I learned much about his life, but I learned even more after his ascension to heaven.

He appears to me in many guises and conveys his feelings. He tells me of those sorrowful souls who are in the spiritual world now. He meets and talks with the very people who once crossed his life on earth. They share with him things that only they could know, confessing their frustration and sorrow for not having understood him. Through those spiritual visits, I came to understand all of them and the important events of their lives, particularly those moments that directly or indirectly had an impact on Jesus' life.

Who was Jesus? Who was his father? How was he born? What profound truths was he trying to convey to us?

It is necessary to say that his life was not an ordinary life. Jesus was an incomparable man, and his life was exceptional even before his birth.

CHAPTER 1

IT WAS EARLY AUTUMN, seventy years after the birth of Jesus of Nazareth, and Mary Magdalene's wrinkled face and dark eyes reflected both the joy and the sorrow in her spirit. She pondered her long life, which had begun in a fishing village by the Sea of Galilee. Her mind was still keen enough to recall many events during the four decades since the tragic crucifixion of Jesus.

She was an old woman whose heart was scarred by the painful memory of God's precious one, chosen to make the blood of Abraham known to all the world. He was nailed to a wooden cross on the hill at Golgotha, slowly suffocating as Roman soldiers mocked and ridiculed him at his feet. She and other faithful followers had stood nearby, wanting to comfort him, yet too frightened to do anything but watch.

Mary Magdalene fixed a silent gaze on the distant horizon of the Aegean Sea, its choppy waters dotted by sailing craft. The soothing sound of a steady breeze moved through the leaves and branches of nearby trees. Sighing, Mary brooded over the shocking reports of General Titus' army destroying the Holy Temple in Jerusalem. Roman Emperor Vespasian and his indomitable legions were now masters of all lands encircling the Mediterranean Sea, and the once proud Judean capital of Jerusalem was strewn with lifeless bodies amid crumbled walls and dwellings. She had heard that as the victorious Roman soldiers gathered the wounded and emaciated survivors of the forty-seven-day siege, a horrific wailing echoed the shattered hopes of terrified children and women as they mourned lost fathers and husbands, who had been either butchered or sold off into slavery.

General Titus, acting upon the directives of his father, Emperor Vespasian, had brutally subjugated Jerusalem and other Jewish enclaves that opposed Roman rule. After the fall of Jerusalem, Titus marched his army northward to the towns along the western shore of the Sea of Galilee. At Magdala, they inflicted particular cruelty on the inhabitants, killing every single one of them, leaving the once peaceful town bare of any human breath. Many of the residents had attempted to flee by boat but instead met violent deaths by the archers on the Roman vessels. Titus had hoped his victory over the Galileans would teach a harsh lesson to the zealous Jews who had recently dared to compete with the divinity of the emperor.

Mary Magdalene knew well why the Roman generals had been so eager to destroy Magdala. The emperor himself had likely heard of a new community of believers sprouting up from within the Jewish population. After all, a few years earlier Emperor Nero had burned down much of Rome. In a wily move, he shifted the blame for the fire to a mysterious group of people who worshiped a Galilean carpenter who was *resurrected from death*. Though he was born a common man, his followers believed he was the Son of the One God, a Savior for all people on earth. So a few days after the fire, the Roman elite had become aware of this radical group of believers and their glorified Savior, whom they called Jesus the Christ.

What was General Titus' real objective in destroying Magdala? What were Roman soldiers actually looking for when they sacked the town before slaughtering its entire population?

The answer was very clear in Mary's heart. "I have known and attended the most remarkable man who has ever walked upon the earth," she muttered under her breath. Over the decades, she had repeated this statement many times. Since Jesus' crucifixion, she had been as strong as a watchtower, protecting her secrets from those who meant him harm. What precious knowledge had she protected all these many years?

Here I am, on the island of Patmos, she thought, glancing at the hopeful faces of the men, women and children sitting around her. *Yes, I am old and tired ... tired of a life in which I had to hide my true identity from those who have no mercy for our Lord. The enemies of our Lord are eager to destroy all traces of his life ....* The thought trailed off as the sound of crashing waves rose from the rocks below. Yawning, she sat on a wooden bench under a fig tree as the sunlight filled the landscape. She looked too frail to control her emotions, yet she drew strength from some inner force.

With a sudden smile, she uttered, "Although I am sick and weary, I delight in the company of my two children, Isaac and Sara, who share this serene island with me. Like you, we live in a violent world, but here on Patmos I have found peace by keeping my identity a secret. Yes, there are moments when I want to shout into the wind, telling everyone that I am the most fortunate woman in the world, because I knew closely the most magnificent man the world has ever known."

She paused, taking a deep breath as if to push back the sting of longing for her beloved. "My heart longs to pass into the divine world invisible to human eyes," she lamented. "The kingdom of my beloved Jesus is a bright world within my heart. Yet this world of flesh often distracts me from living fully there with our Lord.

"Naturally, I would have wanted Jesus to remain with us during our journey through this earthly world. There were many instances when I needed his guidance. Yet he did appear to me, at times, addressing me in a comforting tone, saying, 'Mary, you know the ways of the Lord. I will always be with you.' I knew him, and I have tried to help others come to know him through me. Yet, I am a woman without the gift for telling stories like those Jesus had told to the souls of defeated men. If Jesus had remained with us for many years, how much more could he have shown the world? And our children would have known a father like no other. Jesus was a true father to us all, loving us completely and unconditionally. Each man, woman, boy, and girl was a child to him, even those who had committed horrible crimes. He never turned one person away, nor did he ever turn one person against another for his sake. Even those who mocked and brutalized him, and eventually murdered him, were his children whom he could not hate. Even before Jesus' death, our own children and I lived like nomads, finding no place to settle in peace."

Overcome with emotion, Mary Magdalene paused to catch her breath. Who was she speaking to? Who was this story for? As she watched the gulls flying overhead, she recalled the conversation with the scholar who had given her the news of General Titus' conquest of Jerusalem and other Jewish strongholds.

A few hours later, Mary had decided to devote her final years on earth to creating a record of Jesus' life. She would draw on her personal experiences with him, no matter how painful it might prove to be to revisit those distant years of their friendship.

With a clear vision that renewed her strength and resolve, she had approached the scholar and instructed him in a motherly tone, "Take this pouch of coins and purchase writing tools for me."

As Mary replayed the scene in her mind, she soon realized that her obligation to record his life story was similar to what Jesus must have felt upon accepting his fate. His story, as accurate as she could record it, had to be put down on papyrus so his words and deeds would remain eternally alive, just as he lived eternally.

Bringing her thoughts back to the present, Mary observed the scholar as he positioned himself in front of a simple board table under the shade of a date palm. With a serious expression, he set the writing tools on the table and closed his deep-set eyes as if in prayer. Moments later, he opened his eyes and pressed the pheasant quill pen against the papyrus scrolls, paying close attention to Mary's words as she continued speaking.

"I remember the first time I saw Jesus," she thought aloud, looking at the people sitting around her, eager to hear her testimony. "I was taking a jug of water to my father and his workers at the shore. My father owned several fishing boats and was in need of a skillful carpenter to repair a few of his battered boats and build some new ones. Others had refused because they felt that my father didn't pay enough for the labor he demanded.

My father was not an easy man to please, so he had to look outside the town of Magdala for skillful carpenters. Through word of mouth, the name of a reliable carpenter from Nazareth came to his ears.

Jesus had been raised as the son of a carpenter. And for a young man who possessed an open mind, along with a great vision for life, the village of Nazareth had become too small for his dreams. So he began lending his services to villages and towns by the Sea of Galilee, where he had perfected his skills in repairing fishing boats.

"One afternoon I left the house, searching for my father, whom I found by the boat moorings. On the way there, I noticed Jesus' silhouette. He was returning to get a tool he had left behind at the house. When we drew close, we gave each other a polite greeting. I offered him a friendly smile, and our eyes met. He focused intently upon my face, seeming to look deep into my soul.

"Blushing, I felt as if I were suddenly naked. I couldn't hide anything. But Jesus' eyes radiated kindness and serenity. This took me by surprise because I was so used to coarse men who undressed me with lustful stares. Though Jesus' stare was more intense than that of other men, there was no hint of lust. It both revealed and erased all past unpleasant stares. I felt that Jesus was replacing them with a sense of honor."

Mary paused and moved her eyes to the coastline, fearing that it would be impossible to convey her first impressions of Jesus. As if speaking to the sea breeze, she murmured, "I recall that while his eyes penetrated mine, his lips produced the sound of greeting, a voice that opened a new portal to my soul. The tone was cordial, but firm and resolute. I sensed that I was in the presence of an unusual energy.

"During the following days, my initial impression of Jesus remained with me as he continued his work with zeal. I could see that he wanted to create a perfect boat for my father. He scrutinized his own work, often doing a particular task over and over again. He wasn't even satisfied when my demanding father commented it was the best craftsmanship he had seen. In fact, Jesus labored as if he were trying to raise the standard beyond the highest expectations. His work humbled my father to the point where for the first time in my life, I heard my father remark, 'I am very pleased with your efforts,' as he paid Jesus in advance the full price he had promised.

"Believe me, this was very different from previous scenes when a worker asked for his pay after a completed job. Somehow my father always held onto a portion of the pay, causing the worker to argue and scream before stomping away, angrily spitting at the ground with curses directed toward him. I always feared the repercussions of the curses upon our family. But my father righteously defended his actions and his standards as a covenant with God. He held a high standard for himself and his family. We followed the Mosaic laws to the letter, measured by the strict tradition of our ancestors.

"Once, I returned home well after sunset on the Sabbath, upsetting my father. So I was punished by having to stay in a dark room for a whole day. My mother delivered meals to me with sympathetic expressions. Yet she never once criticized my father. So I remained isolated from the full light of pity and love. My father approached all people with severe scrutiny. Amazingly, this Jesus of Nazareth was beyond my father's scorn by exceeding his high standards, not only in workmanship but also as a man and a follower of the laws of Moses.

"Jesus stayed with our family, and soon we all noticed exceptional qualities in this kind and intelligent Nazarene. Some people said he was not only a diligent carpenter but an honest and trustworthy man who couldn't rest until he fulfilled a commitment. Yet there were others who traded in vicious gossip about him, claiming he couldn't be trusted because the identity of his real father was unknown. When I first heard these rumors, I couldn't help but feel confused and saddened.

"I looked forward to seeing Jesus whenever I delivered water and bread to him and the other workers. His smile, his appearance, his behavior and way of speaking had a strange power over me. I came to realize that Jesus' character was as pure as gold, and he brought a kind of perfection to his every word and action, as if by doing so he was bringing us all closer to the very likeness of the Lord God.

"From the moment of our first greeting, my mind was preoccupied with thoughts of Jesus. I found myself oddly attracted to him. Though comfortable in his presence, I also felt extremely timid and unsure of myself. I sensed that he was somehow profoundly familiar with my life, even more so than members of my own family. At the same time, I felt that I knew nothing about him. My feelings ... the rumors ... every smile and glance and whisper ... it was all spinning inside my head like a whirlwind coming off the stormy sea.

Soon I yearned to be alone with Jesus, without having the eyes of others fixed on us. Yet such a situation was unacceptable for a maiden such as myself. As the days passed, I felt trapped in a labyrinth of social courtesies. I could only greet Jesus in public under my father's sharp gaze. I could never inquire about his life or family ties, much less ask him to dispel the malicious rumors. Fortunately, about four weeks after his arrival to our town, a moment arose when Jesus and I had the opportunity to meet without others nearby.

As we ran into each other on a footpath near a grove of olive trees, he did not seem surprised, and he gave me a luminous smile. "Mary, how are you today?"

"Fine," I blurted out, not able to look him in the eyes.

He stared at me a long moment, the afternoon sunlight caressing his reddish-brown hair. Finally he said, "You are a polite and gentle young lady, but your heart is heavy. Is something bothering you?"

I was a bit startled, yet not completely surprised by his candor. Fumbling for something to say, I replied, "It's a lovely morning. Where are you going?"

"Yesterday your uncle asked me to repair some tables at his home." After a long pause, he added with a twinkle in his eye, "You want to know more about me ... who I am, and where I am from."

Speechless, I nodded.

"But you know me, don't you?" he said. "You watch me work beside your father, and I share meals with your family. You have even watched me while reading prayers."

I gave a noncommittal shrug, glancing at two singing sparrows on the fragile branch of a nearby sapling.

Looking softly into my eyes, Jesus added, "Mary, the real questions to ask should be directed at yourself. *Who am I, and where did I come from?*"

His statement so confounded me that I wanted to point at him and shout that he was a demon and run to the safety of my home. Yet I stayed, allowing his words to travel through my heart, hoping they could take rein over the wild thoughts and feelings possessing me. By this point neither of us could look into the other's eyes. I felt him speaking to me, yet he was not talking aloud.

When he finally did say something, it was with concern. "Am I keeping you from your chores?"

Yes! I suddenly recalled that I was on my way to get a fish for our evening meal. I hadn't noticed the sun lowering in the sky, so I would need to hurry. "I must hurry. I am helping my mother with dinner."

"Don't worry, you have enough time. Always carry out your tasks with joy. I'll see you at supper." He dipped his head in respect and allowed me to pass.

As I hurried off, I felt the experience of our encounter living within me, and I attended to my various tasks with a lightened spirit. In fact, I enjoyed preparing the evening meal so much that I didn't notice my father and Jesus sitting at the table in the next room, engaged in a serious discussion.

Dinner was delightful. Everyone ate bread, grilled fish, beans, and melons. I listened to Jesus as he spoke to my parents about Jacob's twenty-one years in Haran while working for his Uncle Laban. After the meal, my father thanked me for making the fish so delicious and asked me to sit with them while my mother cleaned up.

When she left the room, my father took my hand and said affectionately, "Marion, my little blossom ..." I was surprised, for he hadn't called me this pet name since I was a child.

After a few seconds, his eyes grew moist, as he continued, "My precious daughter, you have grown into a beautiful woman. This past year I have noticed how some men have begun to look at you. So I've been praying for the Lord to grant me the ability to protect you until He sent the right man for you, someone whose love would be even greater than mine." He paused, making a subtle gesture at Jesus. "Mary, I believe that man has arrived."

My heart leaped as my father added in a level voice, "Jesus and I have been discussing the future. With my blessing I want you to discuss the possibility of your future with him."

This last statement baffled me. I was expecting my father to have already made the betrothal contract, as a father would usually do before speaking to his daughter.

Seeing the confusion in my eyes, my father added, "As Jesus requested, the two of you shall talk before any decisions are made. After I turn in for the night, you can remain here and discuss the matter with him."

Feeling a shortness of breath, I remained silent as my father pushed back his chair and stood, his gaze lingering as he walked toward the corridor leading to his room at the back of the house.

When I returned my gaze to Jesus, I noticed his concerned expression.

"Are you all right?" he asked quietly. His lips curled upward. "Is there a problem with your father's request?"

Too ruffled to express my thoughts, I wondered if it was Jesus or my father who had first broached the subject of marriage.

Jesus cleared his throat. "Do you have any questions?"

I chose my words carefully. "Tell me what you expect of me," I said plainly.

He replied in a serious tone, "Mary, are you ready to travel with me on a road never traveled before?"

Although to this day I remember these words exactly as he said them, at first they took me by complete surprise.

Turning slightly, I glanced at the moonlight outside the window and tried to relieve the dryness in my throat by swallowing. As I considered Jesus' question, I realized that sharing my life with this man would be very different from anything I had known before in our village. I shifted anxiously in the chair, trying to imagine what my life would be like if I were his wife and where on earth would this untraveled road lead to?

Leaning forward, his hands folded, Jesus added matter-of-factly, "Mary, I sense in you some very special qualities not apparent in other girls your age ..."

"I'm not a girl," I inserted. "I will be seventeen next ..."

"I know, I know." His eyes danced with amusement. "Unlike other young women, you have many fine qualities that I find, well, admirable. You're loving and caring, and you maintain a humble attitude of service toward your parents, as well as toward others in the community. This brings great joy to my Father in heaven."

As I digested his words, I felt that Jesus wanted certain qualities in a woman, so that upon marriage she would be receptive to his guidance. But why? How could I, in my ignorance, imagine the weight of responsibility

I would have to carry in future years? And how could he claim such intimacy with *his Father in heaven*?

Jesus and I spoke for several more minutes, and then I asked him if I could retreat to my place of prayer before making a decision.

He agreed to my request and that night I could not sleep a wink.

Since this Jesus of Nazareth was a special person, I knew he would require a special woman to be his wife. Yet he must have thought I was a good and decent woman, or he wouldn't have made the offer.

On the other hand, what trials and hardships did I have to overcome in order to fulfill my potential? And did I want to place myself in a position of such pain and anguish? Jesus had already challenged me in unexpected ways, yet I hoped that the sweet joy that I would experience with him would supersede all difficulties that may lie before us.

Since childhood I had known that I wouldn't become an ordinary fisherman's wife. Yet, I never imagined someone like Jesus for a husband. If we married, I knew intuitively that what I learned from him would far exceed anything I could accomplish on my own. The adventurous nature within me rejoiced at the thought, but my more cautious side resisted the notion of accepting his proposal.

Throughout my long night of uncertainty, I was unaware of Jesus' own concerns about me. Years later, I learned that he was aware that if I became his wife, then my course would be as difficult as his. He knew that he would at once be teaching me and needing my support.

During my early years with Jesus, I couldn't fully comprehend much of his thinking. His reality was not my reality, and his vision for the world was not my vision.

CHAPTER 2

I AM EMBARRASSED to admit that I didn't enjoy good relations with the mother of our Lord until I grew stronger in my faith and began to follow Jesus more seriously. It was only during the latter years of his ministry that my mother in-law and I grew close, our souls merging. I cherish my memories of those days when we were able to spend quiet time together, getting to know each other intimately, both of us terrified for the fate of the man we loved.

One particular day remains very clear in my memory. It was a lovely spring afternoon in Capernaum. Jesus was in the countryside with his disciples. Mary and I were drinking tea in the courtyard, and she began to share her feelings about her son's conception and birth. Although Jesus had told me some of the stories surrounding his birth, Mary was more interested in revealing the personal struggles that she and her family faced during her pregnancy. She was only fifteen at the time. Caesar Augustus was emperor of the Roman Empire, and Herod was king of Israel, which for the past four centuries had been under the subjugation of the Persians, the Greeks, and now the Romans.

Mary had a kind and generous nature, and she was totally dedicated to her family. Unlike most other girls her age, she nurtured in her heart a profound faith in God, while humbly serving both friends and strangers, dutifully following the laws and commandments. With an innocent and pure soul that inspired almost everyone who knew her, Mary was betrothed to Joseph, a young man living in the same town of Nazareth.

This is a small, peaceful town in the mountainous region of Galilee. As the crow flies, Nazareth is about seventy miles north of Jerusalem, and twenty miles to the east of the Great Sea. About six miles west of Nazareth is Mount Tabor, and near its base passes the main road for traffic between Egypt and Damascus, and beyond to the great cities of interior Asia.

The honored tradition of our culture is parents' choosing a husband or wife for their children. This was the case for Mary and Joseph, whose engagement had been arranged by their parents. All the same, Joseph and Mary had been fond of each other as children, and a deep sentiment of love blossomed as they grew older. Indeed, as Mary revealed to me, by the time they were engaged they were very much in love and looked forward to the day of their marriage. Caleb and Azuba, the parents of Mary, were very pleased because they had enjoyed a long and cordial friendship with Joseph's parents. So both families joyfully took to the task of making plans for the wedding celebration that was to take place in Nazareth in about three weeks.

One typical summer day, Mary and her father were returning to Nazareth riding on two donkeys. Mary grew happier by the moment as she pictured embracing her dear mother whom she had not seen in more then four months. Mary had been staying at the home of her cousin Elizabeth and her husband, Zechariah, the elderly priest in Ain Karem, a village west of Jerusalem in the hill country of Judea.

Zechariah and Elizabeth had been childless during their long marriage. Yet one day while Zechariah was tending to his sacred duties at the temple, an angel of the Lord appeared to him. Trembling with fear, Zechariah listened in amazement as the angel Gabriel announced that Elizabeth would give birth to a son. This child was to be named John, and he would become a great man who could lead the people back to the righteous ways of God, preparing the way for the coming Messiah. Since both Elizabeth and Zechariah were quite old, he questioned Gabriel's prophecy. In anger, Gabriel made Zechariah temporarily mute, which shocked the local inhabitants. Yet after a period of time, Elizabeth was indeed with child, and five months later her cousin Mary had come to stay with her.

Separated from her parents, Mary had waited anxiously for her father to come and bring her back to Nazareth. As soon as Mary saw the outer houses of Nazareth, one of her cousins spotted them approaching, so he hurried to their house and gave the good news to Mary's mother.

Azuba shouted out with joy. After months of separation, she could finally embrace her lovely Mary! She dropped what she was doing and hurried to the front room. She stuck her head out the open window and looked down the roadway, longing to see her husband and daughter. They had just turned the corner by the time she stepped outside to receive them, barely containing her happiness. But she remained on the porch, waving her hands and calling out their names as they drew closer. To Azuba, it felt as though the sun were shining its light through Mary's beaming smile. Clearly her emotions could be read on her face.

As Mary's father helped her off the donkey, Azuba scurried over to her. "My darling, Mary!" she cried out, with a leaping heart. She wrapped her arms around her daughter's shoulders, tightly embracing her.

Through muffled sobs, Mary uttered, "Mama, I'm so happy to be home. I missed everyone so much." Perhaps, Mary admitted to me later, there was something obvious in this display of emotion.

"Oh, we have missed you too." Gaining control of her emotions, Azuba stepped back from her daughter and saw that her clothes were covered with dust. Noticing her pale skin and the sickly look in her eyes, she couldn't help asking, "Are you ill, my child?"

"I believe so. It must be from the journey." She pushed a smile to her lips. "There's no need to worry. I will feel better after a long sleep. But first, I want to see Joseph."

"He's not here," replied Azuba. "Last week he left for the coast. His cousin in Caesarea has a boat now. So he asked Joseph to come lend a hand with the fishing."

Mary couldn't hide her disappointment.

"Don't pout. Joseph will be back soon."

For the next two days, Azuba went about her daily tasks while Mary rested in her room, bedridden with a stomachache and periods of dizziness.

Early the following morning, Mary suddenly awoke with an awful pain in her stomach. Without forethought she crawled from the straw bedding and made it outside just before vomiting several times. Her eyes burning, she wiped her mouth and straightened up to see her mother standing beside her, a concerned look on her face.

That afternoon, Mary grew sick again. Dark shadows beneath her eyes, she went to her mother and hugged her as tears rolled down her cheeks.

A bit frightened, Azuba soaked a clean rag with cold water, then placed it on her daughter's neck and forehead, hoping she was merely suffering from a minor ailment contracted during her journey. But Mary's headaches and nausea grew worse, and Azuba became more anxious with each minute.

A week had passed since Mary returned from her visit. The very thought of food made her sick, so she refused to eat any meals. And though she rarely left her room, she began losing weight, causing both her father and mother to speculate that maybe she had been stricken with a serious illness.

The next day, Azuba awoke from her usual afternoon nap and sat on the porch reflecting on the health of her daughter. She began to have suspicions that something terrible had happened to Mary while she was staying with Elizabeth.

Although she didn't want to admit it, Azuba soon realized that Mary's symptoms were those of a woman carrying a child in her womb. But to think that her young, unmarried daughter could be pregnant was beyond any comprehension.

That same afternoon, Mary awoke from her nap and got dressed for the first time in two days. After deep thought, she knew the truth would come to light and she would be confronted with the idea that she might be with child. She stepped onto the porch and sat next to her mother. They remained silent for a few minutes, afraid to say what they were both thinking. With a tiny sigh, Mary scooted closer to Azuba, resting her head on her mother's lap, just as she had done so many times as a child.

Azuba stroked her daughter's long, silky hair, wondering.

Wishing she had never visited her cousin's home, Mary straightened up and looked at her mother's face. "Mama, I have to talk with you."

Azuba tried to suppress her emotions. "Yes, my dear."

Mary stammered, "Try to keep calm."

"Did something happen to you?"

She shook her head. "No, Mama … I don't know how to tell you …" Mary's voice trailed.

Azuba's sun-weathered face turned even redder, her eyes wide open as she tried to read her daughter's thoughts. "Mary, you are scaring me." She waited a long moment. "What happened that caused your … illness? Tell me!"

The girl took in a gulp of air. "Mama, it's been a while since I had menstruation."

"What?" she blurted out, as if the news were a shock.

Mary avoided her mother's icy stare. "Mama, I am not certain, but I could be pregnant …"

"What? But how? I won't believe it!"

"I'm sorry …"

"How? You aren't even married yet!" Breathing with difficulty, Azuba made an angry gesture.

Not wanting the neighbors to hear, she took a deep breath and spoke in a hushed voice, "Oh, that Joseph. I could strangle him." Azuba lowered her eyes in despair. "Why?"

"Mama, we didn't." Mary's voice was barely audible. "I promise, we didn't."

Azuba wasn't even listening. "What will I tell your father?" she moaned, half to herself. "Even though you and Joseph are promised, this is forbidden. And your child! Everyone will treat your child with disrespect."

"Mama! I haven't been with Joseph …"

"My God! What are you saying? Don't make this worse than it is."

Mary shook her head again. "No, Mama … It wasn't my betrothed …"

"My God! My God!" cried Azuba. "What have you done to yourself? Your father will kill you with his bare hands. Have you no shame?"

Mary was so distraught she couldn't find the strength to utter a sound in defense of herself. She stared blankly at the cloudless sky, wishing she were a child again.

Wringing her hands, Azuba cried, "Your father and I don't deserve this. Think of the disgrace it will bring down upon us." Pausing, she looked directly at her daughter's tear-stained face. "If it isn't Joseph, who then? Tell me!"

Hoping to keep her secret close to her bosom, Mary replied in a tense whisper, "Mama, I cannot tell you what happened. I am sorry … but I cannot tell you."

Azuba tried to make sense of the situation, but she only became more befuddled. *It must have happened in the town where Elizabeth and Zechariah live,* she thought with growing concern.

Not wishing to worsen the state of her daughter's poor health, especially since she was carrying an unborn child, Azuba put a calm tone to her voice. "My dear, we can talk more calmly after a day of prayer." She stood and pulled Mary to her feet, giving her a reluctant hug. "Considering the situation, it's wise for you to stay with your Aunt Sara. I will try to explain your condition to your father. He'll be hurt and angry. But hopefully he won't harm you. After a few days, maybe you can return and discuss the matter with him and Joseph."

Mary went to Sara and Maleb's farm just south of Nazareth, and Azuba remained at home, nervously waiting for Caleb to return home from work. She knew it wouldn't be easy to speak to him about their daughter's condition, but she tried to keep control of her fears.

That evening at her aunt's house, Mary began to feel better as she mended an old quilt that had belonged to her maternal grandmother. When Mary arrived unexpectedly late that afternoon, Sara was surprised to see her, and was even more surprised when her niece asked to stay for a few days. Sara had just reached her sixty-eighth year on earth, as apparent by the slow movements of her aching body and a fleshy face lined with deep wrinkles. Of course she welcomed her young niece, but when Sara discovered that Mary had been quite sick since returning from Judea, this aroused her curiosity. After a light dinner, she asked in a subdued manner, "Mary, did your parents have an argument?"

"No, of course not. Those two rarely disagree on anything."

She persisted. "Well, did you and Joseph have a spat about something?"

Mary shook her head, realizing too late that it had been a mistake to go there. But she kept a placid expression as she continued working on the quilt.

Vexed by Mary's reluctance to be forthcoming, Sara complained, "Ah, my blessed niece! You are quieter than a butterfly. I don't understand why you cannot open up to me."

Her throat tightening, Mary drew a deep breath and prayed her aunt would stop prying. She also prayed for a restful sleep later on, without the menacing dreams of the past two nights. But Sara intended to get to the core of the problem. She surmised that Mary and Joseph must be at odds concerning their future marriage. If so, perhaps Mary simply wished to be alone to ponder the matter.

Setting a hand on her niece's shoulder, Sara added in a sincere tone, "Don't worry. Soon everything will be fine, and you can prepare for the wedding day whatever the problem may be."

With tears brimming in her eyes, Mary found her voice. "Auntie, no mortal is able to solve my problem. Especially Joseph. He doesn't have anything to do with this." She hesitated an awkward moment, exhaling a breath. "There is a divine plan in all this," she added faintly.

"*Divine?*" echoed Sara, frowning.

"Yes," the girl murmured, realizing that if she wished to have peace of mind, she must accept her circumstances. She thought aloud, "My real problem is how to convince others that God is in this. I had a deep experience while …" She stopped abruptly, not wanting to reveal what had happened.

"What are you talking about, Mary?" asked Sara, growing more confused. "I'm only a humble housewife like your mother. Don't start talking about spiritual issues. Matters of faith can only be discussed by men of God. Perhaps the priest Zechariah can help you. He has great knowledge, as well as the respect of our tribe. If you believe there has been a divine intervention in your life, then speak to him."

Mary gave her aunt a light nod, but didn't dare open her mouth.

"You look exhausted," uttered Sara, assuming a motherly tone. "Are you feeling any better?"

"Yes, my headache is gone, but I am still a bit nauseous." Stretching her arms, she let out a soft yawn. "Auntie, where can I sleep tonight? I am so tired I could drop upon this very floor and doze forever."

"You'll stay in the room next to mine. Let's pray that God will search your heart and give you the necessary strength to confront the new day."

Yes, thought Mary, as she struggled to her feet, *tomorrow I will certainly need God's help… Oh, dear Lord of Lords. Grant me both the strength and the courage to face my parents with the truth of my pregnancy, and touch Joseph's heart so he can understand that we are your humble servants to treat as You wish.*

After a day of hard work in his pottery shop, Caleb returned home, where his wife awaited him. "Why are you late?" asked Azuba, trying to keep her voice steady.

Caleb answered, "I took some bags of grain to my parents." His eyes darted about the room. "Where is Mary?" he asked as he began washing his thick hands. "She's still in her room?"

"Eat your meal," said Azuba gesturing at the table to a large bowl of fish stew, freshly baked bread, and dishes of lentils and cucumbers. "I told Mary to stay with some relatives tonight."

"Why?" he asked, tasting the hot stew. "She's not still sick, is she?"

"We'll speak about that later," she replied, putting off the inevitable.

Azuba pushed the bread and jar of wine closer to him, then decided to pour the wine into his cup as she had done during the early years of their marriage.

Humming softly, she let her thoughts drift back to those pleasant days as Caleb raised the cup to his mouth, sniffing the pleasant aroma before taking a taste of the sweet wine.

"Tonight I want to relax," he said, breaking off a chunk of bread. "I'm going to my cousin's home. Some friends will be there, joining together around a fire at the front of his house. It has been a while since we shared company, talking and drinking the good wine that he made last year."

"Caleb, it's better if you stay tonight," said Azuba, in a firm yet respectful tone. "We need to discuss an important issue."

"Issue?" he muttered, not catching the tenseness in her voice.

"Finish your meal. Then we can sit and talk about Mary's future with Joseph." With a low sigh, Azuba refilled his empty cup. "Here, drink more. Maleb and Sara made it themselves. It's good for your health, and it puts you in a good humor. My father used to say that when backed by a good cask of wine, there's no problem too big to deal with. Here, drink more … All problems can be made right. I once heard …"

"Enough of this babbling! Woman, what's wrong?" His lips spread into an uncomfortable grin. "How many cups of wine have you drunk? More than me, I suspect."

"She dropped into the chair across the table from him. "You need a calm mind before we begin our discussion."

"What discussion?" he snapped. "I told you I'm going to my cousin's …"

"No! We need to talk about Mary's condition. It can't be put off."

"Azuba, what's going on?" He kept his eyes on her face as he raised the cup and drank all of the wine in one gulp. "Why is Mary somewhere else tonight? You still haven't told me where she's staying."

"She is safe with one of my relatives."

"Safe from what?" he grumbled, not liking the tone of her voice. She stared at her stew in silence while he reached for the jar of wine and refilled his cup. He took a sip, hoping he could leave soon. His cousin's house was a five-minute walk east of Nazareth, through fields of beans and garlic, with a stream cutting through the groves of trees.

Then Caleb noticed the nervous, frightened look in his wife's eyes. This was unusual, for Azuba was always cheerful, never letting problems take her over.

Realizing she was about to dispense some serious news, Caleb gave her a searching look as he leaned forward, speaking in a brusque tone, "So what's this important thing you have to tell me?"

"Caleb, we have a serious problem. I can't deal with it alone, so you have to promise to control your temper. Please don't go into a rage …"

"Ah, good woman! You're starting to worry me. What could be so bad?" He put a light tone to his voice. "Have you gambled away all of our land?"

In no mood for his bantering, she said flatly, "We have a serious problem with Mary. Something happened during her stay at the home of my niece, Elizabeth." Her eyes lowered to the dishes before him. "There is a reason why she's not here with us."

Straightening up in his chair, Caleb looked Azuba straight in the eye.

He couldn't help thinking that Mary was seriously ill, perhaps near death. "You shouldn't have fed me such a big meal. My stomach is coming up through my throat." He felt his heart pounding. "Has our daughter's illness taken a turn for the worse?"

Almost in tears, Azuba said in a trembling voice, "It's not an illness ..."

"Then what's wrong?" She hesitated before stammering, "Caleb, our problem is that your ... daughter ... Please don't get upset ... Our daughter is pregnant."

At first Caleb thought his ears were deceiving him. "What did you say?" adding in disbelief, "How is it possible for our daughter to be pregnant before marriage?"

"She seems to think so. She hasn't had her blood for over two months, and though she didn't name the person, her words and actions lead me to believe she had intercourse with someone ... someone other than Joseph."

Clenching his fists, Caleb's face turned red, the anger swelling within his heart. He rose from the chair and pounded a fist on the table, rattling the dishes. But he wished he could direct his anger toward the one who had done this to his daughter. "Why would our Mary commit such a sinful act? How?"

She made no reply, bracing herself for her husband to erupt in a fit of rage.

"Azuba, this goes against the laws of God." A worried note entered his voice. "It might lead to death for Mary. If the elders and religious authorities discover that she's pregnant, they can have her stoned to death."

"I know, I know," sniffled Azuba. "Caleb, though she did wrong, I am not prepared to lose a daughter. We have no choice but to send Mary away, far away, where no one knows her or our family. We must leave as quickly as possible."

A distraught look crossed Caleb's face, the storm of his anger quieting. "It's the end of Mary, and the end of my honor and reputation," he concluded in despair. "I am destroyed here. My life, my family, the relations with my relatives and friends ..."

Now the anger swelled within Azuba. "Don't think only of yourself," she admonished him. "Mary is in a dangerous position." She gulped. "Where can we send her? There must be a safe village or town where I can accompany her without fear."

Caleb paid no attention to her words. "Where is Mary now?" he demanded. "Where did you send her?"

After a long minute, Caleb spoke in a faraway voice. "There's no place for Mary to hide. The only solution is for her to marry the father of the child." Moving over to the chair by the window, he muttered to himself, "What will I say to Joseph's parents?"

"Don't worry about them," Azuba responded ruefully. She sat on the floor at his feet. "Our main concern is to find out who fathered this child."

As though he hadn't heard a word from her mouth, Caleb passively stared out the window at the setting sun, a forlorn look on his face. "A close friendship will be destroyed," he said in a grave tone. "Aaron and Marta have been our friends for so many years. He and the whole town will turn against us. Everyone knows Mary is betrothed to Joseph. How can we remain here?"

"This isn't the time to worry about the feelings or actions of others," Azuba responded forcefully. "Tomorrow we can speak to Mary and try to convince her to reveal the father of the baby. We must do it for her sake, as well as for the sake of the innocent child now forming inside her body. All right?"

Caleb turned and gazed into his wife's eyes, now reddened with tears.

"Yes, you're right," he whispered, a look of sorrow passing over his face.

The following morning Caleb awoke sick at heart, barely summoning the strength to complete the short walk to his pottery shop. Azuba, on the other hand, had a distinct bounce to her step as she gave everyone a friendly smile while hurrying along the dusty roads between her home and her sister's farmhouse.

Trying to conceal her worries, Azuba greeted her sister in a breezy manner.

"Sara! Thank you for watching over Mary."

"I didn't expect you so early." Sara closed the door as her sister entered the front room. "Mary's still in bed. She isn't feeling well. Last night she was fine, but early this morning she threw up on my clean floor!"

"She must get up now," stated Azuba. "She has to return home and have a talk with her father," she said. "Perhaps you should join us. I trust your judgment in times of crisis."

"Crisis? What are you talking about?"

Azuba breathed a sigh of relief, speculating that Mary had kept her pregnancy a secret from Sara's prying questions. "Did Mary happen to mention anything about her visit to Zechariah's home in Judea?"

Growing suspicious, Sara gave a shrug. Her voice grew wistful.

"Azuba, you remember how much Elizabeth loved Mary when she was a baby?"

"Of course. And to think that your Elizabeth just gave birth to a boy child announced by Gabriel himself. What a miracle!"

Sara nodded and smiled. "It must be a miracle for an old man like Zechariah to sire a child in Elizabeth's empty oven!"

Despite the turmoil in her heart, Azuba couldn't help giggling along with her sister.

Thinking that Sara would eventually hear about Mary's pregnancy, Azuba decided let her in on the harsh news. "Sara, you and I are very close. We have always shared our secrets."

Sara turned and faced her sister, sensing she was about to divulge something. "What's the matter?" she asked with growing concern. "You don't look well yourself."

"When you and Mary spoke last night, did she give any hint that something bad happened to her while at Elizabeth's home?"

"Absolutely not!" answered Sara. "In fact, I have no clue what Mary is thinking or feeling. Your daughter hasn't spoken over ten words since coming here."

"Sara, you are my closest relative, so you should know as well what has happened. Your niece Mary is pregnant."

These were the last words that Sara had expected to hear from her sister. Confused, she gazed at Azuba with incredulous eyes. "How can it be?" she sighed.

"It's the truth," added Azuba, shaking her head. "Mary has missed her bleeding. She must have had intimate relations."

Obviously shocked, Sara blurted out, "May the Lord God have mercy on us!" She took a deep breath, a mixture of fear and anger building in her heart. "Oh, for all the prophets! The Messiah cannot come soon enough!"

Wondering if Mary were awake or still asleep, Azuba caught her sister's attention and gestured her to speak quietly. "We need to talk privately, so we don't disturb Mary."

"I had presumed Joseph and Mary severed their relationship," remarked Sara, her voice softer. She released a hollow laugh. "But the opposite! Apparently they sealed their relations!" Pausing, she considered the ramifications of their premarital union. "Aaron and Caleb have been friends many years. They are determined to unite their blood through their grandchildren. The only solution, it seems to me, is to accelerate the wedding preparations."

Azuba now spoke in a somber tone, "Yes, yes, but the problem is more serious than that. Mary claims that Joseph isn't the father."

"What!" exclaimed Sara. "But Mary is quite fond of Joseph. I can't believe that she would violate her promise. They were destined to become husband and wife. Now what? Is Mary to marry a person that we don't even …?"

She stopped speaking as Mary entered the front room, a sleepy look on her face. She warily approached her aunt and mother.

Before Azuba could inquire about her health, Sara said in irritation, "For the love of Heaven! Who did you have relations with? Which family does he belong to?"

Startled that the secret was out, Mary gasped, "Mama?"

Sara wouldn't be silenced. "My dear niece," she uttered, placing her hands on Mary's abdomen, "this child has no future if he doesn't have his father's name."

Mary turned away from her aunt, her puffy eyes falling on her mother's face. "I told you yesterday that I cannot reveal his name. No one would believe me, even if I did."

"Do not concern yourself with that," Sara said, her voice now soft, trying to win her niece over. "Your father and I will speak to him and his family. The law is very strict about an unmarried woman having intimate relations before her wedding day."

"Auntie, I realize my life is in danger. But believe me when I say that it is impossible to reveal the baby's father."

An imploring tone entered Sara's voice. "Mary, for the sake of your eternal life, we must contact this man and his family."

"Please try to understand. I cannot compromise his position."

"Are you saying this man is already married?" pressed Azuba, hoping to get the truth from her daughter's heart. "Does he have a wife and children?"

With a frustrated sigh, Mary said quietly, "Mama, do you remember the dream I had about the archangel Gabriel? It was the night before I left for Judea when …"

"Enough of this!" said Azuba, interrupting Mary's account. "I don't want to hear such nonsense. No angel appeared in your dream, announcing you would have a special son through divine intervention. For the love of God, now, tell us who sired this child for real!"

A calm feeling came to Mary's heart as she turned to her aunt. "I am convinced this child is very special. Aside from the dream and other divine signs given to me, his father is a special man in God's eyes."

"A special man?" repeated Sara, caught off guard by her niece's claim. "If he is a special man, he should live in a special place, carrying out important duties." She considered the possibilities. "Tell me, is he perhaps an official at Herod's palace?"

"Since you have found such a special man, at least tell us who he is," said Azuba, her voice full of contempt and sarcasm. "If you do not reveal it voluntarily, I am afraid your father will attempt to persuade you through different methods."

A defiant look crossed Mary's face. "Why should I reveal his name? This man can never marry me, for he has a wife ..."

Azuba's face turned red. "Oh, dear Lord, what have you become, Mary? To have intimate relations with a married person is abhorrent in the sight of God!"

Mary looked at the two women. "I beg your forgiveness for the pain and sorrow this may cause you, but the father of this child is the priest Zechariah."

"Zechariah?" repeated Azuba in astonishment. "In his own house?"

With a stern look, Sara demanded sharply, "Mary, are you accusing my son-in-law, the husband of my daughter, a righteous and esteemed priest of God, of defiling you?" Trying to control her temper, she shook her head. "No, Mary, I cannot believe that Zechariah would betray Elizabeth." A thin smile crossed her lips. "Young lady, if you must conjure up a tale, create a more plausible one."

"It's the truth, I swear," retorted Mary, a hard knot in her jaw. "This child is the son of Zechariah. The seed of Zechariah is very special. Both he and I had spiritual experiences with the archangel Gabriel." Pausing briefly, she turned to her mother. "Mama, I promise that Zechariah is the only man who has known me intimately. This child was conceived during my stay at Elizabeth's home. No man was there except for Zechariah. And each time I left the house, I was accompanied by other relatives who ..."

Shaken by Mary's account, Sara threw her hands in the air. "Azuba, all this becomes more unbelievable and outlandish with each passing moment! If your daughter is speaking the truth, then we have no recourse but to protect Zechariah, a man who is highly respected."

Staring at her older sister, Azuba stated plainly, "Are you worried about Zechariah, or your daughter Elizabeth?"

"I am worried about my daughter, just as you are worried about Mary." Her eyes fell to the floor. "How could such a thing happen?"

"I have no answers," murmured Azuba, befuddled. But still not convinced that Mary had given them an accurate account of what happened at Elizabeth and Zechariah's home in Judea, she turned to her daughter with a look of compassion. "Whatever the truth may be," she said, "we will find it. For now, however, the most important matter is the child's health, as well as yours. Let's return home and feed you a hot meal. When your father returns, we can discuss this matter concerning Zechariah."

Mary nodded sheepishly, hoping the Lord God wouldn't abandon her during these difficult days.

Sara found her voice, speaking in a subdued tone. "My dear niece, I will speak with your Uncle Maleb. He's a wise man who understands the ways of God. Perhaps he will agree to meet with Zechariah and get to the truth of this matter."

"Don't speak to Maleb yet," said Azuba. "Let's first hear what Caleb has to say. I am certain he'll have definite ideas on what we should do."

"Without a doubt," replied Sara, then, thinking of her niece's and the child's well-being, adding, "but maybe Mary should remain here until her father has time to digest this awful news. There is no way to predict what he may do."

"How true," Azuba conceded. "In that case, come with me to talk to him. Two voices are stronger than one. Together we can reason with Caleb." She went to Mary and gave her a loving embrace. "If this is truly God's divine plan, then keep your faith and somehow it will work out for the best."

"I hope so, Mama." After a little yawn, she asked in a tiny voice, "Are you sure that I should remain here?"

"Your aunt is right. It's better for you not to see your father yet." She glanced at her older sister. "Sara, let's go and prepare lunch for Caleb. A lion with a full stomach is easier to confront than one who is starved!"

Both Mary and Sara watched Azuba as she moved toward the front door with the determined look of a warrior heading into battle.

CHAPTER 3

NOT WISHING TO INTERRUPT the testimony of Jesus' mother, I took small sips of tea while she reflected on that distant period of her life. Although her voice was surprisingly peaceful, I could see in her eyes the pain and sorrow she had felt upon learning about her pregnancy, then the horror of having to reveal the news to her mother and aunt.

As Mary mentioned, in order to understand what transpired between her and the priest Zechariah, it is necessary to backtrack before the conception to when her parents decided that she should visit her cousin's home in a village near Jerusalem.

It was a hot and humid morning in Nazareth when Azuba's eldest sister walked along the road leading to Caleb's home. Usually Sara was lighthearted and full of optimism, yet today she was rather downcast, with a haggard look. The night before, she had slept little, for she was consumed with worry over her daughter, Elizabeth.

Azuba was outside sweeping the porch when she noticed her sister approaching the house with a bundle wrapped in white cloth atop her head.

Pleased to see her, Azuba put the broom aside and walked to the road to greet her.

"Good morning!" she called out. "Tell me, are you lost? Or have you dropped by to prepare lunch for us?"

"Neither," she uttered, breathing heavily, beads of sweat glistening on her forehead and cheeks. "I came to see my niece. Is Mary home?"

"Not at the moment," said Azuba, removing the bundle from her head. "Have you lost your mind? What are you doing out in this heat?"

Feeling faint, Sara made no reply and followed her sister through the doorway.

While Azuba stepped into the small cooking room, Sara made herself comfortable on a cushioned chair by the open window, letting a slight breeze refresh her flushed face.

"So what brings you this way so early?" Azuba asked, returning to the room with a cup of water from the well. She handed it to her sister, adding, "Is there a problem at your house?"

After a sip of cool water, she gathered her thoughts. "Well, Elizabeth's situation worries me. My poor daughter is having a difficult pregnancy."

"This surprises you?" stated Azuba, a caustic note to her voice. "A woman her age should expect nothing but misery during a pregnancy."

"How true," sighed Sara. "All of my pregnancies were difficult, and giving birth was even more painful." She drank another sip of water. "As you know, it was truly a miracle that Zechariah and Elizabeth could make a child at their advanced age. But her longtime trustful servant has died and my daughter doesn't feel at easy to have a stranger inside the house at this time, so for now she has to take care of her husband and take care of herself and the unborn child. Elizabeth needs her rest, but I am too old to be much help."

"Even if you were able to go help her," remarked Azuba, pulling a chair over to the window, "I doubt that Maleb would allow you to leave. Our husbands are like children without us."

"This is why I trudged here to see Mary," Sara confessed, shifting her position. "You and Caleb would be doing me a great favor by permitting your daughter to stay with Elizabeth until her child is born. My daughter loves Mary so much, and hopes she can join her as soon as possible."

Surprised by the request, Azuba sipped from her cup of water while considering the matter. "This is a busy time for our family," she finally said. "Mary's thoughts are on her coming wedding with Joseph. He and his parents won't be pleased if Mary suddenly disappears."

"I realize my Elizabeth is asking much of your two families. But Mary may jump at the chance to visit Elizabeth's home. Ain Karem is near Jerusalem. Has Mary been to the Temple and other holy sites?"

Azuba nodded, her mind going back about ten years before, when several families from Nazareth made the pilgrimage to Jerusalem for the feast of Passover.

"Sara, I'm sorry, but I can't give an answer now. You have to wait until I speak with Caleb. If Caleb consents, then he will inform Joseph and his family." She hesitated. "Why can't the family of Zechariah help Elizabeth?" she said bluntly.

"I have no idea. In my mind it seems the family of the woman should resolve these kinds of situations. Elizabeth is my daughter, and your daughter Mary is a suitable choice, I thought." Smiling for the first time,

Sara added, "I know that Aaron has great respect for Zechariah. I doubt he would oppose Mary visiting Judea to help the pregnant wife of an esteemed priest."

Azuba laughed and said, "Dear sister, Caleb should have you speak to Aaron and Joseph. You could convince a Roman legion to turn their swords into plowshares."

Shaking her head, Sara said with a sigh, "Only the Messiah can achieve such miracles. I am afraid the Romans won't leave this land until Elijah comes down from the clouds with a band of angels."

With nothing else to discuss, Sara drank another cup of water before leaving.

As Azuba began preparing a light meal for Caleb, she reviewed the conversation with her sister and decided that perhaps it was not such a bad idea for Mary to live with Elizabeth for several months before embarking upon her new life as a wife, and eventually a mother. After all, Mary was still young and should take advantage of this opportunity to see the hill country of Judea and visit the holy sites in Jerusalem again. Even though Elizabeth's husband wasn't a member of the religious hierarchy in Jerusalem, he was held in high esteem in nearby rural areas and occasionally performed sacrificial duties at the Temple. So Mary would be in good hands while taking care of Elizabeth.

When Caleb returned home an hour later, Azuba was in a cheery mood as she placed dishes of fish, vegetables, and fruit on the table. "You're early today," she observed while he washed his hands.

"My potter's wheel broke," he grunted. "I was making a set of bowls and lamps when the axle cracked and splintered," he explained, sitting down at the table. "Joseph's father is repairing it now." After offering a prayer of gratitude for the meal, Caleb tasted the steamed fish. With a satisfied expression, he reached for the flat bread and dipped it in vinegar, then ate a big bite and savored the flavor while absently examining the small cut on his forearm.

"My eldest sister visited today," Azuba said, setting a pitcher of water on the table. She sat across from him and tried to keep a casual tone. "Sara's daughter Elizabeth is having a difficult pregnancy. Her most reliable servant passed away not long ago, and Sara inquired if Mary could stay at Zechariah's home and attend to Elizabeth's needs until after the child's birth."

Caleb looked up from his plate of food. "When is the baby expected?"

"In about four months. It is said the archangel Gabriel announced its future conception to Zechariah."

Caleb gave her a dubious look. "That's what the old priest claims!"

"Why would Zechariah invent such a tale? There are many signs that Elizabeth's child will become a special man for God. For one, Zechariah lost his voice while burning incense, and such a phenomenon was related to the angel's prediction."

With a dismissive shrug, Caleb continued eating.

Azuba studied her husband's bearded face and realized he hadn't changed much over the years. Though rather gruff at times and short-tempered, he was always kind to her and their daughter, as well as to strangers looking for a cool drink or a bite to eat.

"Woman! What's wrong with you today?"

"Caleb, I believe we must help Elizabeth. Her and Zechariah's child will grow up to be a great leader of our people, so we must send Mary to their home."

"If Elizabeth needs her help, then Mary can go. But not without the consent of Joseph and his parents."

"Of course," nodded Azuba, pouring more water into his cup.

On the other side of the village, where Mary's paternal grandparents resided, there was a deep well that provided water for the local households. The well was also a popular spot for residents to meet and exchange gossip. After finishing her chores at home, Mary would usually spend an hour each day there, helping to fill the pails and other containers brought by the women and children.

Today, however, Mary had no time to linger and chatter with others. She had just filled two ceramic jars and was walking toward her grandfather's house. About halfway there, she encountered Joseph. He was with his elder sisters and their children. Judith had three young sons, and Anna had a daughter who was almost two, and another child due in a few months.

At eighteen, Joseph was a handsome and energetic man of average height, with a neatly trimmed beard and dark curly hair. He was an obedient son with a generous heart, and everyone who dealt with him considered him a fair, honest, and hardworking fellow who helped in his father's carpentry shop.

"Mary, where are you going?" Joseph asked, glancing at the jars cradled in her arms. He took them from her and said through a small yawn,

"I was on my way to your father's house."

"To see my father, or me?" she teased.

Blushing a little, Joseph said good-bye to his sisters as they hurried off to complete some errands for their mother.

With a sudden smile, Joseph said in an exuberant voice, "Mary, I just had a long talk with my father. He promised that his workshop, along with all the tools and materials, will be given to me in several years, after we have children. Meanwhile, I will continue working with him to acquire more experience."

"How wonderful! Such news makes me very happy, especially if it pleases you. We are so blessed to have generous parents." She took the jars of water from him and continued down the road. "I must hurry to my grandparents' home. They're waiting for me."

Walking near her side, he said, "Let me carry the water for you."

"I can manage. You should return to your father's workshop."

"As you wish," he replied, admiring her plucky spirit.

A few minutes later, Mary arrived at the home of her grandparents. They were getting along in years and were recently in bad health. Both were thankful for having a dutiful granddaughter who possessed a serving heart.

Stepping into the front room, Mary announced breathlessly, "Here's the water!"

Her grandmother smiled faintly as she stood with difficulty, gesturing at the far corner of the room. "Put the jars on the table by the barrel of wheat flour. And would you fill two cups for us?"

After serving them, Mary kissed her grandfather's forehead. "Do you need anything else?"

"No, sweetheart," said her grandmother. "You can go if you like, but first let me give you a kiss."

Mary stepped over to her and turned her cheek slightly as the old lady pecked her.

"You are our precious treasure," she smiled. "Joseph is fortunate to be marrying a lovely girl with such a good nature and pure heart."

Her grandfather cleared his throat and said, "Mary, let me tell you something that I've wanted to say for a long time." He squinted at her. "I want you to know how special you are."

"Naturally," she giggled. "In God's eyes, all His children are special."

"No, no, I mean it," insisted the old man, a serious look on his craggy face. "We come from a special blood lineage."

His wife sighed. "Daniel, don't start on that story about your father now. Mary has to return home and help Azuba with household chores."

He paid no attention to her. "Mary, your great-grandfather, my father Matthew, once told me that his father, whose name was Levi, and his father, who was Mélkí, had a secret that has been passed down through the generations of our family."

Suddenly curious, Mary said to him, "What secret?" Then with a wry smile, she said to him, "Did old Noah land his ark of animals in Nazareth?"

"Stop your jokes!" he snapped. "It's not proper for a woman to joke so much."

"Sorry, Grandfather." Putting a serious look on her face, she stood near his chair and rested a hand on his shoulder. "Now what is this secret your father told you?"

"Well, dear … our blood lineage is straight from that of King David of the tribe of Judah, who as you know, was a son of Jacob himself!"

Mary thought about it. "You mean that King David is our ancestor?"

"Yes, his bloodline." With a contemplative look, the old man gazed toward the window as if he were reliving the sacred stories of the past. "Mary, one day soon the Messiah will come to our troubled land and liberate us from evil forces. And it is written by God's prophets that our Savior will be of the house of David."

"Yes but the prophet Isiah has also indicated that the Messiah is an Everlasting Father, Wonderful Counselor and Prince of Peace. And it has been said, since the time of the prophet Zechariah that he will come from a family of priests. Therefore, he will be an Everlasting High Priest," added grandmother who had heard it from her father.

Patiently waiting out the end of the tale, Mary gave her grandparents a kiss on their foreheads.

"Dear," her grandfather added with emotion, "you are the only child of your father, who is my only child … And as you know, I was the only son of my father, who was the only child of his parents, who were …"

Growing impatient, his wife interjected, "Daniel, she understands the point of your story! Don't keep her any longer."

He was quiet for a long moment, praying silently that his only grandchild would realize the seriousness of what he had said. "Mary, you must produce offspring to continue the lineage of King David in our family. Don't ever forget this secret!"

She gave a solemn nod. "I will always carry it in my heart." After kissing him one last time, she gave her grandmother a warm embrace.

As Mary was stepping through the doorway, her grandfather called out, "Child, tell your father to come for a visit. I need to talk to him."

Mary nodded and hurried off, making her way along the congested road in the direction of her father's home. It took only several minutes when walking at her normal pace, if she didn't stop to chat with friends or relatives. Though several of her friends called out to her, she merely waved and continued on her way. Due to the heat, there were only a few people on the streets, along with a few carts and wagons pulled by mules and donkeys, loaded with fruits and vegetables to be sold at the outdoor market.

As Mary entered the small courtyard in front of their house, Azuba shot her an angry look. "Where have you been?" She was by the oven, having just lit the wood so she could bake bread. "Gossiping at the well?"

"Not today," Mary replied with a light laugh while removing her kerchief. She fanned herself and dropped upon the stone bench near the oven. "Sorry for taking so long. Grandfather was telling me that Papa is a descendant of King David."

"Little good it does us," muttered Azuba, mixing the flour and water together. As she began kneading the dough, she added with a sigh, "Mary, you have no time for rest. Your father is already home. While I'm making the bread, go feed the hens."

"They won't starve. I fed them earlier." She knelt by her mother's side. "Let me do that for you. The dough is tough and hurts your fingers."

"My hands are fine today, praise be to God." Her manner changed. "But you can wash the vegetables and clean the fish."

When Mary entered the house, she found her father sweating profusely as he repaired his favorite heavy oak chair.

"Hello, Papa! Are you enjoying yourself?"

Caleb grunted an inaudible reply, his mind focused on the task.

As Mary began dusting the dinner table, he glanced at her and asked, "Did you help your grandparents this afternoon?"

"Yes. Grandfather says to come by when you can. He needs to speak with you."

"Oh, early this afternoon I was only a short distance from their house. I had to meet with Joseph's parents." Pausing, Caleb put the mallet down and reached for his chisel, then scrutinized the chair.

Mary looked curiously at her father, waiting for him to say more. But Caleb remained quiet as he worked intently on the chair, thinking it would be wiser not to elaborate on his discussion with Aaron and Marta. After his talk with Azuba concerning Elizabeth's situation, Caleb had decided to walk over to Aaron's workplace which was attached to the home.

He met and talked to Joseph's parents about Elizabeth's health and the need to send Mary to Ain Karem. Aaron and Marta gave their approval and all agreed to postpone the wedding until three weeks after Mary's return.

Slowly the light of day gave way to darkness. After their evening meal, Azuba wanted to speak to Mary about Sara's request. But Caleb was exhausted from a combination of too much wine and the stress of the past few days and went to bed early.

Azuba and Mary sat in the courtyard, chatting with some women who lived nearby, with Mary pestering for details about the first year of their marriages.

Later that night, while Mary was sleeping, the archangel Gabriel appeared to her in a dream, proclaiming that she had been chosen to give birth to an extraordinary child. Gabriel announced that a divine seed would enter her womb, and nine months later she would give birth to a child unique in all the history of mankind. He would be called the Son of the Most High, and the Lord would give him the throne of David, and he would reign over the house of Jacob for eternity, and his kingdom would never end.

The next day after sunrise, Azuba was preparing the morning meal while agitatedly muttering to herself. Hearing the sound of her mother's voice, Mary awoke but remained in bed while reflecting on the incredible dream she had just experienced. She wanted to share its significance with her mother, and quickly got dressed and stepped into the cooking area of the small house.

"Good morning, Mama," she said, smiling as she gave her a peck on the cheek. "Why are you up so early?"

"Your father was snoring all night. Whenever he drinks too much, he sounds like a grouchy old hog."

Laughing at the thought, Mary reached for a spoon and tasted the soup from the pot on the cooking stove. Then she began to tell her mother about the dream. Azuba interrupted her, though, feeling the urgency of Elizabeth's situation. "Mary, yesterday Sara came here with a special request. Elizabeth is having a difficult pregnancy and needs somebody who can assist her. So your father and I, with the consent of Joseph's parents, have decided that you should go and visit the house of Zechariah, helping your cousin with ..."

"Mama! You agreed to send me there without even talking to me first?"

"Your Aunt Sara has done many things for our family. It won't hurt you to help Elizabeth until her baby is born."

In a mild state of shock, Mary moved away from her mother, wondering if Joseph had been informed about all this.

Azuba added strongly, "Your father will go with you. It's near Jerusalem. You're leaving today, so get a few items of clothing together."

With tears in her eyes, Mary said imploringly, "But what about my wedding? I saw Joseph yesterday. He was so happy that our day of union was nearing."

"Aaron and Marta have decided to postpone the wedding until your return." She paused. "I suspect it will take place three weeks later."

"But, Mama!" she cried out. "I don't want to leave Nazareth so close to my wedding day. Why can't Aunt Sara find someone else to care for Elizabeth?"

"There is no other relative who is single and as capable as you."

A little sigh escaped Mary's lips. "How long will I have to stay there?"

"Two weeks after Elizabeth's child is born, your father will come for you."

Thinking she might be able to change her father's mind, Mary took a few deep breaths, trying to regain her composure. "Mama, last night I had an unusual dream," she said slowly, easily recalling the vibrant details. "Gabriel appeared and declared that I have found favor with God and that I would bear a great child who will be called the Son of the Most High."

"The archangel visited you in a dream?" Azuba inquired, raising a brow. "My daughter, all women dream of being the mother of a great child."

"But Gabriel told me that I was to name him Jesus, and that the Lord would give him the throne of David." Her voice dropped. "Gabriel also said I am not to worry because God would provide all necessities for me and the child."

"God provides by giving us good minds and strong bodies. If you don't use your God-given abilities, then you will starve. When you and Joseph are married, this is the first thing you should teach your children."

"Mama, are you even listening to me? The archangel Gabriel came to me in a dream and told me that I would conceive and give birth to the Son of God."

"Daughter, although you are precious in the eyes of your father and me, why would the Almighty send the archangel to a country girl?"

Not knowing what to reply, Mary uttered, "Mama, why did I have such a dream? How could I give birth to the Son of God? I am not even married yet, and now I may never be, if you force me to go to Judea. Why do I have to leave Nazareth? Do I really have to?"

After a fruitless effort to dissuade her father, Mary realized she had no choice but to obey their command to go. About mid-morning Azuba hastily folded some of Mary's clothes into a tight bundle, then led her outside, where Caleb awaited. They mounted two large donkeys and started their long journey southward toward Ain Karem, situated in a mountainous area of Judea.

Zechariah was a senior priest of God, very respected and loved by the people. Even as a girl, Mary had been aware of his reputation and standing in the community. The parents of Elizabeth had considered it a great marriage, for their daughter had brought honor and blessings to the family by marrying a descendant of the tribe of Levi, who was one of the sons of Jacob. The Levites were special in the eyes of God. At the time of the exodus from Egypt, when Moses had been commanded to take a census of all the men of Israel, God had ordered him to take a separate census of the Levites, for they were of special blood. It was the Levites who kept the tradition of the fathers of Israel during slavery in Egypt, by practicing the circumcision, venerating God, and rejecting false gods. And during the exodus to the Promised Land the Levites also kept great loyalty to the God of their fathers when disgruntled Israelites constructed and adored the golden calf.

During their journey southward, Caleb reminded his daughter of the importance of her role in the house of Elizabeth and her husband.

"Mary, take care of your cousin just as you would look after your mother and me. Due to her age, Elizabeth will be mostly bedridden during these final months of her pregnancy. So you must watch her closely, while also doing household tasks. And don't forget that her elderly husband is a senior priest. Approach Zechariah with reverence, for he is close to the one true God, who is the Creator of all life on earth and in heaven, the God of Abraham, Isaac and Jacob, and thus the God of Israel. And remember that we belong to the chosen people of God. And Zechariah is His priest, for he comes from the blood lineage of the Levites, from which God chooses His holy priests …"

Three days after leaving their native land of Galilee and passing through the wild countryside of Samaria, Caleb and his brooding daughter finally reached the heart of Judea. Although Caleb was tempted to visit the Great Temple in Jerusalem, he decided against it and escorted Mary directly to Zechariah's modest dwelling in Ain Karem.

It was early evening when Caleb and Mary dismounted from their weary donkeys. As her father approached the gate to the front courtyard, Mary reached for her bundle of clothing, moving with difficulty, each step painful, for her entire body ached from the long journey over rough terrain, the dry, scorching weather leaving her sensitive skin burned.

Mary joined her father just as Elizabeth opened the door. The inside of the house was dimly lit by candles, so it took a few seconds for Mary's eyes to adjust and distinguish her cousin's face, now roundish and puffy under the eyes. "Uncle Caleb?" Elizabeth said, her voice faint.

"Elizabeth!" he replied with a broad smile. "How good to see you! I hope we didn't disturb you from a peaceful slumber."

She shook her head, her eyes falling upon Mary's face. "What a joy to see you!" She reached out and gave Mary an affectionate embrace. "My goodness, you've grown so much since our last meeting. What was that, four years ago?"

"Hello, cousin," she said, trying to keep the surprise from her face. She had forgotten that Elizabeth was only a few years younger than her own mother. "Pregnancy seems to agree with you. You are lovelier than I remember."

"And you are a terrible liar!" Elizabeth replied. "Yesterday I was very ill. Soon I have to return to bed to rest." Pausing, she gestured them to step inside. "Please come in. How was your journey?"

Caleb spoke up with a frown. "It was arduous, yet I am thankful we arrived safely." As his eyes adjusted to the dimness, he added with reluctance, "Though many in Israel despise the Romans, we have to grant them the fact that they have built good roads. Fortunately, there were many other travelers … families, traders accompanied by Roman soldiers … so we never felt in danger from bandits."

Walking awkwardly, Elizabeth led Caleb and Mary through a series of rooms to the rear of the nicely furnished house. The back area appeared to be a recent addition. The paint smelled fresh, and the room opened up to a patio enclosed by two layers of netting to keep out flies and mosquitoes. "You will sleep here,. It is cool, with a light breeze from the west."

"This is fine," said Caleb with a smile, taking the bundle from Mary's arms. "Elizabeth, I can only stay one night. Tomorrow I plan to visit

Jerusalem and offer sacrifices at the Temple. Then I must return to Azuba before she comes after me."

Looking disappointed, Elizabeth said, "I wish you could stay longer, even though I wouldn't be much of a host. Here I am with child … at my age. It is like a dream!"

Mary said dryly, "The water in this town must have magical powers."

Caleb couldn't hold back a chuckle, but he grew serious when he noticed the agonized expression on Elizabeth's face.

Supporting her bulging abdomen with her hands, she dropped upon a blue cushioned chair. Grimacing, she spoke in a faint voice. "Mary, each time you speak, my son starts kicking up a storm."

"Don't try to stop him," she replied, smiling for the first time. "This region could certainly use the rain!"

Elizabeth tried to smile. "Dear, I don't remember you being such a humorous child."

Caleb gave his daughter a severe look of disapproval. But as he began to admonish her, Elizabeth's voice cut him off. "Dear lady, I apologize for upsetting your marriage plans. Actually, it was my husband's idea to send for you. After three days of prayer, he had a sudden inspiration to contact my mother about getting help for us."

Yawning, Caleb sat in a nearby chair. "By the way, where is Zechariah?"

Elizabeth turned to him. "He left a short while ago for the synagogue to offer prayers. Silent ones, I imagine. As you may have heard, Zechariah lost his voice when the archangel Gabriel appeared to him in the Temple, foretelling my pregnancy and the birth of a great son whom we are to name John."

After a light meal of bread, fruit, and nuts, Caleb and Mary began to retire for the evening. Both were quite tired and hoped to sleep late into the next morning. But just as they were thanking Elizabeth for her hospitality, they heard the front door open and heavy footsteps in the corridor. Seconds later, the priest Zechariah appeared in the dining room. A smile of evident satisfaction crossed his gray-bearded face when he saw Caleb and Mary sitting at the table with his wife.

He opened his mouth to speak, but then willfully pressed his lips together, remembering that his power of speech had been taken from him several months earlier when he had angered Gabriel.

Stepping over to Caleb, he gave him a warm embrace, patting his back a bit too ardently. Then he turned and looked at Mary, communicating his grateful feelings with a warm smile and placing his hands over his heart.

He joined them at the table, and Caleb spoke up in a jovial manner. "Earlier your wife was telling us about your future son. Perhaps he will become a great leader who drives the Romans from our land ..."

This statement drew immediate responses from both Mary and Elizabeth, and for the rest of the evening, the three of them discussed a number of issues while Zechariah remained in his chair, rocking back and forth, listening attentively while praying in his heart that God's will be done on earth, with his future son becoming a righteous priest and servant of the people.

The following day Caleb stood in the courtyard with his daughter. He reminded her again to treat Elizabeth as if she were her own mother. Mary seemed to accept the situation, lowering her head submissively as he kissed her brow. Then Caleb walked to the road where Elizabeth and Zechariah were waiting, holding the reigns of the larger donkey, the hot sun already beating mercilessly down upon their heads.

Caleb and Elizabeth talked for several minutes about her parents' health, and then she and Zechariah returned to the house after watching Caleb ride off toward Jerusalem.

During the first week of Mary's stay, the days lumbered by. Elizabeth seldom left her bedroom. Since she was weak and incapable of doing even the simplest of tasks, Mary kept quite busy while trying to maintain a humble spirit and a reverence toward Elizabeth and Zechariah, both of whom admired her deep faith in God and obedience to the laws and commandments.

As Mary would tell the story years later, when she served Zechariah during her stay there, she would bow before him as a sign of respect. At times she felt that when looking upon his noble face, it was like seeing the face of God. As the weeks passed and she grew closer to Zechariah, she felt closer to God, the closest she had ever felt to the Creator of heaven and earth. For Mary, to serve Zechariah was like serving God, and she began to look forward to being in the presence of the old priest, who always treated her so kindly.

When Elizabeth wasn't sick or overcome by a longing for sleep, the two cousins enjoyed sharing their thoughts and feelings. Mary was happy to discover that Elizabeth was quite smart. When feeling well, she was able to help Mary understand the sacred writings that Zechariah had given her to study.

Many of these sacred scrolls had belonged to Zechariah's grandfathers, who had taught him the great significance of his role as a descendant of the tribe of Levi. Zechariah had spent his youth in the company of wise scholars whose lives had been dedicated to the service of God and adherence to His laws and commandments.

As Zechariah grew older and well versed in the history of his people and their various struggles during those periods when their faith had abandoned them, he became even more determined not to stray from God.

As the long-awaited day of the child's birth drew close, Elizabeth grew weaker and needed even more care. Mary served her elder cousin with kindness and a good-natured fortitude that didn't go unnoticed by Zechariah. He was aware of Mary's spiritual qualities and recognized in her a certain internal beauty as she served both him and his wife without complaint.

In the evenings while Elizabeth rested, Mary would prepare food and serve Zechariah while he read the Scriptures from papyrus scrolls.

Zechariah was drawn to Mary's innocence and deep heart, and he was impressed by her profound desire to study the Scriptures. Like Mary, the old priest enjoyed their time together. He also felt her admiration for him, which infused him with more vitality as he read about the history of the chosen people.

Mary had an insatiable curiosity about Zechariah's roots. One day while the two cousins were having tea, she asked Elizabeth about Zechariah's roots.

The older cousin explained that the priest came from the lineage of Aaron, the brother of Moses, whose parents were both from the tribe of the Levites. "God told Aaron that their sons had the responsibility to attend the sanctuary as priests. That is why he is a priest," said Elizabeth. She paused for a moment sipping from the cup. "The Levites are the ones that God consecrated to serve Him directly through the generations. They were the ones who transported the Ark of the Covenant and now take care of the Temple," she added.

Drinking from her cup, Mary asked, "Is that why they do not inherit material possessions?"

"Yes, the privilege to serve the Lord God is their inheritance. God told them to take one tenth of what the people offer to the Lord. So this is what they do."

Elizabeth paused in contemplation. "We do not know when the Anointed One will come but we do know he will be a Holy Priest."

Elizabeth's testimony about Zechariah's roots only reaffirmed Mary's conviction that he was a unique man of God, also she wouldn't reflect on the words of her grandfather regarding her roots to King David.

As time had passed, she had grown to revere the priest and always felt God's presence when with him. She honored Zechariah and looked forward to those times when they were together.

One evening while he was having dinner, Zechariah gestured to her that the stew was delicious and asked her to share the meal with him. Her fascination deepened as she sat beside the priest, enjoying her meal. She felt she was sharing a meal with the Almighty.

Due to Elizabeth's weak condition during her pregnancy, Zechariah had not been intimate with his wife for many months now. And though he was a priest, he was still a man.

In that moment while Elizabeth slept, Zechariah and Mary felt the presence of spiritual forces filling the room with a special magic. When their eyes met, it was as if they were in a trance, with Zechariah seeing only God's femininity in Mary, and her seeing only God in Zechariah. Drawn by admiration, innocence, and spiritual forces beyond themselves, Zechariah and Mary joined in a physical relationship.

Zechariah's precious seed entered the womb of Mary. A union transpired between a man of deep faith, a priest from the tribe of the Levites who had served God all his life, and a pure and innocent maiden called by God for a holy purpose. That evening, inside Mary's womb the tribe of Levi and of Judas had become one.

CHAPTER 4

REFLECTING ON MARY'S CLAIM that Zechariah had been intimate with her, Azuba hurried along the road leading toward her house. Sara was a few paces behind, sick with worry as she chastised herself for having asked Azuba to send Mary to Judea. Now, Azuba was intent on informing her husband about Mary's supposed encounter with Zechariah.

Azuba slowed her pace to allow Sara to catch up with her. Although they had tried to avoid being seen, they couldn't help coming across some of their relatives and friends doing errands, taking advantage of the early hours before it became too hot to be out. A few noticed the anxious expressions on their faces and called out to them, but the two sisters ignored them and continued making their way along the web of roads in Nazareth.

All morning Caleb had been battling a whirlwind of emotions and bitter thoughts as he kept going over his conversation with Azuba. Having slept little, he was now on edge and ready to explode if his wife didn't return home soon with Mary. For the past few hours, he had tried to keep himself busy by inspecting each room of the house, looking for things to repair. But all the doors, shutters, cabinets, and pieces of furniture were in good condition. So he began to pace about in nervous agitation, a thousand questions pounding in his head as he prayed to God that his daughter wasn't with child.

"Caleb! We're home!"

Hearing his wife's voice, he stopped pacing and stared at the front door just as it flew open. Sara entered first, a tense look on her face, followed by Azuba.

Caleb glanced at his sister-in-law, then moved his burning eyes to his wife.

"Ah!" he barked. "I see you've brought company."

Taken aback by his scowling face, Sara replied in a sheepish voice, "Azuba asked if I …"

"You did your duty. Now you can leave."

"Caleb, don't be rude!" Azuba responded sharply. "Sara is aware of Mary's situation, so I want her to join us. We need whatever ideas we can get."

Caleb motioned to a chair near the window.

"I will get us some water," Azuba said as she headed for the cooking room.

Still perspiring, Sara settled herself by the open window, while Caleb pulled a chair closer to her and sat down.

Trying to read her thoughts, Caleb asked abruptly, "Sara, where have you and Azuba hidden my daughter?"

"Calm down, Caleb." Though she was trembling inside, Sara somehow was able to put on a brave face. "You shouldn't see Mary until you hear everything that happened while she was in Judea."

"So something *did* happen at your daughter's house?"

Sara exhaled a deep breath, not knowing how to begin. Thankfully, Azuba returned to the front room with a tray of freshly sliced pears and cups of cool water.

After setting the tray on a small table near Sara's chair, Azuba gave her husband a cup of water before sitting next to him. There was sour look on his face as he tried to imagine what had happened to his daughter.

Collecting her thoughts, Azuba uttered a silent prayer as she looked deeply into his eyes, hoping he wouldn't lose his temper upon hearing what Mary had said. She told him everything starting with Mary's dream.

"What?" gasped Caleb, his eyes popping wide open. A sudden pain struck his chest as if he had been hit by a heavy mallet. "Is it possible?" he thought aloud, glancing at Sara. "How is it possible that a priest of high standing would commit such an act with an unmarried girl? And worst of all, the husband of your eldest daughter!"

Sara lowered her head in shame.

After a long drink of water to steady his nerves, Caleb set the cup down and gave his wife a searching look. "Are you certain you heard Mary correctly?"

"Quite certain," answered Azuba.

"I know she would never lie to us," he sighed. "Do you think she might have dreamed or imagined the whole event?" he added, looking at her quizzically.

With a hollow laugh, Sara said, "That child in her womb is not a dream."

Feeling no resentment toward his sister-in-law, Caleb patted her hand and continued in a milder tone, "I simply cannot believe that Zechariah could bring such dishonor to our families. Especially with all that has happened with the conception and birth of his first child. Why would he jeopardize the reputation of a young virgin and her family, along with his own image as a representative of God?"

Azuba's voice turned cold. "Men don't cease to be men simply because of advanced age or religious devotion. Elizabeth was ill for many months, so she wasn't …" Her lips curled into a scowl. "Why should we be so surprised? Elizabeth's husband isn't the first married man to stray from his wife's bed."

Feeling a bit embarrassed and admonished by such an observation, Caleb stared out the window, mumbling in confusion, "But still, Zechariah should have controlled himself, keeping in mind that he is a priest and that Mary is his wife's cousin. He should've known his attraction to Mary was wrong, then either subdued his desires or sent her back to us."

Azuba said, "Though Mary should have known better, she is still just a 15-year-old girl who was probably impressed by Zechariah's position and great knowledge."

Sara said dolefully, "Whatever happened, I assure you that my husband and I will find the reasons."

"In the meantime," said Caleb, glancing at Azuba, "I must speak to Joseph's parents. Aaron and Marta have the right to know about Mary's condition. But no one else is to hear of this matter, until we have a complete understanding of what happened. Mind you, I am not trying to hide or justify the sins of my daughter. But since both our families will be affected by Mary and Zechariah's illicit actions, each one of us here must take special care to be circumspect. Understand? If the religious authorities learn about Mary's condition, they can take her away from us and sentence her to death."

With an imploring look, Sara said to him, "Then why must you tell Aaron? It should be kept secret."

Caleb's face went sour. "Then what shall I say to my friend?"

"When the proper time arises, then you can speak to him. Until then, why upset him and his family?" With a conciliatory smile, Sara added in a soft voice, "I don't know what caused my son-in-law to do such a thing. Since he is the husband of my daughter, I feel responsible."

"Nonsense," said Azuba. "How could you be blamed for Zechariah's actions? He is an elderly priest who should have remained loyal to both his wife and God, not to mention his newborn child, who was conceived by divine intervention."

"Speaking of divine involvement," said Caleb, with some wariness, "I want to hear more details about Mary's so-called dream. Gabriel appeared to her the night before our journey to Judea?"

Azuba nodded and began slowly, "As I said, she claims the archangel Gabriel appeared to her in a dream, telling her that God was with her, and that she would give birth to a child who is to be called Jesus. He will be blessed by God, and one day he will become the king of Israel ..."

Shaking her head in wonder, Sara exclaimed, "Oh, what a difficult situation the Lord God has put us in! First, John is conceived under miraculous circumstances, and now this child inside Mary's womb appears after Gabriel's prophecy." Her eyes shone. "If John is special, why shouldn't this child be special? Both of them come from the seed of Zechariah, a dedicated priest of God. Since John and Jesus have the same father, it would make them half-brothers whose mothers are pure and pleasing in God's eyes."

Caleb's first instinct was to baldly reject Sara's interpretation of events, yet as he considered her explanation of Mary and Zechariah's relationship and his own Davidic roots, it oddly seemed to make sense to his wounded father's heart.

"Sara, what you say is very moving. But unless Gabriel comes to me and echoes your sentiments, I have to handle the situation as I see fit. This means I must inform Joseph's family. Although we may be able to hide the child's paternity, we cannot hide Mary's condition much longer. In two months' time, everyone will notice ..."

Azuba interrupted him with an idea. "Why can't Mary and I travel to a land near the border? After the child is born, we can return here or settle near Jerusalem."

"What about our grandson?" retorted Caleb stiffly. "If he has to be a special person, as Gabriel predicted, how can you leave him in a foreign land with strangers whose beliefs differ from those of our forefathers?" Pausing, he let out a low, quiet sigh. "Besides, you and Mary cannot suddenly hasten off without explanations. There are many people in this region who know about Joseph and Mary's upcoming wedding, many relatives and friends in common with both families." Shaking his head, he added in a weighty voice, "Azuba, our daughter is to remain in Nazareth. And to break relations between Joseph and Mary without giving a clear explanation to his family is inexcusable."

"You're right. However, before speaking to Aaron and Marta, let's go with Sara and Maleb to Judea. We can visit on the pretense of seeing their newborn child. Then after judging Zechariah's demeanor around us, we can then broach the subject at hand."

A frightened look crossed Sara's face. "Sister, please stay here. Maleb and I should first discuss the matter with Zechariah in private. Though I trust Mary, I still wish to meet with Zechariah alone to hear his account of what happened."

Caleb thought briefly, then said in a firm tone, "All of us must go. And as soon as possible." He looked at his wife. "Since we are Mary's parents, it is imperative for us to speak to Zechariah directly."

Agreeing with her husband, Azuba stated, "We can leave tomorrow."

Sara realized it would be no use to argue with them, so she relented and said in a faint voice, "If it is meant to be, all four of us will make the journey. I suppose Mary can stay with my cousin's family until our return."

"No!" said Azuba. She cast Caleb a quick glance. "Mary has to come with us. Without her there, our accusations carry no weight or substance."

With a grunt, Caleb nodded and said flatly, "Now, where is Mary? She must return promptly and have a good night's sleep before making another long journey."

Azuba studied his face for any hint of anger. "Caleb, if Mary returns now, do you promise not to lay a hand on her?"

A look of surprise crossed his face. "Woman, don't test my patience. I have a right to be angry! This sordid matter has touched the deepest part of my heart, leaving a deep wound that will never heal." He looked away a moment. "But I would never hurt my daughter. You know that."

"Anyway, we must take Mary to Judea so that Joseph won't speak with her and possibly discover her plight."

Sara took her leave, in order to prepare her husband for the trip they would all be making to Elizabeth's. Later that afternoon, Mary returned home.

Caleb observed his daughter intensely, but he refrained from talking to her for fear that his tumultuous emotions would overwhelm him, causing him to either explode in anger or break down in tears.

Since Mary was too ashamed to speak to her father or even glance at the sorrowful expression on his face, she avoided him, taking dinner in her room before falling into an uneasy sleep, not knowing that she would be traveling back to Ain Karem the following morning with her parents.

CHAPTER 5

THE FOLLOWING MORNING Mary's parents awoke at sunrise, their senses keen on what lay ahead during the upcoming days. Mary told me years later that during that trip she could sense a new dedication in them. After their morning prayers, they quietly packed items of clothing for themselves, as well as for Mary, who was sound asleep.

When everything was ready, Azuba stepped into her daughter's room and gently shook her shoulder. "Wake up, Mary. It's well past sunrise."

Lying on her side, Mary opened her eyes and focused on her mother's face.

"My child, you need to get up and eat your breakfast. Soon we will be leaving for Sara's home. Hurry up!"

Not quite understanding what was happening, Mary got out of bed and quickly dressed. When she walked into the dining area, she noticed a small bowl of porridge on the table. Since returning from Judea, she hadn't consumed much food due to her dizzy spells and stomach cramps. Yet now she was feeling better and realized that she needed to start eating more, if not for herself then at least for the child growing inside her.

She sat at the table and was just about to pray when her mother entered the room, a distracted look on her face. "Don't take long. We have a lot to do."

"Did you and Papa already eat?" asked Mary, glancing at her.

"Yes. Your father is waiting for us. I've already packed what we need for the trip."

"Trip?" echoed Mary. "Where are …"

Mary couldn't finish the question, for her mother was already out the front door.

Sensing trouble, Mary poured honey over the hot porridge. After a prayer of gratitude, she dipped her spoon into the bowl and tasted the thick oatmeal. Though it tasted good, she couldn't enjoy it because she could hear her parents chattering in barely contained angry tones.

After a few minutes, Mary stepped outside and was surprised to see the two donkeys that she and her father had recently ridden from Judea.

Mary studied the bundles of clothing strapped together and draped over the backs of the donkeys, leaving just enough space for riders. Mary wasn't certain, but she thought her mother had said they were all going to Sara's home. Was this the "trip"?

With a strange feeling in her gut, Mary stepped over to her mother. "Mama, where are we going? To Aunt Sara's?"

Azuba nodded and moved aside as Caleb approached. Giving Mary a brief intense look, he placed his hands on her waist and lifted her atop the smaller donkey's back. Then he helped Azuba mount the large donkey.

It didn't take long for Caleb's family to reach the outer fields of Maleb's farm just south of Nazareth. As the donkeys approached the fertile valley where Maleb and Sara's farmhouse stood, Mary craned her neck, and in the distance she could see her aunt and uncle standing outside by a wagon hitched to two oxen. Instantly thinking her parents intended her to give birth in another land, Mary sighed ruefully and murmured beneath her breath, "Our family leaving Galilee, and we are never coming back. Will I ever see my beloved Joseph again?"

When Sara spotted Caleb's family on the main road bordering their land, she let Maleb help her into the rear of the wagon. Although Maleb was well over sixty, Mary watched him effortlessly climbed atop the wagon and make himself comfortable as the oxen began their slow yet steady march toward the road leading southward to Jerusalem.

Caleb stopped the donkeys when his family reached the winding road to Maleb's farmhouse. Inhaling a deep breath of the warm morning air, he let his eyes wander over the fertile land.

It took several minutes for Maleb and Sara to reach Caleb's family on the main road. Exchanging only a few words with his wife and daughter, Caleb helped them into the back of the wagon where Sara was waiting, a light blanket covering her legs.

Distraught over the vague notion that she'd never see Joseph again, Mary snuggled close to Sara, whose calm expression belied the feelings of dread that were certainly building in her heart.

Caleb tethered the two donkeys to the gate of the wagon and sat next to Maleb on the driver's bench. The oxen had been like Maleb's children for over fifteen years, so when, in his raspy voice, he gave the command, they began moving forward, effortlessly pulling the weight of the wagon and its five occupants.

As they moved southward, Mary uttered in a tiny voice, "Aunt, where are we going? To the home of Maleb's brother near Joppa?"

Sara didn't answer, as her eyes shifted to Azuba's face.

After a long silence, Azuba spoke crisply to her daughter, "We need to visit Elizabeth and Zechariah to clear up this matter."

Mary let out a gasp. "Do we *have* to?"

Azuba nodded, and since she had slept little the night before, she stretched out her body and rested her head on a clump of hay, desperately hoping the upcoming meeting with Zechariah would be without rancor or discord.

After a few minutes of awkward silence, Maleb put a hand on Caleb's shoulder and said in a sincere tone, "I want to apologize for what has happened. My entire family should deeply repent to God for the sins of my son-in-law."

Caleb remained silent for a while, ruminating over Sara's interpretation of Mary's dream about Gabriel. "Maleb, if the actions of Mary and Zechariah are in accordance with the Lord's will, then no one needs to repent. Yet if my daughter and your son-in-law truly defied God's divine law, they are the ones who need to repent, although we and others will also have to suffer retribution for their sins."

For three days, Maleb's oxen pulled the wagon about twenty miles a day across the rugged terrain of Galilee and Judea stopping only the night rest. A blistering sun beat down upon the land from early morning until late afternoon, but Caleb and the others weren't feeling much discomfort. In fact, all were giving thanks to God for being able to travel in this rickety wagon instead of walking or riding donkeys like many of the other wayfarers.

There was only a tiny sliver of light in the evening sky as Maleb pulled his wagon into Ain Karem. Although Mary had left the place only two weeks before, it seemed like years to her. The long days of serving Elizabeth and Zechariah were now but a faint memory, a hazy dream that had no bearing on her present life. Yet Mary realized this was foolish thinking, for she was carrying Zechariah's child, and she well knew her father and mother were planning to confront him about seducing their young, virgin daughter. Mary grew more fearful by the minute, as the team of oxen pulled the wagon and its occupants past familiar buildings and closer to Zechariah's house. Maleb and Sara, too, felt increasingly nervous about the impending encounter, but they also couldn't help being excited at the thought of holding their baby grandson.

Seven years had elapsed since Maleb had last been to Ain Karem. But his memory was still sharp for a man of his age. So he guided the oxen directly to Elizabeth's home, where several dogs were sleeping near the gate of the courtyard.

After helping the women out of the wagon, Maleb and Caleb led them through the courtyard and knocked on the front door. A minute later the door opened, and Elizabeth appeared with a baby cradled in her arms. Sara's shriek of joy momentarily startled Elizabeth, yet she gained her composure as her eyes darted about the faces of the people before her, first her parents and then Caleb, Azuba, and Mary. Why were they all here? she asked herself.

With tears in her eyes, Sara stepped forward and gently took the sleeping child from her daughter's arms. "Oh, John! What a handsome boy!"

Maleb kissed Elizabeth's flushed cheeks, then stood next to his wife, smiling with pride as he studied the child's perfectly shaped head and noble face, with dark brown eyes, straight nose, and large, rounded chin.

The sudden anxiety in Elizabeth's heart was eased by the joy at seeing her elderly parents. It had been over four years since she and her husband had celebrated the eight days of Hanukkah with them in Nazareth.

After Sara placed the baby in Maleb's arms, she turned to Elizabeth and gave her a long hug, tears streaming down the cheeks of mother and daughter. "Mama, why didn't you send a messenger with news that you were coming?"

"You surprised us with a grandson, so we decided to surprise you with a visit!"

Laughing with the others, Elizabeth showed them into the house and began to tidy up as her parents sat in chairs by the open windows, while Caleb and his family quietly stepped into the adjoining room and sat in chairs at a table.

Looking for something to say, Azuba remarked in a casual tone, "Elizabeth, you look remarkably well after giving birth."

"I feel much better," she admitted, "now that John has seen the light of day." She took some parchment scrolls in her arms and placed them onto a low table in the far corner of the room. Then she lit a candle, giving Mary a subtle glance. Since her cousin had a skittish look on her thin, pale face, Elizabeth realized that she and her parents had not journeyed all the way from Nazareth just for a casual family visit.

"Papa, I wish I had been told ahead of time. I would have prepared a special welcome for you."

Twirling a finger through baby John's sparse black hair, Maleb looked up and said in a flat tone, "Dear, seeing you and our grandson is special enough." He hesitated a moment. "Actually, your mother and I, along with Caleb and Azuba, have an important matter to discuss with Zechariah."

Her heart now pounding, Elizabeth lowered her body into the empty chair at the dining table. "He's not here at the moment," she stated, trying to keep her voice steady. But noticing the bleak expression on Mary's face, she added, "Zechariah is at the synagogue talking to the Rabbi. If this is important, I can send my neighbor for him."

"Yes, please do," said Caleb, forcing a smile on his face.

Wishing he were back in Nazareth at his pottery shop, Caleb reached for Mary's hand and patted it gently as Elizabeth left the room.

After a few moments of tense silence, Azuba said quietly, "I think she's aware of what happened. Something in her manner is different, as if she can read our thoughts." Turning to her elder sister, she added with sudden pugnacity, "Zechariah has tarnished the reputation of our daughters, and ruined any hope of happiness for our families."

She stopped as Elizabeth returned and stood near her father, who was rocking the infant in his arms. Seeing the look of contentment on John's face, Elizabeth stepped over to the dining table. It was clear to Mary that she had been crying. Her eyes were red and puffy.

Her heart moaning in sympathy for her niece, Azuba said to her, "John is such a precious child. Does he cry much?"

"No. Almost never. He eats well and rarely wakes during the night."

"He has the eyes of my father," said Maleb, studying his grandson's face. "But his nose and mouth are those of Zechariah." At that moment, the baby reached out and latched onto his grandfather's middle finger, squeezing it tightly. "Whoa!" he said, laughing. "This child is as strong as a bull. He will become a great prophet of God."

"Elizabeth, you must be quite proud of him," said Azuba. "Is it true that Zechariah got his voice back upon naming the child?"

"Yes. Amazing, isn't it?" said Elizabeth. She grew silent for a few moments, as if deciding whether it was all right to go on. "On the eight day after his birth, the priests came to circumcise him. I was to name him John, as Gabriel had instructed Zechariah about ten months earlier at the Temple in Jerusalem. But everyone protested, insisting that he be named after his father. But when Zechariah wrote the name John, he suddenly regained his ability to speak and predicted that our John would prepare the way for the coming Messiah."

"Praise be to God," said Sara, smiling and taking the baby from Maleb's arms. "You will have to find the best scholars in Jerusalem to teach him the laws and commandments, and how to be a righteous man in the eyes of our Lord God."

"Who is a better teacher than Zechariah … and me?" replied Elizabeth. "As he grows older, John can help me serve the people here and in the neighboring villages, and his father is considered one of the wisest priests in the region." A frown suddenly crossed her face. "I don't wish for John to associate with the priests of the Temple hierarchy in Jerusalem. The shrewd Sadducees, led by the high priest Annas, are more interested in their power and wealth than in serving God and the people."

Sara promptly retorted, "Daughter, please don't make enemies. Our lives are difficult enough having to deal with Herod and the Romans without alienating ourselves from the religious authorities in Jerusalem."

Elizabeth began to respond but thought better of it and stepped away from the table. She raised her arms above her head, stretching from side to side.

"My back still hurts from carrying John many months," she remarked. "I have a new admiration for women who do this countless times."

Azuba caught her attention. "Would you like to have more children?"

"At my age?" she replied, laughing outright. "Aunt, just giving birth to John was a great miracle. Without God's divine intervention, I couldn't have carried this child for half the term." Lowering her arms, she dropped into the chair again, her eyes on Mary's grave face. "Cousin, I want to thank you again for taking care of me. Without your love and support, I couldn't have managed the household, much less kept from falling into poor health, which would have seriously jeopardized John's birth."

Avoiding her eyes, Mary said dully, "I didn't do anything special. My parents wanted me to come, so I came."

Suppressing a sigh, Elizabeth said to Caleb, "Uncle, may I offer something while we wait for Zechariah? Figs or dates? Something to drink?"

Caleb shook his head. "During the past three days, I have drunk enough water to float a Roman galley."

"Don't bother preparing a meal for us," added Azuba. "We ate before our arrival."

"How long will you be staying? A week at least, I hope."

Caleb shook his head again. "We must return to Nazareth soon."

Elizabeth nodded gravely, wringing her hands as they all nervously awaited Zechariah's arrival. "Uncle," she uttered, facing him directly.

"I believe that I know why you came to our home. You wish to discuss Mary's relationship with my husband ..."

"So you *do* know about it!" Sara cried out, the blood rising to her face. "How could you have permitted such a thing? Mary was a virgin when she left Nazareth, but she returned stripped of her innocence!"

Surprisingly, Caleb felt a certain calm as he said to her, "Elizabeth, what exactly do you know of their relationship?"

"Several days after regaining his voice, Zechariah came to me and confessed that he had an intimate relation with Mary." Pausing, she drew a long breath and looked at her cousin. "Mary, I'm truly sorry. As you know, I could barely make it out of bed during those days. And due to his age and deep faith in God, never once did it enter my mind that you and Zechariah would grow close in such a manner."

Making a small gesture, Maleb spoke in an impatient tone, "Daughter, you should know that lustful desires are stronger than reason, stronger than even the law. Mary is a clever girl, full of grace and good humor. Any man would be attracted to such a sweet and lovely woman. Even a devoted priest like your husband!"

"Papa, what could I have done? I was bedridden. Though some men stray from their wives, during all our years together not once has Zechariah committed such an immoral act." Trying to control her emotions, she moved her eyes to Azuba and Caleb. "Oh, how will you ever forgive me?" she said, her voice low and stricken. "Believe me, I would rather die than have had this deplorable thing happen to Mary."

"There is nothing to forgive," replied Azuba. "But I agree with you. How could you, or any of us, ever suspect that a pious man like Zechariah would yield to temptation with the young cousin of his wife?"

His eyes on Elizabeth, Caleb spoke deliberately, "Your husband has always had our confidence and respect, for we consider Zechariah a responsible man whose beliefs and actions have reflected a deep devotion to God."

"This is why I am so confused," uttered Elizabeth, dismay and confusion in her eyes. "After so many years of study, teaching, prayer, and fasting, how could my husband succumb to such a vile temptation and lose control of himself?"

Maleb thought this over, then said in a somber tone, "When Zechariah came to you and confessed his intimacy with Mary, did he give any justification for his unthinkable behavior?"

Elizabeth nodded mutely, recalling that stormy evening when her husband entered their room while she was nursing the baby. "It was so unexpected," she began slowly, "that at first I simply thought he was joking. But when he kept apologizing and expressing regret, breaking down, I realized his union with Mary had actually taken place."

She paused, then added, "My memory is hazy, but it seems Zechariah told me that during Mary's first month with us, he felt an increasing spiritual attraction to her. On the night of their union, he came under the influence of a powerful force that stimulated him to consummate their relationship. At the time, he sensed it was a holy act sanctioned by the Divine …"

Mary raised her voice, confessing, "Yes, this is also what I felt." A peaceful glow shone from her eyes as she gazed at her cousin. "There was nothing tawdry about our union. When we were together that evening, I felt an invisible force pushing us together, as though God Himself were offering a blessing on our union." Her eyes moved to her mother's face before settling upon her father. "I felt as though I was fulfilling Gabriel's prophecy of conceiving a child who would become God's Son …"

Mary hesitated, taking a deep breath. After a moment of reflection, she added, "Papa, I know it's difficult for you and Mama to understand, but that evening I felt that God needed my womb, and that it was with the seed of Zechariah that we would create His divine child." She leaned forward in her chair, her hands folded upon the table. "From the depths of my heart, I know this child is from God. He should be born without the threat of violence or any danger to his life …"

"I don't understand," said Elizabeth, a confused look in her eyes. "Mary, what child are you talking about?"

Caleb cleared his throat. "Elizabeth, Mary is in a dangerous position."

Elizabeth looked at him in perplexity. "Uncle, you speak as though this matter cannot be kept secret. Who is to know?"

Rising to her feet, Sara said in a brusque tone, "Are you so naïve that you cannot fathom that your cousin is with child? Look at her! Mary is carrying Zechariah's offspring at this very moment!"

"Oh, my God," murmured Elizabeth, feeling faint. She drew a long breath and looked at her cousin's belly. "Are you pregnant with my husband's child?"

Mary nodded. "Gabriel said he should be called Jesus, and that he will reign over the house of David."

Grimacing, Maleb got to his feet and said gruffly, "Now do you understand the urgency of our visit? Not only is Mary and her child's life at risk, but your husband may also be in grave danger."

Elizabeth dropped her face into the palms of her hands, letting the tears flow freely.

When Elizabeth's neighbor reached the synagogue to deliver her message to her husband, Zechariah was deep in study and at first did not want to be interrupted. "But, your wife's parents have just arrived at your home, and Caleb's family is with them."

"What? Mary is here with her p-p-parents?" he mumbled, nearly passing out.

"Yes. Your wife says you need to return home immediately."

Panic-stricken, Zechariah realized that his relationship with Mary must have come to light in her family's household.

As he left the synagogue and headed for home, a jumble of emotions clamored in his heart. What could he say to Mary's parents? How could they understand what had happened? How could he apologize to them? How would his own son be able to contend with such disgrace and ridicule while growing into manhood?

Each step Zechariah took was a battle with his body. His legs felt so heavy that he had to practically drag himself down the road to his house.

Suddenly short of breath, he stopped walking for several moments, hoping some miracle would save him from facing Mary and her parents.

He had no rational explanation for them. That evening when he and Mary were alone, they both had sensed a spiritual presence guiding them, as if God had created the circumstances that had drawn them closer together until finally they were one in heart and body. And, indeed, they had felt a certain fulfillment in their union.

Yet after John was born, and Mary departed days later, Zechariah's heightened sense of the spiritual meaning of their union gradually vanished and was replaced by more common human thoughts and feelings. He had begun to feel guilty about his actions, until finally he was forced to reveal the truth to his wife.

Zechariah's breathing soon became laborious, and his heart thumped louder as tears slid down his cheeks into the thick gray whiskers of his beard. By the time he entered the courtyard and opened the front door to his house, he was frantic. He entered the room slightly hunched over and breathing heavily and noticed that Maleb and Sara were standing together near the open window, frowning severely at him. He bowed his head in respect and uttered a proper greeting. Then he turned and saw Elizabeth sitting at the dining table with Mary and her parents. John was cradled in

Mary's arms, and as she looked up and caught sight of Zechariah coming her way, she gave him a sweet smile of understanding. Startled by his appearance, Caleb and Azuba rose to their feet, not knowing what else to do, or what to expect. His lean face was beet red and covered with glistening tears, making his dark eyes look like islands in a stream.

Before Elizabeth could voice any angry thoughts, Zechariah dropped to his knees and prostrated himself on the floor before Caleb and Azuba.

"Please forgive me!" he cried out. "I have sinned with your daughter! Forgive me … forgive me … forgive me …"

Seeing this genuine act of repentance from the elderly priest, the parents of Mary were struck mute momentarily. Certainly they were indignant and bitterly concerned about the fate of their daughter, but how should they respond to a representative of God who was lying prostrate before them in such a humble manner, his face streaming with tears.

Zechariah continued wailing in a voice full of sorrow, "I am sorry … I am truly sorry … Hold me culpable for this fool act … Mary has no fault to bear … All the guilt and punishment should fall upon my soul …"

Watching him, the hot anger and resentment melted from Caleb's heart. Feeling sorrow for the elderly priest, he bent over and lifted him to his feet. Looking him straight in the eye, he said in a gentle yet firm tone, "Zechariah, it is only the Lord God who can judge men's weaknesses. Although I am Mary's father and am deeply pained by your actions, I cannot put my hands on you in anger and revenge."

With a low sigh, Caleb added, "But I want you to understand this very clearly. Mary's life is in imminent danger. Mary is carrying your child."

Zechariah gasped, his reddened eyes growing big as he turned and stared at Mary.

"You are pregnant?" he said in disbelief.

Mary gave a silent nod, feeling sympathy for the elderly priest.

Her father said to him, "Mary's condition cannot be hidden for long. Her mother and I intend to keep the birth of the child a secret. However, if it becomes necessary, you will admit you are the child's father. Understand? And if the religious authorities try to harm my daughter, you will inform them that you seduced her. You will stand before everyone at the Temple and state clearly that you are wholly responsible for my daughter's condition. Understand?"

"Yes, Caleb, I will do what you say," Zechariah blubbered, as he silently questioned how he could father two children at his advanced age.

Maleb raised his voice in anger, adding, "You will also protect

Elizabeth and John from any harm by religious zealots. Is that clear?"

Zechariah nodded vaguely as he moved his eyes to Mary's mother, who was staring at him with contradictory feelings.

"Azuba, I'll do what must be done. I pledge to do whatever is necessary to shield the lives of Mary and her child. I am solely culpable, and I am willing to admit this before all of the Temple priests … if it becomes necessary."

With a hint of a scowl, Azuba said, "Since you already have a wife and baby child, how can we expect more from you?"

Two days later, after resting and making plans for Mary to stay with a distant cousin in a village near Syria, the five started their journey back to Nazareth.

Although the confession and penitence of Zechariah didn't alleviate their pain, both Caleb and Azuba now felt more sympathy for Mary, and in private they wondered aloud if Gabriel had actually come to her in a dream, as she had professed.

Whatever the case, Caleb firmly resolved that upon his return to Nazareth, his first duty was to promptly visit Aaron and Marta's home and have a heart-to-heart talk with them about the situation with Mary.

CHAPTER 6

IT WAS EARLY EVENING when the weary oxen halted near a gnarled old tree by the rutted road leading to Sara and Maleb's farmhouse. There was still an hour of light before darkness settled over the region along the eastern shores of the Great Sea. After saying their good-byes to the elderly couple, Caleb helped his wife and daughter mount the donkeys. Then he uttered prayers to the Lord God as they headed in the direction of Nazareth, arriving at their house as the sun dropped below the western horizon.

Azuba arose early the next morning, and though she was exhausted and filled with nervous apprehension, she found the strength to wash clothes at a nearby stream before preparing the first meal of the day.

Soon joined by Caleb and Mary, she ate in silence while the two spoke about their visit to Zechariah's home. At one point, Azuba indicated that Elizabeth seemed to harbor resentment toward Mary and Zechariah for conceiving a child while she was bedridden during her own pregnancy.

Leaving Mary alone at home, Caleb went to his workplace and Azuba walked to the home of Joseph's parents. As she had expected, Aaron and Joseph weren't there, but Marta was working in her vegetable garden. Marta was a short plump lady with graying hair and big round eyes that seemed to see through a person. Pleasantly surprised to see Mary's mother, Marta invited her to stay for tea and help make plans for the children's upcoming wedding. Azuba politely declined and asked if Marta and Aaron could meet with her and Caleb early that afternoon to discuss a matter of grave importance. This was an unusual request from Mary's mother, and it alarmed Marta, who couldn't imagine what *grave* event had prompted her visit so early in the day. But she kept her confused thoughts to herself and readily agreed to receive Mary's parents after the midday meal.

As she was leaving, Azuba asked in a casual tone, "By the way, how much longer will Joseph be fishing with his cousin?"

"You didn't hear?" said Marta, as the two women stepped through the courtyard gate. "Joseph returned from Caesarea yesterday. He was so anxious to see Mary that he went straight to your home even before saying anything to us."

With a perfunctory smile, Azuba replied, "I'm sorry we weren't there to receive him." Then she said a quick good-bye and hurried down the road.

Caleb returned home shortly before noon. His nerves on edge, he listened to Azuba and Mary read psalms of David. Then the three of them offered deep prayers to God, seeking His help and guidance.

While Mary rested in her room, Caleb nibbled on some fruit, as he and Azuba waited for Sara and Maleb. They finally arrived just as Caleb and Azuba stepped onto the front porch. During the walk to Aaron's home, the four of them exchanged few words, for they knew their meeting with Joseph's family would be a gut-wrenching experience, causing hurt feelings and bitter resentments that would likely last for many years.

When Marta had informed her husband about Azuba's unexpected visit and request for a meeting, Aaron had remained silent and merely nodded his understanding. Like his son, Aaron was a robust man of average height. But Aaron had grown heavy in recent years, and his curly hair and full beard had patches of white hair, which Joseph often kidded him about. Although he was hungry, Aaron declined any food and stepped into the courtyard with a cup of water. Clearly worried, he dropped into a chair and drank the cool water while contemplating the upcoming meeting. He had heard from a friend that Caleb's family had left Nazareth the week before and journeyed south to Zechariah's village near Jerusalem, accompanied by Maleb and his wife. On its face, their sudden departure didn't seem unusual. It was only natural for Maleb and Sara to visit their daughter's home so they could give blessings to their baby grandson. But why would Caleb, Azuba, and Mary go with them? After all, Mary had just spent over four months there. She had been back in Nazareth for only few days before suddenly leaving again with her parents. Very strange.

Murmuring a prayer for a calm heart, Aaron stepped onto the road outside the walls of his courtyard. After greeting several people passing by, he caught sight of Caleb and Azuba slowly approaching his house. But why were Maleb and Sara accompanying them? And why the solemn expressions on their faces? *Has my Joseph committed some act to displease them?*

"Welcome, my friends!" he called out, pushing a smile to his lips. As they drew closer to the house, he gave a short bow and respectful greeting to Maleb and Sara, who were held in high esteem in Nazareth due to their deep spirituality and good deeds.

Then looking at Mary's father, Aaron added in a dry tone, "Though my birthday celebration isn't until next month, I will gladly accept any early gifts today."

His heart ready to break in half, Caleb said in reply, "I am still waiting for your gift that you failed to bring to my last party."

"Hah!" exclaimed Aaron, giving his friend a slap on the back. "You always have a clever retort." He turned to Azuba. "How can you live with such a creature?"

"It's not easy," she replied. "Just ask Marta. I imagine she experiences the same frustrations with you."

Aaron made no comment as he guided everyone into his house. Marta was waiting in the front room and gave them a warm greeting that was more formal than usual.

After everyone was seated, she gestured at the low table covered with dishes of cakes, bread, and fruit and cups of spring water. "Please. Our home is your home, so take as much as you like."

Aaron sat across from Caleb and Azuba. "Marta, be careful of what you offer. Caleb just may take all our furnishings to his palace."

"Palace, you say?" Caleb minced his voice. "Aaron, my humble abode could fit inside this room twice. If I had one-tenth of your wealth, I could easily purchase enough food to feed all the beggars of this land."

"Beggars?" he echoed. "I am the only beggar you know, and not once have you given me the crumbs off your plate."

Sara frowned. "Aaron, why do you men constantly badger one another?"

Maleb promptly interjected, "We men have few joys in this world, so allow us the pleasure to insult each other. It's just friendly banter."

"Well spoken!" said Aaron. "Maleb, when I reach your great age, I hope that my wife treats me as well as Sara treats you."

With a grimace, Sara said, "If I didn't take care of this old goat, he wouldn't know how to cook an egg, much less prepare a fine table such as this."

"Thank you," said Marta. "I apologize for not having more to offer you."

"This is more than enough," remarked Azuba.

As everyone retreated into their own thoughts, the room grew quiet, and a sudden tension thickened the air.

Aaron hesitated, then asked, "Maleb, how was the journey to Zechariah's home? I heard that you and Sara visited your daughter and new grandson."

"Thankfully, our journey went without difficulty. For an old man like me, these things are no longer easy."

"Maleb, you still look very fit," remarked Aaron, wishing Caleb would get to the point of their visit.

After several moments, Marta said, "Tell me, who does Elizabeth's child resemble?"

No one answered at first, but then Sara said in a faraway voice, "Well, John has some facial features of Maleb, but the child takes after Zechariah a great deal. While we were there, John cried only a few times. But when he did, you could hear his wailing all the way to Jerusalem!"

Marta nodded and shifted anxiously in her chair as everyone lapsed into another lengthy silence.

Just as Caleb began to explain the purpose of their visit, Joseph called out from the courtyard. Moments later he came into the house, a look of surprise crossing his face when he noticed Mary's parents, along with her uncle and aunt, sitting with his father and mother in the front room.

"Who is this rugged young man?" joked Maleb, rising to his feet and giving Joseph a fond pat on the shoulders.

After greeting the guests in a respectful manner, Joseph turned to his parents and said quietly, "Father, am I interrupting anything?"

"Will you join us?" stated Caleb, gesturing at the chair next to where Marta was sitting. "Our discussion concerns you and Mary."

A puzzled frown crossed Joseph's face. "I haven't seen my betrothed since she left for Ain Karem over four months ago. So yesterday morning when I returned from the sea, I went to your house. But your neighbor said that all of you had departed last week to visit her cousin's home near Jerusalem. I assume he was referring to Elizabeth and Zechariah's village."

"That's right," Sara said with a nod. "Naturally, my husband and I had a strong desire to hold our new grandson. And since Caleb's family had to meet with Zechariah, they were kind enough to accompany us on the journey south."

Joseph squinted at the elderly woman. "If Mary is as sick as she says, then your long journey there and back must have been difficult for her."

Azuba said sullenly, "It was very difficult for us all."

Caleb regarded Joseph in long silence, thinking he was too clever for his own good, just like Mary. That was probably why they were drawn to each other.

After clearing his throat, Caleb spoke in a somber tone. "Aaron, I apologize to you and Marta for coming to your home on short notice. What I have to say to you is not easy, but quite necessary due to a situation beyond our control …"

"Is there a problem involving Joseph?" asked Aaron, gesturing at his son. His eyes moved to Azuba's rigid face. "Has my son done something to offend you?"

She shook her head no, and Caleb broke in with a wavering voice. "Aaron, other than my relationship with God and my family, I value our friendship more than anything else in life. So I hope what I am about to convey will not destroy the love and trust that we and our families have for one another."

Sara's voice was wistful when she added, "Even though our lives are often toilsome, we can consider ourselves fortunate in that we have many relatives and friends in this region.

Her eyes thoughtful, Marta said dryly, "Sara, is this the reason why you and your husband have come today? You hope to provide wisdom and guidance for us?"

Sara replied with a limp shrug. "Yes, but first someone needs to provide wisdom for me."

Aaron smiled at the statement, but there was still a certain tension in the air that caused his uneasiness to heighten.

Maleb added flatly, "The wisdom of man can be put into a small cup. What's needed now is the wisdom of the Lord … and the strength to abide by it."

Raising a brow, Aaron said to no one in particular, "Come now, it couldn't be all that bad. Does Mary wish to postpone the wedding for some reason?"

If I don't tell him now, I never will, thought Caleb, sighing inwardly.

"Aaron, what we speak about today must remain in this room. If others hear about our discussion, it could result in serious consequences that may jeopardize the life of my daughter."

Pausing, his eyes fell on Joseph's face. "Young man, do you understand? What I am about to tell you will be shocking and maybe even repulsive to you. But if you truly love Mary, then you will not utter one word to anyone. Understand?"

Joseph nodded hesitantly, trying to imagine what Mary could have done to prompt her father to speak so sternly.

Breathing slowly to steady his nerves, Caleb glanced at his wife, who looked as if she were about to be executed. He turned back to Aaron and Marta and began to explain in a level voice, "During Mary's stay at Elizabeth's home, something took place that no one in this room would have ever believed could happen."

As Aaron weighed Caleb's statement, his expression became more intense, almost severe. Yet oddly, Marta had a placid look on her face, as though she were prepared to accept whatever Caleb was about to dispense.

"Azuba and I have no proof of this," he went on, "but Mary claims that Gabriel came to her in a dream. He announced that she would give birth to a special child who would be called the Son of God …"

Joseph held up a quick hand. "So you are saying that Mary and Zechariah had very similar experiences with the archangel?"

"Not quite," uttered Azuba, her hands now trembling. "Zechariah was burning incense in the Temple when Gabriel appeared at the altar, whereas Mary was dreaming when the archangel supposedly came to her."

Although his parents had doubtful looks on their faces, Joseph nodded thoughtfully and said, "What is shocking about such a dream? Usually prophets, priests, and other holy people have otherworldly experiences with the Divine and His angels. I find nothing strange about a pure woman like Mary having such an experience." He glanced at his father but not, it seemed, for approval. "In fact, I suspect that many people have contact with angels, yet they are too timid or frightened to tell others about it."

Aaron made no comment but gave Caleb a searching look. "So this is the reason for your visit?" A note of sarcasm entered his voice. "You are asserting that my Joseph will become the father of God's Son?"

Caleb didn't smile. "Aaron, I desperately wish it were Joseph's fate to marry my daughter." He paused a moment. "It pains my heart to inform your family that Mary is already with child. She conceived while staying at Zechariah's house."

Upon hearing that his betrothed was pregnant, Joseph jumped to his feet, staring intently at Caleb. "No … not Mary … not my Mary!" He turned to his parents and nearly shouted, "Mary's father must be mistaken! How?"

Her eyes growing large, Marta motioned for him to sit down, before looking at Mary's mother in astonishment.

For several long moments Marta was speechless as she began to sense the deep anguish that Azuba and Caleb must have been feeling all these days.

"Azuba," she finally said, "you and I have known each other for many years. Is your husband speaking the truth?"

"Yes, Marta. You can imagine my shock when Mary told me. It was after her return from Elizabeth's home that I discovered the awful truth."

Marta glanced at her husband, who had grown pale, a sickly expression in his eyes. Aaron was obviously too startled to utter a word to anyone. So she studied her son's contorted face. "Joseph, is this your child?"

He rose from his chair again. "Of course not!" His voice began to break. "Mary was a virgin when she left Nazareth."

Marta's face clouded. "Caleb, do you know who fathered the child?"

He nodded vaguely. "Yes, but I cannot reveal his name at this time."

Her lips tightened as she pondered this. "If you are certain it isn't Joseph, then his father and I cannot permit him to marry your daughter, even if they may love one another."

"Azuba and I understand your position," said Caleb in response. "We don't expect Joseph to accept Mary in the present circumstances."

Stroking his beard, Aaron thought aloud, "So, you do know the identity of the man who was intimate with Mary?"

Caleb gave a silent nod, glancing at Maleb and Sara. Though their wrinkled faces showed little emotion, their wise eyes told him to be cautious.

"Is the man a native of Galilee?" pressed Aaron. "Or does he live in Jerusalem or one of the surrounding villages?"

"I am very sorry," Caleb stated, more forceful this time. "For the sake of everyone involved, it is better that I not disclose the identity of the child's father."

Trying to collect his thoughts, Joseph stared at Mary's mother. "Tell me more about her dream," he said, his voice a bit calmer. "Mary actually believes that Gabriel came to her and announced she would give birth to the Son of God?"

"Yes," murmured Azuba. She hesitated. "She had the dream the evening before she and her father journeyed to Ain Karem. Then while Mary was visiting her cousin's house, she claims that a powerful spiritual force influenced her to be intimate with a special man, who asserts he was also affected in a like manner."

Aaron's brows knitted. "You mean you spoke to the man who seduced your daughter? Is he an acquaintance of Zechariah's family?"

Marta tried to hold back her tears.

"Azuba, this is a tragedy that has struck both of our families. We have always considered Mary like our own daughter."

"And Joseph has been like a son to us," Caleb replied, resisting the urge to embrace his close friend. "Aaron, I am so sorry …"

Joseph blurted out, "When is Mary going to wed the child's father?"

"There will be no wedding," murmured Azuba, her eyes on the floor.

Seeing the stunned look on Joseph's face, Maleb said to him, "Your heart mourns in deep sorrow, along with bitter feelings of betrayal. Yet I assure you this agony will pass, and over time you will regain hope and experience God's love as your parents find a suitable woman for you to join in marriage."

"But I want to be with Mary!" insisted Joseph, rising to his feet. He approached Caleb and Azuba. "Is Mary at home now? Can I visit her?"

"No!" said Aaron, grasping his son's arm. "You are not to speak to Mary ever again. She is carrying the child of another man."

As Maleb and Sara stood near the front door, Marta said with growing concern, "What are we to tell our relatives and friends? They will be suspicious …"

"You're right," said Aaron. He looked at Caleb and Azuba. "You cannot hide Mary's pregnancy much longer."

"Mary cannot remain in Nazareth," Marta insisted, her voice almost a shout. "Your family will be ostracized and even persecuted. Mary might even face trial."

Caleb said curtly, "Marta, I am well aware of the possible ramifications. Azuba and I are now working on a plan to secure our daughter's safety. All we ask from you is to remain silent for a few days until we quietly leave town."

Aaron set a firm hand on his shoulder. "With the help of the Lord God, you will find a solution that will spare Mary's life."

Near tears, Caleb embraced him. "My friend, if God is truly behind the birth of this child, then He will protect both the child and his mother from harm."

Aaron and Marta made no response, waving their hands furtively as the four left the house. With Caleb in the lead, they walked quietly toward his home, where Mary was alone, wondering how Joseph had taken the news of her pregnancy. Much of what had just taken place she would not learn until years later, bit by bit, from Joseph.

CHAPTER 7

AS HIS PARENTS BEGAN to discuss the shocking turn of events, Joseph went to his room and shut the door. Lost in a daze, he let out a tormented groan like some woeful spirit trapped on this hellish earth, his limp body falling on the bed as if the breath of life had been sucked from it.

With growing despair, he stared vacantly at the ceiling while trying to make sense of it all. A storm of thoughts swirled about in his mind. *Dear Lord, how could Mary be with child?* He murmured in disbelief. Though he was angry and full of indignation, he couldn't help but feel great sadness for Mary. *Is the girl that I have always loved actually pregnant? How could Mary allow herself to be touched by another man? Didn't she realize it would destroy our lives?*

The hours drifted by as Joseph continued to mourn his lost bride. Several times his father and mother came to his room, trying to comfort his grieving soul. Yet he turned them away each time. So Aaron and Marta would return to the front room, holding hands and desperately appealing for divine intervention in their son's life. They fervently prayed for the Lord God to give solace to Joseph's desolate heart, and also to lighten the burden of fear, guilt, and shame in Caleb's distraught family.

After hours of confused and tortured thought, Joseph still hadn't completely accepted the fact that Mary was carrying another man's child. *If she is really pregnant, who is the father of this child?* wondered Joseph, hoping this was a bad dream and that he would soon awaken to the pleasant reality of life as it was before Mary had left Nazareth. "What exactly happened while Mary was in Ain Karem?" he uttered, sitting up in bed.

After a while, Joseph asked himself: *What should I do? Should I obey my parents and try to forget Mary? Am I able to wipe away her memory? Or should I confront Mary and force the name of this man from her? If so, what then? How could I persuade him to marry her and fulfill his obligations as a father? If he refuses to make Mary an honest woman, should I raise my hand in anger and strike him down?*

Joseph knew that he could never harm another man or woman. So how could he support Mary in her time of great need? Should he accept her as she was? Yet to accept Mary meant to have a confrontation with his parents, his mother in particular. He knew that his mother would never welcome a daughter-in-law who had given birth to another man's child.

Joseph loved and respected his parents. To accept Mary would mean creating discord in his family. At the same time, what would Mary do with the child once he was born? How would most people in Nazareth treat the child if he were born fatherless? His birth and presence alone would be a source of shame and bitterness between members of his own family. The child would constantly remind people of the shameful act that had occurred between Mary and *this man* from Ain Karem.

Joseph realized that his bitter feelings caused by Mary's betrayal would never vanish from his mind … or from the minds of his relatives and others living in the region. *Perhaps Mary would gradually forget her misdeed and accept the child with a mother's love, but could he ever forget?*

His head somewhat clearer, Joseph got out of bed and stood by the open window overlooking the vegetable garden. He soon realized that if he forgave Mary and took her as his wife, then he would have to accept the shame and ridicule. Moreover, he realized he would be obliged to care for her child, loving and taking care of him as his very own.

Although Joseph genuinely loved Mary, he realized that he could never devote himself completely to her and the child in her womb. His parents were right. There were too many dangers and complications awaiting him if he proceeded with the wedding.

After a short, restless nap, Joseph had a meal with his parents. Strangely, the subject of Mary's pregnancy wasn't even mentioned. His father was suddenly very curious about Joseph's experiences while fishing with his cousin; he asked detailed questions about the boat, nets, water, and wind conditions on the Great Sea.

When his parents left home to take some food to the rabbi's family, Joseph quickly washed his hands and face before stepping onto the road in front of his house. Then walking in the opposite direction from that taken by his parents, he headed toward Caleb's home. He intended to have a serious talk with Mary and hopefully discover the truth. After all, the only information about her condition had been provided by her parents. Perhaps Mary could shed more light on what actually occurred during her lengthy stay at Zechariah's home in Judea.

Besides, thought Joseph as he quickened his pace, *this was the longest period that the two of them had ever been separated.* In the deepest part of his heart was the need to be close to her, to look into her eyes, and to hear the sweet sounds of her enchanting voice.

As Joseph rounded a corner and entered the road leading to Caleb's house, he spotted Mary about a hundred paces in front of him. Thankfully, she was alone, carrying a bucket of water in the direction of her home.

"Mary!" he called out, walking faster as he waved his arms. As he got closer, he saw the water sloshing over the rim of the wooden bucket. "Mary! Please stop!"

Surprised to hear the husky voice of her betrothed, Mary turned and smiled tentatively upon seeing him. "Joseph!" she said, setting the bucket on the ground. "Where did you come from?" She was not sure whether to touch him or not.

"I came from my parents," he said dryly, casting his bitter thoughts aside. Desiring to hold her hands and draw her closer, he added in a light tone, "Where did you come from? A dark cave in a mountain?"

"Oh, you haven't changed a bit. You're as silly as ever!"

"And you are prettier than ever," he said, stepping closer.

"Joseph, be careful," she warned, backing off. "People will see us and talk."

He gave a little shrug, momentarily forgetting she was with child. It was like they were children again, talking and laughing without a care in the world.

Glancing about, Joseph noticed the open gate of a courtyard up the road. So he grasped onto the handle of the bucket and led Mary into the secluded area. They sat on a stone bench, butterflies fluttering about the flower bushes along the walls.

"This is so peaceful," sighed Mary, staring at the tiny pink blossoms. "What happened to you while I was away?" she said, touching the sunburned skin of his nose. "Before I left here, you were thin and pale. Now you look like a brawny fisherman."

"Being out on the sea is exhilarating. I found a certain freedom that I've never known before." Pausing, his eyes unconsciously moved down to her mid-section. He quickly caught himself and feigned a yawn as he turned his head toward the azalea bush. Yet Mary had seen the movement of his eyes and caught the scornful expression on his face before he turned away from her.

"Joseph, you don't have to hide your anger. I understand."

Closing his eyes, Joseph inhaled a deep breath of the fragrant air while trying to gather his jumbled thoughts. Earlier in the day, there was so much that he wanted to express … so much anger that he wanted to vent upon her, so much sorrow in his heart that he wanted her to feel and experience. But now that Mary was nearby, inches away, he couldn't bring himself to expose his deepest thoughts to her.

"Joseph, what have I done to you? Forgive me. I'm terribly sorry that I've caused you so much pain and heartache."

Opening his eyes, he turned and faced her. "How could it happen? Did you forget about our marriage plans? Why, Mary? Tell me, please."

"Forgive me, Joseph. Truly I don't know what to say. It happened, and I cannot explain how …" She stopped speaking as the barking of a dog came from inside the house, startling her. When the barking stopped, she added in a soft voice, "Joseph, I love you and no one else. I have always loved you …"

"You have always loved me?" he said sharply. "Even when you were in the arms of *that man* from Zechariah's village?"

Lowering her eyes, she murmured, "Even for me, it is difficult to understand. So how can I explain it to you?"

Wanting to understand what had happened, Joseph placed his fingers under her chin, lifting her head. "This afternoon," he said flatly, "your mother claimed that Gabriel appeared to you in a dream before you left for Elizabeth's home. If so, do you believe what happened in Ain Karem has any connection to that dream?"

"I do," she said simply, looking into his intense eyes.

Joseph stared at her for a long moment before turning away, desperately wanting to believe her illicit relationship with *that man* was acceptable to God.

But how could it be? The laws and commandments strictly forbid intimacy between a man and woman outside of marriage. Several years earlier, he had witnessed two adulterers being stoned to death in the streets of Nazareth, and he had heard of similar events taking place in other villages and towns throughout Galilee, Samaria, and Judea.

"Joseph, I feel so alone, so afraid." Mary's hands were now trembling, and her voice wavered. "Though my parents try to comfort me, I know they are ashamed."

"Despite what happened, I still love you," he replied. "How could I ever harbor resentment against you? Yet, how can I forget what you have done? And what about this child growing in your womb? If we were husband and wife, how could I be the father of a child who's the fruit of your transgression? Your child would be an obstacle to us having a good marriage. The child would always come between us!"

"I know, Joseph. If we did marry, you would constantly struggle with your hurt feelings and bitter thoughts. And each time you would look at my child, it would be like throwing salt in a wound that never heals."

Nodding reflectively, Joseph considered her words. "Yes, though one part of me wants to forgive and accept the situation, another part wants to lash out in anger, hurting both you and this child."

Mary's eyes fixed on him. "I cannot change what you feel toward me and my child. But I want you to realize that never once have I betrayed you in my heart. Due to a profound spiritual experience in Ain Karem, I offered my body to a holy man whom I believed was also inspired by God …"

"A holy man?" he repeated harshly, frowning at her. "So *this man* who seduced you in Ain Karem was a priest?"

"He didn't seduce me," she retorted, reaching for the bucket. "From our union, we conceived this special child who is to be called Jesus."

"Jesus?" echoed Joseph, his voice losing its edge. Scratching at his beard, he added curtly, "Mary, if you need to believe that God is behind the conception of this baby, how can I convince you any differently? Yet my parents and I cannot accept such an implausible tale, and neither will other people of Nazareth. If your father and mother are truly concerned about your life, they will take you far away from here!"

Before Mary could reply, Joseph jumped to his feet and left the court-yard, not looking back as he slammed the gate, leaving her there alone as the old lady of the house stepped outside and scolded her for being there.

When Joseph returned to his home, he was still muttering angrily to him-self as he considered his miserable situation. His encounter with Mary had made him even more bitter and distraught. As he passed through the front room, his mother studied his face and guessed that he had met with Mary. Yet she said nothing, silently praying that her son could over-come this trial and hardship, and somehow learn from the experience to become closer to God.

After getting undressed, Joseph fell onto the bed and stared blankly at the ceiling for a long time before drifting off to sleep. Strange dreams dis-turbed his rest all during the night. Then just before sunrise the next morn-ing, the archangel Gabriel appeared to Joseph in a dream, announcing that the Lord God was very pleased with Mary, and that Joseph should take her as his wife. "Joseph, do not be afraid of what your relatives and others may say, for Mary's child is special in the eyes of the Lord God."

When Joseph awoke to the light of day, he felt a strong spiritual presence around him. At first it frightened him, because he was not sure if he had fully awakened from his dream. He closed his eyes and tried to sleep more, but the words of the archangel reverberated in his mind like the echoes of a faraway drumbeat. Unnerved, he got up and quickly dressed, as if to run away from it all. It was only when he was almost out the door that he felt a sense of peace come over him and realized what he had to do.

Wishing to share the dream with his parents, Joseph stepped briskly into the dining room. Aaron and Marta were already seated and eating their morning meal, talking in hushed tones about yesterday's events, quietly speculating who might be the father of Mary's child.

After greeting them, Joseph dropped into the chair across from his mother.

Rather surprised by the calm look on his son's face, Aaron put down his spoon and said to him, "Are you feeling better?"

Joseph nodded. "Yesterday I was so hurt and angry that I couldn't think clearly. Yet now I know what must be done." Glancing at his mother, he added in a casual manner, "We will hold the wedding on the scheduled day."

"What?" she said with a frown, thinking she didn't hear him correctly.

"I plan to wed Mary," he stated, more forcefully this time. "The Lord God is pleased with her and the child she is carrying."

Aaron stared at him in astonishment. It was as if the whole world were going mad. "Joseph, don't you realize your betrothal to Mary is no longer valid? Caleb and I agreed to sever your relationship. Don't worry about Mary's situation. You are no longer bound to her."

Meeting his eyes, Joseph said defiantly, "Father, you're mistaken. Mary is still my betrothed, and I intend to become her husband." He turned to his mother. "I have known Mary since childhood. She has always been a part of my life, especially since you and her parents arranged our betrothal. So I will not terminate our relationship simply because she doesn't meet your expectations."

"Meet our expectations?" repeated Marta, almost shouting. "Don't you understand that Mary will give birth to a child unrelated to your blood? If you marry her, what will people think once the child is born?

There will be gossip and accusations, and an investigation soon following, for which we already know the outcome!"

"Mother, if Mary and I quickly have a wedding, and I shelter her from criticism during the remainder of her pregnancy, then we can endure whatever persecution may come our way after the child is born."

Aaron's face took on a somber cast.

Clearly recalling Gabriel's instructions to him, Joseph remained calm. "Even without your consent, Mary and I will be married next week."

"Without *our* consent?" snapped Marta, flushed. "Joseph, you know very well that in our tradition sons and daughters only marry with the blessing of their parents. Though Mary is the daughter of our dear friends, it would be very difficult for your father and me to bless your union."

"Listen to your mother," said Aaron, sternly. He already sensed that his position on the matter had no persuasive effect on his heartbroken son. "She and I have removed Mary from our thoughts, and we urge you to do the same. Soon we will begin to look for another girl from a good family, who is worthy to become your spouse and the mother of your children, as well as our grandchildren!"

Although his father's remarks were upsetting, Joseph managed to keep the anger from his voice. "I understand how you feel," he said calmly, stroking his beard. "Even though you may not feel affection for Mary and her child, we are still young and will give you many grandchildren. Over time, our sons and daughters will bring you and Mary close together again."

Aaron gave thought to this, then responded in a constrained voice, "Joseph, such things aren't as simple as you think. When people begin to ridicule Mary and her child, along with you, their judgments will cut right to your heart and damage your pride. Even though you might accept Mary, it will be very difficult to accept a child that is not yours. Her child will constantly remind you of what took place between Mary and the *mysterious man* in Ain Karem." A shadow passed over his face. "Your mother and I aren't certain, but we believe that Mary had a relationship with Zechariah …"

"You mean Elizabeth's elderly husband?" uttered Joseph with a skeptical look.

"Why not?" retorted Marta. "Mary doesn't know anyone in that village, other than her cousin's family. While Elizabeth was confined to bed during her pregnancy, Mary and Zechariah spent many hours together. I suspect they grew quite close."

For a long moment Joseph was left without words as he reflected on his talk with Mary in the courtyard. Could the priest Zechariah be the *holy man*?

Pulling himself together, Joseph passed off his mother's remarks with a soft laugh. "Why make wild speculations? I assure you, Mary will never reveal the identity of the child's father. It could be anyone ..." His voice trailed off as he tried to recall Gabriel's exact words to him in the dream.

"Joseph," said his father, bringing him back to the present, "if you take Mary without our consent, where will you and she live? Do you honestly expect me and your mother to welcome Mary and her illegitimate child into our home with open arms?"

With a silent gaze, Joseph considered this. "Father, I don't blame you and Mother for rejecting Mary," he reluctantly conceded. "I felt the same until I had a wonderful dream early this morning during my sleep. This sounds almost unbelievable, but Gabriel came to me and comforted my soul. He told me not to worry about taking Mary for my wife, for the Lord God is pleased with both Mary and her child."

"You had a dream of Gabriel, too?" said Aaron somewhat derisively. He couldn't help laughing. "This is too much!" he bellowed, turning to his wife. "First, the old priest claims that Gabriel took away his voice. Next, Mary claims that Gabriel told her she is to conceive the Son of God. And now our Joseph has a dream in which Gabriel tells him to marry a girl who is carrying a fatherless child!"

Marta's face went pale. "Aaron, be careful what you say!" she warned. "Our small minds cannot always fathom the will of God, much less know how His will is to be achieved. Though God is perfect, He must deal with us imperfect creatures."

"How true," Aaron replied, turning serious. "Yet I doubt the Creator of the universe would send the archangel Gabriel to our clumsy son." Pausing momentarily, he saw the determined look in Joseph's eyes and immediately regretted what he had said. "Son, I am not denying that you dreamed of Gabriel. But perhaps you somehow conjured up his appearance and had him say what you wanted to hear, eh?"

"Father, I didn't conjure up anything!"

A grim smile crossed Marta's lips. "Perhaps you invented this dream to influence our hearts to accept Mary and her child?"

"I did not invent it. My dream of Gabriel was real, even more real than us sitting here right now." His voice grew stronger. "For reasons that I cannot comprehend, the Lord God wishes for me to wed Mary. What choice do I have? I cannot turn my back on God, or on Mary and her child. I won't allow her to face a situation where people might try to harm and even kill her and the child." He rose slowly to his feet, staring down at his bewildered parents. "This is my final decision."

"So be it!" remarked Aaron, also rising. There was no sense in his son's plan, but he had lost a daughter-in-law and was not going to lose a son, as well. "You are our only son, and because we love you dearly, your mother and I will somehow find a way to accept Mary and her child. But it won't be easy." Growing silent, he contemplated the new situation for an extended moment. "I suppose I should pay Caleb and Azuba a visit and try to explain the reasoning of your heart."

Marta gave her husband a hard stare. "You are a bigger fool than he is if you think we can keep Mary's pregnancy a secret. In a few months our relatives and neighbors will clearly see that Mary is already plump with child. And since Joseph and Mary were separated for months, everyone will realize he is not the child's father!"

Trying to hold himself together, Aaron gave his wife a helpless look, as though he were sinking in a pool of quicksand with no one to lend him a hand to get out.

"As I see the situation," he sighed, "we have no recourse but to insist that Joseph is the father of Mary's child. If we stand together, no one can prove differently."

Marta gave a shrug. "Unless, that is, the real father steps forward and demands control of the child once he is born."

Frowning with grave concern, Aaron muttered an inaudible reply as he draped an arm over Joseph's shoulder. "Son, I hope that Gabriel won't stray far from Nazareth!"

Joseph kissed his mother's cheek before following his father into the courtyard, where the two men decided to speak with Maleb and Sara, as well as Caleb and Azuba. "Don't forget about Mary," said Joseph. "She will definitely have an opinion about our future marriage."

"No doubt," uttered Aaron, hiding the fear simmering within his heart, for he realized the coming months would be unlike any they had ever faced before.

Early that evening, Joseph and his parents left home and headed toward Caleb's house, although it was over Marta's protests. She was still angry and quite disappointed in Mary for betraying her son's devotion. At the same time, however, she did feel some compassion in her heart for Caleb's daughter and hoped local religious leaders wouldn't find out about her pregnancy. After all, society's judgment is simply not fair at times. It is the woman who receives denunciation and punishment for having an illicit relationship, whereas the man usually receives little chastisement.

Nevertheless, as a caring and attentive mother who cherished her son, constantly praying for his health and success in life, it was extremely difficult for Marta to embrace a pregnant daughter-in-law who was carrying someone else's child.

Marta could not discount Joseph's exhortation. To abandon Mary would be an act of cruelty.

Couldn't Mary be considered a person who is poor and needy? Marta rationalized. *I have treated Mary as my own daughter since childhood. And considering Mary's immoral behavior while she was away from Nazareth, it is a matter of life and death to extend love and forgiveness at this crucial time in her life.*

When Joseph and his parents arrived at Caleb's home, they greeted him and Azuba with warm smiles. Obviously surprised by their unexpected visit, Caleb invited them inside his humble dwelling, his heart dancing with joy at seeing his close friend so soon after informing him of Mary's transgression.

"I am delighted to see you," Caleb said, fondly patting Aaron's shoulder. As everyone stepped into the front room, he added in a jovial tone, "Please make yourselves comfortable while Azuba slaughters a Roman horse for our evening sacrifice."

Laughing softly, Aaron said to him, "Caleb, it cheers me to see that you haven't lost your sense of humor." He and Marta sat in chairs near the open windows, while Joseph sat on a stool next to Caleb.

"Excuse me," uttered Azuba, hurrying from the room to get fruit and cakes.

"Bring some wine!" called out Aaron. "We must drink to God's great sense of humor."

Puzzled by Aaron's remark, Caleb agreed nevertheless, adding, "True, even in times of sorrow and great hardship, we should maintain our sense of humor. This is the reason why our people have endured so much persecution and misery over the long centuries. We know the One God is always with us, sharing both our tears and our laughter."

"How true," Joseph remarked. "I imagine many funny stories were told by our ancestors while they were building pyramids for the pharaohs." He glanced at Mary's father. "What do you have when all of Herod's concubines are gathered together?"

Caleb thought briefly, then said with a shrug, "What do you have?"

Joseph said dryly, "A full set of teeth …"

As Caleb and Aaron broke into laughter, Marta gave her son a vexed look.

"Joseph, don't be crude. Such jokes are unworthy of you, especially at a time like this!"

"Mother, if I were any more serious, blood would pour from my eye sockets."

With a brief sigh of frustration, Marta turned away from him and stared vacantly out the window. Grinding her teeth, she was thankful her parents weren't alive to see the spectacle of Joseph and Mary's shameful wedding.

Aaron leaned forward with folded hands. "Caleb, this afternoon I visited Maleb's farm. I had a long talk with him and Sara about Mary's situation."

Caleb stared at him in silence. "Tell me, this is the reason you dropped by tonight?" he said, his voice subdued. "Have you and Marta decided to rid Nazareth of unwelcome vermin who destroy the moral climate?"

"Nonsense," Aaron responded with a frown. "The Romans and their corrupt gods are the only vermin we need to get rid of. Hopefully that day is not far off."

"You could be right," said Caleb, glancing at Azuba as she returned to the room. She couldn't help but feel nervous as she carried in a tray with dishes of olives, dates, sliced apples, and honey cakes, along with large cups and a bottle of wine.

Marta rose and moved a small table to the center of the room, where Azuba set the tray. After handing everyone a cup and filling them, Azuba sat next to her husband and gave Marta a searching look, trying to guess the purpose of their visit.

Aaron raised his cup in the air. "Caleb, may the Lord God pour His blessings upon my son and your daughter."

After a sip of the wine, Caleb scratched his head in bewilderment. "Aaron, your toast would have been fine about four months ago, but now?"

"Yes, indeed," he responded. "There are changes in the wind, and I have brought my headstrong son here to explain them to you."

"Changes?" repeated Caleb, not daring to hope. "At times, the wind can be as fickle as a woman's heart. Let's hope these changes aren't fickle, eh?"

Not amused by his comment, Marta was about to speak her mind, but she held onto her thoughts at the last minute when Aaron subtly reached for her hand and gave it a hard squeeze.

As all eyes turned to him, Joseph felt the blood rush to his face. He had expected his father to inform Mary's parents of his decision to marry her. But now it was upon his shoulders to take control. This seemed only right, he realized, for he would need to be strong and decisive in the coming months if there were to be any hope of saving Mary's life, as well as any chance of their making a wholesome family in the future.

"I gather that Mary is not at home," Joseph finally said, looking at her mother.

Azuba shook her head. "Mary cooked dinner for her grandparents. She ought to be back any moment now."

Joseph half nodded, thinking it was better to speak to Mary's parents first before revealing his innermost feelings to her. Hopefully they could take a long walk by the stream and clear their hearts of all doubts and fears before preparing for their wedding day.

Looking at her parents, Joseph spoke in a level voice. "For the time being, it isn't of great importance why I made this decision. What's important is that if Mary still wishes to marry me, then I am willing to have the ceremony next week. As for …"

"Oh, Joseph!" Azuba cried out. "May God bless you! Mary will do everything in her power to be a good wife to you, and a good daughter-in-law to your parents!"

"Of course she will," said Aaron, smiling at her. "Mary is a warm-hearted person who serves everyone in our community in a caring, sacrificial manner."

"How kind of you to say that," remarked Caleb, wondering if this were Joseph's idea, or if Aaron and Marta had prodded him into sacrificing his pride. Whatever the reason, he felt a tremendous burden had been lifted off his shoulders. "Aaron, I am pleased for both Mary and Joseph, but even more pleased that relations between our families won't be damaged. Joseph's decision will help to preserve our friendship."

"Our friendship was never in jeopardy in the first place. Even if Joseph and Mary decided not to get married, you and I would have remained close until the end of our days on this earth."

"Hopefully after that!" added Caleb with a smile. He moved his eyes back to Joseph. "I believe it is important for me and Azuba to hear the reason behind your decision to marry our pregnant daughter."

"Yes, of course," replied Joseph without hesitation. "As I told my parents, I was visited early this morning, just before sunrise, by the archangel Gabriel. In essence, he told me that I should marry your daughter, and not worry about the thoughts and criticisms of others."

After a long moment of silence, Caleb said stiffly, "Joseph, so the reason you wish to marry her is because you had a dream about the archangel?"

Aaron said dryly, "Before visiting my airy son, I wish Gabriel would have consulted with me. I would have given him a piece of my mind, blasphemous as that might sound." He chuckled nervously.

"No doubt," muttered Caleb, his previous joy evaporating. He took a big gulp of wine, then added in a weary tone, "Yes, yes, perhaps blasphemous; and of course we mean no disrespect to the Lord God, but I am growing rather impatient with all these angelic visitations."

Frustrated by their dismissive attitude, Joseph stated, "I know it sounds unbelievable, but Gabriel came to me and announced that God is pleased with Mary. It was as real as the sound of our voices." He made a small gesture, adding strongly, "I know Mary well, and she would never lie. She believes the Lord God inspired her to be close to a holy man who …"

"Holy man?" echoed his mother, adding curtly, "Is that what Gabriel told you?"

Joseph shook his head. "I spoke to Mary yesterday while you and Father visited the rabbi's home. Mary said she was intimate with a holy man, which seems only natural, since Gabriel had announced she would give birth to a very special baby."

Marta sighed. "Are you such a fool as to actually believe that incredible tale?"

Shifting uncomfortably in her chair, Azuba quickly changed the subject with Joseph. "So, when you awoke this morning after your dream with Gabriel, you made the instant decision to take Mary as your wife?"

"It wasn't instant or thoughtless," he retorted. "It's difficult to explain, but I feel that God wants me to marry your daughter. I believe He has assigned me the task to protect Mary and her child."

Marta looked at Azuba and said in a sharp tone, "To be honest, I am completely against Joseph's decision … disturbed by it. Though I love Mary, I don't want my son to marry a girl who's carrying another man's child. If you were in my position, you would feel exactly the same. I cannot tolerate the thought of having my son raise Mary's illicit child, especially in my home."

"Who can blame you?" replied Azuba. "But what do you want from us? If your Joseph is willing to shoulder the responsibility of caring for Mary and her child, then Caleb and I will do everything possible to help them."

"Thank you," said Joseph. "I *will* assume responsibility for her pregnancy. If we can hide the fact for several months, then people may not become suspicious ..."

Marta raised a quick hand. "Not suspicious?" she guffawed. "You are both stubborn and foolish! As Azuba will be the first to tell you, older women know when a young woman is bearing, even during the early months. It's as clear as the nose on your face!"

"If so," Joseph retorted with confidence, "then Mary and I will leave Nazareth. A week after our wedding, we can offer a plausible story that explains our journey to another region. After the baby is born, we can stay there, or live somewhere else for a few years before returning here."

Caleb spoke up in a tired, self-deprecatory tone. "As everyone here knows, I'm not a wise man. Yet I am old enough to know that such plans rarely develop according to expectations. So don't expect that every little thing will fall into place as you hope."

"That's good advice," remarked Aaron, turning to his son. "Joseph, you and Mary should stay here for as long as possible. Carrying a child is difficult enough in one's hometown, but it'll even more complicated if Mary travels to a strange place with no relatives to help her."

"I agree," Azuba said, a hopeful look on her face. "Each morning Mary can come here. That way, I can watch over her until nightfall. You and Marta won't have to concern yourselves with her daily needs. She could even have the child here, if that would please you."

Aaron was silent for a moment. "Caleb, though my wife and I have accepted Joseph's decision, we cannot promise that our disappointment in Mary will vanish. Nor can we promise to show any affection for her child ..."

Azuba's eyes widened. "Believe me, I am more hurt and disappointed than you and Marta. But what about Mary's dream of Gabriel? What if this child is truly a gift from the Lord? When I pray deeply about Mary, her dream, her experience in Ain Karem, then my heart cannot help feeling that God is there somehow."

"That could be," responded Aaron. "Yet Marta and I haven't had any dreams or visions about this. Until we do, I doubt that our thoughts will change. In the future, when Joseph and Mary have their own sons and daughters, then our grandsons and granddaughters may help to alleviate our bitter feelings toward your daughter."

A look of sadness crossed Caleb's face. "I understand, and I apologize that we have put you in this difficult position." He paused. "Words cannot express my gratefulness to Joseph for helping Mary in this manner. Since her life is still in great danger, we should prepare for the wedding as quickly as possible …"

"What wedding?" said Mary, standing at the doorway. As her eyes darted about the room, she was surprised to see Joseph and his parents there. They were smiling, as if the events of the past few months had never taken place. Joseph rose to his feet and approached her with outstretched arms, and she realized that somehow he was willing to accept her as his wife.

CHAPTER 8

THE FOLLOWING WEEK, Joseph and Mary were joined together in a traditional ceremony similar to that of their parents, grandparents, and scores of ancestors. Fortunately, during the festive occasion, only their parents, along with Elizabeth, Sara, and Maleb, knew that Mary was pregnant.

That evening Joseph led Mary to his parents' home, but they didn't sleep together due to her delicate condition. Though he felt trepidation after the ceremony, Joseph was determined to be a good husband and a dutiful father once Mary's child was born. As the weeks slowly passed, some of Aaron's neighbors began to chatter among themselves, wondering how it was possible for Joseph's wife to have such a noticeable bulge only weeks after their wedding. Everyone naturally assumed the two young lovers, during a moment of weakness, had been intimate before their marriage. But since Mary and Joseph had soon married, almost all who guessed at it were not upset and didn't make a public issue of it.

A few weeks before the baby was to be born, Aaron's home had become an almost impossible place to live in for Joseph and Mary. The marriage was difficult enough for Joseph without his mother's endless criticisms of his pregnant wife. Whenever Marta was alone with Joseph, she would disparage his wife's character and not too subtly try to persuade him to end the marriage and find a new bride. His two elder sisters and their husbands also treated Mary coldly, once they had been told that Joseph was not the child's father. In fact, Joseph's relations with his family deteriorated to such a low point that he decided it would be better for him and Mary to leave Nazareth and move south to Judea, where his Uncle Jonah worked as a tentmaker and leatherworker in Bethlehem.

Although Mary felt like a menial servant in Aaron and Marta's home, she wanted to remain in Nazareth because her father had been suddenly struck by a strange illness that not only severely affected his power of speech but also left him with no strength in his legs, so he could barely walk. Devastated by the hopeless condition of her husband, Azuba tried to care for both Caleb and Mary as best she could. But soon after, Azuba's health declined due to worry and exhaustion. She had no recourse but to move Caleb to the farmhouse of Sara and Maleb, and she sank into a deep sadness and fever of regret over the dire fate of her family during the past year.

During an intense discussion late one evening, Mary finally relented to her husband's wishes to move from his home. Still thankful for the great sacrifice he had made by marrying her, she didn't wish to disobey Joseph or give him a reason to annul their marriage and put her life in danger before the birth of her child, who was growing bigger in the womb each week.

On the morning before their departure from Nazareth, a major rainstorm passed through the town. A cold wind blew from the northwest, and the roads were muddy as Joseph held the reins of the donkey upon which Mary sat. As she sobbed, Joseph glanced at his distressed wife. "Mary, I promise that one day we will return here. My parents are good people. Their hearts will eventually soften, especially if we have children of our own."

Mary gave no response, gravely concerned about giving birth among strangers. And who would help care for the baby during its first months on earth? She was not sure she knew what to do.

Thinking about her poor mother, Mary finally murmured, "Perhaps we can return after your parents learn to accept us as a family. When we have our first child together, you can take over your father's carpentry shop. Your mother will feel kindly toward me by then. Right?"

Joseph guided the donkey around a big puddle of water. "Mary, it may take a long time for her bitter feelings to pass." He hesitated. "Actually I can understand my mother's hostile behavior toward you. Since I am her only son, she was anticipating a grandson from my seed to continue my father's lineage. Who knows if you will be able to have children with me."

Joseph's words stabbed Mary like an ice pick. Despite all her efforts to allow him to feel loved and honored by her, he continued to demonstrate hurt and resentment toward her in moments like this. Suddenly she felt the child kick within her, reminding her that they were not alone.

Shivering from the cold wind, Mary's heart spoke to her child. "Yes, we are together in this situation. I am blamed for conceiving you, and you are blamed for being conceived. But the Lord God will watch over us both, and you will fulfill your destiny.

Joseph and Mary were silent during most of the journey to Bethlehem, the ancestral home of Joseph's father. He had chosen Bethlehem in hopes they would have a better chance to create a new life together with the help of his father's relatives. He didn't know how exactly, but he felt that being away from his mother and the malicious whispers of neighbors would relieve tensions between Mary and himself. As a child, he had visited his paternal relatives in Bethlehem several times, staying at the home of his father's younger brother. His Uncle Jonah was quite fond of him, and Joseph believed that he would be supportive at this difficult time in his life.

During the long journey south, Joseph replayed in his mind various ways he could explain to his relatives the reason he was bringing his young pregnant wife to Bethlehem. He finally decided to emphasize his desire to have *his* and Mary's son to come into the world in the village of his ancestors. However, almost five years had elapsed since Joseph last visited his father's relatives in Bethlehem. The village itself is nestled in the southern portion of the Judean Mountains, about six miles south of Jerusalem. The Abrahamic matriarch Rachel had died and was buried near Bethlehem. Yet the village is especially noted for being the birthplace of David, and also the place where he had been anointed king of Israel by the prophet Samuel.

To Joseph's consternation, the traveling was slow. For almost two weeks he led the donkey over the rough terrain at a turtle-like pace. Since Mary had bad headaches much of the time, and occasional pains in her abdomen, they often stopped along the way so that she could lie down and rest.

When Joseph and Mary finally arrived in Bethlehem late one afternoon, they found the dwelling of Joseph's uncle. To the young man's surprise, the reception was anything but warm. Jonah's family and other relatives gave Joseph polite greetings, but were overtly ungracious to Mary, who received icy stares from the womenfolk. Several weeks before, Mary would learn many years later, rumors of her early pregnancy had reached Bethlehem by way of Marta's niece, who was friends with Jonah's wife.

Regretful for having left Nazareth, Mary suspected even then that Joseph's relatives knew that the child in her womb was not related to them. After an hour of painful casual talk, Joseph realized that no one would offer them lodgings for the night, due to a lack of sympathy for their situation, as well as not wanting to take on the burden of two more mouths to feed, with a baby soon coming and disturbing the peace of the household.

When Joseph and Mary departed from his uncle's home, the moon had already risen over Bethlehem. With growing concern about his wife's condition, Joseph had no choice but to look for an inn to spend the night at. Since it was now too painful for Mary to ride atop the donkey, she held Joseph's hand as they trudged through the streets in search of a room. There were only a few inns in the village, and none had space for them. So they walked to the outskirts of Bethlehem and noticed an isolated house. Nearby was a cave in the side of a hill that was used as a stable. Hoping this could provide shelter for the evening, Joseph humbly approached the owner and asked if he and his pregnant wife could stay there. The owner readily agreed, feeling sympathy for the young married couple.

Shortly after they were settled comfortably among the animals in the stable, Mary started having severe pains in her abdomen, much more severe than those she had felt during the journey from Nazareth.

Joseph helped Mary as she lay down on some blankets over a bed of straw. During the next hour, the pains intensified as Joseph massaged Mary's lower abdomen while praying fervently for God's intervention. When Mary's groans grew louder, Joseph realized the baby might be born at any moment. So he went to the stable owner and asked if his wife could assist Mary during the birth process. Since his wife had a serious illness, the owner suggested a local woman who acted as a midwife.

Joseph hurried back to Mary in a panic, and quickly told her that he must leave to find a midwife. Though the night air was turning colder, her pale face was covered with beads of perspiration, and she trembled with fear at the thought of being alone under such dreadful circumstances.

When Joseph disappeared, Mary's heart filled with terror at being all alone in a dark cave with farm animals milling about. She felt more fragile and abandoned than ever, especially since Joseph's relatives had treated her so badly earlier that day. Her heart dark with fear and sorrow, she began sobbing, a lost child longing for her parents. As the blackness of night surrounded her in this strange, unknown place, she gasped for air as the stabbing pains increased, causing her to question whether she and her child would survive the night.

Summoning all her strength, Mary tried to sit up as she called out to the God she loved and trusted, the One God who nearly a year before had sent Gabriel with the promise that she would give birth to the future king of Israel. But as hard as Mary continued praying, there was no comfort, only unbearable pain as she fell backward on the blankets.

As Joseph hurried along the narrow roads of Bethlehem, his heart grew even more distressed over the callous way he and Mary had been treated by Jonah's family. So he had no desire to return there and ask for help, even if he couldn't find the midwife.

Upon stopping at a small dwelling just off the main road, Joseph knocked repeatedly at the door until a tall, middle-aged woman appeared, with a half-eaten apple in her hand.

"Are you Devorah?" he blurted out. "Please, I need your help!"

As soon as she saw the frightened face of the young man, she knew that he must have a wife who was struggling to give birth.

"My wife is ..." But before he could finish, the woman turned away and walked toward the rear of her home.

Praying that Mary was still all right, Joseph was about to collapse from nervous exhaustion as the woman returned and pushed a heavy basket into his hands. "Is this your wife's first child?" she asked.

He nodded and almost stumbled as Devorah brushed past him and started walking in the opposite direction from which he had come.

Joseph called out to her, "Mary's in a stable on the other side of town."

Devorah seemed concerned as she turned to say, "Since this is her first child, I will need assistance."

Soon she came to the house where two elderly sisters lived, both of whom often gave her advice and help during complicated deliveries.

While she was inside the house, Joseph blew on his hands to keep them warm.

"Why did I force Mary to leave Nazareth?" he muttered, berating himself for being so foolish. "Lord, please spare her life!"

When Devorah emerged from the house, she was accompanied by two wrinkle-faced ladies who gave Joseph warm smiles. Both were quite short and stooped over, and bundled up against the cold weather.

"Lead me to your wife," commanded Devorah. "She's in a stable?"

Joseph began walking quickly, then broke into a run. When he looked over his shoulder, he was surprised that all three women weren't far behind him.

"Where are you from?" inquired Devorah, near his side now, taking the long strides of a tall man. "By your accent, you must be from Galilee."

"Yes, our families live in Nazareth. But Mary and I want our son to be born in Bethlehem, like all my ancestors." He hesitated, realizing he had said *our son*. "Do you know Jonah and Rivka's family? They live close to your home ..."

"You are related to Jonah?" she questioned, with a look of surprise.

Joseph nodded. "He is my father's younger brother."

Confused, Devorah grew silent as Joseph turned onto the trail leading to the cave.

As the women drew closer, they could hear the groans of the woman, who was clearly in great pain.

Relieved that Mary was still alive, Joseph broke into a run again. When he entered the stable and saw Mary writhing in pain among the smelly animals, he repented in his heart for having harbored any ill feeling toward her during the past months.

A faint smile flickered across Mary's face when she saw Joseph and the three women, who rushed over to her.

Joseph knelt beside her, breathing heavily as he reached for her trembling hand.

"Mary, don't worry. These women are going to help you give birth to the child."

Squeezing his hand, Mary nodded.

The midwife touched Mary's pale cheek. "My dear, you have such lovely skin," she said in a soothing voice. "I am Devorah. Over the years I have brought many children into the world." Pausing, she gestured toward the other women. "This is Abira and Nasya. They are here to pray for you and the child during its birth."

Through half-closed eyes, Mary glanced at the two sisters and was comforted by the smiles on their faces. "Have faith," said Abira, her voice clear and sweet. "God is watching over you, and His angels will protect your child from harm."

Devorah turned to Joseph and said firmly, "Go to the owner and get several candles or a lamp. Then bring us a bucket of fresh water from the well. And hurry!"

No sooner had he left than Mary grimaced with intense pain and latched onto Nasya's bony hand. "Oh, I feel the baby moving within me!"

The old lady said in a loud whisper, "Mary, try to have pleasant thoughts and your baby will come out smiling!"

"Breathe deeply," uttered Devorah, her strong fingers massaging Mary's abdomen. "That's good. Keep breathing deeply."

Mary closed her eyes and concentrated on her breathing. She thought about her mother and her aunt, imagining they were there in this drafty cave, taking care of her during this time of suffering and hopeful expectations.

The waves of pain became almost tolerable, now that she sensed a divine motherly presence through the images of her mother and aunt.

Praying in whispers, Devorah continued massaging Mary's abdomen, then glanced at Joseph as he returned with a bright lamp and a bucket of water. He set them near her side, feeling a surge of confidence while studying her resolute face.

Stroking Mary's damp hair, Devorah said gently, "You are strong for such a young woman. You did very well on the last contraction." Then she examined the vaginal opening again and saw it was growing larger. "Mary, your child is coming. Why don't you stand and try to walk a little. The baby's weight will help it come quicker."

With their support, Mary was able to move a few steps until another round of strong contractions sent a wave of pain throughout her body. This time Mary screamed when she felt pressure on her pelvis as though something were trying to split her in half.

Devorah responded in a reassuring tone, "Mary, that's it. You are doing great. Keep breathing deeply and your child will soon be in your arms." Pausing, she turned to Abira. "Is everything ready?"

"Yes," she smiled at Joseph as he stared at Mary with moistened eyes.

She is still so young, he thought, recalling an afternoon only a year earlier sitting in the shade of an olive tree near Maleb's home, talking with her about their future. Just a few weeks later Mary had suddenly left for Ain Karem, and their lives had never been the same since that time.

Joseph was pulled from his reverie as Mary clenched his arms and cried out. Noticing her tousled hair and the sweat on her cheeks, he felt she was stunningly beautiful as she struggled to give birth to the child. The physical pain of her contractions was like the emotional pain he had been enduring in his heart. Yet his love and concern for her was even greater than his pain.

As Mary's contractions grew more intense and closer together, Devorah told Abira in an urgent tone, "Abira, I want you to squat next to Mary. Cup your hands and be ready to support the baby's head when it comes out …"

The elderly woman smiled as she got into position to receive the child. Even though she had done this hundreds of times, Abira always acted as if it were her first experience.

"Very good, Mary! Keep pushing … That's good … Breathe deeply and push … Oh, I can see the crown … Nasya, while Abira supports the head, you pull gently on the shoulders … Mary, keep pushing … Push!"

Mary inhaled deeply, and then exhaled a long breath as she used all her strength to push the baby through the birth canal.

Nasya announced calmly, "Devorah, I have the shoulders."

"Very good … Now gently pull the child while Mary pushes hard one last time … Push … Push … Push, Mary!"

Though she tried with all her might, Mary felt she had no more power. Then a force seemed to take control of her body, providing the strength she needed to push hard one last time. Almost immediately, the pressure on her pelvis eased into a ghostly presence as the baby passed through the final portion of the birth canal and into the hands of Abira.

"I have him!" she exclaimed, carefully handling the newborn.

Standing near her side, Nasya uttered a prayer before cutting the umbilical cord and slapping the child's buttocks hard, causing him to wail out as he took his first breaths of air amid the animals in the cold stable.

After many exhausting hours, Mary silently thanked God for helping her give birth to her son. Joseph and Devorah led her to the bed of straw and supported her as she lay down upon the blankets. With a satisfied look, Devorah began singing a psalm while she removed the placenta and washed Mary's lower parts,

Thankful that both Mary and the baby were alive, Joseph knelt beside her and dabbed her sweaty face with a wet towel. Curious about what the child looked like, he moved his eyes to Abira and Nasya as they washed the blood off his face and body. They wrapped a soft quilt around him while murmuring prayers for its good health and a long, fruitful life.

Relieved the ordeal was over, Mary closed her eyes and listened absently as the two sisters joyfully cooed, "Praise God for his birth … He's a handsome boy with well-formed hands and feet … Just look at that high forehead … Yes, this one is going to be a scholar … maybe even a holy man!"

"What will you call him?" asked Devorah, looking at Joseph.

He hesitated, then gestured at Mary. "My wife has named him Jesus."

"Jesus," murmured Mary opening her eyes. "May I hold him?" she said weakly.

"Of course," Devorah replied, smiling warmly. She took the whimpering baby from Abira and gently placed him next to Mary.

A grateful smile crossed her face as she cradled the child in her arms. She couldn't help wondering if Gabriel and the other angels were now present there, watching over her and Jesus. "He's so precious," she uttered, studying his facial features.

Kneeling again, Devorah guided the baby's tiny mouth to Mary's full bosom. After a few moments, the child began sucking milk, causing Devorah to smile with satisfaction as she rose to her feet and joined Nasya and Abira.

Now that they had finished their task, the women looked quite tired and ready to return to their homes for a well-deserved rest.

The stable was now lit by moonlight as strong winds cleared wispy clouds from the night skies over Bethlehem. Humming softly, the new mother studied her tiny son's face and clearly detected traces of her own features in his. His darkish, round eyes and large mouth were similar to hers and her father's. Yet, the child definitely had Zechariah's forehead and slightly hooked nose. In fact, she thought with concern, if Jesus and John were placed side by side, some people might suspect they were brothers.

As the newborn baby continued feeding at his mother's breast, Devorah approached Mary with a cup of sheep's milk in her hand. "Here, dear, drink this to strengthen you while you nourish the little one. You need to restore your health." She lifted Mary's head a few inches and placed the brim of the cup under her cracked lips. As Mary drank the sweet milk, she felt Jesus' tiny lips loosen, pause, then suck again. Her eyelids soon fluttered and closed as she drifted into a deep slumber.

Devorah told Joseph to monitor his young wife closely during the next few days. Since she had lost so much blood, she would need to remain in the stable for at least a week and rest until she was strong enough to travel. Joseph listened with concern to Devorah, and then he thanked the three women with some of the few copper coins he owned. After the exhausted women left the stable, Joseph walked among the animals with growing apprehension in his heart, knowing he was now fully responsible for the two lives beside him.

While mother and son rested during the night, Joseph remained awake, his mind turning over thoughts of how their lives would be from now on. Certainly, Mary would invest her life into caring for her son. Joseph knew that if he had any hopes of having a child of his own seed, he would need to help Mary with the care of this little one, so that she could regain the strength to bear his children. In the meantime, he had to plan how to build a life in Bethlehem to support his young wife and this child.

As Mary stirred from her sleep, Joseph knelt by her side and reached for the baby, feeling a little clumsy at it. As he lifted the delicate child from her side, he was careful, though, to hold the head sturdily in his palm while supporting the back with his forearm.

Mary opened her eyes, seeing his blurry image. "What are you doing?"

"Sshhh … You lay still while I bring the child to your other breast."

Using both hands, Joseph placed the child's mouth next to her other bosom. The baby latched on, and soon the stable was silent again.

Joseph watched as the baby sucked voraciously. He realized that Mary needed much nourishment to sustain such a demand from the little one. So he took the cup and got more milk from the sheep, then brought it to her, watching the child suckle.

For several moments, Joseph felt a tinge of jealousy. The woman he loved so deeply, who had sparkled for him, was now smiling while engrossed in love for her son.

Strangely, he felt more like a servant than Mary's husband. Yet he still loved her, even as she gave her full attention to Jesus.

Kneeling by her side again, Joseph lifted Mary's head and shoulders while bringing the cup to her mouth. After a few sips, she turned her face away from the cup.

"Try to drink all of it," he implored, moving the cup to her lips. "You need to build up your strength for the baby."

It took a while for Mary to drink the milk. She murmured incoherently and then drifted off to sleep again while the baby continued feeding at her breast.

Once again Joseph was alone with his assorted thoughts. Although his heart was burdened by many concerns, he finally surrendered to sleep as the first slivers of light from the morning sun began to brighten the skies above Bethlehem.

During the following days, there were still no rooms available in town, and since Jonah's wife showed no sympathy for the situation of her husband's nephew, Joseph and his small family had to remain in the stable. Though the weather grew milder, Mary's weakness forced her to rest as the baby alternately slept and fed at her breast.

Feeling compassion for the young couple, the landlord cleaned the stable and brought them a carpet, pillows, and more blankets, giving them fresh water each morning for drinking and bathing. Around noon each day, Devorah, Abira, and Nasya came by to care for Mary and her child, bringing nuts and fruits, herbs, bread, and goat's cheese, as well as jars of soup made from ox bones, while some shepherds brought fresh sheep's milk. Devorah also persuaded the landlord to make another manger, and when it was finished, Jesus slept there when not in his mother's arms.

Even under these humble circumstances, Mary and Joseph felt abundantly blessed. They thanked everyone deeply, while praying that God would give them blessings for their goodness. On the eighth day after his birth, Jesus was brought to the town's synagogue. The child was offered to God with song and prayers. Then the rabbi performed circumcision on Jesus as God had commanded for all the offspring of Abraham.

The following day, Joseph swallowed his pride and walked to the home of his Uncle Jonah, asking if he could help find work for him. Jonah was ashamed of the way his family and other relatives had treated Joseph and Mary upon their arrival. So he sincerely apologized and decided to introduce Joseph to an older man named Benjamin, who was a respected carpenter in the region. Since Benjamin had more work than he could handle, he gave Joseph some old doors to repair and observed him in silence as he went about the task. It didn't take long for Benjamin to realize that the Galilean was a skillful craftsman. So he let Joseph's family move into the small room behind his workshop, which stood next to his home on the outskirts of Bethlehem.

As the weeks and months passed by, a sense of normalcy crept back into the lives of Joseph and Mary. During the daytime, Mary and baby Jesus usually stayed in the main house with Benjamin's wife. Tirza was a kind and humorous woman who spent much of the day at her upright loom, mostly weaving rugs that were sold in Jerusalem. Since she and Benjamin were childless, she doted over baby Jesus and his mother, whose health was still poor due to her difficult childbirth and the stress of the past year.

Although Joseph missed his family in Nazareth, he found that Benjamin reminded him of his father. The older man liked Joseph a great deal, and the two of them were often together for over twelve hours a day, working on various projects.

Now that Joseph was a father, he became more serious and began planning for the future, especially since he hoped that he and Mary could have at least three or four children of their own. This goal gave him great energy and strength to work harder and save his money, with the thought of returning to Nazareth in the future.

About a year after their arrival in Bethlehem, Mary seemed to have returned to her old self. She was more gregarious than ever and had made friends with some other young mothers with children about Jesus' age. Now that he could walk, Jesus wandered about the house and courtyard, poking his nose into each thing he found and getting his hands into everything.

Unfortunately, Mary's cheery mood did not last long. Late one afternoon, as she and Benjamin's wife were preparing for the Sabbath, a messenger delivered news from her Aunt Sara in Nazareth. Both Caleb and Azuba had recently died, only a few days apart. It was a blow for Mary to lose her beloved parents. She felt a mixture of sadness and regret over having not been there to comfort them during their final years on earth, on top of having caused them so much grief upon her return from the home of Elizabeth and Zechariah.

Although Mary deeply mourned her parents' death for many weeks, she realized that life had to go on, and she was grateful to the Lord God for blessing her with a good and hardworking husband, along with a cute, bright-eyed son like Jesus, who was a constant source of joy and delight for everyone who came to know him.

Late one evening, Joseph was sitting on a cushion in front of a low table, reading a portion of the Torah written on an old scroll, which he had borrowed from Benjamin. He was having difficulty concentrating on the scripture. Though the flame of the oil lamp provided enough light to read, Joseph could barely keep his eyelids open. He had gotten up at dawn that morning, and all day he and Benjamin had been laying heavy timber beams for the roof of a new house.

Tired and hungry, Joseph returned to the small room behind the workshop to find a dish of vegetables, some fruit, and strips of roasted mutton waiting for him, all prepared by his dutiful wife. Since Mary had no cooking room or outdoor oven to bake bread, she would prepare the meal at Benjamin's home under Tirza's guidance.

"Where is Jesus?" he had asked, kicking off his sandals.

"At Benjamin's house," replied Mary, serving him a cup of wine. "Jesus played there all day with the children of Tirza's niece. Then shortly after sunset, he collapsed from exhaustion. So Tirza is watching over him."

After a sip of wine, Joseph said shortly, "Don't take advantage of her good heart. You should go get Jesus now."

"Tirza doesn't mind," said Mary, sitting across from him. "She knows this room is too cramped for the three of us."

Joseph made no response and uttered a prayer of gratitude. He ate the meal in silence as Mary knitted a head scarf, an occasional smile crossing her face whenever Joseph looked at her.

She kept on knitting until Joseph asked in a hopeful tone, "Are you pregnant with our first child?"

She shook her head, adding playfully, "But it's not from a lack of effort," and chiding him again for sometimes acting like a rooster in a henhouse at night.

"But there's only one hen in this house, and she's the loveliest hen in Bethlehem."

She giggled and watched as he rolled up the scroll, then moved to her side of the table and held her hands. "Mary, I loved you when we were children, and I love you even more today."

"Oh, Joseph, I have always loved you. I want to give you sons and daughters of your own flesh and blood." As she wrapped her arms around his thick waist, he gave her tender kisses on her forehead, her cheeks, her lips. "Listen to our hearts beating together. It is like we are one in flesh and spirit."

"Yes, for always," she murmured, her heart thumping as he led her toward the bed.

Never before did Joseph feel so in love and confident that Mary would conceive a new child for them, a child who would be the fruit of their union. They were convinced that God had united them in sacred marriage so that they could experience the greatest of the divine loves, the love between husband and wife, as spiritual as it was physical, a love fulfilled in their long nights together in each other's arms.

CHAPTER 9

JESUS WAS JUST OVER TWO when Joseph and Mary returned to Nazareth. Their marriage was now strong and stable, and Mary was five months pregnant with their second child, so Joseph prayed that his parents had undergone a change of heart and would now accept Mary as a daughter-in-law and perhaps in time, even the child Jesus as a grandson.

Joseph led the donkey carrying his wife and child toward his parents' home. As Jesus chattered excitedly, Joseph prayed under his breath that smiles would appear on his father and mother's faces upon seeing his family return from Bethlehem. But against their grandest illusions, even though Aaron and Marta received Joseph with tears of joy, they greeted Mary and her son with cool indifference. At first Joseph let it pass, excusing his parents' behavior by assuring himself that it wasn't that Aaron and Marta disliked Jesus, it was simply that they didn't know how to relate to him and his mother. Or so he told Mary the following day.

But in the months to come, Joseph's parents showed little warmth or affection toward the boy. Mary could plainly see that Joseph's parents were incapable of displaying any sort of familial feelings for her son. And though she had accepted the fact that Aaron and Marta would never forgive her for having another man's child, she couldn't bear the thought of Jesus not being doted on by his grandparents. If her own parents were still alive, she often brooded, Jesus would surely be receiving their love and guidance, and in turn would be treated more kindly by others in Nazareth.

Nevertheless, Mary was pleased to be back in her family home. Though things weren't perfect, life seemed as near to normal as it had ever been, with Joseph filling his days working at his father's carpentry shop. Mary was grateful to him for marrying her.

The years passed quickly, and Jesus grew into a sturdy young boy of strong spirit. Though he was usually content and always friendly to other children and respectful to his elders, Mary noticed that during quiet moments he became contemplative and sorrowful, as if he had lost something of great value. Before he was nine, Jesus had heard that Joseph was not his real father. It happened one winter afternoon near the end of Mary's fourth pregnancy, while Jesus and his younger brothers stayed at the home of their grandparents. Jesus was helping Marta rearrange bags of grain in the storeroom, and he asked her why she never hugged or kissed him like she did his brothers and cousins. All of a sudden Marta blurted out that he was an illegitimate child and that only his mother knew who his real father was.

Jesus soon realized that many others thought this way. Sometimes when he played with his cousins, they would argue and ridicule him, saying that he didn't belong to their family because he wasn't a true son of Joseph's. And in Nazareth and the surrounding villages, there were many people who taunted him, saying that Joseph wasn't his real father, and that his mother had been intimate with a stranger. Naturally, this angered Jesus, and it both intensified his loneliness and made him curious about his true lineage.

With the passing of time, Mary noticed how her son often sought refuge in a world that only he seemed to inhabit. He was sensitive and warm-hearted, with great love for the birds and animals. And though he was quite sociable, he also had a reflective side, quietly observing people burdened by sorrow, poverty, and sickness as they struggled under the heavy yoke of Roman rule. Jesus was also very curious. He had so many questions for anyone who would listen to him. He wanted to know why so many people suffered, and why there was so much violence, misery, and injustice in the world. Unlike other children in Nazareth, he displayed a precocious compassion for those poor souls going through difficult times.

Often, other children refused to play with Jesus, and were even quite mean and hostile to him. One afternoon, while he was sitting on a large rock watching several boys play, one of them shouted out, "Hey, bastard, do you want to play?"

As Jesus got up and ran onto the field to join in the game, another boy yelled at him, "Don't even think about it. We never play with idiots like you. Go away!"

Tired of being ridiculed, Jesus ran home. In his mother's arms, he uttered in a trembling voice, "The other boys often tease me and won't let me play with them. Some even call me a bastard, as though I don't have any parents."

"Of course you do," replied Mary, stroking his hair. "I am your mother, and Joseph is your father."

"But when he's upset with you, why does he look at me with such angry eyes? It's as if I have committed some great wrong that he cannot tell me about."

"Jesus, that's only your imagination." Though wrenching inside, Mary pushed a smile to her face. "It's normal for couples to have disagreements. But after your father and I argue about something, the anger soon passes and we talk and laugh again like usual."

"But when you aren't here, he often speaks harshly to me. Sometimes I think he hates me. He loves my brothers and sisters, but not me!"

`"Jesus, I am sure that's not true. Though your father may seem discontent at times, he loves you very much. And so do I."

Noticing how disturbed his mother was by his comments, Jesus gave her a sweet smile and a kiss on the cheek. He remained quiet for several minutes, eating the hot fresh bread that she had just taken out of the small oven at the rear of the house.

"Mother, why doesn't Grandmother Marta love me? She's nice to Simon and James, but so cold to me. When we are at her house, she offers them food but usually ignores me."

Mary felt a craggy rock in her throat while she listened to Jesus. Her dear son! How could she, an insignificant woman in Nazareth, protect him from the cruelty of this world?

She took a deep breath and managed to speak in a calm voice. "Jesus, all people are different. You can't expect everyone to be the same. Your grandmother is getting old and sickly, so she hasn't been in a good mood recently. But she can still be affectionate in her own way."

Mary always encouraged Jesus and gave him support, consoling him with loving words and warm hugs whenever she sensed he needed them, which was often, the older he got. But since there were now five children in the family, Jesus received less of his mother's affection, and he couldn't help but notice how Joseph doted over the others while ignoring him.

Nevertheless, Jesus' spirit strengthened day by day. Mary taught Jesus to be caring and helpful to his younger brothers and sisters, and they loved him very much. Yet as they grew older and realized that Jesus had a different father, even they sometimes teased him to the point where he would run from the house and walk alone in the countryside.

Several times a year, many of Mary's relatives would come together for religious celebrations or family events such as weddings and birthdays.

Jesus was twelve years old when Mary's great uncle celebrated his seventieth birthday. Some of his relatives, including Elizabeth and Zechariah, along with their thirteen-year-old son, John, came from outside of Nazareth.

Zechariah seemed very uncomfortable in Nazareth, for he obviously knew that Jesus was his son. But he took advantage of this opportunity to quietly observe the handsome young man. Trying not to call too much attention to himself, the old priest stole furtive glances at Jesus, scrutinizing his facial features and mannerisms.

John enjoyed getting to know Jesus and his other cousins. Jesus wasn't as loud and boisterous as the others, but he took part in the various games, even those that called for rough, aggressive behavior.

Unlike Jesus, John had an assertive character and a loud voice, and being the son of a notable priest, he was well educated and treated with great respect by his relatives. Jesus, on the other hand, was somewhat reserved and humble in appearance, so in occurrences like this his relatives paid little attention to him. Although Mary's relatives were more considerate of Jesus than Joseph's relatives had been, they did tend to treat John with greater respect due to his status as the son of Zechariah.

Ironically, a similar situation existed between Mary and John's mother. Elizabeth was educated and well thought of for giving birth to John under miraculous circumstances. And being the wife of the elder priest, Elizabeth had more prestige than Jesus' mother, who was considered someone of low social position within her own clan. So from Elizabeth's viewpoint, which had gradually changed over the years, Mary was now a cousin of little importance, someone with whom Zechariah had foolishly engaged in a moment of weakness.

The details of Jesus' conception had remained a well-kept secret, Mary's parents taking it to their grave. But it was not enough to avoid the suspicions of relatives and neighbors alike. And when the subject came up, they asked each other the same questions over and over again. How could Mary have had an advanced pregnancy just a few months after the wedding? And if she had been intimate with Joseph before their marriage, then how could Jesus' conception have taken place, since Mary was staying at Zechariah's home at the time?

"Maybe the old priest had something to do with it?" they had wondered aloud, with a mixture of scorn and amusement. Yet no one had the courage to say anything publicly, especially in the presence of Elizabeth and the elder priest.

Over the years, John's mother had guarded the secret in her heart, hoping that Mary's family would do the same. And though Joseph and Mary's relatives suspected that something horrible had taken place in Zechariah's home, they still felt great respect for him. They were too proud of having a member of the family holding a high and prestigious social position. It was in their interest to keep their suspicions to themselves, masquerading any circumstantial evidence with evasive smiles while Zechariah and Elizabeth were in Nazareth. Why jeopardize Zechariah's important visit with embarrassing questions?

Besides, they had no actual proof of Zechariah's moment of weakness, and no one would dare to question a man of his prestige. So on those few occasions when members of their clan reunited, almost everyone believed it was wise to simply ignore the issue as if it did not exist.

John was proud of being Zechariah's only son and liked the attention he received from adults and other children. He was the undisputed leader of any group of young ones, and he always decided which games were to be played and what roles each boy had to carry out. He spoke well for his age, with a rich vocabulary, so other boys rarely confronted him or challenged his authority.

On the third day of his visit to Nazareth, John was looking for lizards when he came upon Jesus, who was returning from the rabbi's home.

"What are you doing?" he asked, watching curiously as John scampered toward a flowery bush. His hand shot out at a shadow on the leaves, then went limp as he straightened up and looked at his cousin.

"I am trying to catch a lizard," he answered with a frown. "In my town they are larger and have a brownish color. Here they are different." Stepping closer, he added, "My father says I was born six months before you."

"That close?" uttered Jesus, shading his eyes from the sun. "Did you know that my mother was living at your home when you were born?"

John shook his head, his eyes darting about in search of another lizard. After a few moments, he said absently, "Your father is a carpenter, right? Is that what you want to do?"

Jesus nodded. "Sometimes I help my father at his workshop. It's interesting to make cart wheels, tables, and chests."

John gave him a long look. "Why are you so quiet? When we play games, it seems like you're afraid of everyone."

This surprised Jesus. "I am not afraid of …"

"You sure act like it. And you usually have a sad face. One of our cousins told me your father isn't your real father."

Startled by John's comment, Jesus pulled back and uttered, "My mother told me not to pay attention to them. They're always making fun of me."

"Then why don't you fight them? Don't you have any friends who can help you?"

Jesus thought about it. "I don't like fighting."

"But if some evil-minded boys attack you and your friends, wouldn't you fight back?"

"Of course. When one boy treats another badly, then I protest and try to convince him to change his ways. But if he persists, I will defend the other person."

"Good," said John with a nod. He studied Jesus' face. "Can you come to the synagogue with me? We can study the Torah and learn the traditions of our forefathers."

Jesus said, "Our rabbi often teaches me and my brothers about the Mosaic law and the teachings of the great prophets."

Suddenly losing interest in catching lizards, John sat on large rock. "Do you know that as children of Israel, we belong to a people who believe in a single God? And the priests like my father are God's representatives among us."

Jesus nodded and said, "The God of Israel is the God of the law. Yet for me, God is also a Being of deep love. On days when others are treating me badly, I take refuge in the Lord. I feel a spiritual presence around me. He is my comfort like a loving father almost."

"What are you talking about?" John asked cynically. "The God of Abraham, Isaac, and Jacob is the God of the law. Through Moses and other prophets, God has given us the law, which we must obey. God is pleased with those who follow the law, and all others will burn in hell."

"Yes, this is what the religious authorities often claim." He hesitated, but when he spoke, his voice was assured. "When I experience special moments with God, I can feel that He is my father ... and I can even sense His presence."

John gave him a strange look. "My father has taught many things about the Torah to me, and we respect all the traditions. So if God were to approach anyone in this family, it would be my father, who is a devout priest ... or even me, since I am his only son." His voice had grown hard, condescending. "Jesus, it seems you don't understand the laws and beliefs of our people."

Jesus began to reply, but John held up a quick hand. "This doesn't surprise me," he added. "You are merely the son of a carpenter. It's not your fault. You should study the sacred Scriptures. I'll ask my father to find somebody to teach …"

John stopped in mid-sentence as he saw Mary approaching them.

"Oh, John! Here you are. Your mother is looking for you."

John said good-bye and hurried off as Mary drew closer to her son.

"Jesus, what did you and John talk about?" she asked with a note of concern. He smiled at her. "I was telling him about my close relationship with God."

"Still on the same subject?" she said with some irritation. "If I were you, I wouldn't tell others about your *close* relationship with the Highest."

Jesus' voice grew serious. "Who is the Messiah? And what will he do when he finally arrives?"

Mary remained silent, suddenly recalling Gabriel's prophecy that her unborn child would become God's Son, who would lead the descendants of Jacob …

"I don't know that much," she finally said, glancing at Jesus. "I have heard that God will send a Savior to our people who will be the king of Israel, and who will help free us from the tyranny and injustices of our enemies …"

"So the Messiah is a great warrior who will strike down the Romans?"

Smiling briefly, Mary shook her head. "The Messiah will be a man of peace who brings the love and glory of God to our people. But all the kings on earth will bow down at his feet. Some people like your grandfather believe that Israel will rule the world, and the Messiah will take vengeance on all our enemies."

Jesus' eyes widened. "Do you believe that?"

Mary gave it some thought and gave a little shrug. "Over the years, I've heard so many different interpretations of the various prophecies that I am not sure what to believe."

"But how could God send a Messiah who slaughters others? If so, the coming of the Messiah will stain Israel with blood, even if it's the blood of our enemies. Our God cannot be so cruel or our Savior so violent."

Mary made no reply. She merely dropped upon the rock and stretched out her legs as she inhaled a deep breath of the fragrant air.

Jesus soon added, "Mother, what good is a Messiah who arrives with a knife in his hand, cutting arms and heads of our enemies like King David did? This kind of a Messiah would not be sent by the same Lord God that I have come to know."

Turning to him, Mary answered with a rising voice, "From what you've told me these last few months, it seems your experiences with God are quite different from other people's, even the rabbis' and priests." She grew silent a long moment. "You may not remember this, but when you were a child, I told you about a mystical experience I had. One evening an angel of the Lord came to me in a dream and proclaimed I would give birth to a special son. Indeed, you are very special and much different from the other boys your age."

Jesus considered this. "If I am different, it is because I have a very special mother, who loves me so much."

A smile bright as noon crossed Mary's face. "Jesus, I am happy that you feel spiritually close to the Lord. But don't ignore your studies of the Torah. Maybe one day you can become a respected rabbi or a great priest like John's father."

"Mother, I know it's difficult for you to understand my relationship with our Father in Heaven. But the God that I know is also within me. When Father treats me badly, I suddenly feel that God is with me, comforting me. And when other boys make fun of me, or when Grandmother Marta ignores me and acts like I am not her grandson, God says to me that I am His true son and that He loves me very much!"

Mary raised a brow. "Do you hear a voice speaking to you?"

"Yes, I can hear God's voice. It's difficult to explain, but it's like a shifting force within me. It takes hold of me and fills my entire body with divine love." Pausing, his eyes shone brightly. "This is God! I can speak to him as naturally as I am talking to you or Father."

After reflecting on this, Mary thought about their already shaky standing in the community. "I understand, but just don't go telling others this. They'll think you have gone mad and take you from our family."

Jesus couldn't help but laugh and continue to share. "Everyone should have this kind of experience with God." His eyes narrowed. "How could a loving God send a Messiah who tries to save Israel with force and violence? I believe that our religious leaders have a mistaken concept of God and of the Messiah."

Mary sighed inwardly, surprised that her eldest son could be so eloquent about such complex ideas at the tender age of twelve. "Jesus," she said confidently, having just made the most impulsive decision, "there are certain facts about our family that you need to know. Unlike your brothers and sisters, you are the fruit of my purity and devotion to God when I was only fifteen years old …"

Puzzled, he tilted his head. "What do you mean?"

"At the time, you were conceived by my faith and love for God," she replied, smiling at him. "In other words, I thought that by being intimate with a man who was close to God, then I could also be close to the Lord."

Jesus looked away for several moments, then studied her face. "Are you saying that Father isn't my real father?"

She nodded ever so slightly. "Though Joseph isn't your real father, he loves you as if you were his own son."

"That isn't true. Often he is ashamed of me. When he meets his friends and they talk about their children, Father speaks of Simon and James with pride, but not of me. To him, I am something to be hidden behind a door." Jesus took a deep breath, trying to hold back the army of new thoughts amassing in the back of his mind. "Mother, who is my real father then?"

"Dear, your father is a good man, a servant of God who follows His righteous path." Pausing, her gaze remained on her son's face as he stood quietly, looking straight into her eyes. "For some divine reason that I cannot explain and have never been able to explain" she added, "You are a child who was announced by the angel Gabriel."

Jesus half-nodded, an intense look on his face. "You say my father is a servant of God. Does that mean he is a priest?"

Mary nodded in silence as she recalled the night of their union.

"Mother! You have to tell me this name. Is he still alive?"

"Yes, he is in Nazareth this very day. But promise that if I reveal his name, you will not say anything to him, or do something that draws the attention of others."

Jesus gave her an expectant look, staring deep into her soul as though he could read her innermost thoughts.

Against her better judgment, and pushed by her guilt over his suffering at the hands of bullies, Mary decided to finally be honest with her son. She cleared her throat and heard herself say, "Your father has much prestige in our clan … He is the priest Zechariah."

"John's father?" uttered Jesus, remaining still, as his mind absorbed this new discovery. Yet the shock was evident on his face as his cheeks flushed red.

He had never imagined that someone like Zechariah could be his actual father, and that John could, in fact, be his brother. *How tragic*, he couldn't help thinking. *Two brothers of the same father, but each treated in a different way. John is placed on a pedestal, whereas I usually gravitate to the lowest of positions no matter what group I am with.*

Later that afternoon, Jesus drew near a gathering of his relatives, hoping to find his father among them. He soon noticed John speaking with a group of some of the other cousins. Although Jesus had been with him earlier, he now looked at him with different eyes, as if this were the first time he had actually seen him.

His perception of John had been shattered within a matter of seconds. Before his mother's confession, Jesus looked upon John as a cousin. But now John was his elder brother, whom he had to serve and respect.

Jesus made up his mind that he had to cultivate a loving sentiment toward John, but without his half-brother sensing it. If this feeling could be kept hidden during the coming years, it would hopefully give them more opportunities to meet and exchange ideas about God.

Moving his eyes away from John and the other boys, Jesus continued his search for Zechariah. Moments later, he saw him seated alone a few meters away from a group of young men. The men were exchanging disparaging remarks about King Herod's family, but Zechariah seemed to be reflecting on something else, perhaps a sacred passage from the Torah or some verses of an ancient prophet.

Cautiously, Jesus advanced in the direction of the elderly priest and stood at a short distance, quietly studying him with eager eyes unlike anyone who had ever gazed upon the old man before. Zechariah noticed the boy and could not avoid staring at him. Like a magnetic force, their eyes met and locked. And soon their minds and souls locked together as well. At that moment, Jesus understood that his true father, the one who comforted and took care of him, the one who gave him love and support, was the Father in Heaven. He, not this priest, was the one dwelling in Jesus' heart, mind, and body.

From then on, Jesus' primary task in life became to deeply know his true Father, the Creator of all life on earth and in heaven in all His glory and fullness.

After his mother revealed the truth of his origin, Jesus felt a strong urge to learn more about the traditions of the chosen people of God. He began to study the laws, the prophets, and the Scriptures of the land of Israel under the supervision of a scholar recommended by Zechariah.

The old priest did this in secret, for he didn't want anyone, especially Elizabeth, to discover that he was involved in Jesus' education. Jesus soon developed his own interpretation of everything that he studied.

During the passing years, as he approached manhood, Jesus developed a great devotion to God, along with a great love for humanity and all the creation. He began to live a life of constant prayer that reflected his immense desire to communicate with the Lord. Due to his personal experiences with God, he had a new perspective on God's nature, along with a deeper understanding of the original nature of humanity, which he realized was created in the direct image of the Creator.

Day by day, the relationship between God and Jesus grew more intense and intimate. He understood why God had taken care of him, had sustained his emotional needs and helped him endure all his vicissitudes for so long. He realized why God had revealed Himself to him like a father, allowing Jesus to see and communicate with the invisible world. He understood why God revealed to him the meaning of the laws of Moses, the words of the prophets, and the Scriptures.

"Who could be the Messiah?" He had often wondered as a child. But now he realized that he was the one destined to become the Savior. He had been chosen by God to understand the visible and the invisible realms of all creation.

With tears pouring from his eyes, Jesus prayed deeply and inquired to the Lord whether this were certain. And God told him that truly he was His favorite son, the one who had pleased Him, the one He had been spiritually close so that he could assume the responsibility to educate and save humanity.

At this stage of his spiritual maturity, Jesus swore to the Father that he would do all he could until his last breath to bring salvation to the land of Israel and to humanity. Jesus wanted to share with others what he knew about the nature of God, the true nature of man, the relationship between God and man, which he called The Truth. He believed that everyone should be enlightened about how evil came into the world, and learn how to free themselves from their dark side and develop their divine nature.

He would reveal a new message whose profound meaning could be understood only by humble people with receptive hearts, a message that Jesus was still perfecting in his soul.

CHAPTER 10

DURING MY LONG YEARS, I have passed through many different towns and cities in Israel and other lands bordering the Great Sea. My favorite of them all is Magdala, where I grew up in a tightly knit family. I remained there during the first years with my husband, Jesus, and our young children. Magdala hugged the western shore of the Sea of Galilee, making it an active center of fishing, as was Tiberias to the south, and Gennesaret and Capernaum to the north.

The Sea of Galilee is a freshwater lake thirty miles east of Mount Carmel, which overlooks the deep grayish-blue waters of the Great Sea. The lake is some twelve miles long and about six miles across at its widest point. Due to the long, sweltering summers in Galilee, we were often at the mercy of violent thunderstorms that suddenly came from the surrounding hills, causing small fishing boats to be dangerously tossed about by the big waves. But most of the time, the large lake was as placid as a sheet of parchment, giving a silvery sheen that always took my breath away.

Like others in our town, my family had been fishers for many generations. My father sold and distributed dry salted fish throughout Galilee, particularly in Tiberias. Having been raised in a family of fishers, I became an expert at an early age.

During the two-year period before the arrival of Jesus in Magdala, my father's business had declined. My elder brother and sister, Lazarus and Martha, had moved to Bethany, a small town just to the east of Jerusalem. With no one to help my father, it was impossible for him to complete all his daily tasks. So Jesus arrived in our village at the right time.

Initially, it was easy for my parents to accept Jesus as a new member of the family. They felt I was fortunate to have married such a good man, for he was honest and upright, exhibited high intelligence, and had much initiative. More importantly, at least in the eyes of my father, Jesus was a skilled craftsman who could build and restore fishing boats to mint condition. For my parents, all these qualities had offset his reputation as an illegitimate child. My parents felt Jesus was a perfect match … for me and for them!

Our wedding took place about two months after his arrival, and he was welcomed into our family. Our custom requires that a new husband reside in the town of his wife, particularly if the man doesn't have a definite paternal origin. So Jesus came to live in my parents' home.

Naturally, the day of our wedding was a special one for both of us. Jesus' mother, his two sisters, and his brother James were present, as was my brother and sister. It was a jubilant feast with much singing, dancing, and plenty of food for everyone. Oddly, though Jesus seemed pleased, he was also rather solemn and withdrawn.

Shortly after the ceremony, he announced to me in a somber voice, "Mary, today is a very important moment for Heaven."

I looked at him and smiled. I was just happy for the day and needed no explanation from him.

After the sun dropped below the horizon, Jesus and I walked toward our modest dwelling. The sun was replaced with a beautiful full moon that illuminated the surrounding landscape, just as our love brightened our hearts.

Guided by the light of an oil lamp, we stepped into the house and closed the door behind us. At last, I thought with a nervous breath, we were alone and free to express our love for each other. We clasped hands. Then, to my amazement, Jesus bowed his head and started praying to God, thanking Him for our marriage blessing. I followed his lead and bowed my head also, quietly listening to the profound words coming from deep within his heart. His eyes filled with tears as he expressed his deep love for Him whom he called Heavenly Father. At the end of the prayer, Jesus stepped closer and laughed softly, letting our noses touch.

He squeezed my hands, and speaking with conviction said, "Mary, the circumstances of my life, along with my destiny, have brought me here to this village. Of all the women I have observed, you are one who has the most of the necessary qualities to support me in the building of God's kingdom on earth."

"*God's kingdom on earth?*" I echoed feebly.

Jesus nodded, a gentle smile on his face. "We will grow together as husband and wife, and soon as parents, and form a godly family. Our children, our family, will belong to God. We shall become an exemplary family for all families to follow, where the love of the living God will be expressed in our relationships. You and I will show God's parental heart by loving all people as we love our children."

My nervousness had passed. I had forgotten about the flesh momentarily. I remained quiet, his profound words flowing through my ears and into my spirit. At that moment I felt so connected to Jesus, although I didn't have a clear understanding of what he was actually saying.

"Mary," he said, his eyes boring into me, "the Lord has revealed so much to me these past few years. I hear His voice day and night ..."

His words perplexed me, for he was talking about the Lord God as if He were living with us in the same house. "What does God say to you?" I uttered, somehow concerned that I had not known what I was bargaining for when I consented to this marriage.

"I cannot reveal everything at this moment. Your heart is not ready to receive more. Be patient, and from now on listen carefully to whatever I say. Also, at times my behavior may startle you. So before judging me, offer prayers to the Lord and ask for His guidance."

Admittedly, now I was definitely disturbed by what my new husband was telling me. But I also felt a sense of shame because of my inability to fully understand the meaning of his words. What was he actually saying to me? What did he want me to do? The only thing I was really sure of was his presence in front of me. His eyes, his mouth, the curve of his lips, seemingly modeled by God in perfect harmony with mine.

"Mary," he whispered, "although I am a man in the image of God, you as a woman are of equal value, and you are a partner in my mission."

What mission? I repeated inwardly. It was not our custom to consider the wife an equal to the husband. *How did he mean it then?* I asked myself while waiting for his kisses.

Slowly, he lowered his head and moved his lips toward mine. As he wrapped his arms around my shoulders, I felt as if my entire body was dissolving.

He moved his face to my bosom and listened to my rapidly beating heart, the moment now arriving for us to discover intimate secrets reserved only for a husband and wife. Soon we became one in spirit and body, giving ourselves in an unabashed way that I never imagined possible. And as we gave each other pleasure, our souls merged in the presence of God loving spirit, forming a sacred union never to be broken.

In the following weeks, the light of the sun rarely found us apart from each other, and soon our hopes were high for the arrival of our first of many children.

After our first month of marriage, it became evident to my father and mother that Jesus was a good husband to me and a fine son-in-law to them. The hearts of my parents melted from the power of his warm smiles and the respect he constantly showed them, not to mention his industrious work habits and the courteous manner with which he treated people.

About a year after our wedding, Jesus began to oversee much of our family's fishing business. Those were times of prosperity, and the business flourished. It was also a period of personal joy because I was about to deliver our first child.

When Isaac was born, I could hardly contain my joy, scrutinizing him from the crown of his head, covered with thick black hair, down to his little toes. His body was strong and beautiful, and I couldn't help thinking he was a miniature copy of his father. I felt the splendor of motherhood.

Jesus took the child in his arms and counted his tiny fingers, then gave his forehead a thoughtful kiss before uttering a prayer of gratitude to the Lord God. We gazed at each other and realized that our lives had been elevated to a new height. It was a glorious feeling, as when the first rays of the rising sun banish the darkness of night while illuminating the morning clouds in hues of yellow, pink, and orange.

Jesus looked into my eyes, and I felt his happiness penetrate my heart. And for some reason that I couldn't fully fathom, I felt that I was a woman of destiny, his destiny. I felt like a spoiled child over the constant love and care he offered. I believed our relationship was so strong that nothing could break the bond between us. But despite living close together, my spiritual experiences and understanding of the world were very different from his. Yet I tried to open my heart to him and always listened attentively during those times when he was teaching me.

We had numerous conversations about God and the angels, and spoke about our duty to fulfill God's will on earth. Though Jesus' teachings were profound, I came to realize that I needed to discover the reality of God with my own spiritual eyes, something Jesus himself encouraged me to do.

The months seemed to fly by with few concerns. Sara was born about two years after Isaac. She was an adorable baby, and Jesus and I were just as enthralled as we had been as first-time parents.

Smiling with great contentment, I put Sara in Jesus' arms. His face beaming with joy, he held our daughter as though she were a fragrant bouquet of flowers.

I was so happy during the following months as my life revolved around my husband and our two children. Jesus' intention was to educate me in such a way that I would be guided toward a deeper understanding of God's nature. But I seldom understood what Jesus was trying to teach me. After all, before marriage I was used to living in my own little world, scarcely aware of people and events outside of our fishing village, much less what Jesus was talking about when he stated that the Lord was offering me the opportunity to become a perfect model of the divine femininity. *What did he mean?* I couldn't help wondering.

Jesus dedicated his life to his family, and to the work of educating me. It seems he never overlooked a single opportunity to speak about spiritual things. I listened as closely as I could, between one task and another. Many times I apologized to him for not having time to give him my total attention. And as the children grew older, our discussions were often interrupted by one crisis or another.

"Oh, I don't have time now," I would say abruptly in an apologetic tone. "After feeding the children, I need to help my mother at the marketplace."

In the evenings after dinner, I was usually so tired that when Jesus spoke to me about some matter, my gaze would lose its intensity and I would drift off to sleep. Since my brother and sister had moved to Bethany, I was the only child around to help my parents, which compounded by responsibilities at home.

Although Jesus had just as many responsibilities, he somehow found the time to go fishing every once in a while. He relished life on a boat in the company of the endless blue waters and open skies. At those times when he was quite tired, he usually took one of my father's boats onto the lake to pray and meditate, inevitably falling into a deep slumber, from which not even strong winds or rough seas could rouse him.

As Isaac and Sara grew older, they would run about the house and courtyard making joyful sounds. Jesus adored them both, and enjoyed carving toys for them.

I'll never forget one afternoon when Isaac was almost four and they were on the floor, playing with large pieces of wood, pretending they were boats. Jesus laughed deeply as he watched Isaac act as though he were catching many giant fish from his odd-shaped boat.

From my first moments as a mother, I discovered the unconditional love that mothers have for their children. My days were filled with the endless task of serving my son and daughter, dutifully tending to their needs with all of my heart.

Meanwhile, Jesus kept trying to enrich my mind. One day he said to me, "Mary, I can only give you partial guidance along the path leading to our Heavenly Parent. You have to find your own way without my help. Your heart must grow quickly so the Lord God can dwell within you as a model daughter, wife and mother."

I gave a hesitant nod, growing more bewildered with each passing moment. What did he mean by *model wife and mother*? And how could the Lord God dwell within a human being, especially a simple woman like me?

The years went by, and our married life continued without problems. Although those were peaceful times for me, I could tell that Jesus was carrying a great burden upon his shoulders and preparing for other things. He seemed to live beneath a shadow of anguish that wouldn't allow him to fully enjoy life in our small community. I wasn't certain, but as I began to observe him more closely and listened to his private prayers, I realized that he felt responsible for the sins and sorrows of mankind.

We had been married about five years when Jesus awoke one night with a muffled shout. After lighting a candle, I saw a solemn look on his face. He sat up and stared into my sleepy eyes. "My Heavenly Father just came to me, saying the time is near for me to start my mission outside family boundaries."

I knew that this would be the beginning of a kind of separation between us.

The next morning neither one of us mentioned what had happened during the night. But we had not forgotten it. I knew that Jesus stood at a major crossroads, considering whether he should live an ordinary, peaceful life in this Galilean fishing village or dedicate himself fully to what he believed was his destiny to save humanity.

Naturally, I wanted Jesus to cast aside this grand destiny that I felt was impossible to achieve. And I foolishly thought I could convince him to remain with me by pleasing him day and night. But instead, he talked more and more about God and His suffering children throughout the world.

One time, Jesus went three days without speaking to me. Frustrated, I hurried to the two-room structure by the lake shore where my family conducted our fish business. When several customers departed, I stormed inside and confronted my husband. "Is it me? What have I done to displease you?"

"How could a gentle creature like you displease me?" he uttered with an amused smile. He touched my cheek. "I have so much to reveal to you about Heaven's will. But words are not enough. You need to have your own experiences with the Lord."

Not really understanding his reply, I began to sense an underlying threat to my security and peace of mind. I turned away from him in tears. All I cared about was living a normal life with my husband and children. And although Jesus was a caring husband, I knew that he loved God more than anything else in the world, even more than his own family.

Within a few weeks, he began leaving Magdala for two or three days at a time. Since he had trained a couple of young men to assume his duties, my father never complained or criticized him in front of me or our children.

But Jesus gradually prolonged his absences, staying away from Magdala longer and longer with each journey. At first, sensing how important it was to him, I tried to be supportive. But I soon turned angry over what I judged to be his increasing disregard for the well-being of his family.

One morning, after having returned home only the day before, Jesus told me that he had to visit one of his relatives, who could help God to fulfill His plan for the redemption of Israel.

"How long will you be gone this time?" I asked dutifully, my voice trembling.

"A long time," he said flatly. "John leads a community of believers who live in the wilderness near the northwest coast of the Dead Sea. It will be a treacherous journey, but it's important that I meet with him."

I was petrified. What could I do in the face of such determination? I wanted to understand Jesus and support his efforts for the Lord, but I couldn't shake off my desire for us to be like the other families in our village.

Was it wrong to want to enjoy the small comforts of daily life? Couldn't I be a worthy wife and a good daughter of God by serving my husband and children as they went about their normal routines? In my opinion, there was no better place to find God than my village, my home, and my family. So what could I do if my husband loved this other vision of God to the point of leaving me to care for the children alone?

The following morning Jesus woke up early and began preparing his clothes and food for the journey. But before he had a chance to leave, I grabbed him by the arm and begged him not to leave me.

"Please stay with us," I implored, trying to pull him back into the house, into our lives. He made no reply, merely staring at me with his calm eyes. It was almost as though he hadn't heard my plea.

I knew it would be useless to say anything else, and after a long moment of silence he kissed my forehead and left without looking back.

I followed him outside and stood in front of the house, looking at the back of his head as he took long strides along the dusty road. Weeping softly now, I covered my mouth with my hands to hold back a scream of desperation. I felt that my love was locked in my husband's heart, but I was helpless to keep it near and I wondered whether I would ever see him again.

Later that day, I offered feeble prayers to the Lord and slowly realized that my desires were selfish, not in accordance with His will.

"This is the real problem," I reluctantly told myself. "It would be impossible for me to persuade Jesus to be something other than what he is. To change his nature to suit my pleasures would be like trying to put sunbeams in a glass jar. Jesus had become one with the Lord God, and his will was to do his Heavenly Father's will, even at the sacrifice of himself and his family.

CHAPTER 11

THE SUN BEAT DOWN UNMERCIFULLY upon Jesus, and though his head was covered with a white hood, he was sweating profusely and his mouth as dry as the scorched desert sands under his sandaled feet. After days of searching, he had finally reached a community of Essenes near the Dead Sea. Unlike the Lake of Galilee, seventy miles to the north, the Dead Sea had no fish. When I was just a child, I often heard my grandfather call it the Sea of Salt. The two inland bodies of water are connected by the Jordan River, winding through a deep, fertile valley with flowers and singing birds year-around.

The Jordan flows into the northern point of the Dead Sea, about fifteen miles west of Jerusalem. But the wilderness of Judea, along the western shores of the Dead Sea, is anything but a paradise. It was here that small of group of Essenes lived as hermits, away from the cities and towns dominated by Rome's pagan culture and a safe distance from the political affairs of the Temple priests, scribes, and Pharisees. These groups of children of Abraham had a low opinion of the character of women. So although some of them married, it was for the continuance of the human race. Those of them who believed in an extreme abstemious living preferred to adopt children than marry to procreate. So doing they would get around the Mosaic laws. But there were also those who engaged in charitable works, they often took care of orphaned children.

Members of the Essene community led austere lives of prayer, study, and service in the hope that God would soon put an end to this evil world. Like other religious Jews, the Essenes expected God to send the Anointed One, the priestly Messiah who would commence a new chapter in the history of the chosen people. The Essenes were mostly farmers or simple craftsmen, and they often came together to debate the moral issues of the day, as well as interpret the sacred books of the forefathers. Sometimes, groups of Essenes formed communities in the solitude and purity of the desert, strictly adhering to the law and focusing on rituals to purify their souls. After the death of his parents many years before, John was taken in by various groups of Essenes. He spent his youth devoutly praying, fasting, and studying the Scriptures and the words of the prophets of ancient Israel.

Jesus estimated this community of Essenes had several hundred adherents, yet he couldn't find John among them as he explored a series of buildings. In one there were several rooms, one of which had about twenty men who were studying the Scriptures under the guidance of a white-bearded man. Then, as Jesus approached a smaller building used to make pottery, he spoke to a young fellow who told him that John was living in a cave in a nearby mountain. After an hour of searching, Jesus finally came across John as he walked among the rocky hills of the desert.

At first glance, Jesus could easily tell that this was a holy man who led a disciplined life of self-imposed hardship, someone who was very serious about the God he loved. Though rather thin, John's arms and legs were hard with muscle, and his squarish face was darkened from exposure to the sun and the strong winds of the desert. The robe he wore was made of camel hair, and he had piercing brown eyes under thick brows, with curly hair and a matted beard.

John recognized Jesus immediately, flashing a smile and opening his arms. The two men embraced with genuine affection. Then they retreated to a nearby cave to seek relief from the intense desert heat.

His legs stiff and sore, Jesus stretched out upon the cool rock floor and drank water from a goatskin bag. Soon, John grew comfortable and began reminiscing about their first meeting when his family traveled from Ain Karem to Nazareth for a relative's birthday celebration. John had fond memories of the journey and his visit to the farm of his mother's parents. But he had especially liked playing games with his cousins, and talking to Jesus about God and the Prophets.

Nodding reflectively, Jesus was surprised that John had such vivid memories. In spite of the twelve years that had elapsed since then, Jesus' stormy emotions upon hearing from his mother that Zechariah was his true father were still fresh in his mind. The elderly priest had been dead for many years now, and Jesus often couldn't help mourning for the father he had never gotten to know.

Passing the water bag to John, he said in a subdued tone, "I am pleased I found you. Since we last we saw each other, I've been blessed with many spiritual experiences. I knew nobody better to share them with."

"Yes, I imagine you have much to tell me." After studying his brother's face for a long moment, John added abruptly, "Jesus, I know about our father."

He gazed at him, surprised. "Our father?" he uttered, straightening up.

"For years I've known about the relationship between my father and your mother." He drew a deep breath. "It was hard on me at first. I didn't want to accept the fact that my father, a consecrated priest, could have committed such an immoral act with his wife's cousin, a mere girl at the time.

Jesus lowered his eyes as John put a hand on his shoulder. "My father told me just a week before he was murdered, almost as if he knew what awaited him."

Jesus recalled the sorrow and dread when the news came to Nazareth of Zechariah's death by the hands of a mysterious assailant.

After a long silence, John said to him, "I can still hear the sound of my father's voice when he first explained the spiritual occurrences surrounding my conception and birth." A proud note entered his voice. "My father was a great priest from the bloodline of the Levites. He wasn't a false teacher like those Hasmoneans, who claim the office of high priest." He paused, a distant look on his face as he recounted his father's tale. "He told me that I had been chosen by the Lord to announce the coming Messiah. And when my father admitted you were his son and my brother, he also told me that God granted special grace for his act with your mother, and that God even considers his blood lineage a special one. He believed that my destiny was already marked by God ... But he was uncertain about your future."

Jesus nodded. "We both have special missions for the Lord."

"Then take a bold decision to live among the Essenes," offered John. "In this community there are no human activities to clutter your mind with petty desires, nor any distractions as you strive to obtain a deeper connection with the Divine, in order to fully receive His grace and mercy." He made a sweeping gesture outward with his hand. "If you stay with me in the desert, you will hear the Lord's voice in the quiet of the night," he continued, making a smaller gesture directed inward. "Fasting also helps to hear God's soothing voice. Fasting purifies your feelings, increases your clarity of thought, and can help you to resist harmful temptations."

Jesus nodded and crossed his legs. "But fasting and living like a hermit should only be a temporary lifestyle. John, you shouldn't separate yourself from the world. Righteous leaders are needed now more than ever to guide people and bring them the knowledge of God."

Yawning, John was surprised to hear such words come from his younger brother.

Jesus added, "We are not meant to sit idly, contemplating the universe during the heat of the day and cold of the night. The Lord God wants us to eliminate the evils of this world by uplifting the hearts and minds of people." He paused a moment. "Besides, I am married and have children," he added offhandedly.

"You are married?" John uttered, looking disappointed and puzzled. "I know it sound strange for a Jew but growing up among the Essenes who consider women low creatures and view pleasures as evil and conquest of passion to be virtuous I come to believe that celibacy is a better way of living that brings us closer to God."

Jesus shook his head, speaking slowly. "In God's eyes men and women have the same value. Don't you know that God's desire was to have a close relationship with Adam's family?"

"Perhaps. But the body is corruptible, and staying away from women is the best way to reach union with God."

"There is nothing impure between a husband and wife. In fact, it was through the family of Adam and Eve that God wanted to fulfill His hopes for humanity." Jesus' voice deepened. "God is better reflected in the family because He manifests Himself in the husband and the wife."

Frowning, John held up a quick hand, "I know, I know, he uttered, "God has created us in His image, male and female. But are you ascribing human characteristics to the Lord God?"

"I am ascribing divine characteristics to humans. Since we are God's children." A little smile crossed his face. "Marriage is the fundamental venture for human spiritual advancement. It increases joy in our hearts and brings us closer to God."

John gave him a skeptical look. "But marriage does not resolve the evil nature of the human character. All men and women live in contradiction, seeking both good and evil. And the reality of evil is that it always remains in our hearts. Only a life of complete isolation and abstinence, the full denial of desire, can empower the mind to control the body."

Jesus sighed, glancing at the bright sunlight outside the the cave and wishing that he and John hadn't been separated all these years. He enjoyed talking about these things with his brother, even when they disagreed.

"Evil is part of human nature," said John, an insistent note to his voice. "Our fleshly desires can only be suppressed by practicing extreme self-denial."

"John, don't you see?" Now Jesus made a grand gesture to the world outside the cave. "Even in nature there are male and female animals, and likewise in the plants and trees. If God made all the creatures, then He, too, must have both male and female aspects."

John's eyebrows arched, and he stared at Jesus. "How true," he affirmed, "Most of what you say is not new or shocking."

"Yes," replied Jesus. "But it's plain that God wants a husband and wife to become one in flesh. We all know that children are the fruit of the sacred union of their parents' flesh and blood. But without God's blessing, marriage cannot be judged as sacred. We Jews know that If Adam and Eve had not fallen, they would have given birth to children who were free of sin. Then at their death, they would have gone to the highest level of the spiritual world, living with God in ultimate joy for all eternity."

John considered this briefly. "Are you actually saying there is no way to become the image of God without the wife being equal to man?"

Jesus nodded. "The Lord God derives great joy from a happy marriage where husband and wife are one having same value, which brings forth children who reflect His nature."

John's mouth tightened as he moved his eyes from Jesus' face. "You have many strange concepts," he said, as if weary of listening. "The woman has brought misfortune to man. How can people be without flaw when sin has dominated our lives since the Garden of Eden?"

"This is why humanity is in dire need of the Messiah," stated Jesus. "Since Eve failed by listening to Satan and the first Adam failed by listening to Eve, the second Adam comes to redeem that failure, thus, the Messiah will restore a woman in the position of Eve, and they will be united in marriage by the Lord God. They will accomplish what the first human parents failed. How else can mankind be saved?"

"Saved?" John repeated, staring at him suspiciously. "Have you lost your mind? Even the Messiah won't be able to save humanity."

Under John's scrutinizing eyes, Jesus persisted. "The second Adam and his restored bride will establish God's blood lineage of goodness."

John straightened up, meeting Jesus' eyes. "Where in the Torah do you find such nonsense? What prophets have predicted the Messiah comes as the second Adam?"

"Why should the Messiah repeat old truths? The Anointed One will come with a new message." He grew erect and raised his voice. "For thousands of years humanity has struggled in limbo between good and evil. The commandments, as well as the Scriptures and the teachings of the prophets, merely serve to encourage humans to correct their past failings and choose the path of goodness."

"Then you do agree with me!" John barked, jumping to his feet and pacing back and forth in agitation. "Even now as we speak, the struggle between good and evil continues. Man is not free from his contradictions. If a person hopes to draw closer to God, then abstinence and isolation from the rest of the world are the best means."

Realizing it wouldn't be easy to change John's mind, Jesus forced a smile. "John, the time has come to discover God in all His truth. The sons and daughters of Israel know of the origin of evil but not how to eliminate it from their hearts." As Jesus paused for a drink of water, he noticed the skeptical look on his brother's weather-beaten face. "John, it is essential that you understand the message of the Messiah. Why exactly is the Messiah coming? What is his real mission? And how can we find him once he is born on earth?"

John narrowed his eyes, still pacing the grounds of the cool cave, in turmoil as he considered Jesus' words.

After a prolonged period of this, he muttered, half to himself, "I do believe we live in messianic times. In fact, I believe the Messiah will soon come, preceded by the return of Elijah. He will be a high priest from the Aaronic line, as a legitimate priest." Frowning, he added bitterly, "The Messiah won't be a corrupted and false priest like the ones now controlling the Most Holy Place in the Temple in Jerusalem."

"The Messiah is also the legitimate king coming from the Davidic line," reminded Jesus. "But above all else, it is the Messiah who will expose the original sin to all humanity and establish God's pure blood lineage, linking his family to all people on earth."

John stopped pacing. He glared at Jesus. "You are wrong!" he blurted out. "The time has come for a washing away of sins. This is the true purification."

Turning grave, Jesus warned, "Please strive to open your heart to the possibility of a deeper truth."

John grew quite irritated at hearing such advice from his brother who had no formal training or any followers. "Jesus, what God needs now is an iron fist … not love, but fear of God's wrath that will turn people back to …"

Weary, Jesus slowly rose and stepped closer to his brother. "Fear of the Lord is not the way to defeat the evil in our souls. Promising the eternal pain of hellfire will not stop people from committing sins."

John shrugged, glancing at Jesus with an expression of uncertainty.

Not wishing to alienate his brother, Jesus said in a doting manner, "What are your plans? Will you remain here much longer?"

"Where God leads me, I will go. Until that day, I will fast and pray ardently for the salvation of our people."

"Praying for the renewal of Israel is wise, but your life has a purpose. And surely it is not to live in the desert forever. John, it's important to do God's will by loving Him and serving humanity."

"Prayer, the denial of self and sex and withdrawing from this corrupted world is the best way to get in touch with God " said John, thinking it nothing short of absurd that Jesus was giving him spiritual advice.

Setting a firm hand on his brother's shoulder, Jesus added, "You and I need to work together in order to save humanity."

John dismissed the suggestion offhandedly.

Jesus stayed with John for a couple of months. But as he would do with me, for a long while Jesus kept John unaware about his real mission and the nature of his role in the redemption of lost souls. His brother was simply not ready for it. However, during those two months John came to the realization that the time had come for him to go back among the people."

CHAPTER 12

OUR SIXTH WEDDING ANNIVERSARY fell on a lovely April day. Wildflowers dotted the fields and hillsides near Magdala, and the trees around our home were bursting with white and violet flowers, their sweet fragrance filling the air and attracting many bees, butterflies, and singing birds, all of which totally enraptured Isaac and Sara.

When I awoke that morning, I rolled over in bed to find that Jesus had already gotten dressed and left the house. He spent from dawn to dusk at the top of the mountain to the west of Magdala. He fasted the entire day, praying and imploring God to show him what to do to resolve human suffering. During the last several months, he had often gone without food for three days at a time, continuing to pray intensely. He prayed for me and our children, for his mother and siblings, for Nazareth and Magdala, for Israel and the entire world. He was often quite anxious, living with a sense of urgency about a matter that only he could deal with. I often found him crying from a secret pain that had enveloped his mind.

It was well after sunset when Jesus finally returned home, his eyes raw as if he had flayed them while weeping. After a quiet dinner, he prayed with the children before putting them to bed, kissing them and wishing them a good night.

Then he walked over to me, looking deeply into my eyes for a long moment. We needed to have a serious talk, a more serious talk than we had ever had.

"Let's sit outside," he suggested, brushing my hair with his fingers.

I nodded and followed. We sat in the wicker chairs near some potted plants. Remaining silent, Jesus gazed at the branches of the pomegranate tree just outside the courtyard. "Mary, it's such a glorious evening," he said softly, glancing at the heavens, lit by thousands of stars.

"This is my favorite time of the year," I thought aloud. Moving my eyes to his face, I began to wonder whether his feelings for me had changed over the years.

"Because of the way you've been acting lately, I feel that I'm becoming less and less important to you."

He shifted his body, to face me fully.

"Why do you neglect me?" I snapped. "It's almost as if I have done something to make you angry."

He grew serious. "You have never made me angry …"

"You aren't planning to abandon me, are you?"

"Don't be silly," he responded, almost as if he were chastising a mischievous child. "Mary, you are my wife. You make me whole. God created you for me, just as he created Eve for Adam. So naturally I love you."

Even though I believed him, I couldn't help saying, "Do you?"

"Of course I do. I'm blessed to have met you."

"And you are a good man, Jesus. But there is something that you are hiding from me, something that is pulling you away from our family."

He didn't respond, although his eyes remained fixed on me.

"For a man who has such a bright smile, you rarely smile or laugh anymore." I reached for his hand. "What's the matter, dear? You can tell me."

"Mary, I have come to learn things about God's heart that sadden me."

"I know you've been praying. So even when I am caring for the children, my thoughts are with you. I try to pray, too."

Taking a deep breath, Jesus let his eyes wander to the starry sky.

After a minute, I confessed in all honesty, "I can't help thinking you don't love me as you once did. Have I become less in your eyes as God reveals greater things to you?"

Leaning toward me, Jesus took my face in his hands. "Please, believe me, Mary. I love you more now than on our wedding day."

I couldn't hold back the tears, of both rage and helplessness, as I choked on my next words. "If you pray so much, why hasn't God revealed to you how much we need you in the home?" My voice dropped to a whisper. "I want to fall asleep with your arms around me, and awaken each morning with you beside me."

After a moment of thought, he responded in a patient tone, "God does show me how much my family needs me. From this, I have learned how much God's children need Him. But sadly, God's suffering children are lost and near death, wandering about in a spiritual desert with no leader like Moses to guide them."

"Jesus, that sounds well and fine. But we have to deal with our situation. I only know our feeling of loss and longing for you as a father … and a husband!"

"Mary, I understand your hurt and loneliness. I am truly sorry for my absence." He kissed me tenderly on the forehead. "As I've told you before, you are a very special woman. God is calling us both. You are an integral part of His plan."

"But you have such a strong mind and determined heart. Am I the right woman for you?"

"Mary, never doubt my words again. Disbelief and distrust are Satan's weapons." Frowning, he spread his hands in exasperation. "After all I've taught you over the years, don't you realize who you are?"

"Though you have taught much, I have understood very little." Rising from the chair, I stepped over to the gate to make sure it was locked, then turned around. I stared at Jesus and wondered whether he were planning to visit John again in the desert.

"Jesus, I need you here! You spend too much time in prayer and contemplation."

"This is who I am. Just as you need water and bread to sustain you, I need meditation and prayer to satisfy the thirst of my soul." He paused as I returned to the chair, dropping into it with a low, angry sigh. "Mary, while in deep thought and prayer, the Lord talks to me and I talk to Him."

I stared at him, not wanting to hear about his relationship with God.

"The Lord vitalizes my heart and strengthens my will," he went on.

With an indifferent heart, I blurted out, "I need you, just as you need God! Why can't you understand that?"

"I do understand." He put a hand on my shoulder, not losing his composure. "You and I have been entrusted to help others to become close to the Lord God. He wants us to leave our comfortable lives and rescue the lost sheep of Israel and beyond."

This made me even angrier. "By neglecting our family?"

"Mary, you must understand that our family is part of God's will. The Lord will ask nothing of us that we cannot do."

"Sorry, but I am getting tired of your dreaming. If you want our family to remain together, then you have to change your ways."

Obviously surprised by my remark, Jesus forced a smile, while I stared at him with a mixture of concern and condemnation. He said nothing as he gazed upward at the distant stars, as though he were imploring God to come down from the heavens and soften my hard heart.

The silence grew ponderous, and a dark mood clouded my thoughts. Several more minutes passed before I abruptly got to my feet and walked inside the house, leaving him alone with his God to ponder the fate of our lives.

Early the next morning, Jesus rose and prepared to go to the mountain for his daily prayer and meditation. Usually I watched him wash and dress with half-closed eyes, but I kept my eyes shut tight and turned my face when he approached the bed and leaned over to kiss me good-bye.

"Still angry with me?" he uttered, a sad note to his voice.

Even though I wanted to remain silent, I couldn't control my tongue and said with irritation, "You cannot shoulder the burdens of the whole world. It's an impossible task."

"Mary, I have been called to bring God's lost sheep back to His bosom. I must devote myself to the task." There was absolute certainty in his voice that was new, as if he had lain awake all night perfecting it.

I turned my face and looked into his reddened eyes. "I admire your loyalty to the Lord and your steadfast commitment to His will. But I simply will not commit to helping you, mainly because I don't understand what is expected of me, or where that leaves our family."

Jesus began to make a reply, but suddenly thought better of it. After a quick kiss to my forehead, he reached for his water pouch and left the house before I broke into tears, regretting the day he had first come to our village.

To my surprise and delight, Jesus returned home before noontime, with a vibrant step and shining eyes. He asked me to pack some food for a family outing to the nearby hills. Taking the dog with us, Jesus and I held hands while Sara and Isaac skipped along the trail, singing gleefully, as if there were not a problem to worry about in our land.

About an hour later, we had eaten lunch and were relaxing near a stream flowing through a high, grassy area overlooking the assortment of fishing boats dotting the calm waters of the lake. A flock of swallows had been circling overhead, occasionally swooping down just above the upper branches of the trees on the hillside.

Her eyes wide with curiosity, Sara said to her father, "Do they ever land and drink from the stream?"

"Of course," he replied. "All creatures need water, just like you and me. Even the tiniest insect needs nourishment."

Isaac said, "Way up in the sky, the birds look so small."

Jesus patted his head. "They are small when compared to other birds. Some hawks and eagles have wing spans a few meters across."

For the next hour, Jesus taught the children about the different types of birds and animals native to the region, and how they lived in harmony with nature.

Afterward, Jesus and I played tag with the children while the dog raced among us, barking and snapping at our legs. For the first time in months, I felt relaxed and grateful for the small pleasures of daily life, and I realized that nothing on earth is as beautiful as parents and children spending time together, laughing and enjoying a peaceful afternoon. Our shouts and laughter filled the surrounding hills and valleys like the songs of birds. When the children grew tired, Jesus opened his arms wide and uttered a prayer of gratitude as they snuggled against his chest. Then looking in my direction, he gave me a loving smile that made me feel as if I were a part of that embrace.

I returned his gaze with a measured smile, wary of what might lie ahead of us. Despite that, my heart pulsated with love for him, and I listened with delight as he began imitating the calls of various birds and animals. This drew humorous comments from Isaac and Sara and hilarious attempts to mimic him. I couldn't help giggling as he prowled toward me like a big bearded cat going after his mate. Then he jumped to his feet and tossed Sara into the air as she laughed uncontrollably. When he stopped, Sara caught his face between her hands. The feel of the child's little fingers pressing against his cheeks made Jesus' heart sing out with joy. He put her down and tossed Isaac into the air a few times before giving him a big hug.

Later that afternoon, dark clouds rolled over the village and the sea, a sudden breeze from the west announcing the approach of a storm. We rushed down the hill toward the village, hoping to reach shelter before the rains came. But just as we came to the road leading to our home, the rain began pouring down, followed by claps of thunder from the ominous skies. Moments later we were soaked. But we didn't care about our wet clothes or the water running down our faces. We were delighted to be caressed by Mother Nature as we finally reached our house and dashed through the doorway, amid joyful laughter.

Two hours later, dinner was prepared, and we all sat around the table and bowed our heads in prayer. After Jesus gave thanks to the Lord for the meal, the dog sat near his feet as usual, waiting for scraps of food.

"Papa, why do we pray before dinner?"

Jesus looked at him. "We should always show our appreciation to the Lord God and His creatures for sustaining our lives. So before you eat a meal or start any activity, you should offer thanks to God and ask for His guidance and blessing."

"Does the Lord always hear our prayers?" asked Sara, between bites of fish and lentil soup.

Jesus smiled at her. "God listens and answers your prayer in the best way that helps you and others around you."

His answer must have satisfied her, for she made no comment or asked any more questions about the matter. After dinner, he put the children to bed and prayed with them before returning to the room. "Mary, you seem happy this evening," he remarked, as he lowered himself on the soft pillows on the floor.

"The children enjoy your company," I told him. "Dear, why can't we do things together more often?"

"Believe me, it's not because I don't want to." A sad look crossed his face. "I must …"

"You must what? Why? Who says? What are you looking for in life?"

"You know the answer, Mary. You know …"

"What I know is that from now on I want more of you each day!"

"I would like that, but I cannot disregard my responsibilities. Please understand that I wasn't born to live the life of an ordinary man."

"That's obvious," I retorted, sarcasm in my voice. "Lately I've been wondering who I can compare you to. *Is my husband like a priest, a rabbi, or a philosopher?* But you are so different from even them. I've never met anyone like you before!"

"To understand me, you need to hear about my past, my experiences with my Father."

With an inward sigh, I fixed my gaze upon him and wondered what art of persuasion he would try on me, at first thinking he was going to talk about Joseph, the only father that he had ever known.

"When I was a child," he stated, "God began communicating with me … in strange, frightening at first, yet wondrous ways. I gradually sensed that I was a special child with magical powers, for I could heal other sick children. Naturally, I was cautious and kept my powers a secret from everyone, at first afraid that no one would believe and as I got older because I knew they would think me mad. It was between God and me. Not even my mother knew. I was only thirteen when I realized the extent of my powers."

As I listened, I kept my skeptical thoughts to myself, leaning forward a little as he continued with his fanciful story, a bit concerned that he had never told me any of this. "With just the touch of my hand and prayerful thoughts," he continued, "I could cure someone who was sick. One time a friend of mine had a high fever and a frightening cough for a few days. When his parents left his room, I tearfully asked the Lord to assist me in healing him …"

Jesus stopped in mid-sentence for some reason, as if the memory of the event were too much to bear, and swallowed hard, closing his eyes. He drew a deep breath, then opened his eyes and added quietly, "After praying, I put my hand on my friend's chest and told him that I wished he would be cured of his sickness. He stopped coughing, and the next day he was back to normal and playing with the other boys." He paused, although not to gauge my reaction. "That evening while deep in prayer, I realized that I was a Hebrew by blood but the son of God in heart and spirit."

Overwhelmed by this, I sat there and stared at Jesus, trying to make sense of what he had just revealed to me. I wasn't sure if I believed his story, or if I wanted to believe it. Yet I knew one thing with absolute certainty. There was no evil in him. And he told the innocent tale with such conviction that even if he had no powers, he was absolutely convinced that he did. But if he truly had such magical powers, how come no one had ever known about it? What other "miracles" had he performed.

As if reading my thoughts, Jesus said in a matter-of-fact voice, "Like I said, I learned at a young age to be cautious around others. So I used my healing power only when I was certain no one would discover it. I wanted to keep my power a secret until I could fully understand the meaning of it."

I promptly asked, "What about the time you cured your friend of the fever and bad cough? Didn't he tell his parents?"

"Yes, of course. They would have noticed the great change in him anyway. But when they came to my house and questioned me and my parents, I acted witless and claimed it wasn't me who helped him. *It just happened,* my mother suggested, throwing me a strange look." A brief smile crossed his face. "Obviously, I would only help those children who had a minor sickness, so their recovery could be explained by natural forces or God's mysterious intervention."

He paused again, waiting for me to comment on this. But I was so startled and confused by what he had just divulged that I couldn't form any coherent sentences, although I tried at first. After clearing his throat, Jesus added in a level voice, "Mary, I was born to be a vessel of God's love and truth, allowing His power to save humanity from both spiritual and physical sickness. When it comes to illness and disease, many of them have a spiritual cause. As the healer, it is best to treat the cause or source of the sickness. For example, the boy with the cough was deeply grieving over the loss of his grandmother. He felt that she was the only person who could ever love and care for him. By touching his chest, I took out that pain and replaced it with the knowledge of God's deep love for him. Of course, the boy had no awareness of any of this, and I was only half-conscious of it myself."

I stammered, "You actually believe you are meant to be a vessel of God's love and truth to the suffering people of this land?"

"To all people," he stated, without a hint of arrogance. "The Lord God loves all His children, not just the Hebrews. This is the reason why I need you. Unconditionally! We have a great task ahead of us."

I remained silently stunned as Jesus told me about his conception, the story of his mother's encounter with the priest Zechariah, which his mother affirmed to me years later. As the shock wore off, I listened eagerly as Jesus told me about his birth and childhood. My heart ached at the loneliness and difficulties he had experienced due to his birth and the horrible circumstances he faced during boyhood.

"Though I spent most of my early years in Nazareth," he went on, "I had no close friends. I was the despised bastard of the town. So I often found myself alone, desperately searching for God's heart. But as I grew older, the Lord God began to manifest His presence to me in various ways. Sadly, there were also long periods when God remained hidden, silently observing me in the midst of terrible misery and loneliness."

Jesus grew silent momentarily, gazing toward the open window. Then after a long moment of reflection, he continued in a subdued voice, "As I grew older, I often wondered why other children didn't feel the way I was feeling, and why my mind was so active for my age. What was inside my heart that was absent from the hearts of others? Why were my feelings so deep, and why was I so sensitive to the suffering of others? How come I was not like the other children? Usually they laughed, ran, and played with no concern for wounded animals and sick people? And why did others, even some of my relatives, try to degrade me and make me feel that I didn't belong?"

Pausing, Jesus became silent again, a distant look on his face. "Although I am uncertain about this," he uttered, half to himself, "I believe that God was displeased with my situation, but He allowed it to exist so that, like Adam and Eve in the Garden of Eden, I would be isolated in such a way that I had no one to turn to but Him and His loving presence, thereby fostering my relation with Him."

A cool breeze coming through the window shook the flames of the two oil candles, causing their light to dance about our faces.

With a sudden shiver, I slid out of the chair and joined him on the pillows, resting my head upon his chest.

Soon he murmured, "I knew that my path was unique, and that God had a plan for me. However, there were certain days when my pain was so deep that I hoped that God would have left me alone."

Jesus' voice trailed off as he placed his hands on my cheeks. "Other children sensed something different about me … normal boys considered me strange. Yet in my heart of hearts, I knew that God was real and that for some reason He needed my help to fulfill His will."

I suddenly heard claps of distant thunder as the wind grew stronger outside.

Jesus' face took on a somber cast. "Even with all the power granted to me by God, I will not be able to heal the imperfections of this world unless the people will open their hearts and allow me to guide them back to His loving spirit."

I gave him an understanding smile and rose to close the shutters, then moved toward our room. "It's time for bed," I said sleepily.

In a moment he was near my side, gently grasping my arm. "Mary," he whispered, caressing my hair, "let's use this time to strengthen our relationship. Soon, there will be many forces that will try to pull our family apart."

Even though his words frightened me, I swiftly pushed them away, for I didn't want anything to come between us during the long night. We went to bed and clung to one another, my worries of an uncertain future cast aside as our bodies became one in flesh and our souls one in spirit. For some reason, I felt oddly at peace with myself as heavy rains beat against the shutters and the rumblings of thunder echoed in the dark skies over Magdala.

CHAPTER 13

CAIAPHAS WAS THE HIGH PRIEST of Israel, the thirteenth appointed by Herod the Great. Caiaphas had served longer than all the high priests before him, holding his position for many years. It was evident that Caiaphas enjoyed the power and prestige that came with the position, not to mention the wealth and material possessions he had accumulated over the years.

Seeking to understand recent events along the banks of the Jordan River, Caiaphas had summoned a few elders of the Sanhedrin, the supreme political religious body of Israel. Also joining the discussion were some Levites, who were the priests of the Temple. They had gathered in a chamber room of the Temple typically used by priests to decide who would be chosen to enter the Holy Place on that day. It was airy and spacious, and thus Caiaphas had chosen it for the council meeting.

The high priest had also summoned Saul, a young Pharisee from Tarsus, the capital of Cilicia, just northwest of Syria. Saul was of the tribe of Benjamin, and he was appreciated by Caiaphas because he was both a Roman citizen and a Greek-educated scholar. Moreover, Saul was a staunch defender of the Mosaic law. And he wasn't afraid to speak his mind on any subject.

Arriving late to the meeting, Saul hurried into the chamber room. He dropped into a vacant chair and offered a nod to Caiaphas before subtly glancing at the stone-like faces of the men around the long table.

The high priest had known Saul since the days he had been a student attending the great Hebrew Academy of Jerusalem. Although Caiaphas was a Sadducee, and not particularly fond of most Pharisees, he appreciated the zeal with which Saul upheld Jewish traditions.

After a sip of water from his silver cup, Caiaphas spoke in a low, guttural voice. "As you were told, I have gathered you together to discuss some unusual activities at the Jordan River." His eyes darted about the table. "Does anyone know the fanatic who calls himself John the Baptist?"

One of the Levites said in reply, "John is the son of the late Zechariah, who was a respected priest in the village of Ain Karem."

With a look of mild surprise, Caiaphas uttered, "Yes, I knew Zechariah. He was a devout and righteous servant of the Lord."

The Levite added in a reflective tone, "John was about fifteen years old when his father was assassinated, a crime that was never solved, but all signs lead to Herod Antipas as the architect."

"Why would he kill Zechariah?" inquired Saul, a troubled look on his face.

The others glared at him as though he had no right to voice his thoughts among such learned elders.

"A struggle for power, I assume," stated the same man. "Rumor had it that Herod felt Zechariah was undermining his authority. The old priest had declared that John was chosen by God to prepare the way for the Messiah."

"In other words," said one of the elders, "Herod felt that Zechariah was devising a plot to destroy him by presenting a false prophet and later a false Messiah."

"Do you believe this to be true?" said Caiaphas, astonished.

The elder nodded. "As you know, Herod will go to any extreme to protect his power. Though John was harmless at the time, Herod decided to silence Zechariah's voice."

Caiaphas looked at Saul. "Do you know this John the Baptist?"

He shook his head. "I was told that he lived in the desert for a period, in one of the Essene communities by the Dead Sea. Then about a year ago, John began what he calls a process of purification for the chosen people. Now he has growing support among the villages along the Jordan."

"Saul, you and I spoke to the same person," a heavy-set priest remarked with a chuckle. Turning to Caiaphas, he added in a flat tone, "John's influence is spreading among the common people, who respond to his call for baptism. He is a fiery speaker who exhorts people to live righteously so as to avoid hell."

Caiaphas considered this. "Has he declared himself a prophet?"

A long silence followed, for no one knew for certain what this John the Baptist thought of himself. But the high priest persisted, impatient for an answer, "Well? Is he some kind of desert prophet?"

Saul spoke in a quiet voice. "I'm not the person to address such a complex matter. Yet on the basis of what is known, John is baptizing people in the Jordan, claiming their sins are forgiven by his water purification rites."

Caiaphas was taken aback. "Only the Anointed One of God has the power to forgive sins," he said sharply. "Does this John the Baptist think of himself as the Messiah?"

Once again there was no response from the men at the table. Some had unreadable expressions as they drank water from their cups, silently chastising this John the Baptist for disturbing their peaceful daily routines.

Making a gesture, Caiaphas moved his eyes to Saul's face. "I want you to go to the Jordan and speak to this man personally. We need to understand what he is doing there, and who he claims to be, and under what authority." After a brief pause, he added with finality, "Choose four people to accompany you on the journey. And don't return here without absolute clarification."

Three days later Saul and four high priests arrived in the area along the Jordan River where John had been preaching and conducting baptisms. It was early November, and the air was fresh from a light rain that had fallen during the night. There was a heavy growth of reeds along the banks of the river, standing up to eight feet in height. The river water flowed lazily southward, reflecting warm rays of the midday sun as groups of men, women, and children stood on a broad, grassy slope leading down to the bank, now muddy from several days of people wading into the river to be baptized by John. And there was John, wearing a tunic made of a coarse material often used to make grain sacks. In a powerful voice, John was calling out to the people to confess their sins and wash them away in the cool waters while also imploring God to forgive them as they prepared their souls for the imminent arrival of the Messiah.

Since boyhood, John had been convinced that he was a child of destiny. Due to Zechariah's spiritual experiences at the Temple, which he had often conveyed to his growing son, John was certain that he had been called by the Lord God to prepare the way for the long-awaited Messiah. In fact, his father's words of encouragement still resounded in John's heart.

John gazed meditatively at the crowds that had gathered around him before wading into the waters of the Jordan, with Jesus near his side. A few years had passed since Jesus' first visit, and now they were together again. Jesus had spent the last three weeks assisting John in the immersion of the repentant into the cleansing waters. It was the last day of Jesus' visit to the area, and he prayed inwardly that his elder brother could understand the great significance of their relationship.

Standing waist-deep in the slow-moving waters, John turned and signaled a small group of men to enter the river. With solemn yet hopeful expressions, the men stepped into the waters and drew close to John and Jesus, their anxious gestures betraying uncertainty that their lives would actually change much after being baptized by this charismatic preacher.

"The Anointed One is coming … and soon!" proclaimed John, with a sudden gesture.

He approached the first man in line and set both hands on his shoulders, uttering a prayer of repentance before immersing him into the water. Seconds later he pulled him up and said in a fervent voice, "Brothers, all signs indicate the last days of God's judgment are upon us!"

Most of those present nodded in agreement as John added loudly, "Soon we will see the Messiah with our very own eyes! We must purify our bodies and cleanse our minds because God's kingdom is coming!"

John prayed for the next man in line, immersing him into the cool waters. Then after raising him up, he glanced at Jesus. "The Messiah's word will be like a sharp sword separating the wheat from the chaff."

"Surely God's judgment will come," Jesus answered with a nod. "But the Lord is also the merciful God of infinite love and goodness. When the Messiah comes, his mission is to convey God's love, truth, and compassion."

John scowled momentarily. "Saving Israel and humanity with love and compassion?" he thought aloud, immersing another repentant soul. After baptizing him, he said firmly to Jesus, "Already we have the Mosaic law and the commandments. The people of Israel need to live in accordance with the commands that God gave us through Moses and the prophets. What need is there of another truth when we have the truth now?"

"John, there is a higher degree of truth, and God has revealed it directly to me. My mission is to reveal that truth."

Unsettled by Jesus' remarks, John threw him a look of disapproval as he stepped away from him and toward another group of people who were entering the river.

During the following hour, John felt the power of the Lord flow through him as he baptized a throng of men, women, and children, with Jesus supporting him with strong prayer and words of encouragement to the newly baptized.

Still standing in the river, John moved closer to Jesus and grasped his upper arm strongly. "Your mission is to reveal God's truth?" It was a rebuke. "I hope you know what you are suggesting. You are greater than the Messiah?"

Jesus made no reply, brushing away John's hand.

John puffed out his chest and said testily, "Unlike your grand scheme, my mission is to *merely* prepare the way for the Anointed One. I am to reawaken the people to the spirit of God. I will continue baptizing and converting the sinful so they comply with the commandments and Mosaic law."

"What you are doing is important," stated Jesus.

John smiled crookedly, his voice losing its bite. "Though I disagree with many of your beliefs, I still feel there is something in you. Despite the fact we were sired by the same father, you were born outside his house and were treated rather badly as a child. But you have never harbored any resentment against me. Though we are often at odds, the same blood flows through our hearts."

"God has placed His hopes on our family. We must be united until all of God's children come to know His divine light." A wry smile crossed Jesus' face as he spoke. "Can't we agree on that much?"

Laughing deeply, John gave Jesus a slap on the back. Soon John noticed some finely attired priests among the crowd on the rise of land above the river. He studied their faces, wondering whether they had come to be baptized or merely to observe his unorthodox activities.

John called out to them in a booming voice, "Brothers, don't be timid! Come into the river and cleanse your souls of all sins and impurities!"

Saul took a step forward and signaled the two men to come out of the water. "We wish to speak to John," he stated, his authority apparent in his bearing.

Not liking the hard expressions on their faces, Jesus said in a whisper, "John, it appears you are drawing an elite flock today."

As the brothers waded toward the muddy shore, one of the priests asked in a clipped tone, "Which one of you is John, called the Baptist?"

"I am the one," uttered John, stepping on the shore. As they walked upon the slope, he gestured to his left. "This is Jesus, my cousin from Nazareth," he told them, not wanting to reveal they were actually brothers. Then shading his eyes from the bright sunlight, John added in jest, "Have you come with treasures or good tidings?"

"Neither," said Saul, smiling briefly. After he introduced himself and his companions, he got to the point. "John, there are some people in Jerusalem who wish to know who you are. And what is your purpose here at the Jordan?"

"Some people in Jerusalem?" echoed Jesus, staring at a heavy-set priest who was eyeing him skeptically. "Do you mean the common people? The ones who labor all day? Or the haughty ones called priests who siphon the offerings of the poor and downtrodden?"

Though the others bristled at this, Saul didn't seem offended by the remark. Keeping his eyes on John's face, he said mildly, "The ruling council of the Temple has asked us to come here. There are serious rumors in Jerusalem about your activities."

Before John could respond, the heavy-set priest said brusquely, "Do you consider yourself the Messiah, the one everyone is longing for?"

John shook his head. "No, I am not the Messiah."

"Then who are you?" asked the priest to his left. "Are you Elijah?"

"No, I am not Elijah …"

Not wholly satisfied, Saul gave him a penetrating look. "So, do you deny being the prophet Elijah, the one who is to announce the coming Messiah?"

"I am not the Elijah," John stated firmly, denying for the second time his spiritual role. "Since you are well educated, you know it is written that Elijah rose to heaven in a chariot of fire, and he will return in the last days to usher in the Messiah."

Spreading his hands upward toward the cloudless sky, he added in a mocking tone, "I assure you that I've never ascended to the skies in a chariot of fire."

"No, I wouldn't think so," uttered Saul, looking at John's companion. There was something familiar about him, but he couldn't place from where.

An elderly priest with gentle eyes found his voice. "John, help us to understand your mission here. We need to return to Jerusalem with a clear answer."

"I am God's humble servant. I was called to prepare the way for the Messiah."

Saul's brow furrowed. "Yet you claim not to be Elijah?"

John nodded, surprised by the persistent line of questions.

The heavy-set priest gave him a grave look. "If you aren't the Messiah, then why are you baptizing people, claiming you can wash away their sins?"

"Yes, I do baptize, with water … but only to prepare people to receive the baptism of the Lord. He will baptize with the grace of the Holy Spirit."

One of the Levites spoke up. "If your mission is to prepare the way for the Messiah, then tell us when he is coming. Tomorrow? Next week? Or perhaps when you are old and toothless and can no longer shout out his arrival?"

This drew laughter from several people in the crowd who were listening intently to the exchange between these learned men and the two.

Jesus said in a clear voice, "When the time comes, only the innocent eyes and pure hearts of children will be able to recognize him."

The heavy-set priest raised a hand in anger. "Are you contending we priests will be blind to the Messiah's arrival?"

Growing impatient, John said in a rising voice, "The Messiah will come after I prepare his way. However, I am unworthy to untie the leather of his sandals."

"I am a Pharisee," stated Saul. "The Temple leaders who sent us here don't approve of your baptizing rites." He added with indignation, "Do not pretend to be something that you are not. As you know, there are many people who are desperately seeking hope during these chaotic times."

"Don't promise hope where there is none there," added the heavy-set priest. "So be careful with what you say. We are scrutinizing your words and movements."

Stroking his chin in contemplation, Saul said in a level voice, "John, even though you claim to be neither Elijah nor the Messiah, there are many people who believe differently. So you have one last chance to declare yourself. Who are you, and who gave you the authority to perform these actions?"

With an annoyed look, John uttered, "I have said what I had to say. Now return to Jerusalem and tend to your rituals, while I do the work of the Lord among these good people who thirst for love and guidance."

After hearing this, with the implication that they were not providing these things, Saul and his companions turned and walked away from the crowd, grumbling among themselves.

That evening, a full moon rose on the horizon as John and Jesus stretched out their tired bodies upon a grassy area just east of the Jordan. In the near distance there was a mass of tents, about twenty altogether. They had become temporary shelters for John and his followers these past months as they traveled to the villages along the Jordan.

When John and Jesus had completed their prayers, they rested near a campfire while discussing the heavy burdens that the Lord God places upon the shoulders of His holy servants.

With his head resting on his clasped hands, Jesus thought aloud, "To be chosen by the Lord is an honor, yet frightening at times."

John nodded. "Fulfilling God's will has never been easy. His words of truth aren't something that most people like to hear ... or to obey."

"You're right," said Jesus. He rolled onto his side, looking at his brother. "It was for this reason that God promised the coming of Elijah to announce the Messiah. The Lord hopes the Anointed One can avoid misunderstanding and suffering. This is why Elijah must come and prepare the people to welcome the Messiah with open minds and willing hearts."

John hesitated. "What if Elijah does come on the clouds and announce the coming of the Messiah? Who would deny such a thing?"

"Only a fool. If Elijah did come on the clouds, no one could deny it." Jesus sat up and held his hands closer to the dancing flames of the fire. "John, consider this. What if Elijah is already here, and what if his fiery spirit is working through you."

Jesus' suggestion was so unthinkable to John that he merely shrugged it off.

"John, I am serious. What did our father tell you when you were growing up?"

John hesitated a moment. "That the archangel Gabriel told him that I would be born in the spirit and power of Elijah and that my mission was to prepare the way for the Messiah."

"Yes!" His voice rose. "God wants the best people to gather around the Anointed One so that his influence can spread as quickly as possible."

After tossing more wood onto the fire, Jesus added reflectively, "Since childhood I have opened my heart and soul to God, desiring to understand everything about Him. I wanted to learn about His nature, His creation, His relationship to mankind, and His will for me. Mostly I wanted to understand why humanity is mired in sin and such anguish."

John glanced at his brother, realizing he knew very little about him.

Jesus soon added, "After years of tearful prayer and deep meditation, I concluded that God is our loving Parent, and we were created as His children …"

Looking bewildered, John said faintly, "At times I can understand what you say. Yet I am baffled by your beliefs. In your heart of hearts, what is the truth for you? As for me, I am guided by the law and God's commandments given to Moses on Mount Sinai. Why did God do this? Because we are sinful creatures who need strict regulations, as well as prayer, repentance, fasting, and abstinence. But for those haughty people who continue sinning without remorse, there is the fire of hell for eternity."

With a weary expression, Jesus said to him, "But how could a God of goodness punish His children in such a cruel manner? In fact, our

Heavenly Parent's utmost desire is to save each of His lost sheep as quickly as possible."

"Jesus, why do you insist on referring to God as our *Heavenly Parent*?"

"Because He wants us to become His precious children and share in His divine nature."

John made no comment, but focused on the rising moon and wondered what would happen after Saul and the other priests returned to Jerusalem, reporting to the Temple authorities their discussion with him.

Jesus added in a level voice, "In order for God's kingdom to become a reality, Israel and all humanity need to understand the original destiny of human beings and why it remains unfulfilled. You know that in each person there are characteristics of those angels who have fallen which I call Satan, along with divine qualities that come from the Lord God ..."

"So you actually believe that each person has divine qualities that come from God."

"Yes, isn't it obvious? Unfortunately, as you well know, there is also the existence of evil in human nature. God's desire is for all mankind to eradicate the malignant nature that we inherited from Satan. But purification is not enough. God also wants us to connect to His divine light. Simply put, each person needs to develop the divine nature that God gave to us."

As if he hadn't heard a word of Jesus' explanation, John shook his head and said adamantly, "Our nature will never change! Only baptism can purify our corrupt hearts, and only obedience to the laws will control our sinful behavior. This is the truth."

"People need a transformation of heart more than anything. Only God's love and truth can make that happen. We need to discover our true nature given by God, who created us in His image. He never intended for us to be His servants. We were created to be His sons and daughters ..."

"You're wrong!" shouted John, jumping to his feet. Stepping away from the fire, he muttered to himself, "Humans are too evil and impure to even approach the Lord God." He turned around and stared at his brother with feverish eyes.

Sighing, Jesus responded in a patient tone, "John, I know this is difficult for you to grasp. First, you need to understand how evil originated. What truly happened between Adam, Eve, and the archangel whom I call Lucifer? Without a complete understanding of evil we won't be able to eliminate its pervasive influence in our lives."

John's face clouded over as he pondered this for a long moment. "The sin of Adam and Eve was an act of disobedience," he said firmly.

"The Lord God gave them the command not to eat from the Tree of the Knowledge of Good and …"

Taking in a slow, deep breath, Jesus said without visible emotion, "John, the story of the Fall shouldn't be taken literally."

John offered a dismissive shrug, moving his eyes to the faint light from a group of stars on the western horizon.

"Have you ever met a serpent that could speak?" asked Jesus, trying to hide his irritation. "Though Satan has spiritual power, it's not possible for him to make a serpent talk. The author of Genesis compares Satan to a serpent because he tempted Eve with his poisonous lies. Besides, since God is our loving Parent, why would He have placed a harmful fruit in the Garden that could have caused the death of His children?"

John sat across the fire from Jesus, staring at him over the flames. "The Lord wanted to test Adam and Eve to see if they were capable of following His orders. If they had obeyed, then God would have trusted them. But due to their disobedience, God had to cast them from the Garden." After a short pause, he added loudly, "For this reason, we must repent and obey the Lord by complying with all the laws and commandments!"

"So you think that God is a heartless ruler who dictates laws and orders, with the threat of punishment. People shouldn't be motivated by fear but by a desire to become better people and vessels of love."

Jesus stood up and stretched his arms for a minute, looking off to his left as a burst of laughter came from the men in one of the tents. Then he dropped to the ground and crossed his legs. "The Lord made the earth and sky, the seas and mountains, the plants and trees, the fish and animals. John, look at nature around you. God made all these things for us to enjoy. As our loving Parent, after the earth was prepared, God made His children to live here. Indeed, God used physical laws to create the universe, but the motivation came from His loving heart."

John turned away and remained silent, not wishing to engage in further conversation with a man whom he felt was expressing beliefs that were not totally in line with his.

Feeling a sudden coldness in John's heart, Jesus said in a clear voice, "Your antiquated beliefs in a God who is a strict and merciless master is not in harmony with the loving God who is my Heavenly Parent."

John was taken aback upon hearing this. Shifting his body, he glanced at Jesus and saw in him not someone who was a learned scholar and great teacher, but a younger brother with whom he had become acquainted during the past few years.

"Jesus, I simply cannot accept your reasoning or your insults. Since God is both omnipotent and omniscient, He has no need for the companionship of man."

"John, nobody can live alone for eternity. Even the most powerful kings on earth need to share their thoughts, feelings, dreams, and ideals with those who can respond to them. God Almighty is no different. The Lord needs children who can respond to His love and ideals."

"What you speak is blasphemy," accused John. "How dare you raise man up to the same level as the Lord God!"

"You are misinterpreting my remarks."

Before John could jump in again, Jesus quickly added, "When you feel sudden joy after something good happens, do you embrace a tree and whisper your good news to the trunk and branches? Of course not. You look for another person, someone quite like you, who can understand your heart and respond to your joyful feelings. Am I right?"

John nodded reluctantly, giving him a conciliatory smile.

"The same is true of the Lord God," Jesus continued. "Our Heavenly Parent desires to share His love and joy with a being who understands His heart and respond to His thoughts and feelings. God graced us with His characteristics so that we could have a reciprocal relationship with Him and be His eternal partners of love."

John looked at Jesus as he considered all this. It was too much for his tired mind to grasp. He had gotten up before dawn and spent the entire day preaching to the crowds who had flocked to the river to hear him.

"We'd better get some sleep," John muttered, rising to his feet. "Tomorrow is a new day, and there will be many more for us to baptize."

Jesus nodded and accompanied John back to the nearby village where they were staying. When John awoke early the next morning, Jesus was gone after having had a dream instructing him to return to Nazareth …

The next day the sun was high in the sky when Saul, still accompanied by the four priests and Levites, returned to Jerusalem. Tired from their journey to the Jordan River, they kept their thoughts to themselves as the small caravan passed through the city walls, beneath the Temple Mount, and then toward the upper parts of the city.

As they passed the Temple Mount, Saul looked up and noticed a lone silhouette walking slowly in the direction of the upper city. Squinting, Saul realized it was the high priest. Caiaphas was approaching the narrow causeway that connected the Temple to the roads and buildings of the upper city. In a matter of minutes, Saul and his companions caught up with Caiaphas and greeted him obsequiously. "Shalom!" they called out, approaching him.

"Shalom," he uttered, an anxious expression on his face. "Were you able to find this John the Baptist? Did you speak to him?"

"We found John at the Jordan, about ten miles north of the Sea of Salt," responded the heavy-set priest. "He is a rough-looking fellow, but with a sweet and powerful tongue that hypnotizes simple-minded people."

Caiaphas shifted his eyes to Saul's face. "What is your estimation of Zechariah's son? Any chance John could be a prophet?"

"I am not an expert on prophets," he said dryly. "But in my opinion, this John doesn't fit the role of a prophet, especially one who might announce the coming of the Messiah. I could be mistaken, but John simply doesn't strike me as being a glorious person like the prophet Elijah."

"That's what I thought," remarked Caiaphas. He looked at the others. "Well, do you have a different perspective on the matter?"

The priests and Levites shook their heads, deciding to keep their thoughts to themselves for fear of saying something that might come back to haunt them in the future.

After a long moment of silence, Saul spoke up in a level voice. "We came across a number of people along the Jordan who believe that John could be the Messiah. But I am convinced that he is neither the Messiah nor a pretender. Upon questioning, he absolutely denied having any aspirations to be deemed the Anointed One."

The heavy-set priest laughed. "John is just a simple man who's been in the desert sun too long. In a few weeks he will regain his senses and return to his village and take up farming."

As chortles of laughter filled the air, Caiaphas felt a surge of relief and was pleased to know that no great prophet would challenge his authority or try to take over his exalted position at the Temple.

But one of the Levites cleared his throat and said, "We were surprised to find that John has many disciples. He was with a relative by the name of Jesus. Though humbly dressed, there was a certain dignity about that man. In fact, he seemed more like a prophet than John."

Some of the others nodded, while Caiaphas' interest piqued. "And who is this Jesus? Have you seen him before?"

Saul said offhandedly, "John told us the man is his cousin. There was clearly some special bond between them."

Frowning, the heavy-set priest remarked in a brusque tone, "This Jesus was an impudent upstart with a clever tongue. Whatever we said, he twisted our words to try to make us look foolish."

Trying to hide his apprehension, Caiaphas barked, "So we have a lunatic who draws crowds of people into the Jordan for baptisms, and his cousin whose sharp barbs pierced my overly sensitive priests. Is this your report?"

Wanting to return home, Saul stated in a tone of finality, "We have told you what we saw and felt. If you aren't satisfied, you can always send others to observe John and his followers."

Caiaphas' lips tightened into a thin line. "Let's keep a close eye on John and his cousin. Time will reveal what mischief those two are planning."

"We should watch this Jesus fellow closely," said the heavy-set priest. "His tongue seems more dangerous than John the Baptist's."

"Is John married?' asked Caiaphas.

"He is not," answered the same priest.

"No!" exclaimed in astonishment the High Priest. "Doesn't he know that for a Jew marriage is a sacred obligation? Not to marry is to diminish the likeness of God."

"That is something we can pint point against him next time we see him, and if this relative of his is unmarried too…well, he will hear our disapproval," said the heavy-set priest.

Caiaphas thought aloud, "I know people in Galilee who can assist us. But let's wait a few months and see how things unfold." There was a moment of silence as Caiaphas stared at Saul. "You can stay longer in Judea, can't you?"

He shook his head. "I must return to Tarsus. I haven't seen my family in two months."

"Fine," Caiaphas said, nodding. "But don't stay away too long. Jerusalem is teeming with all sorts of fools and fanatics who hope to start another war against the Romans. So I need you here. Understand?"

Saul dipped his head in respect and began to walk off, absently wondering if John the Baptist and his cousin were more dangerous than some of the priests and sect leaders who participated in Temple affairs while secretly vying for greater power and wealth.

CHAPTER 14

THE YEARS PASSED TOO QUICKLY as Jesus divided himself between his public mission and our family life, including my father's fishing business. By the time Jesus was twenty-nine years of age, he was ably handling an assortment of tasks and duties associated with the business with the help of some assistants. Although he was quite busy and usually out of the house from early morning to late evening, he somehow managed to make time for trips to meet with John the Baptist or other people who seemed interested in his unorthodox beliefs.

The children and I pleaded with him to stay home as much as he could. I understood when he had to leave town on business activities, but when he would suddenly depart without notice to visit John, sometimes for weeks, I would sink into a sullen mood, occasionally venting my frustrations on those people who came around asking for him.

One late winter, when Jesus returned home from a long trip, we were surprised by his unexpected arrival. Overjoyed, the children ran up to him, shouting "Papa! Papa!" With tears in his eyes, Jesus opened his arms and gave each child kisses and a warm embrace.

After a light meal, during which Jesus told us about his recent travels, Isaac asked anxiously, "Papa, how long are you going to stay this time?"

"I'll be here for a while. I promise you," he told them in a way that left no doubt that he meant it.

Isaac had become a strong, vibrant boy, while Sara was a sweet, generous girl with a humorous personality. They both resembled their father in many aspects, particularly Isaac, whose husky body was crowned by a rather large head, with sparkling brown eyes that took in everything around him.

When Jesus was home, he was a dedicated parent giving his full attention to the family. He would take long walks with the children, explaining various aspects of God's creation, such as the habits of different animals and what their sounds meant.

"God has blessed me with special gifts," he once told them when they noticed that some animals would approach him without fear.

Sometimes at night Jesus would take us up to the hills and explain the various patterns of stars and the mysteries of the heavens. I was content and hopeful during those outings, for I could see that Jesus and the children treasured each other's company. Jesus delighted the children by teaching them how to carve little human forms out of wood ... tiny, detailed sculptures that looked real.

Often Jesus would talk to them about the Lord God and His purpose for creating the natural world. Isaac and Sara sat beside him, giving him their total attention.

He wanted to raise them in the knowledge of God and His deep love for humanity.

When Isaac asked what love was, Jesus replied, "Love is an unselfish emotion. It is expressed through the thoughts and deeds of devout men."

Spring came, and Jesus and the children began spending time together in our large vegetable garden behind the house. Early each morning, before it grew hot, they worked, briskly weeding the garden, tilling the soil, and planting new seeds. I was amazed to see how meticulous Jesus was, liking to keep their daily tasks well organized. Whatever he touched shone with its own special beauty.

One night, after the children were put to bed, Jesus and I went outside and sat on the stone bench by the garden. There was a quarter moon in the sky, and a soft breeze graced us with an enchanting mixture of fragrances from the flowers decorating the bushes about the area.

Jesus looked at me. "Mary, God is not a philosophical concept. He is a living reality within the hearts of all men and women. By discovering your own nature, you will come to know God as our celestial Father and Mother, and truly feel you are the daughter of God."

He paused, studying my face. "Open your heart to God, and His spirit will always be there. Allow God's spirit to guide and support you. Allow God to give you His full love. He wants to talk to you, share His life with you."

I gazed at him. "Unlike me, you are so sensitive to God's heart. Though it is easy for you to relate to Him, others might find it difficult to feel the presence of the Almighty in their lives." Patting his hand, I added with a smile, "The children and I are so happy when you're here with us. Don't you feel content when you are home with us?"

"Of course I do. My family has always been important to me."

"So how come you leave home so often to meet with your brother and others?

"I know this is hard to accept … and it may seem selfish on the surface … but I meet with others for your sake and for the children, and for the sake of other families as well. Every day, I see people are walking around spiritually dead, not knowing God. I have to bring them back to life. I have to help them understand their value in front of God, and teach them to create model families where spouses are loyal and children are respectful to their parents."

He paused and leaned toward me. "God has called upon us to form such a family. We have to educate our children so that they will know the existence of God in their hearts."

"I don't oppose the idea of our children knowing the Lord," I said in reply. "But at the same time, I cannot understand why you spend so much time away from home, teaching things that people might not even care about, spending time that is not theirs but ours."

A good-natured smile appeared on his face. "If anything, you are an honest woman who is not afraid to express your feelings."

"I know you hope to see changes in me," I uttered. "You want me to be aware that I can be more than what I am now. But I have my limits in striving for your ideals …"

My voice trailed off. I was distracted by a shooting star on the northern horizon.

Afterward, I remained silent, feeling his eyes on my face. With a small sigh, I turned to him and said, "Most husbands are pleased to have a wife who takes care of the children, the chores, and cooking. But you keep pushing me to go beyond the normal boundaries of family life. I simply cannot do it. I am just an ordinary woman."

"There's nothing wrong with being ordinary. But whether we like it or not, we both have a special destiny. You were born to be the wife of a man who has been called by God to commence a new era of peace fostered by love and truth. However, I do not even know yet how long it will take. It depends on the response of those very people whom I came to free from the bonds of ignorance. But I cannot ignore that call. What kind of a lesson would that impart to the children?"

I turned my face, inhaling the mingling of smells and fragrances carried into our courtyard. After a minute of troubled thought, I gave Jesus a subtle look and realized there was a part of him that I would never fully comprehend, just as there were parts of me that he wouldn't grasp.

"Housekeeping and watching over the children are never-ending tasks," I pointed out. "I would just like to keep my feet on the ground."

"Mary, you are a descendant of many generations of women who were blessed by the grace of the Lord. You must realize that God has invested much effort to purify the wombs of a particular line of daughters of Israel."

Puzzled, I murmured, "What do you mean?"

"I believe you were born of the same blood lineage as my mother," he explained. "Many generations of women in our families have lived in full respect of the laws of Moses and the teachings of the prophets."

I thought about the lives of my mother and grandmother, and then considered my own situation. Despite the fact that Magdala was close to the corrupt environment of Tiberias, a city constructed by Herod to please the Romans, and the fact that I often came into contact with a variety of men due to our fishing business, I had kept myself clean and in good faith to the God of Abraham, Isaac, and Jacob.

"I know," said Jesus with a smile, giving me a look as if he could read my thoughts. "This is one reason I chose you to be my wife. My attraction to you goes beyond your physical aspects. You are a woman of strong heart and mind. Although you were exposed to evil and temptation, you remained unscathed by it. You were able to maintain your deep faith, while keeping both your heart and body pure."

Somewhat embarrassed by this effusive praise, I said nothing as I glanced at the wispy clouds crossing the lower tip of the moon.

Catching my attention, he added in a serious tone, "Sexual purity is especially important. In fact, it was part of the problem that led to the human fall."

A bit confused, I stared at him. "As a girl I was taught that Adam and Eve's sin was their disobedience when they ate the fruit offered by the serpent."

"But it's not that simple. The serpent and fruit shouldn't be interpreted literally."

"Oh?" I uttered with sarcasm. "I suppose the Lord told you that, huh? Did God also tell you how He created everything in six days?"

Jesus smiled wanly. "Mary, remember that for God a thousand years is like a day, and a day is like a thousand years. The Scriptures say that God created the sun and the moon on the fourth day. Right?"

I nodded, wondering where he was leading with this, and if it was a trick to catch me in something.

"Days and nights, as they occur on earth, did not exist when the Lord created our vast universe. The main point of the Creation story is that everything develops over a period of time."

"So God cannot make a huge mountain with a blink of the eye?"

"Of course not. An enormous period of time was necessary for the Lord to create the heavens and earth. Just as God is present in our lives today, He was present during each step of the creation process, watching over all growth and development."

"That seems natural," I said absently as I watched two frogs near the courtyard gate. They were croaking wildly, perhaps in the middle of a mating ritual.

Jesus followed my eyes and focused upon the frogs. Then he turned back to me and added, "God's development of man and woman was a meticulous and attentive process. The Lord put all His efforts into creating the perfect physical body. When everything was ready, God breathed a spirit into the bodies."

Questions were pounding my mind. I felt the need for answers.

"Going back to Adam and Eve," I said to him. "If the Lord knew the fruit was poisonous, why didn't He stop them from eating it?"

"Because in doing so He would have taken away human freedom and creativity. God left it up to them. Unfortunately, Lucifer, knowing the spiritual immaturity of Adam and Eve at that precise moment, wanted to compromise their spiritual growth, destroying their innocence with deception."

"I always believed that God made man by modeling him with the dust of the earth, giving him life by blowing in his nostrils!"

"Mary, this is a story for children," said Jesus with a compassionate smile. "Everything needs to follow the universal laws of growth."

"Is that the reason why God didn't create man and woman already full-grown?"

Jesus nodded silently, rising to his feet and stretching. He stepped over to the furrows in the ground and squatted by the first row, where tiny shoots had recently emerged from the ground. He scooped up a small handful of the soil and brought it up to his nostrils, sniffing it for several moments. "We ought to have a good crop this year," he uttered as he stood upright.

"So Adam and Eve had to grow physically as much as spiritually?" I asked.

"Yes. They had to grow into their maturity. They were born from a physical mother as any baby is. And in their physical aspect, they were not different from the previous generation. However, at the moment of their birth, God endowed them with internal characteristics that distinguished them from the others. The angels were responsible for assisting Adam and Eve in the process of spiritual enrichment."

Jesus paused again. His gaze swept across the stars in the sky, then fell upon me. "Those early years were important for God's creation because the first humans had to learn their identity and begin the journey toward their destiny. The role of Lucifer in this process was fundamental. If he had cooperated with God's will, he, too, would have attained his perfection."

"Seems that things didn't go as God planned," I commented, the distant sound of barking dogs breaking the silence of the night.

Jesus shook his head. "Instead of extending his love and sense of duty toward Adam and Eve, Lucifer plunged into a jealous and resentful frenzy. Among all creatures, he had been the angel with the highest position in the angelical world. But he became too prideful and refused to give up his power to Adam and Eve, although he knew that it was God's plan. Lucifer was not capable of foreseeing the advantages and blessings in store for him, had he just done the will of God. Instead, he waited for a suitable moment to spiritually destroy the first human beings."

Jesus took a stone and tossed it into the flower beds. "Adam and Eve were growing from adolescents to young adults," he explained. "With the coming of her menstrual blood, Eve had become a woman. It was right at that moment that Lucifer approached her with his sinister plan."

"From what I know of the Scriptures," I said, "in the middle of the Garden of Eden there was a tree of life and a tree of the knowledge of good and evil."

"Mary, as you know, the Garden of Eden represents the earth before the Fall, a pristine paradise without evil or suffering. But it also represents on another level the bodies of Adam and Eve, which are the supreme creation in the universe and thus a paradise. In the middle of the Garden, which means also in the middle of the body, there are the sexual organs. So, in reality, the trees symbolize the sexual organs. And as you know, trees produce flowers and fruit."

"And in the fruit, there is a seed with its generating power," I said, amazed. "So what you are saying is that the tree of life is Adam."

"As well as his sexual organ. And the fruit is the sexual love. It is how life begins."

"So, the Garden of Eden is Adam?"

"Yes. The life giver."

"So the tree of life symbolizes Adam and his sexual organ!" I was suddenly so excited by this new knowledge that he was revealing!

"Yes, Mary. Adam and Eve should have become husband and wife when God told them to. Not before! Thus, they would have created a family in which God lived."

"So Adam and Eve would have become parents just like God!" I thought aloud, delighted to discover such truth.

Jesus looked pleased. "Mary, the sexual organs are the most sacred part of a man's body. They are sensitive because they carry the seed of life. Man and woman complement each other, and their relationship as husband and wife and, eventually, parents is eternal. The children will always have the same parents …"

"And parents should always have the same spouse," I interjected. "The family unit lives forever."

Jesus nodded. "Conjugal love, or the sexual act, is the most intimate experience between a man and a woman. It is the moment when both should be in complete unity and harmony." He returned to the bench, sitting next to me and reaching for my hand. "The intimate moments between a husband and wife are meant to draw them into a perfect state of harmony. It is the supreme expression of love," he said, looking into my eyes.

I nodded, then thought aloud, "What does the tree of good and evil represent?"

"It symbolizes the sexual organ of Eve."

"So Lucifer waited for the moment when Eve reached the age where she could bear children."

Jesus nodded. "Though Eve could communicate with God and the various angels, both she and Adam were spiritually immature. Lucifer, as an archangel, wanted to keep Eve away from those angels loyal to God. So he was often by her side as he began the process of seducing her. Since Eve was so innocent, she didn't understand the danger of such interactions, especially since Lucifer had been guiding her and Adam since her earliest memories."

I noticed that while telling the story Jesus adopted a sad expression, as if the story were about some personal woe.

"Since Eve had not completed her spiritual growth, her purity and peace of mind were disturbed by this illicit sexually charged intimacy with the archangel. Over time, her sexual attraction became stronger as she and Lucifer spent intimate moments together. And though she felt distant from God, Lucifer told her this was the fastest way to become like God.

While considering his explanation, I inhaled a deep breath of the cool night air and realized that since the story was more complex than I had imagined, the same could be said about our lives, which we lead mostly in secret from one another. "So you believe that Lucifer manipulated the truth, distorting it for his own selfish purposes?"

Jesus nodded. "Even when Adam and Eve were children, the Lord could foresee the possibility of what might happen with the archangel. This is why when they reached adolescence, God gave them the Commandment. God told Adam and Eve they could play with the animals, enjoy the rivers and mountains, and eat any fruit they desired, except for the fruit of their immature love."

I reflected on this. "So God wanted young Adam and Eve to enjoy themselves while growing up as children and adolescents." Then, feeling as if the breath had been knocked out of me, I asked. "After seducing Eve, did Lucifer encourage her to get closer to Adam and tempt him?"

"Something like that," replied Jesus. "As Eve's contact with the archangel intensified, she began to realize that she was supposed to be with Adam, not the archangel. In her desire to return to God, she then went to Adam and encouraged him to be intimate with her. Adam was physically mature, although not quite an adult yet, but he had not yet become one in heart with God. So he wasn't serious enough about keeping God's Commandment to reject her advances."

"So Adam was as guileless as Eve had been when Lucifer first seduced her?"

"Exactly. In his innocence, Adam succumbed to Eve's charms and they had sexual relations. Their desires and attraction to one another became stronger, whereas their relationship with God suffered." A look of sorrow crossed Jesus' face. "Adam and Eve's purity and innocence were replaced with anxiety, fear, uncertainty, and a sense of abandonment as they felt lost and separated from the Lord God."

"So, instead of developing their inner character and connection to God, they focused on the sensation of sexual pleasure," I added.

Imagining the scene in my mind, I couldn't help but ask, "Is this the reason why Adam and Eve covered their sexual parts with leaves?"

"When we do something wrong, we usually try to hide it from others. Adam and Eve disobeyed God's Commandment not to eat of the fruit, so they covered that part of their bodies that had sinned." His voice rose. "Through the story in Genesis, the Lord wants us to realize that a misuse of the sexual organs led to the fall of humankind."

"The Scriptures also say that God looked for Adam, calling out his name."

"God already knew where to find Adam and Eve, don't you think?" With a little gesture, he added, "The fact is that because of the Fall, Adam stopped growing spiritually and was cut off from God. So God, in grief and anguish, was calling out for the true Adam, for the uncorrupted and virtuous character of perfect Adam."

"This makes so much sense," I muttered, pondering the implication of his words. "Everything seems so clear now."

Jesus nodded solemnly. "Adam and Eve inherited the divine nature of God, but also the evil nature of the fallen archangel Lucifer. Therefore, Adam and Eve could not give birth to sinless children. Since then, both goodness and evil dwell within the spiritual nature of Adam and Eve's fallen descendants."

"Is this why I seem to be pulled in different directions by good and evil?" I asked.

Jesus nodded. "We have God's divine characteristics, yet also Lucifer's fallen traits, such as jealousy and thirst for power, fear and rage, ignorance and pride. With the birth of the children of Adam and Eve, the dual presence of good and evil became a central part of the makeup of humans." Pausing, he looked directly into my eyes. "This is the Messiah's mission. To return humanity back to God's lineage."

I was again bewildered, as if I had just entered the labyrinth of my own life. *Who is this man, and how did he come to know this information about Adam and Eve?*

Silence fell upon us as a chilly breeze blew off the lake, making the dark night seem even more lonely and foreboding as I considered the implications of his words.

CHAPTER 15

IT HAD BEEN A QUIET MORNING in Magdala, but then an unpleasant event took me by surprise and upset the tranquility of my life for many months afterward. I was cleaning the road just outside the courtyard. When I was almost finished, I noticed three rough-looking fellows approach the house, all of them glaring at me.

Nervous, I backed off a few steps, hoping they weren't burglars and thugs. As they drew closer, the tall fellow with a black beard gestured at me. "Are you the wife of a man called Jesus?"

I nodded in silence, my hands trembling.

A stocky fellow with a reddish beard said in a brusque tone, "We want to talk to him. Is he here?"

I shook my head. "He's out of t-t-town," I stammered. "He left several days ago and won't return any time soon."

"Don't lie to us!" snarled a short fellow with a big mole on his forehead. "Is Jesus hiding in the house?"

"My husband doesn't hide from anyone," I replied, somewhat emboldened.

"Are you sure he isn't here?" demanded the red-bearded fellow, his eyes moving to the open gate of the courtyard.

"Of course, I'm sure," I retorted with relief, for I realized these ruffians weren't here to harm me or the children. "Who are you?" I uttered, feeling the anger build inside my chest. "And why are you looking for my husband?"

Raising a fist, the short one spoke through gritted teeth, "We want to have a long talk with Jesus. If he says the right things, maybe we won't break his head open."

The other men laughed gruffly, nodding their heads as if to confirm what their partner had threatened. In fact, their expressions were so menacing that now I again feared that they might just harm me and the children in jest.

While the red-bearded fellow stepped over to the courtyard gate and looked inside, the tall one said, "What lies have your husband and John the Baptist been spreading?"

I looked at him in utter confusion. "Oh, this is about Jesus helping John the Baptist?"

"Woman, you well know why we were sent here! Jesus and his cousin John have been preaching along the Jordan River. John is proclaiming he's preparing the way for the Messiah. They are making trouble by baptizing gullible people from villages near the river."

"Honestly, I don't know what John is saying or doing. I hardly know him. But I do know that my husband is a good man incapable of hurting anyone."

The short fellow said stiffly, "We have a message for both of you. We will kill anyone who takes part in a conspiracy to undermine the authority of Herod Antipas." He shook his fist again. "Is that clear? When you see your husband, tell him to break all ties with this John the Baptist and his followers!"

I felt as though the earth were shifting beneath me. Trying to keep the fear from my voice, I said to him, "If you already know where he and John are preaching, then why did you come here? Merely to frighten a helpless woman?"

He grinned crookedly. "We didn't receive orders to travel to the Jordan. We are only interested in troublemakers in this part of Galilee."

His statement made me realize that whoever sent them to Magdala had to be someone from the area surrounding the lake.

Turning slightly, I noticed the red-bearded fellow still searching near the house, I supposed for a sign that Jesus might be nearby.

"You won't find my husband under the flower pot," I called out foolishly, which promptly drew harsh looks from the others.

The red-bearded fellow walked in my direction. "Woman, do you want your beating now? If so, I can oblige you!"

"*Why is this happening to us?*" I whispered, realizing for the first time that Jesus' obsession to fulfill what he perceived as God's will had now begun to jeopardize the safety of our family.

I gasped as the tall fellow latched onto my wrist. "Can we count on you to control your husband's activities?" he said, smiling coldly.

"What can I do? I'm only his wife."

"You know what must be done. Convince him to shut his mouth and stop seeing this John the Baptist at the Jordan." His grip tightened. "But if John and your husband continue to stir up trouble, then you and your children will be danger's path …"

"Serious danger," added the red-bearded fellow in a menacing tone. He gave me a hard shove, causing me to stumble and fall to the road.

I felt as if they had indeed given me a thorough beating as I picked myself up off the ground. My muscles hurt to the bone. Somehow my mind tried to deny the reality of this ugly scene. *My life, the lives of my children, are in danger? Impossible! This cannot be happening to us!* Yet the evil men standing around me told a different story. Until that moment, I had never encountered any danger in our peaceful fishing village by the calm waters of the lake. But now I felt invaded and terrorized, and I was amazed how the solitude of my heart had changed so drastically within the space of only a few minutes.

The carefree sounds of children's voices reached the ears of the men. They turned their heads and looked up the road. Isaac and Sara were returning home after playing with friends. Without hesitation I broke into a run, my legs churning as though a wild animal were chasing me. Worried about their safety, I wrapped my arms around Isaac and Sara's shoulders, drawing them close to my body. Terrified, I glanced over my shoulder and saw the men coming quickly toward us.

The short one took a dagger out of his belt, while the other two grabbed Isaac and Sara by their arms.

Fear became the master of my heart. I was trembling and could hardly control the shaking of my hands.

"No! Please don't hurt the children!" I begged, pulling helplessly at their strong arms.

Sara began whimpering as the short man pushed me backward and waved his knife in front of my face.

"Do you want your mother to die?" he growled at the children.

They shook their heads, both now whimpering and then screaming as if they were facing a mad demon intent on devouring us all.

Suddenly the red-bearded fellow gave Isaac a slap to the face, hard enough to draw blood from his nostrils. When he wiped his nose and saw the blood, Isaac cried out in panic. "Mama, I'm bleeding … I'm bleeding!"

Without hesitation, I rushed over to him and embraced him tightly.

Scowling, the tall one spat out, "We plan to return soon to deal with your crazy husband. So you'd better convince him and John the Baptist to stop this nonsense about the coming of the Messiah."

The red-bearded fellow added loudly, "Herod and others are watching

John and his followers closely. If Jesus doesn't cut his ties with them, we will return … and we won't be so gentle! Understand?"

They gave us a fierce look, then turned and hurried toward the lake, because a small group of townspeople had noticed the commotion and were approaching from the opposite direction. Not wishing to put Jesus in grave danger by divulging what had just occurred, I latched onto the children's hands and pulled them inside our house, locking the doors securely.

Though I tried to forget it had ever happened, the three ruffians and their evil threats became the new reality in our life. In fact, their harsh words had more of an effect upon my thoughts and emotions than the thousands of words spoken to me by my husband over the years, the present situation more tangible than the coming kingdom that Jesus was always talking about.

As I washed the blood from Isaac's tear-stained face, I lamented over the fact that he and Sara would never forget this horrible experience, which might drastically change their lives in the years to come. I knew that from that moment on, I had to fight to protect my children. And in order to do so, I might be at odds with my husband more than anyone else. Because I worried that he might understand the seriousness of his mission but not the seriousness of the threats to his own children.

The thriving city of Tiberias sat on the western shore of the lake, about three miles to the south of my family's home in Magdala. The center of the land on which it stood had been a Jewish cemetery when I was a child. But over the vehement objections of many Galileans, Herod Antipas had transgressed Jewish law and gone ahead with the construction of the city. The fancy new capital of Galilee with Herod's sumptuous palace on the acropolis was named after Tiberius, who had become the Roman Emperor after the death of Augustus about six years earlier.

Nebat was a crafty Galilean leader and one of the wealthiest and more powerful men among the Herodians, a political faction that supported the dynasty of the Herods. Nebat's fortunes were heavily dependent upon the fate and influence of his close friend, Herod Antipas, who was one of five sons of Herod the Great. Yet only Antipas and Philip were still alive, the father having murdered their brothers during the turbulent years before his own death.

Now that Rome was firmly in control of Palestine, the region had been divided into three major districts. Herod Antipas had been charged with ruling over Galilee and Perea, and Herod Philip ruled over Iturae and Trachonitis, while the Roman governor directly administered affairs in Judea and Samaria. Herod Antipas and his friends had envious eyes on Judea and its capital of Jerusalem. His heart full of greed and deceit, Herod hoped the present governor, Pontius Pilate, would soon place the Judean territory under his rule, thus enlarging his kingdom and influence.

Nebat's stately house was built in the Greco-Roman style. It over-looked the main road near the central market of Tiberias. Always eager to strengthen his bond with Herod Antipas and his powerful advisors, Nebat was watchful of any suspicious activities that could be perceived as a danger to Herod's reign. Willing to do anything to help Herod expand his territory, Nebat was also always looking for an opportunity to advance his own interests in the region and increase his wealth.

As he sipped wine from a silver cup, Nebat stood by the open window and studied the dark clouds gathering overhead. His eyes roved down-ward to the congested roadway, teeming with vendors and streams of men and women passing before their stalls and shops.

About a minute later, a pleased smile crossed Nebat's gray-whiskered face when he noticed three men approaching his house. With a clap of thunder, the rain began pouring down in heavy drops, causing the men to break into a run. It didn't take long to reach the gates of the front court-yard, and they rapped hard on its polished wooden surface to make sure the servants heard them.

Seconds later, the door swung open and a young servant boy gestured at them to come inside. After bolting the door, the servant boy ushered the three men into a spacious, ornately decorated room with candle chan-deliers. The men took off their cloaks, giving them a quick shake before tossing them over a high-backed chair covered by a shiny green material.

They waited a few minutes, and another servant appeared. She had dark skin and a friendly smile, and tried to make conversation with the red-bearded fellow while leading them up marble steps to the second floor. They had been there before, so they walked into the room on the left, the one with gray-speckled granite pillars along the walls.

Nebat stepped away from the window and studied their faces, trying to guess whether they had brought good or bad news. After several moments, he concluded they had failed in their mission. Hiding his dis-appointment, he finished the wine and set the empty cup on a table. Then, after a bored glance at their wet sandals and feet, he spread his hands, palms up. "Well, did you find this Jesus fellow?"

"He wasn't in Magdala at the time," answered the taller fellow, whose name was Benhad. Stroking his black curly beard, he added with a nod, "But we confronted his wife and children. Believe me, they won't ever forget us."

Nebat frowned at him. "I hope you didn't leave any cuts or visible bruises."

"Just a bloody nose on the young boy," said the red-bearded fellow. His name was Chesed, and he and the others had been doing Nebat's dirty work for years. "The woman was a feisty demon," he said gruffly. "But as we were leaving, I looked back and saw her shaking with fear. I bet she gave this Jesus an earful when he returned home."

"Good," said Nebat, smiling as he rubbed his hands together. He glanced at the short fellow with the mole. "Rechab, we have to make sure that false prophets don't become popular and manipulate people's minds."

Yawning, Rechab remarked, "There will always be false prophets, along with false Messiahs making false promises to the imbeciles who follow them."

"Maybe so," replied Nebat. "But frustrating their efforts is the best defense against self-proclaimed Messiahs, especially those who attempt to subvert Herod's authority."

Benhad cleared his throat. "But John the Baptist has denied being either a prophet or the Messiah. And this Jesus fellow is a harmless fisherman who goes around telling people the kingdom of heaven is at hand. I don't see what danger he poses."

"Harmless?" echoed Nebat. "I suspect both rascals are lying to cover a scheme to incite revolt across the land." A challenging note entered his voice. "It doesn't upset you that John the Baptist is roaming the countryside, announcing the Messiah is about to come? We have Herod, we don't need any false Messiahs to overturn our golden pot of silver and jewels. Our goal is for Herod to take over Judea. When that day comes, each of you can live in a mansion like this!" Smiling at the thought, Chesed got to his feet and said to Benhad, "We have to silence John's booming voice before he conjures up his false Messiah."

His eyes darting about their rough faces, Nebat ordered impatiently, "Do your good deed as quickly as possible. John's popularity increases every day." He focused his dark eyes on Rechab. "Yesterday I received a message that John is making too much noise. So he cannot be ignored any longer. If we don't silence him now, he may well endorse some charismatic figure as the Messiah and next king of Israel."

Rechab scratched his cheek. "Has John given any indication who he might select?"

Nebat shook his head. "Shrewd devil, keeping everyone in suspense."

Benhad said, "Each time John is questioned about the coming Messiah, he responds by saying that he's unworthy to even strap the sandals of the Anointed One."

Concerned, Nebat said, "If John's *wondrous* Messiah does appear, we cannot allow him to undermine our interests. We must stop him quickly before his influence spreads across the land."

"Not to worry," said Benhad. "My partners and I will make sure that no false Messiahs walk free in Israel."

"We have to be vigilant," advised Nebat. "Otherwise, we could lose everything," he said, his jaw set in a hard knot as he glanced toward the open window. The rain was pouring down in sheets, with strong winds bringing a chill to the air. "These are difficult and confusing times for everyone," he added ruefully. "The common people are desperate. They will believe anyone who comes with a pat messianic message of peace and salvation."

"A flock of fools," muttered Chesed. He was standing by a table with a large silver candleholder with six musk-scented candles. He wondered aloud, "What if the true Messiah does come?"

Nebat narrowed his eyes. "Impossible," he muttered. "This isn't the right time for the Messiah. Rome's mighty legions are invincible. Not even the Messiah could stand up against such power. These times can't be compared with the days of Solomon."

"No, these are times to get along with our Roman occupiers," Rechab asserted gruffly. "We must please them and flatter their vanity in order to win special favors."

"How true," said Nebat, laughing along with the others.

Benhad rubbed the back of his neck. "These days, most people are out for themselves. Even in Jerusalem,"

"Especially in Jerusalem," stated Nebat. "Most of the priests and religious authorities only care about holding on to their power. The high priest Caiaphas has one thought, and that's to preserve his supreme position."

"It all boils down to political power," uttered Benhad.

Nebat continued, "Since Caiaphas wants to stay in charge of the Temple, he has to keep Pontius Pilate pleased by keeping his pockets full. In other words, Caiaphas doesn't want any Messiah king to stand between him and Rome, or any distraction that may give the wrong idea to the people.

"If I were the high priest," remarked Chesed, "I would be worried about Herod's two sons. Both have insatiable appetites for power and prestige. They are like two little boys fighting over the same toy."

Benhad gave Nebat a curious look. "Who do you think should reign in Judea and Samaria, since there is no Jewish ruler in these regions?"

"Surely not a false Messiah," answered Nebat. "You and I both know that Herod Antipas should control all of Palestine." Hearing a rumble of thunder, he stood and moved over to the window as gusts of wind blew rain into the room. "This kind of weather must satisfy John the Baptist," he said with a smirk, closing the window. "I imagine the Jordan is overflowing these days."

Frowning, Rechab said to him, "How many followers does John have?"

"A lot," remarked Benhad. "But no one knows the exact number. They live like Bedouins, and each one seems to think John is a great prophet."

A shadow came over Nebat's face. "As I stated earlier, we must deal harshly with this John and his cousin …"

Chesed raised his voice, "As well as his other followers, who are duping those gullible fools in the countryside."

Nebat nodded and went on, "Though Herod Antipas has many friends like me, I am the only one who realizes the severe threat that John the Baptist poses." His face hardened. "Since Herod is too timid to go directly after John, then we have to take matters into our own hands. Unless we can isolate John and get to him when no one is watching, we must undermine his support by striking at his followers."

"I agree," said Benhad. "This Jesus is the closest relative. If we continue putting pressure on him and break his will, then others will follow suit."

Nebat nodded in agreement, then paid the three men handsomely before leading them downstairs to the dining hall, where they were served fine wines and foods quite unlike what they were accustomed to.

A couple of weeks later, Jesus returned from his journey. Though he was quite tired, I reached for his hand and pulled him outdoors into the fading light of the day.

"We need to have a serious talk," I said firmly. "A terrible thing happened during your absence!"

While we walked along the shore of the lake, I told him about the ruffians who had come and threatened us, treating me roughly and even striking Isaac!

Jesus was sickened, and mentioned offhandedly that he knew who was probably behind the threats.

I rebuked him sharply. "You never told me that Herod is concerned about John's activities along the Jordan." Looking him in the eyes, I asked, "Is your brother planning a revolt against Herod? Is this the reason you've met with John so often during the past year?"

"Of course not," uttered Jesus, avoiding my eyes. He bent over and picked up a shiny black stone. He examined it for a second before throwing it about forty meters from the shore, almost hitting a boat of fishermen in the shallows.

"Mary, it is essential for John to fulfill his mission in a proper manner. If not, the coming Messiah will have a difficult time being accepted by the people, whose beliefs and customs are rooted in the past. John is the bridge between the present era and messianic era."

"I don't understand," I shot back, growing angry and frightened. "If this so-called Messiah ever comes, won't it be easy for everyone to know who he is?"

"Not at all," he replied. "The Anointed One won't come down from the clouds as some people believe. Actually, the Messiah will be a man who looks like other men. Yet spiritually he shines brighter than a thousand suns."

"At times you act like an authority on the subject." Sighing, I added, "If your brother wants to draw the ire of Herod Antipas and his minions, then let it be his problem. He can suffer the consequences. But you need to keep a safe distance from John and his followers." My voice began to break. "Those ruffians were very serious about harming you and our family."

"Don't worry. They won't dare to come back here again."

"How can you be so certain? Do you promise to quit associating with John?"

"Please don't ask me to do that, Mary. My brother needs my support at this time, and I'll need his support in the future."

"Why are you so loyal to him? Because he's your brother? And is he worth risking the lives of your loved ones?"

"It's more than just him. Soon John and his followers will become my disciples."

Upon hearing this, I couldn't help but laugh at him. "Disciples? Will Herod also follow you?" I said in jest. Jesus gave a limp shrug. Though there was a placid look on his face, I could sense that he was deeply troubled.

Grasping his arm, I asked in amazement, "Do you really believe that John is the prophet who is to announce the coming of the Messiah?"

Jesus nodded. "He has come in the role of Elijah. Sadly, John hasn't accepted the fact. This is causing much confusion among his followers, along with others who look up to him for guidance and insight."

"Does he know who the Messiah is? And what is your role in all of this?"

"I can't say any more on the subject. Already I have told you too much."

"As you wish," I uttered, forlorn, realizing the situation was far too complex to be resolved at this time. "For now, will you promise to stay home for a long while?"

"Sorry, I cannot make such a promise. If the spirit of God moves me in one direction, then I have no choice but to follow the path He has set before me."

I began to respond, but held back my thoughts. I knew it was useless to argue with Jesus about such matters. "Tell me, is your brother married?"

Jesus shook his head, gazing at the eastern horizon of the sea. "John has taken a vow of abstinence from all pleasures. Hopefully he will soon realize that family life is closer to God's heart than a solitary existence."

"Well, don't forget that your main task is to dedicate time to your family. Let John prepare the way for the Messiah … not you!"

"Mary, after all that I've taught to you, don't you know that …"

"Jesus!" I said, putting a finger to his lips. "All I know is that I need you here to protect the children. If any harm comes to them, I will never forgive you!"

Looking annoyed, he said, "I promise no harm will come to you or the children."

"I wish I could believe you," I spat out. "Sorry, but at times I regret I married you."

Turning slightly, Jesus gazed at me with solemn eyes. "You shouldn't utter such things. I know you are upset now, but soon you will feel better."

Sighing again, I let my turbulent thoughts drift back to the early years of our marriage when life was more kind to us. "Do you recall when you held Isaac and Sara in your arms for the first time? We were so happy back then! What happened to that? Why do we have to face such danger in our lives?"

Jesus remained silent, his eyes brimming with tears. I could see the frustration on his face as he lowered his body to the ground and crossed his legs. Then putting his hands together, he bowed his head and began praying in a barely audible voice.

He remained in that position for a good while. Finally, I grew impatient and started to walk off, but he called out to me. "Mary, stay here with me a while longer."

I breathed deeply to calm my nerves. "You have to understand that children are the most precious jewels in a mother's world."

"They are precious to me, too. You're not questioning that, are you?"

"No, they adore you too." I sat next to him, resting a hand on his shoulder. It was completely dark now, with only a few boats on the lake, their crews hoping to make one last catch before returning home for the evening.

I couldn't help but feel that Jesus was like those fishermen. He always wanted to make one more catch of people's souls before returning to me and our children.

In the past, I had always been at home waiting for him. Yet now I realized that I couldn't endure his extended absences much longer. Something would have to change in our lives.

CHAPTER 16

IT WAS A BREEZY APRIL MORNING in a large village just west of the Jordan River. Jesus had arrived the evening before and now stood near his elder brother, who was conferring with his chief disciple about the activities planned for the day. As Jesus listened to the conversation, he focused on John's well-chiseled face and knew that he was a decent and righteous man, a humble servant of the Lord, through his caring for the people along the Jordan. Yet Jesus also sensed that deep within John's heart there lurked a certain pride over his *miraculous* conception and birth, along with his upbringing in the home of a respected priest. Thus, John felt a certain superiority toward him, and he was often scornful of people who didn't measure up to his standards of conduct. Though all of this was somewhat troubling to Jesus, what truly disturbed him was the fact that John still wasn't able to comprehend him, and wasn't even willing to try. As a result, John still wasn't aware of his precise role in God's plan for the salvation of fallen mankind. Consequently, even as the two brothers were often working close together, they lived in two very different worlds of thought and sensitivity, which might well drive a wedge between them in the coming months, Jesus feared.

It had rained briefly during the early morning hours, so the flowers and bushes smelled fresh and fragrant as the sun rose in the sky, warming Jesus' face as he gazed into John's deep-set eyes. After a minute of prayerful thought, Jesus had decided that he could not wait any longer to reveal his role in establishing God's kingdom on earth.

When John's disciples walked off in the direction of their tents, Jesus placed a firm hand on his shoulder. "John, let's sit and talk about an important matter."

Though John's mind was occupied with pressing matters, he could feel the urgency in his brother's voice. So he nodded and followed Jesus over to some wooden benches near one of the village wells.

"Even though we have grown close," Jesus began, "I know that you perceive me as a product of my upbringing. Although we are sons of the same father, you still think of me as the son of a poor mother who didn't receive a proper education."

Taken by surprise, John didn't know how to respond to this. Somewhat embarrassed, he kept silent, wondering whether Jesus had a special point in making such a claim.

"John, I realize this may be hard to accept, but the Lord God needed to use the seed of our father, who was a righteous and faithful priest. The Lord also required my mother's innocent nature and pure womb. My mother and our father's relationship was not the result of lustful desires. In reality, their intimate union was inspired by the Lord God, who needed the foundation of their ancestry to create a special child."

Drawing a long breath, John seemed puzzled as he digested his brother's remarks.

"Jesus, I know the Lord God works in mysterious ways, but do you actually believe that your mother's womb had special significance?"

"Yes." He drifted off a moment, then added quietly, "John, I suffered much during my childhood and adolescence. Those were difficult years. Your life has been easier than mine. You have enjoyed many privileges, along with the love and devotion of relatives. Even now, thousands of people flock to hear you preach and to be baptized by you. Everyone loves and admires you, while I ..." Jesus paused as he waved away some flies. "... well, I am insignificant in the eyes of most people."

"That's not true," countered John. "Many of my disciples think highly of you."

A grateful smile crossed Jesus' face. "John, you should realize that you and your disciples must be the first in Israel to receive the Messiah."

"*Receive?*" he echoed, now truly confused. "What do you mean?"

"When the Messiah comes, you must welcome him and follow him, even at the cost of your life." Jesus paused again, looking at him with penetrating eyes. "John, I am the Messiah. With all my heart, I believe that I am the Lord's Anointed Son."

John gazed at his younger brother in bewilderment at first, then his eyes narrowed as he realized the blasphemous nature of such a pronouncement.

Jesus added firmly, "As I travel about to towns and villages, I will need your constant presence by my side. With your full support and that of your disciples, the people will listen to my teachings and directions."

John could barely contain his stormy emotions. "Jesus, how can you believe you are the Anointed One of the Lord? You must be mad to say such things!"

"Even though we are linked by blood, our spiritual powers are very different. I speak with God constantly, and also with angels and other spirits. I can communicate with Abraham, Isaac, Jacob, Moses, and all the prophets of Israel."

John laughed despite himself. "Can you demonstrate your spiritual powers now?"

"You well know that's not possible. The Son of God has a sixth sense that allows him to see those beings who live in the world beyond. Unfortunately, for the rest of humanity this capacity has been deadened by the original sin."

John's face reflected the uncertainty building in his heart. He was still unable to clear the voice from his heart that whispered the same words since hearing Jesus' teachings of what he perceived to be God's Truth. *Much of what he says makes sense. How is possible that he knows so much? Where did he learn such things? Even so, how is it possible for my younger brother to be the Messiah?*

Sensing John's thoughts, Jesus spoke in an even tone. "Don't silence the voice of God in your heart. Don't allow cold thoughts to freeze your heart and obscure the light that is shining within you." Jesus' lips spread into a loving smile. "For now, all I ask is that you simply do not reject the possibility."

"The possibility?" he shot back. "Jesus, I don't know what to make of you! How dare you consider yourself God's chosen one! Even worse, you expect me to consider it!"

"John, it is no accident that our lives have become entwined. You were born to inherit the mission of Elijah. And I was born to be the Messiah. I am as certain of this truth as I am that the sun will rise tomorrow morning."

Now, John spoke in a milder voice. "How can I believe that you fulfill all the prophecies of the coming Messiah, who will establish God's eternal kingdom of peace?"

"If you trust me and follow my directions, we will set an example of unity so that everyone realizes that our objectives are the same." Rising to his feet, Jesus stepped over to the well and helped a young girl fill her bucket. As she walked off toward the village, he turned back to John and explained in an urgent tone, "We must work together in confronting evil, while spreading God's love and truth. If we combine our efforts, then God's kingdom will be established in our own lifetime."

Pausing, Jesus searched his brother's face for some form of acceptance, or a simple a sign of understanding. But what John was hearing had
shaken him to the core, and his expression was one of righteous indignation over his brother's absurd claim.

"Jesus, that's just it. I don't trust you," he said in reply. He got to his
feet and added flatly, "And since I do trust the Lord, I will pray strongly
and wait for His answer."

"John, if your heart is pure and your intentions sincere, then our
Heavenly Father will answer your petitions."

Frowning, John said to him, "Many times I have faithfully studied
the sacred writings regarding the Anointed One. The Messiah will be the
everlasting King sitting on David's throne, and the everlasting Holy High
Priest." His eyes burned with rage. "How can you be a king sitting on
David's throne?"

"John, I need you! You are the one most prepared to listen to me, to
believe me, and to follow me. Without your support, the religious and
social leaders of Israel will find it impossible to accept my teachings. As a
consequence, they will reject and persecute me. Do you understand the
deep significance of your actions at this time?"

After a long moment of hesitation, John nodded his head before turning and walking in the direction of the river shore.

The following morning after a long night of deep prayer, Jesus went to the
same spot on the Jordan where John had been baptizing people during
the past month.

He realized that he must be baptized by John. As my husband explained
it to me later, John the Baptist represented all the prophets of Israel, he
being the last great prophet and the one who was to serve the Messiah
directly. Thus, John's baptism of Jesus marked the transfer of merit from
the old era to the Messiah, who was the supreme representative of God.
The baptism of Jesus by John would be an act of recognition of the new era
of love and truth, deeper and more complete than the old one.

My husband was clearly aware of the profound meaning of this
baptism.

To John's surprise, Jesus came to him in the river and asked to receive
his baptism with the water of the Jordan.

"Jesus! Why do you wish to be baptized?" asked John, looking at him
askance. His voice turned sarcastic. "If you are the Messiah, why do you
need baptism? It should be I who is baptized by you!"

"John, I have come to fulfill what is written. I will baptize you with the Holy Spirit, guide you with the light of truth, and help you discover your true self. Let me help you to develop your relationship with your Father in heaven so that you will live in complete union with His spirit."

Deeply touched by his brother's sincere heart, John couldn't help but feel a profound love for him. In this moment, John's heart was opened, and he felt a powerful sensation fill his entire being. Influenced by the Holy Spirit, John declared, "Jesus, you are better than I. Your heart is purer than mine. Your love for God and Israel is more alive and intense than mine." He paused, gazing at his brother, now with a clear understanding of his identity. "Jesus, your eyes shine with a special light! I see a divine light around your body! Certainly you are filled with the Holy Spirit. You are the Messiah!"

He cupped his hands and dipped them into the river water, then raised them and poured the water upon his brother's bowed head. Jesus was baptized again, but this time with the Holy Spirit. From here on, John and Jesus would have inaugurated a new relationship between themselves. John would have fully accepted his younger brother as his spiritual guide, and moreover would have welcomed him as the Messiah, as the Anointed One. In fact, soon after baptizing him in the river, John would have presented Jesus to all of his disciples, not merely as his brother, but rather as the Messiah. And from that moment on, John would have remained by Jesus' side, accompanying him wherever Jesus went, introducing him as the Anointed One sent by the Lord God. Unfortunately, once the powerful effect of the Holy Spirit had left John's heart, his pride and past skepticism took over again. John fell into the abysm of doubt.

Since Jesus knew how important John's mission was in God's plan to save the world, he decided to remain near the Jordan River, hoping that his brother would soon realize his error and accept his new responsibility. During the next two days, Jesus prayed fervently that John would come to him and repent for his change of heart. Finally, on the third day after early morning prayer, Jesus walked to the area where John had spent the night. The air was cool and damp, the sun hidden by dark gray clouds on the eastern horizon.

John had just stepped from his tent when he noticed his brother approaching in a purposeful manner. Though apparently upset, John pushed a smile to his lips and gave Jesus a wave of acknowledgment.

"John!" he called out, his voice seeming to shake the trees. "Why can't you even consider that the spirit of Elijah is working with you? You should realize that you have been preparing the way for me, the Messiah."

John didn't want his disciples to overhear this, so he latched onto Jesus' forearm and led him over to a bench under a tree.

"Before our father passed away," said Jesus, his voice growing softer, "what did he say about your future mission? You were to prepare the way for the Messiah, right?"

"It's what I've been doing," he replied, trying not to lose his temper. "But you are not the Anointed One, no matter what you say or do!"

Despite the fact that John had briefly understood Jesus' position, he now clearly failed to recognize that the Lord God was working through his brother to establish the kingdom of heaven on earth.

Ironically, the day after he had baptized his brother, John did whisper to a few of his disciples that Jesus was the Messiah. But he gave only a weak, short-lived testimony that was lost in the damp soil along the banks of the Jordan River.

However, some of John's disciples who were leading people into the river had been watching John when he baptized Jesus. They had also heard some of the conversation between the two men, listening carefully to what Jesus had spoken.

Frustrated with John's stubbornness, Jesus walked away with his head down. He decided to leave the Jordan and go to Jerusalem. As he was walking southward along the road bordering the west bank of the river, he noticed that two of John's disciples were following him.

"Rabbi!" one of them called out, hurrying to catch up with him. They were carrying their bedrolls and burlap sacks with all their possessions.

Jesus studied them as they approached. "You are going back to your homes?"

"Yes," answered the larger fellow. He was of medium height and rather husky, his eyes reflecting a hearty passion for the truth. "How do you know where we're going?"

As they continued walking, Jesus gestured at his companion. "It's written on John's face," he said offhandedly. "You are Andrew, and you are from Bethsaida."

"That's right!" said John, with a laugh. Though he was small in stature, he had strong hands and arms from years of fishing with his father and brother. "Are you also returning home?" he asked with curious eyes.

Jesus glanced at him. "Walk with me and you'll discover where I am going."

Andrew said flatly, "What if you walk all the way to Egypt?"

"Then we might be on the road for many weeks," replied Jesus. "It will give you time to ask the many questions cluttering your hearts."

The two young men glanced at each other, glad they had decided to leave when they did. After a short while, John cleared his throat and said, "Rabbi, how do you know our names?"

Jesus smiled at him. "John is a very common name, isn't it?"

He nodded. "You can't take a step without stumbling over someone with the same name." Turning serious, he added shortly, "Perhaps I will change my name, as well as my dull life. I may call myself Caesar, then build a large boat and sail to Rome itself!"

"You're a lost dreamer!" said Andrew, giving him a playful shove on the shoulder. "You'll be a smelly fisherman until you're old and gray like all your grandfathers, that's what you'll be."

"Maybe so," muttered John. "But I wish to be something in this world other than an unknown soul."

Jesus looked at him again. "Is that why you and Andrew have been helping John the Baptist the past two months?"

"Yes, partially. After we were baptized, we decided to follow him and help others to change their lives. But what did we accomplish?" he said bitterly. "We stayed under the shadow for what? I didn't hear any great truth from John. He merely repeated what I've learned in the synagogue over the years."

Andrew said dryly, "Humbly we came, and humbly we go back."

Jesus said to them, "You both should examine your motivations. Looking for the truth is a noble pursuit, but it has to be done with sincerity and wisdom."

The two friends made no response, so Jesus added in a level voice, "There is nothing wrong if you desire to be smart or successful or powerful. It depends on your motivation. If you wish to accomplish great things in order to help the Lord God and touch His deep heart of love, then naturally this can be considered good."

Andrew nodded. "I agree," he said. "But if ambition is not balanced with love, it can ruin your soul." He glanced to his left. "Don't you think so, John?"

He lowered his eyes in shame. "Sometimes I let my selfish thoughts take over my heart."

The three men walked in silence, coming across a good number of local villagers going about their daily chores and tasks.

Still brooding over his brother's failure to support him, Jesus hung an arm over Andrew's shoulder. "How is your life in Bethsaida?" he asked.

"I was born there, but now I live in Capernaum with my older brother's family. Simon and I are fishermen." He gestured at John. "His brother James has a boat. Our two families do quite well."

"Life is peaceful," remarked John. "When not on the lake fishing, we get together with our friends and enjoy all the good things God has given us."

Jesus said humorously, "So your older brothers are working hard every day, while you two are swimming in the Jordan with John the Baptist, eh?"

Andrew laughed deeply. "When I return home, I'm sure that Simon will box my ears!"

Laughing mildly, Jesus said, "As you may know, I live in Magdala with my wife and two children. Though life is simple there as well, I realize great numbers of people experience unbearable pain and heartache each moment of the day."

"Very true," Andrew agreed, nodding. "But what can an ordinary man like me do? Lately, I've been looking for more in life. That's why I came to hear John the Baptist."

"Did you find anything in his teaching that stimulated your heart?"

"Not much," he admitted with a frown. "But John and I heard some of your private discussions with him. We found them very interesting."

Jesus couldn't help laughing. "I did see you two fellows hiding behind trees and bushes. I got some information about you from John's followers. Your longing for truth is great!"

Andrew said, "For many years I've been looking for the truth. I believe we are living in special times, and I'm not the only one. John and I have many friends in Capernaum who are eager for a change, for a new truth."

"Also to find the Anointed One," said John, a wistful look on his face.

Jesus stared at him and Andrew with interest and hope, grateful that God had guided them to him at this difficult time in his ministry.

John added fervently, "James and I have been reading the Scriptures searching for every nuance of meaning in God's holy message."

Andrew hesitated. "Jesus, if you are really the Messiah as John mentioned to some of us a few days ago, then why did he baptize you?"

"Yeah," uttered John, looking puzzled. "Shouldn't you have baptized him and his close disciples, along with others who came to the Jordan?"

His heart anguished as the thought of his last talk with his brother. Jesus said to them, "If you are interested in the truth, remain with me for three days and I will teach you about God's divine nature and His purpose for sending the Messiah."

Andrew and John readily agreed, and they found a good spot by the river to camp. During the following days they got to know one another better, talking about God, Adam and Eve, Noah, Abraham, Jacob, and Moses, as well as the laws and the prophets and God's coming kingdom of heaven.

Early the third afternoon, Andrew and John started their journey back to their families, but not before inviting Jesus to Capernaum to meet their brothers and friends.

Jesus promised to visit them soon, and he watched in prayerful silence as the two friends headed north toward Galilee. Then Jesus passed through the villages near Jerusalem, where he spent over a week preaching his understanding of the Scriptures.

During this time, Andrew and John returned to their homes in Capernaum, on the north shore of Lake Galilee, about six miles from Magdala. Situated near one of the major roads connecting Galilee to Damascus, Capernaum has been considered a major fishing port. As in other towns and villages around the lake, life in those days was good for most residents. Farmers living on the fertile lands nearby grew various grains and olive trees, so there were numerous oil and grain mills, along with large, daily catches of fish by the many fishermen, all which provided ample sustenance for the local inhabitants.

When Andrew and John returned to Capernaum, there was a feast to welcome them back, and naturally they told their families and friends about their experiences with John the Baptist and Jesus. Later, Andrew and John spoke to their elder brothers about Jesus' beliefs, spending the entire night debating the various details with Simon and James, who were at first skeptical about this Jesus' teachings.

A couple of weeks later, Jesus journeyed to Capernaum to visit Andrew and John, along with their elder brothers. He stayed at the home of Zebedee, who was the father of James and John. Jesus went fishing with them each morning, and in the evenings he taught them the word of God.

Both John and Andrew accepted the possibility that Jesus might be the Messiah, but James and Simon continued to doubt. They all listened respectfully to Jesus, however, realizing that he was someone special. Yet since his teachings were so different from anything they had ever heard before, they couldn't fully commit themselves to him. He had spoken about his mission as unique in the history of the chosen people, of all humanity, and that he needed disciples who could devote their lives to him with absolute faith.

Even John and Andrew, who were the most positive, gave all sorts of excuses to justify their unwillingness to respond to Jesus' call. "After all, we're only fishermen, living a humble life," they told him.

Jesus understood these men were not ready for commitment. Naturally they didn't have a clear idea of the spiritual identity of the person who stood before them, nor did they understand the real mission of Jesus as the second Adam, and that the Lord God was giving them the unique opportunity to serve His Son, the Messiah.

After spending three days in Capernaum, Jesus took the road south along the western shore of the lake. Along the way, he met a man named Philip from Bethsaida, who was from the same area where Andrew and John had lived before moving to Capernaum. Philip was traveling to Tiberias for business. Jesus talked with him about God's nature as well as the true human nature, and the mystery of the fall of man. The man believed he had found the one he was looking for.

In Magdala, Jesus invited his new friend to his home, but Philip declined, saying that he first wanted to talk to a close friend in Tiberias.

Philip told his friend Bartholomew that he had found the Messiah. Bartholomew, who was also known by his second name Nathaniel, was highly skeptical, believing that nothing good could come out of Nazareth.

However, Philip managed to convince Bartholomew to accompany him to meet Jesus.

They met and talked for hours. Jesus came to know that the two friends were acquainted with the four fishermen, since they lived in the same area. A few days later, Jesus went to the desert to pray and fast.

CHAPTER 17

DUE TO JOHN THE BAPTIST'S INDIFFERENCE toward him, Jesus needed to prove that he would never abandon his mission, even if it meant proceeding alone without the help of his brother. To demonstrate his determination to the angelic world, and particularly to the fallen Lucifer, Jesus decided to do a fast for forty days in the desert.

Jesus withdrew into the wilderness of Judea, to the dreadful, barren hills around the Dead Sea, and lived there for forty days without food, in deep prayer and meditation.

The desert, a quiet yet hostile place barren of life, symbolizes one's rejection of everything of daily life in which Satan had his footprint. With the failure of the first human beings, Satan came to seize and dominate humankind, as well as the world with all things on it. Satan became the king of the world, of its peoples and cultures.

Jesus' journey to the desert was a way to renounce the world of Satan, with its myriad sins. Jesus' fast and isolation served to prove that he was beyond Lucifer's control, and that he was the ruler of his own body.

He wanted to make clear that his spiritual relationship with his Father, and his understanding of God's nature and His infinite love, were the most important things. His fast was a way of renouncing the pleasures of the flesh and affirming his union with God's spirit. Since Lucifer was aware of all of this, he wanted to discourage Jesus by destroying his dignity as the Son of God.

Lucifer had been successful in bringing about the failure of Adam and Eve, which severed their relationship with God. Lucifer was also hoping to defeat Jesus. Yet at this point in his life, Jesus was already one with God, united in heart and mind.

It was near the end of Jesus' fortieth day of fasting when Lucifer appeared to him. The fallen archangel hoped that in the very last minutes he would find a weak spot in Jesus' will.

Initially Lucifer came as a shadow, and then took his shape. Although he had human form, he was not made of flesh and bones. With malevolent intent, he fixed his gaze on the Son of God. Jesus knew that he was there, in that unearthly place between the physical and the spiritual world. Then Lucifer took a step forward, his intent clear. The confrontation of wills between the representatives of the forces of good and the forces of evil was inevitable. The clash between the Second Adam and the rebellious archangel was about to unfold.

"Jesus, are you so foolish as to continue your mission?" Lucifer whispered, giggling derisively.

Ignoring Lucifer's words, Jesus continued praying in his heart.

Lucifer carried on, chiding him. "Here you are! Alone, hungry, bitter, and misunderstood while persisting with a mission that is destined to collapse. Your fasting will serve no useful purpose. Take those stones and make them into bread. You need to eat in order to regain your strength."

Jesus maintained his calm and answered confidently, "The human body is not the only essence of a human being. Man does not live on bread alone, but also by the word of God."

Lucifer boasted, "I existed long before the first humans. I was the highest creature in the universe. I enjoyed a close relationship with the Creator. I had the respect of all the angels together with the greatest love of God. I had myriad angels under my command. And with God's supervision, we assisted in the creation of the material universe, step by step, from pure energy up to the complex physical world with its diverse forms of lives. Of course, this includes the human body, which houses your spirit." This last sentence, he muttered as an afterthought.

Lucifer paused a long moment, searching for a way to continue. "After having created the sun and earth," he said, deciding to adopt the tone of a teacher lecturing his student, "God created life, with the goal of forming the physical body. Life began with simple forms and developed step by step into more complex forms of life, until reaching the form of the human body. I remember the day when God gave the spirit of life to His first children. He put the final touch on them by giving the spirit in their first vital breaths. Although Adam and Eve were physically born from their mother's womb, internally they were already distinct from the others."

"Yes, I know," said Jesus, trying to remain pleasant, since he knew that the sacred tale was now being used for wickedness. "I know about the beginning of the creation, the starting point of life, and the formation of the first human beings. God gave to Adam and Eve the seed of eternal life, which contained all the necessary elements for them to be the children of

God. Unlike previous creatures, these two were blessed with the ability to create more lives possessing an eternal spirit."

There was a long moment of silence, with only the whispers of the hot desert winds as Lucifer looked directly into the eyes of Jesus. "Before the creation of Adam and Eve," he said, half to himself, "I received the most love from God. Then everything changed with the birth of man. I couldn't bear the idea that these things had been created to receive more attention and love, and would be even greater than I."

"Lucifer, you knew God's plan. So you were aware that one day this had to happen. You were created to be part of God's plans, to help Him with all the details regarding the creation, including human life. The truth is, when you had to face the reality, you were not able to contain your feelings of jealousy and envy. It is also true that some angels committed sins by performing unnatural acts. This was even before the birth of Adam and Eve. Isn't it so?"

Lucifer drew back a little. "Say what you will … But even you won't be able to save humanity. Most people do what I want them to do!" he said in a sudden eruption of anger. He started to move nervously around Jesus. "I give the orders in this world and in the lower realms of spirit world. Humanity is made of wicked sinners who refuse to repent. Humanity belongs to me."

"Lucifer! You have not answered me," insisted Jesus. "Weren't there angels who had sexual relations?" he asked, seeking a full confession from Lucifer, although he knew the details of the events. "Isn't it so, Lucifer? Tell me, aren't you ashamed?"

"Yes! With the creation of animals, it became evident to the angels how material beings procreated. This stimulated an irresistible sexual desire among some of them. Although God made angels with feminine features and angels with masculine features, sexual relations were not allowed until the first man and woman had fulfilled their original purpose," he said resentfully. "Even now our genders are still separated. We had to wait for the birth of Adam and Eve, and then wait for their physical and spiritual growth, and then witness their holy marriage as husband and wife. Then with the blessing of the children of God, we angels would finally join together into monogamous and eternal unions. Many angels had no will to wait, and because there was no way to have contact with the other gender we started to have sexual relations within the same sex. What was an initial curiosity to discover the sexual pleasure became an uncontrollable activity."

"And you have passed on this unnatural habit to human beings. Isn't it so, Lucifer?"

The fallen archangel made no response.

"Lucifer, you have created sentiments and desires that are totally contrary to your true nature, the one that God gave you," Jesus asserted. "And now the spiritual world is like a trash heap. You have created a horrible hell by violating the laws of God."

The reproachful tone of Jesus' voice grew stronger. "Lucifer, you have disobeyed God, and worst of all, you have vanquished human beings spiritually. You have infused the wrong desires into the hearts and minds of men, stripping them of any divine morality. Now men don't know who they are, and live in absolute ignorance of their divine nature and eternal spiritual existence. They live in the physical dimension, unaware of what is waiting for them in the spiritual world."

"They are not different from the rest of us," replied the archangel. "Man is lower ..."

"You have created all kinds of sins and negative feelings," reproached Jesus, cutting him off. "You have substituted hate for love, promiscuity for fidelity, selfishness for the pleasure of giving, anger for peace of mind, deceit for trust, and death for life. You have placed yourself between men and God, obscuring the divine reality and denying men their true nature. You had the responsibility to be the model of obedience and fidelity to God, but you betrayed your Creator and led your angels and humankind to the depths of hell, Lucifer!"

Lucifer shot a murderous scowl at him, but said nothing.

"What did you do to Eve?" asked Jesus suddenly.

"Do you truly believe the people of this land will follow you?" Lucifer said, trying to steer the conversation to his strengths. Making an angry gesture, he shouted, "Open your eyes! The world is mine, and you cannot do anything about it. Men want to live as they are. They get drunk and kill each other, deceive and fight, envy each other and are blinded by jealousy and unable to control their sexual desire."

"What happened between you and Eve?" Jesus asked again. "Lucifer, tell me! Was Eve beautiful in your eyes? Were you attracted to her?"

"Shut up!"

"Surely, Eve was very attractive to your eyes," persisted Jesus. "She was of gentle soul, calm, and of captivating femininity. God had created her to be the wife of Adam. This was her destiny. You among all the creatures were the closest to them. Their physical parents gave them life, helping them to grow physically, but you had the task to guide them in discovering the creation and developing their spiritual senses. This was your responsibility, to make them understand their destiny."

Lucifer gazed at Jesus, a burning hatred in his eyes.

Jesus' voice grew more forceful. "Tell me, Lucifer! What did you do to Eve? Confess your crime."

"To you?" said Lucifer, in a defensive tone.

"Do not hide behind your silence. Confess everything! Tell me what happened between you and Eve."

Lucifer stared at him, fear in his eyes. "Why do you push me to answer? Don't you know what happened?"

Jesus nodded. "You waited for Eve to reach adolescence, and when she reached the age to generate children, you seduced her and caused her to eat the fruit. Instead of helping Eve to develop her spirituality and her love for God, you corrupted her with your unnatural desire for human love."

Lucifer paced about with a scowl, but kept silent as Jesus continued in a firm voice, "You knew that Eve was supposed to experience the fruit with Adam, but only after both had reached spiritual maturity. Lucifer, after you seduced God's daughter, she went to Adam and tempted him with the fruit. Adam, who was unaware of what had transpired between you and Eve, succumbed to her advances and consummated their union before the Lord God could bless them in marriage."

Lucifer feigned a look of unconcern, raising his hands in mock surrender.

Narrowing his eyes, Jesus continued in an even tone, "You knew that if Eve and Adam had premature sexual relations with one another, it would prevent them from achieving a more perfect spirituality."

Lucifer released an arrogant laugh, but Jesus saw right through him. "Lucifer, you knew that Eve was destined to become Adam's wife. You approached her as a thief. You took what didn't belong to you. You invaded her soul, took advantage of her spiritual innocence and of her body that was still immature. Although Eve could communicate with God and the angels, her soul was still underdeveloped."

Although Jesus' body ached with hunger, he added firmly, "As Eve grew older and blossomed into a pretty young lady, you offered counsel, and step by step seduced her. You introduced her to the pleasures of the flesh making her believe that was the way to become in the image of God. You also told her you were the one with whom she should have sexual relations. You were not authorized to instruct Eve about sex."

Lucifer lowered his eyes as Jesus continued on. "Lucifer, you corrupted Eve's spiritual growth by exposing her prematurely to sexual knowledge, and you rejoiced when she went to Adam and offered him the fruit of her physical love."

Nodding, Lucifer admitted in a derisive tone, "Yes, I was happy when that foolish Adam succumbed to Eve's temptation. But you won't ever convince people of what really happened in the so-called Garden. They will not listen. If so, they won't understand. Their minds and hearts are deadened after hundreds of generations of sinful acts." With a swift gesture, he added mockingly, "Give up your futile efforts, Jesus. You cannot accuse me of being solely responsible for the fall of Eve and Adam. They share the blame as well!"

"Lucifer, you deceived them to lead them away from God's original plan," scolded Jesus. "You lied, claiming that if they ate the fruit, they could become parents like God, coming to know good and evil, the evil emotions that you and other fallen angels have generated even before the birth of the first human beings. You deceived them with a half-truth. With the blessing of God, Adam and Eve could have started their life as husband and wife, and given birth to children. Of course sooner or later they would have come to know the evil dwelling in your rebellious hearts. But if Adam and Eve had reached spiritual maturity as the son and daughter of God, they, as perfect man and perfect woman would have guided you to your total restoration. In this way, evil wouldn't have come out of the borders of the spiritual sphere where you dwell. Evil never would have developed in the physical world. And you, Lucifer, together with the other angels, wouldn't have had any choice but to repent and purify yourselves."

"In the beginning," Lucifer said irritably, "the concept of man was only an abstract idea. So I felt no envy or jealousy ..." He fell silent, looking back through time into a dark storm of memories. "But with the creation of man," he went on, swallowing hard, "I became aware of how much God loved His children. All creation had been made for them. This annoyed me, and I refused to accept the idea that I would have to relinquish my authority over these two humans."

"The same way you refuse to submit to me?" asked Jesus.

Lucifer was as restless as ever. He sensed a defeat in his confrontation with the Son of Heaven. He blinked in confusion, unsure of himself.

"Jesus, do not claim such an easy victory!" he finally said. "This world still belongs to me. The people of Israel will not have faith in you. In you they will see nothing but a simple nobody. They have a wrong concept regarding the identity of the Messiah. They built the Temple so the people could develop reverent feelings toward that which is sacred, but instead they have made their Temple into a marketplace."

His heart filled with hope, Jesus responded, "I will help them understand that Israel has been edified to receive this Temple made of flesh and blood. I will tell them that the external part of the Temple symbolizes my physical body, whereas the internal part, which is the most sacred, symbolizes my spiritual body and the spiritual mind where God dwells. They will know their Heavenly Father, and they will accept me as their Messiah, originator of a new blood lineage and Savior. They will join me and help me to fulfill my mission."

Lucifer replied with a surly laugh, "I will build discord between you and your wife and within the people of Israel. All the desires and feelings that I promote, those of the fallen, are alive in the hearts and minds of men. I did it by using their sexual organs. I wanted them to discover prematurely the pleasure of sex, and I made sure they would focus their existence on the gratification of the flesh, neglecting their spiritual growth."

Jesus remained quiet, his gaunt face impassive as Lucifer continued to unmask his crimes against God and humanity.

Stepping away from Jesus, he went into the murky shadows and disappeared.

Later that day, Lucifer returned to torment Jesus with his next temptation. His aim as usual was to discourage the Son of God from pursuing his mission.

"So you are the perfect sinless Adam, the perfect temple who will not fall into the temptations of the flesh," Lucifer said derisively. "Go down, lose yourself. Enjoy the many pleasures of the flesh that this world can offer. Why must you suffer when you can be happy instead? Wine, beautiful women, I can give you anything your lower self desires!"

Shaking his head, Jesus drew a deep breath. "Lucifer, the pleasures of life is mortal traps when motivated by fallen emotions. Sexual intimacy is God's gift, but it can only be experienced within marriage. Lucifer, you knew this!"

"If you are Adam, then where is your Eve?" he said callously.

Although Lucifer's words pierced Jesus' heart, he remained calm, and he controlled his feelings as he thought about his family in Magdala.

Realizing this was a weakness in Jesus' mission, Lucifer was not hesitant to use it, speaking in a harsh tone. "Is Mary willing to follow you? Is she willing to confront the hardships of a life of faith? Is she ready to deal with the persecution and violent threats from all those who will oppose you? And trust me, there will be many. Are you willing even to sacrifice your children to this empty mission of yours?" Pausing, a twisted smile crossed his face. "Jesus, after many years of marriage, Mary still doesn't understand God or the messianic mission you foolishly endeavor to fulfill."

Even though he was quite weak and tired, Jesus responded with sudden vigor, "Lucifer, my wife is a virtuous and righteous woman. Over the years you have tried to poison her mind with unwarranted doubts and fears. Soon God's love and power will sweep over her, and she will understand her position as the daughter of God, and wife of the Second Adam."

"Ah, you poor delusional dreamer! Has the fasting made you lose touch with your common sense?" mocked Lucifer, trying to discourage him. "Don't you know that women want protection and serenity? It is in the woman's nature to seek tranquility and a safe home for her children, while longing for love and attention from her husband. No woman would exchange a stable life for one full of uncertainty and danger. And yet, this is exactly what you are proposing to her. To live as a nomad, wandering from town to town, trying to teach the word of God to witless sinners. Your promises are in the future, but Mary wants a stable life now. Promises for a better future are not enough for her. You know it!"

Jesus listened, knowing that Lucifer was right. But Jesus also knew that presently he was fighting a battle of wills, with words as weapons.

Lucifer said with sarcasm, "So you want to make Mary the mother of humanity? Hah! Do you actually believe your Eve will find the moral strength to dedicate her life to such a difficult mission? Her desires and impulses are mine. The desire to have you all for her comes from me!" He scowled again. "How many times has she been rude to you shutting her ears to your words? Whose anger do you think that is in her face! How many times will she curse your followers, telling them to leave your dwelling? Since she has my nature, I can easily build invisible barriers between you and her."

Jesus was neither discouraged nor disheartened by Lucifer's accusations.

"Soon Mary will unite with God's heart," he said confidently. After a deep breath of the hot, dry air, he added with a nod, "I'll continue helping her to discover the beauty of the soul."

"Your hopes are in vain," scoffed Lucifer. "Neither Mary nor anyone else will understand or follow you!"

Not moved by Lucifer's words, Jesus gazed placidly at the vast expanse of the desert.

"Listen to me!" Lucifer said in desperation. "You should …"

"No," interrupted Jesus, "you listen to me. My Father dwells within me, and I in Him. As the Son of God, I am His representative on earth and in the spiritual world. I am the model and champion of God. I was made in the image and resemblance of my Father. Even before the creation of the universe, the ideal of perfect man and perfect woman was conceived in God's mind. God made the creation for His children and for you too, even for you. I can tell you that the perfect Adam was in His mind and heart before the first day began."

After a pause, Jesus added, "He who sees the Father, sees the Son. I am the physical manifestation of His divine nature. Lucifer, do not tempt me anymore. Do not tempt your God and Master."

Lucifer was obviously shaken by Jesus' words, and he disappeared into the shadows. Though he realized that Jesus was sinless and innocent of any moral crime, Lucifer had no intention of surrendering to God's Son.

Reappearing a short time later, Lucifer moved closer to Jesus and launched a third desperate attack.

"Listen to me, Jesus. You cannot do a thing to stop men from committing unnatural acts and seeking pleasures of the flesh. Even I can't stop people from doing evil. Human beings make their own decisions, shape their own destiny, and the impulse to commit evil is in their nature."

Lucifer's voice had become more desperate, sensing that time was running out. He knew he had only this moment, that afterward he would be unable to do anything to change Jesus' mind. "Jesus, your people have always mocked, persecuted, and harmed those sent by God. They killed so many prophets! How can you be confident it won't happen to you? In this world you have no substantial power."

Jesus gazed at him, seemingly unaffected by Lucifer's claims and final daring attempt to subdue him.

"If you glorify and obey me," added the archangel, "I will make you the most powerful king on earth. Your kingdom will have no borders! And just as you will bow before me and worship me, the people of the earth will bow and worship you! You will gain their respect, something that you will never do through this mission of yours. I will utilize all forms of violence until the last man on earth will submit to your authority and mine."

Jesus responded with even more frank authority, "Lucifer, it is written that you should worship the Lord your God, and Him only should you serve. God's kingdom is made of love and liberty, not violence, death, and slavery. You ask me to revere you. How can God revere and kneel at the foot of His creatures? Neither can the Son, who in all his perfection has received from the Father the love, honor, and authority over the entire creation."

At that moment, there was a fluctuation of power, a flash between wavering brightness and elements from the spiritual sphere where the fallen angels dwelled. Some of these angels who were trapped under the command of Lucifer were sparkling with the desire to join with the Son of God. Lucifer saw it and came to the realization that his attacks against Jesus had no effect on his determined will. He was losing control of his sphere of domain.

"They are too ignorant and unimportant," snapped Lucifer, referring to those repentant angels.

"Each of God's creatures is important to me," Jesus asserted. "All of God's creatures can be redeemed and brought to their original splendor. Even you, Lucifer."

"Never!" said Lucifer, his face full of frustration. "I am offering glory in my kingdom!"

Jesus replied in a firm tone, "I am determined to fulfill the mission my Father has given to me. Lucifer, although you had a close relationship with God, you would have come to God's ultimate love through the hearts of Adam and Eve. You could have become the unquestionable eternal uncle of humanity."

After a pause to catch his breath, Jesus looked at him disapprovingly. "You were made to be a creature of goodness, and to live in harmony with the love of God and perfect human beings. You, Lucifer, have compromised yourself, your existence. The love of God is for every being. Now, with my arrival, not only men but also you fallen angels have the great opportunity to be restored to your original position. In this way, we all can live together in the presence of God."

All of the sudden, Lucifer collapsed downward, like a curtain whose rod had cracked. Moments later, he retreated back to the realm of darkness, his confrontation with God's Son a defeat. The good angels who had maintained their loyalty to God since their creation were all jubilant. It seemed as if the sun itself were exploding in the sky.

Jesus' spiritual victory over Lucifer released a torrent of power that was felt in the angelic realm. God's side had recovered its command. Now it was up to Israel to revive her strength.

CHAPTER 18

AFTER FORTY DAYS OF FASTING, Jesus was very frail and thin, but his spirit was stronger than ever. I couldn't believe my eyes when I first saw him about a week after his forty days in the desert. His battle against Satan had left him emaciated, his spindly legs barely holding up his body. There was nothing under his tunic but saggy, sunburnt skin and bones. I served and nourished him with all my heart. Although I regarded Jesus' lengthy fast as pure madness, there was no doubt in my mind that he would never give up his mission to save humanity, even at the cost of his life.

As the days passed, I remained worried about his health … and seriously concerned about the well-being of our family. So late one evening, while Jesus was relaxing in the courtyard, I dropped into the wicker chair across from him.

"Now that you are feeling better," I said a bit shortly, "I need a clear explanation of your future plans. What role will you play in your brother's sect?"

I detected a look of sadness in his eyes as he uttered, "I am no longer connected with John's activities on the Jordan."

With a relieved smile, I said to him, "Good. Once your health is restored, you can return and help my father with his fishing concerns. And since you love carpentry, you can devote your spare time to building furniture and repairing boats …"

"Mary, I have more important matters to pursue." After a pause, he added in a determined voice, "I must obey my Father's will and fulfill my role as the Messiah."

At first I thought I had misunderstood his words. But as I studied his face and eyes, stupefied, I realized he was utterly serious.

I continued to stare at him in silence, wondering whether the forty days in the wilderness had affected his mind. "Jesus, how is it possible for you to come up with something like this?"

He looked deeply into my eyes for a moment. "Mary, I know it's not easy for you to accept this, but I am the Messiah."

"Oh, Jesus! Everyone knows the Messiah will come in a glorious way, and from the blood lineage of King David."

Once more there was a brief silence between us. He leaned toward me and said pointedly, "Mary, for many years I have tried to guide you to understand the importance of your life. You and I have a special mission for the Lord. You are the wife of the Messiah. I need you by my side."

Feeling scared by his statement, but at the same time wanting to burst out laughing, I moved my chair away from him as a thousand other thoughts crowded my mind. I always believed that he was a special person with unique understanding of the Scriptures, but this notion of being the Messiah! I knew he was certain of his divine calling, just as I was certain of the great tribulations that could devour our family. Quickly my thoughts went to my children, and I knew at that moment my only concern was for their safety.

"Jesus, if you voice those thoughts publicly, true or not, do you know what it means for our family? Both Herod and the religious authorities will try to destroy our family!"

He considered this briefly before answering in a calm manner, "If we have faith in our Heavenly Father, we will be protected."

"Where was your *heavenly* Father when those three men attacked us?" I shot back, feeling the blood rush to my face. "I know you are a good man and an amazing interpreter of the Scriptures, but to actually believe you are the Messiah is crossing the border into insanity. If you don't reconsider your beliefs, it will inevitably bring difficulties to our lives. I have no intention of going along with it!"

"Don't make a rash decision. Not yet," he said, smiling for the first time. "Pray and meditate over it for three days. In fact, why don't we go to the mountainside and pray all night together? The fresh air will help clear your mind."

Closing my eyes tightly, I shook my head. "There is nothing to pray about!"

For the sake of the children, the thought of leaving him entered my mind. I felt that I couldn't be a responsible mother and at the same time be a devoted wife to this fanatic who planned to lead us along such a dangerous path. The two simply couldn't go hand in hand. He had to choose, either his family or his unreal, senseless mission.

"Tomorrow I'm taking the children to my sister's home in Bethany!" I said to him in desperation, hoping that such a threat would shake sense into his stubborn head. But as I tried to control my breathing, I sensed there was no struggle taking place within his heart. His face expressionless and his eyes serene, he was absolutely convinced of his role as the Anointed Son of the Lord God.

He got up out of the chair and knelt before me, offering a reassuring smile as he gently pressed my cheeks with his hands. "Mary, if you feel safer with your sister's family, then perhaps you should stay there for a few months," he said in resignation.

That infuriated me even more. I started to move around nervously, my face red.

"I want nothing more than for you to give up your ideas and dedicate your life to our family!" I yelled in his face.

Right at that moment, several men came to our home, asking to speak to him. I knew they wanted to discuss religious matters, which would consume hours of his time. So in a burst of anger, I let all my frustrations come out and began yelling at the men, demanding they go away and leave us alone. But Jesus promptly intervened and invited them inside. Still angry, I began insulting the men while pushing them away from our front door.

Frightened, the men quickly passed through the courtyard gate, with Jesus hurrying after them. Full of rage, I kept screaming at them like a child who doesn't get its way. The men looked over their shoulders, thinking I was possessed by demons.

When Jesus returned a few hours later, I was still out of control, and I accused him of loving others more than he loved me, and of placing barriers between my heart and his. Looking at me in despair, he silently left the house and went to the mountain to pray.

A week later, Isaac, Sara, and I were in Bethany. Jesus had escorted us there even though he was still rather weak. Two days after our arrival, Jesus was up at sunrise and prepared for his departure. During a light breakfast, he surprised me by mentioning that he was returning to the Jordan River.

Once there, he avoided John and his disciples. Keeping his identity as the Messiah a secret, Jesus increased his own ministry, preaching to small groups of people who were drawn to his sermons about God's infinitive love for all human beings. He also traveled to nearby towns and villages, inviting people to join him by the river.

Soon Jesus started to baptize those men and women who requested it after hearing his powerful sermons. The number of his listeners increased day by day, and some new followers moved closer to the area of the river by Aenon, where there was plenty of water. This was near Salim, where John usually conducted his activities.

He still hoped that John would unite with him and accept the fact that his true mission was to humble himself to the spiritual authority of his younger brother.

Jesus' activities soon became known to John's followers, some of whom became rather irritated that someone else was conducting baptisms.

The lust for supremacy that fallen Lucifer had instilled in the heart of man was poisoning some of John's disciples. They were full of envy and wished that more and more people would come to their master, who, according to them, was the only one with a genuine calling from God to baptize. By elevating the status of their master, they felt elevated as well, and hoped to gain more prestige and authority.

Jacob Ben-Zarah was a man with spiritual ambitions who was John the Baptist's first disciple. Upset over Jesus' activities just up river on the opposite bank, Jacob Ben-Zarah reminded other followers there was no other person in Israel greater than John.

He proclaimed, "Our master is the only one who offers real baptism, and who can forgive sins. So do not let Jesus corrode your faith with his delusions."

However, in a short time, Jesus' popularity began spreading through-out the area. Many people noticed that John and Jesus had different approaches to baptism. Before offering baptism, Jesus would preach first. His voice had the sound of a gentle and caring soul, and his words were full of expectation for a brighter future.

During those days, a wealthy merchant from Jerusalem named Benjamin went to the Jordan to listen to Jesus' words. Benjamin knew that baptism, without a clear understanding of God's will, was merely a bath in the river. He believed that people needed to be guided to a full understanding of God's words in order to choose good over evil. Moved by this conviction, Benjamin went to speak to John's disciples, and they realized that he was more excited listening to Jesus than to John.

Jacob Ben-Zarah was leading a discussion that became rather heated. After a while they came to the conclusion that it would be wise to go directly to John and ask him for a clarification about his beliefs.

As the group approached the river, they saw John on the shoreline talking to several young men. During a break, Jacob Ben-Zarah intro-duced his master to Benjamin, who gave a polite nod of the head.

"Rabbi, forgive us for interrupting," said Benjamin. "With due respect, I need your help understanding baptism as a form of purification. How can a simple immersion in water purify the heart and mind of a person?" he asked, perplexed.

John replied, "The baptism in the water is a symbolic act for the conversion of one's heart and the forgiveness of sins."

The man looked at John, unsatisfied with his response. "But even those who have been baptized continue sinning, because of the evil desires still present in their hearts and minds. How can a person be totally purified so he won't surrender to the desire to sin? It would seem as if the baptism has absolutely no power in diminishing the impulse to sin. Apparently everything stays the same." Throwing his hands in the air in exasperation, he suddenly noticed a crowd gathering around to hear the discussion. "In fact," he added, "most people return to their old way of life without enough will to change their bad behavior and habits. I have seen many people who after been baptized go back to their sinful lives again. Then the same people return here later to be baptized again and again."

Looking flustered, a rarity for John, he said with a forced smile, "This proves they have a desire to change their lives."

Benjamin stared at John intensely, growing more perplexed. "But where in their souls is the moral strength not to commit sinful actions, so they can get closer to God? How can Israel be converted in such a way that its people can finally free themselves from sin and be willing to follow the laws of God? Isn't the purification from sin fundamental, if man is ever to be free from corruption?"

"That is why we are waiting for the Messiah," said one man who had received baptism from John earlier that day. "Only the Anointed One has the authority to forgive our sins," he added.

John's disciples gave the man angry looks, warning him to be quiet. Then they turned back to John, their eyes full of expectation that their master could be more than what he seemed at first. *Perhaps he could be the Anointed One,* their hearts hoped.

Noticing their wistful expressions as they looked at their rabbi, Benjamin said in a reproachful tone, "Rabbi, since you baptize and at the same time forgive sins, do your disciples believe you are possibly the Messiah?"

"I have never claimed to be either the Messiah or Elijah!" retorted John, his voice growing forceful. He looked at Jacob Ben-Zarah and his other disciples. "You are witness to the fact that I've always denied being the Messiah. And although the Lord God has given me the mission to prepare the way for his coming, I have not taken the role of Elijah either, as some people have suggested." He turned back to the merchant. "My sole responsibility is to baptize people in preparation for the Messiah's coming."

After digesting this, Benjamin remarked offhandedly, "There is another man up the river who is also baptizing people. His name is Jesus."

With a cold smile, Jacob Ben-Zarah stated, "We know Jesus well. He is the cousin of our rabbi, and until recently he was a part of our group."

Surprised to hear this, Benjamin said to him in a level voice, "Jesus teaches that baptism has to be understood from a spiritual perspective. He eloquently explains God's divine nature and His purpose for creating men and women. He also asserts that we have to understand the origin of sin and evil so that we can be aware of Satan's traps." A curious look crossed his face as he turned to John the Baptist. "You are a man of God. What is your opinion on Jesus? I have been told the Holy Spirit revealed to you that Jesus is the Messiah."

"Yes, it is true," uttered John, noting the startled looks on the faces of his disciples. "Though he had already been baptized, Jesus requested it again. As I poured water onto his head, I strongly felt the presence of the Holy Spirit. Then I heard a voice inside my heart, as though it were coming from Heaven, or out of my soul."

Benjamin considered a moment. "You say Jesus is your cousin?"

John nodded involuntarily, inwardly debating whether he should reveal the truth about their relationship. Quickly deciding against it, he spoke in a reflective tone, "During the past few years, Jesus and I have engaged in numerous talks about God and other spiritual matters. But recently I have come to know of his profound relationship with God. He has a keen awareness of God's presence, a power unlike any man I've ever met."

Pausing, John turned slightly and gazed at the sparkling waters of the Jordan, thinking aloud, "Jesus speaks of having a special relationship with God, as that between a father and son. Maybe this is the voice I heard."

"You heard God's voice?" questioned Benjamin, staring at him intently.

John glanced at the frowning faces of his disciples. "Ordinary people might not understand Jesus' words because no one seems to know God as deeply as he does."

Jacob Ben-Zarah interrupted him. "Rabbi, what are you talking about?" he said, either angry or bewildered, or both. "Do you seriously believe what you're saying?" He gestured at the others disciples. "We live shoulder by shoulder with you, but this is the first time you have mentioned such things to us. Until now, we have never heard what Jesus teaches … nor do we care."

"His teachings transcend God's laws," retorted John, surprised at his own words. "Jesus is a special man, a true representative of God's heart."

Benjamin spoke with sudden pugnacity, "But Rabbi … if you believe this, why aren't you with Jesus now? If he is such a special man of God, why aren't you and your disciples by his side?"

John gave thought to the question, then replied stiffly, "Although Jesus has unique spiritual qualities, I still have my doubts about his basic teachings. We also have different ideas on how to proceed in the future. His path is one of danger."

Benjamin pressed him. "Rabbi, but you claim to have heard a divine voice."

John took a deep breath, his thoughts going back to that day at the river. "As I said, it was a voice that came from within. It lasted only several moments. At the time, I must have been under the influence of the Holy Spirit. I felt a strong sensation telling me that Jesus is what he claims to be."

Visibly concerned, one of his young disciples said gravely, "Master, what are we to do? Jesus' popularity is growing, his followers increasing in numbers by the hour."

"Well … the fact is that his numbers will increase, while mine will decrease."

Upset by all these unprecedented confessions, Jacob Ben-Zarah barked, "Why should your influence decrease while his increases?"

John grew silent, he eyes staring blankly at the ground.

Benjamin said in a puzzled tone, "Shouldn't both of you grow together? There are contradictions in what you say and what you do. If you aren't Elijah, then why do you claim to be the one preparing the way for the Messiah? Won't Elijah do this when he comes? After all, there cannot be a Messiah without Elijah."

"That's right," uttered several voices from the crowd of onlookers.

Jacob Ben-Zarah said in protest, "Rabbi, I don't understand why you allow your cousin to become popular. He doesn't have the kind of respect and prestige you have gained over the years." He paused as a few other disciples nodded in agreement. "Even though you testified to him several months ago, you now realize it was a mistake."

Remaining silent, John the Baptist suppressed a sigh and couldn't help but question his present feelings about Jesus as he turned slowly from the crowd and stepped into the shallows of the river. *Could my younger brother actually be the Anointed One?* he asked himself in dismay. *If so, should I promptly join him and proclaim to everyone in sight that God's Son has arrived? What if I do this but he turns out to be a false Messiah who leads the people away from God and into the clutches of the evil one? And what would become of me if I had been supporting him? Would I be stoned to death by an angry mob?... Or merely beaten and left alone to wander in shame and dishonor?*

Three days later, Jesus was praying softly as he walked along the bank with some of his followers toward the area where John was baptizing. Once again, Jesus' heart was full of hope that his brother would finally respond to God's divine voice. By preaching and baptizing in a nearby area, Jesus wanted to show John that people were willing to listen to him, and thus John should as well. Also, Jesus wanted to create a situation in which John wouldn't feel ashamed or humiliated by making the decision to unite forces with his younger brother. If his followers drifted over, then so could he.

"Rabbi!" called out Jacob Ben-Zarah, running up to the water's edge. "Jesus is coming here with his followers!"

Hiding his displeasure, John stepped from the river. With the others, he looked eastward and saw his brother approaching with eight men who were carrying baskets filled with bread and fruit. As he drew closer, Jesus waved to him and smiled broadly, genuinely pleased to see him, it seemed. John returned the wave and managed to curl his lips upward, while some of his disciples glared at Jesus and his followers, with a contempt that they usually reserved for Roman soldiers sent here by Caesar himself.

Ignoring their disrespectful manner, Jesus gave them a nod and warm smile. "An affectionate greeting to all of you, humble servants of God!"

"God is with you, Jesus," declared John, giving him a strong embrace.

Seeing this as a hopeful sign, Jesus said to him, "Why don't you and I take a walk and find a quiet place to talk."

They were silent as they walked to a rise of land overlooking the area. As they lowered their bodies to the ground, John said in a clipped tone, "Jesus, I know what you wish to speak to me about. I have no plans to join you, not at this time."

His face clouded. "John, it is not God who divides men, but Satan."

"What do you mean?" John asked in a challenging tone.

"You shouldn't be a slave to petty feelings of jealousy and competitiveness. You should open your heart and acknowledge that we have identical objectives. Remember that in God there is humility, while in Satan there is arrogance. In God there is love and understanding, in Satan hatred and discord. God unites, while Satan divides."

Jesus hoped his words resonated with John, and would inspire him to cast aside his personal feelings and ambitions. Yet as Jesus gazed into his eyes, he discerned that John was unmoved, staring indifferently toward the banks of the river where the crowd of people mingled with the two groups of disciples, everyone talking and laughing while consuming the bread and fruit.

"There are forces of evil that want to attack and destroy us," added Jesus. "These evil forces will act bolder if you and I aren't united in heart and actions." His voice rose passionately. "John, you must understand that the fallen angels actively seek to divide us, and thus undermine our strength, all our efforts, our message."

John remained silent and unresponsive, his eyes glassy.

"Please, John," implored Jesus, "although I look unsuitable for such a position, I am the Messiah. You know who I am, because the Holy Spirit has spoken to you. Do not deny it. Don't let the pride, and doubt, or that sentiment of superiority you have felt toward me, darken your heart."

John said in a defensive tone, "I baptized you and proclaimed to others that you are the Lamb of God."

Jesus stepped closer to him. "It is easy for you to say that to a few people. 'Jesus is indeed the Messiah.' Yet it's more difficult to humble yourself by following me in front of all the people, including your disciples."

John's mind was jumbled by feelings of frustration, uncertainty, and pride toward his younger brother.

Jesus said firmly, "John, the proper course of action is for you to confidently announce to all our disciples that I am indeed the Messiah. Then as we travel about the land, you will testify to the people that the Messiah has finally arrived … and most importantly that I am the Anointed Son of the Lord God."

Pausing, Jesus cupped John's hands inside of his. "My dear brother, we are here together, and together we have to proclaim the kingdom of God. In fact, in these past few months, you and I, along with our disciples, should have already gone through Judea and Galilee, spreading the good news to the chosen people of God. We are already behind."

Jesus paused again, waiting for John to respond in some manner. But his brother pursed his lips, apparently determined not to be swayed by his brother's solicitations.

"John, I have been waiting for many years, hoping you would realize that I am the Messiah and offer your loyalty and tireless support. But I cannot wait any longer. Either you are with me, or we go our separate ways."

After a long moment of hazy thought, John got to his feet and looked toward the river again, where some of their disciples were staring curiously at them.

Standing up, Jesus grasped John's upper arm and pulled him closer, staring straight into his eyes. "I am the one to whom the Lord God has revealed Himself. On the basis of my perfection and personal victory over the forces of darkness, God has given me all power and authority over the spiritual and physical worlds. So do not fear anyone, for if we are united in our mission, we can change the heart of the people of Israel and they will follow us."

Hearing this, John's heart hardened, and he tried to break free from his brother's strong grip. "John, you are my means to reach the religious and social leaders of Israel. On the foundation of your heart and sacrifice, and the tears and blood of all the prophets before you, I can quickly win the people and develop the base to spread God's word throughout the Roman Empire and the rest of the world."

Looking dazed, John was lost in a sea of contradictory thoughts as Jesus persisted relentlessly, hoping to penetrate the barriers that Satan had erected around John's heart and mind. "This can be a time of great harvest for the Lord God, and the bounty of fruit we reap for Him depends on your willingness to support my efforts."

Jesus released his grip and added in a low voice, "At this point, all that I require from you is a test of faith. Acknowledge me in front of the people down by the river. Proclaim that I am the Messiah, and that you and your disciples will follow me to the ends of the earth. Let your mouth echo my words …"

"I cannot," said John, shaking his head as he stepped away from Jesus.

"Why not?" he implored. "If you are constantly with me, many people … young and old, rich and poor, weak and powerful … will take my words seriously. We are in the new season of God's providence. We must teach the truth and move forward across the land, harvesting all that God has prepared."

"I have other duties to fulfill, my brother," John uttered in a barely audible voice.

Growing angry, Jesus said in reproach, "Brother, don't waste time on matters that are distant from God's heart."

With a look of agitation, John retorted, beginning to turn away, "Jesus, I will never stop baptizing or preaching."

"Together as one, we can unleash a huge waterfall of support from the chosen people."

John shook his head, murmuring, "I simply don't have confidence in all this."

"You and I have been entrusted with the destiny to make the world a huge family under the loving parenthood of the Lord God."

John lowered his head in thought, clearly bothered by his brother's insistence on his being the Messiah, and that he must be obeyed at all costs.

When he met his eyes again, John spoke in a weary tone, "Jesus, we have different concepts of the Messiah. But even if we agree on everything you teach, it does not resolve my doubts about you." Placing a hand on his shoulder, he said in parting, "Brother, go in peace, and may the Lord God bless you and your disciples."

Before Jesus could reply, John turned and dashed back down to the river, where he summoned his disciples for a meeting by the river.

As tears rolled down his cheeks, Jesus fell to his knees and fervently prayed that the Lord God could penetrate John's obstinate heart.

Jesus was soon joined by his followers, and together they stood in silence and watched as John and his disciples trudged away from the crowd to go in a nearby village.

This was the last time that he and Jesus spoke directly. John continued to act in accordance with what he considered to be his mission, baptizing and urging the wicked to repent. Despite the fact that he had received a revelation from the Holy Spirit, John never found it in his heart to support his brother. His pride overshadowed the wisdom that God had given him. It was the same pride that had destroyed God's plan for His children and would again compromise His plans now.

John the Baptist continued his activities with his usual strong temperament, not fearing to reproach any sinner, regardless of his social status. He believed God had granted him the authority to reproach arrogant and sinful people, and John did it without weighing the consequences. His actions often angered the Pharisees, military authorities, and particularly Herod Antipas.

Whenever John talked about the sin of adultery and incest, he would denounce the relationship between Herod and his sister-in-law, Herodias. Unbeknown to John, both Herod and Herodias had been told about his condemnation, which ignited their wrath. Herod felt obligated to silence John for a certain period, but due to John's strong influence throughout the region, Herod feared a revolt by his vocal followers. Nevertheless, Herod went against his better judgment and ordered the arrest of John, incarcerating him in the Machaerus Fortress in Perea.

It was during this time that Jesus was baptizing and preaching in Judea. At one point, a group of Pharisees wanted to question Jesus, so they traveled to the area where he usually conducted his activities. As a major religious authority in Israel, the Pharisees were the chief interpreters of sacred writings, one of their tasks to ensure that no false interpretation would gain prominence over an established belief. In keeping with this duty, they rebuked anyone who proclaimed something contrary to traditional doctrine. At times, they would even persuade the secular authorities to jail and punish those people who, according to them, taught false doctrines that could poison the faith of devout Jews.

When the Pharisees arrived at the area where Jesus had been preaching, they were disappointed to find that he wasn't there. So they began questioning his disciples, who were baptizing people in the river.

Later in the week, when Jesus returned, his disciples reported the unexpected visit by the Pharisees. "Rabbi, they are quite angry over your recent sermons. Surely they came here to threaten you."

Jesus nodded absently, his mind on other matters.

Another disciple said, "We were told that John the Baptist has been detained by Herod. Though there was an uproar from John's followers, many more people expressed their satisfaction with his arrest, including the Pharisees. They intend to keep the order in this region, so as not to attract any negative reactions from the Roman authorities. So we were told to leave immediately. If not, we would be severely punished." A weak smile crossed his face. "It was fortunate you weren't here."

After a long moment, one of them said in a worried tone, "Rabbi, what do you want us to do?"

Jesus had a thoughtful expression, as if he were studiously considering the matter. Yet he remained silent, his gaze fixed on the western horizon lined with low hills.

"Rabbi, we believe your life is in danger. Perhaps you should return to Magdala and rest for several months."

Moving his eyes to their tense faces, Jesus gave them a reassuring smile.

"Brothers, we must never forsake the mission God granted to us. Yet we must be wary of evil forces that try to prevent our activities." His tone changed. "If the Pharisees are truly serious about harassing us, then we should move our activities to Galilee. But mind you, I will return to Judea as soon as possible. Meanwhile, those from Galilee can come north with me, but those of you who live here can remain here with your families. Whatever you decide, don't lose faith in me. Continue to spread my teachings to all those who hunger for spiritual nourishment."

Later that day, Jesus began his journey back to Galilee, knowing it would be difficult to overcome the many challenges without the help of his imprisoned elder brother.

CHAPTER 19

JESUS KNEW FROM PAST EXPERIENCE that the Pharisees, Levites, Sadducees, and other religious leaders were not ready to open their hearts and minds to his teachings. Although most of them strictly adhered to the laws and traditions, their minds were shut to any ideas that didn't reflect a close interpretation of their doctrines. I have met many such people during my life. Before I gave my heart to Jesus, I thought only qualified men of God could interpret the laws of Moses. But after discovering the teaching of my husband, including his divine nature and his mission, I began to see that many of these men were alienated from God, partly because they were so rigid-minded. This unwillingness to see things from a new perspective was more apparent in Jerusalem, where the higher religious authorities of Israel dwelled.

But there were other people in Israel, such as the Gentiles, who didn't respect the traditions and laws of Moses. Many of them led a life of violence and immorality, and had little spiritual preparation to accept Jesus' teachings.

The Galileans, a mixture of both Jews and Gentiles, were the ones best suited to accept Jesus. For many centuries they had been in contact with Jewish customs and the concept of a single God. They also lived adjacent to the land of the Gentiles. And since few Galileans held extreme religious beliefs, their minds were open to new ideas. These were the people whom Jesus was hoping to reach, those eagerly searching for God's truth and not indoctrinated by antiquated beliefs.

After the imprisonment of John the Baptist, Jesus made the decision to focus his activities in Capernaum, so he could be close to Andrew and his brother Simon, as well John and his brother James. Jesus felt the four men were special, genuinely looking for a deeper understanding of God's nature and will. Although Jesus had spoken with them on previous occasions, their hearts were still uncertain, however.

One day Jesus wanted to test their faith, so he went to look for them near the shores of the lake near Bethsaida. The day was hot, the sun's bright rays reflecting off the glassy water. He found Simon and Andrew throwing their nets into the waters. Upon hearing Jesus calling them, they stopped and looked toward the shore.

Jesus raised his voice. "I want to meet with you, along with James and John. Where are they?"

"A little farther down the coast," said Andrew. "They went with their father, Zebedee, to mend some fishing nets."

"Let's go find them."

Soon the three men were strolling northward along the path bordering the lake, where they came upon John and James, who were happy to see Jesus and the others. "Hello, Zebedee!" Jesus said, smiling and waving to him. "I see you finally got your sons to do some work."

"Too little and too late," the old man replied with a laugh. He was short and slightly stooped, with a balding head and sparse gray beard. "Have you come to take my sons?"

"Yes, I need to speak with them," Jesus answered, stepping up to them as they rose to greet him.

With a look of concern, John said to him, "Teacher, it has been many weeks since we last saw you. Your face looks quite thin. Have you been sick?"

Jesus shook his head. "There's nothing to worry about. But I appreciate your concern."

A bit later, the five of them arrived at Simon's house. His children were playing outside, and he told them not to come inside while Jesus was speaking.

His wife heard their voices and came out to greet them. She had met Jesus before and admired his genuineness. She invited everyone inside and offered wine, fresh bread, olives, and cakes dripping in honey. Then she excused herself and closed the door behind her, stepping out into the courtyard.

Jesus and the four fishermen sat in a circle on the floor. After collecting his thoughts, Jesus said, "Andrew, did you return to the Jordan and see John the Baptist before he got arrested?"

"No, I was no longer his disciple by the time it happened. As I told you once, John always preaches the same message. My understanding of God wasn't growing any deeper."

Jesus made a little gesture. "But with him you became a better person. You repented for your sins and counseled those who came to seek God."

Simon responded in a sincere tone, "Since being baptized and following the Baptist, my brother has been a changed man."

John remarked, "I do feel less sinful than before. But once I had repented and been baptized, there was really no more reason to follow the Baptist."

After eating a few olives, Jesus said, "John, you and Andrew are men of great initiative. With nobody forcing you, you devoted yourself to a worthy cause of God by serving John the Baptist." He turned and spoke to Simon and James. "If your brothers spent time serving John, who was sent ahead of the Messiah to prepare the way, how much more should they serve the Messiah, who comes to baptize with the power of the Holy Spirit."

Pausing, Jesus looked deeply into the eyes of each man and told them he had been sent by God, and that he needed people of great spiritual strength who could support his mission. "Working together centered upon God's call," he told them, "we will transform hearts and minds."

Jesus went on to explain that God was calling them to complete what the first ancestors of humanity had not fulfilled. The fishermen knew the account in Genesis, about how the fall of Eve and Adam revealed that something abhorrent in the sight of God took place in the Garden of Eden, which cut off humanity from God's direct love and guidance.

Jesus said to them, "If we are to understand evil and its origin, it is vitally important to know exactly what happened. Since God is our father, and we are His children, there should be no mysteries about God. But due to the actions of Adam and Eve, humanity has fallen far away from its Heavenly Parent."

The four men stared at Jesus, listening closely to his every word.

"God knows us, and His desire is for us to know Him." He smiled at James. "Just as you can only put new wine into new wineskins, I can guide you to understand the divine nature of both God and man, as well as the origin of evil, if you open your minds. Once you understand the times that we are living in, then you'll be able to purify your souls and never sin again. But you must have faith in me, and allow me to guide you."

"How?" asked Simon. "We have heard your teachings before. But they were difficult to understand. We appreciate your sincerity and friendship, but we are ordinary people living a simple life."

"Follow me and I will make you fishers of men. I will help you to discover God's infinite love. Together we will convey such love to the people of Israel and all humanity."

James spoke up. "I have many doubts. Though you seem honest and sincere, we don't know you at all, and I really don't understand what you want in the end. You told us you are from Nazareth, and nothing else. We don't know who your parents are, or anything about your brothers and sisters and other relatives."

"Have faith, and I assure that you will understand my teachings in time."

"What do the religious authorities in Jerusalem think about you?" inquired Simon. "My brother feels you might be the Messiah. But if you are the Anointed One, wouldn't it be true that there are no people in Israel better than the Temple priests to understand you?"

Wishing John the Baptist were near his side and supporting him, Jesus answered in a quiet voice, "All I ask is that you listen with an open heart, then pray deeply to …"

James raised a quick hand. "It is prophesied the Messiah will come with power and greatness. If you are he, as John and Andrew believe, then why are you here with us, mere fishermen? You speak to us about Genesis as if we know the Holy Scriptures word by word. All I know is that there is one God, the God of Abraham, Isaac, and Jacob, and that I am a Jew of the chosen people who are waiting for the Messiah."

"Right," Simon added with a nod. "That is why there are high priests and Pharisees. Who better than they can interpret the teachings of the prophets?"

Jesus spread his hands, an imploring note to his voice. "All I am asking is for you to keep faith and have patience. Follow me and with time you will transform yourselves into God's children, and He will readily reveal Himself to you. You will live in complete unity with His spirit. And together we can build His kingdom on earth."

John, who had been keeping his thoughts to himself, quietly listening to the discussion, finally said to Jesus, "How can you expect us to follow you? We have wives and children who need to be fed. We have our work and other responsibilities in the community."

Simon added in an assertive tone, "Where do you want to take us? What will our lives be like by following you?" His eyes narrowed. "I cannot join you, and neither can my brother Andrew," he concluded, throwing his brother a fateful look.

"Neither can John or I," stated James. He took a bite of the honey cake, then washed it down with a gulp of wine. "Jesus, how can we leave our father alone? Perhaps from time to time we could join you. We would like to hear more about your teachings. I have many questions to ask, but not now." Yawning, he got to his feet. "We must return and help our father mend the nets."

All four men were struggling with the same problems that had confronted me before I fully understood my husband's mission and his vision for humanity. John and Andrew, along with their brothers, were so consumed by the routine of daily life that they couldn't imagine a life in the service of God.

When they all stepped outside, Jesus thanked Simon's wife for the food before bidding farewell and walking in the direction of Magdala.

Andrew and the others headed back to work, remaining silent, each one trying to sort out his own thoughts and feelings about Jesus.

Finally, Simon thought out loud, "I simply don't know what to make of him. He speaks eloquently of things no one else says."

"His words make you dream of a hopeful future," remarked James, glancing at Andrew. "Have you ever considered God as your Father?"

Andrew shook his head. "Not even John the Baptist utters things like this." He turned to his brother. "Simon, I don't care what you think, I do believe that Jesus is the Messiah, and I am willing to go with him!"

Simon shot him an angry look. "You told me that John the Baptist proclaimed that his mission was to prepare the way for the Messiah. If Jesus is the Messiah, why isn't John his main disciple? Why didn't John go to the towns and cities, fervently announcing that Jesus is the Anointed One?"

"How can he?" Andrew fired back with a frown. "He's in prison."

Simon grunted. "But you were standing near John the Baptist when he testified that Jesus was the Lamb of God, the Anointed One we all have been waiting for." He glanced at James. "If John truly believed it at that time, why didn't he gather all his disciples and testify to them. It's what I would have done."

James laughed softly. "Perhaps you can become the next John the Baptist!"

After some silence, John said quietly, "Though my thoughts are confused, my heart tells me that Jesus is the Messiah. His words are powerful, and he always speaks with sincerity."

"That's what concerns me," retorted Simon. "He is totally convinced of his mission. I have no doubt that he speaks in good faith. He's a virtuous man with a righteous spirit. However, if he is truly a man of God, why is he spending time with fishermen? He should be in Jerusalem, at the Temple!"

James nodded in agreement. "No Messiah, no king, would spend time in these parts. Where is his power and authority? His grandiosity?" He glanced at his brother. "This Jesus has nothing and is a nobody. He is only a person who foolishly believes he has been given divine powers from his personal God …"

"If Jesus really is the Messiah," inserted Simon, "how does he plan to become king of Israel, with the help of four ignorant fishermen?" He turned to his younger brother, scowling. "Andrew, you will stay here and catch fish, not men!"

James laughed at the remark, but John and Andrew remained silent, continuing along the path toward their boats, both wondering anxiously if they should forsake their present life and follow Jesus into an unknown future.

CHAPTER 20

AFTER SPENDING SEVERAL WEEKS going town to town, Jesus traveled to Nazareth. Every once in a while, he returned to his native town. He never lost hope that his relatives and friends would open their minds to his teachings. He loved them dearly and had no stronger desire than to share with them the gift of wisdom given to him by the Lord God and elevate them spiritually.

As a child growing up in Nazareth, Jesus was often alone, leading a solitary spiritual life. As a man, his life was much the same. He continued to exist on a higher spiritual plane than other people. John, his half-brother, was the person who was most compatible with him. But there was still a huge spiritual gap between them. And, of course, though they were brothers, John was born with his blood tainted by original sin, whereas Jesus was free of all sin, having been born from God's direct lineage.

It is crucial to understand that Jesus had been conceived without original sin due to his mother's faith. Under the influence of the Holy Spirit, she was guided to this act. My husband came from a purified Jewish seed, in which all the characteristics of the Son of God were contained. One of Jesus' responsibilities was to grow into the Tree of Life and ascend spiritually, surpassing all the temptations and barriers that Satan had put between God and men. Jesus accomplished this with a deep sense of responsibility.

In Nazareth, Jesus once again tried to convince his relatives that he was the Messiah. Naturally, it was God's desire for Jesus' family members to be the first to accept him and receive his blessings. The process of salvation had to begin within Jesus' family. With the support of John the Baptist and his family, the rest of the community of Nazareth would have listened to him, thus allowing him to win over the hearts and minds of the religious and social leaders of all Galilee, followed by the other regions and, ultimately, Judea.

The people of Nazareth had never understood Jesus' words, or his mission. Sadly, over the years, most Nazarenes had viewed Mary's son as the illegitimate child of an unknown father, a boy of no importance who was an undesirable to Joseph's parents. So it was incomprehensible and unacceptable that this boy, now a grown man, could be anointed by God for any significant task.

The day after his arrival in Nazareth, Jesus went to the synagogue. When he stood to read, he was given the writings of the prophet Isaiah. Jesus unrolled the scroll and quickly found the passage that read: "The Spirit of God is over me, because he has anointed me. He has sent me to take the good news to the poor, to announce freedom to the prisoners, to give sight to the blind, to release the oppressed and to proclaim a year of the grace of God."

When Jesus returned to his seat, everyone stared at him. Then he declared in complete confidence, "Today this scripture is fulfilled before you." Then he began to teach the meaning of the scripture he had just read, explaining that he was the very person whom God had anointed.

Some of the men immediately accepted what Jesus had proclaimed, but most were quite indignant. Jesus reminded those who voiced their objections that no prophet had truly been accepted in his own place of origin. "I tell you," he said to them, "the chosen people have the responsibility to recognize and to accept the messenger of God if they want to receive His blessings. However, if the chosen ones reject the true words of God and His messenger, then God will give His blessings to other people."

These words infuriated even those who had admired and approved of him earlier. They all came out of the synagogue intending to drag Jesus to the top of the mount, where the town was built, to throw him down. Fortunately, some of his relatives had been informed about what was happening, and they were able to calm the furious crowd, which eventually released Jesus.

Later that day, Jesus decided to visit his mother again before his departure from Nazareth. As he walked up the road leading to Mary's house, Jesus saw her standing outside, near the gate to the courtyard. And as he drew closer, he couldn't help noticing the anxious look on her face.

Mary had already heard from several neighbors about the disturbing events that had taken place at the synagogue earlier in the day, and naturally she was worried about her son. As the sun set, Jesus approached his mother with a loving expression and open arms.

Relieved that he was unharmed, Mary gave him a hug, and he kissed her forehead.

"Are you all right?" she asked.

"Mother, don't cry," he replied with a smile, and she stepped back and examined him. "As you can see, there are no cuts or bruises on my body."

"Oh, my blessed son! How you torture me! What happened at the synagogue? Why did they want to hurt you?"

"Please, Mother. It was a simple misunderstanding."

"Promise to be more careful. No mother wants to see her son murdered by a mob."

Holding hands, they ambled toward the house where Jesus had spent his lonely childhood and adolescent years.

"Son, I know you have strong beliefs, but don't speak or act in ways that upset others. You well know that most people in the synagogues hold a strict interpretation of the Scriptures."

"Mother, you know I have never been like others. I live in another spiritual dimension, where God has revealed Himself to me. He has given me the task to guide the chosen people to a full understanding of His divine nature and our true nature as children of God, and to teach about the cause and process of the fall that took place between the archangel, Eve, and Adam. I cannot hide behind silence."

"Oh, Jesus!" exclaimed Mary, shaking her head. "Do you know the pain in my heart? How can I live with my own son constantly facing death?" Her voice wavered. "I feel so much guilt and sorrow over your past. Son, I love you so much! I have given you life and cannot bear the thought of you being killed by narrow-minded, overzealous believers."

"Mother, I will always be grateful for your love and affection. Thank you for giving me life … for taking care of me … for holding me in your arms … for crying with me during sad moments … for offering me joyful times as a child … Thank you for all the love you have given me over the years."

"Darling, I'm sorry I didn't do more for you. But I had to take care of your father, and your younger brothers and sisters."

"Don't be so hard on yourself," he said, smiling and giving her a warm embrace. "It's getting late, so I must go. Perhaps I will return in a few months."

Noticeably worried, Mary said in a pleading whisper, "Please be careful, Jesus. I was told the religious leaders are planning something."

"Yes, I know their intentions," he replied with a concerned look. "Where is Nazareth's faith in me?"

"Son, take care of yourself. Return to your wife and children. Try to live like others, an ordinary life without danger. This is the only thing that will bring happiness to me."

Jesus kissed her forehead, giving her one last hug before turning and taking long strides along the road. Soon he saw a familiar figure walking in his direction. It was his youngest brother, who was on his way to visit their mother.

Grinning from ear to ear, James ran up to Jesus and threw his arms around him, then nearly lifted Jesus off the ground. "Brother! I am surprised you haven't left yet. How are you? Were you injured this morning?"

"Of course not," he said mildly, not wishing to disturb James, who was a good-natured young man. "I hope you didn't get hurt during the scuffle."

He shook his head. "Since then, almost everyone in Nazareth has gathered around me and asked questions about you. 'What is wrong with Jesus? Could your brother be possessed?' "

Jesus gave him an apologetic look. "I'm sorry." Pausing, he studied his face. "How did you respond to such questions?"

"I told them the truth. There isn't a person in Galilee who is more loving or a more devout Jew than my brother. Then I challenged them to deny it."

Jesus couldn't help laughing. "Did anyone step forward?"

"Only a few elderly men," he answered. "But after a minute of confused babbling, the crowd quickly dissipated." He set a gentle hand on his brother's shoulder. "Jesus, I know you think differently, but not everyone in Nazareth is against you. Especially me! I know your heart. As an older brother, you have always loved and cared for me during hard times, giving me words of wisdom when there was confusion and bitterness in my heart."

As the two brothers walked down the road bordered by humble dwellings and flocks of children at play, James added in a worried tone, "Now that Herod has John the Baptist in prison, do you plan to return to the Jordan River?"

Turning serious, Jesus said, "I will go where God sends me. As of now, I plan to visit some of my followers in Capernaum."

James hesitated. "I know you don't like to speak of John, but I heard that his close disciples believe he is the Messiah. I also heard that religious authorities from Jerusalem asked him directly whether he were the Anointed One."

Jesus nodded. "Yes, I once witnessed a meeting between John and a few Pharisees coming from Jerusalem. But John firmly denied being the Messiah."

James said thoughtfully, "Then could he be a great prophet like Elijah?"

Trying to subdue his bitter feelings from his last meeting with John, Jesus said in a distant voice, "John is the last of the great prophets. His mission is to connect the old era with the new. Sadly, John continues to deny his role as a prophet."

After pondering this, James asked inquisitively, "Why is it that prophets are usually rejected by the people who are closest to them, such as their families and the people of their communities?"

Jesus explained quietly, "James, let's say that God has chosen you to be a great prophet who relays His message and directions to the people of Israel."

"That's not likely to happen," James replied with a chuckle, as they approached the outskirts of Nazareth.

"But if you were to become a prophet," added Jesus, making a little gesture, "then your parents and siblings, along with the neighbors and townspeople, would have a most difficult time seeing you in this new light. After all, they knew you when you were a baby with smelly poop on your bottom, and then later as a playful child with dirt on your face."

James smiled at the imagery. "In other words," he thought aloud, "my friends and relatives already have a fixed idea about me. And if I had been, let's say, a wild boy, getting into mischief, then most people who knew me couldn't accept the fact that I had suddenly become God's prophet."

"Precisely," Jesus affirmed with a nod. "Older people would say, 'How is it possible for this young man, whom we have known all our lives, to be a prophet of God?' And your friends would say, 'We know you! We grew up with you and never saw anything that would qualify you as a prophet!' And your relatives would merely smile and shake their heads in disbelief, thinking you are either joking or perhaps insane!"

"I see," said James. "My friends couldn't understand my new identity and would feel uncomfortable in my presence. My family would be scandalized, and the religious authorities would try to silence me."

"As a result," added Jesus, frowning, "most people in your native land would not accept your spiritual authority as a prophet of God. However, even though your life becomes difficult, you must continue your mission despite ceaseless ridicule and harsh persecution."

James remained silent for several minutes as they continued walking along the road leading out of Nazareth. Near the edge of town, there were only a few scattered houses and buildings. "Jesus, I hope you know I have faith in you. No matter what happens, I will support you."

Jesus smiled gratefully. "You are now the one giving me love and words of wisdom!"

Soon they stopped walking, and Jesus added in earnest, "James, in the future I will ask you to accompany me and my followers as we fulfill God's will in this land. But for the time being, please stay here and help care for our mother."

"Of course," he promptly replied. "And I look forward to the day when I can become one of your disciples."

After a strong embrace, the two brothers parted.

As Jesus turned and walked purposefully toward the distant hills, James watched him and recalled sweet memories of his youth when Jesus had provided him with so much care and affection, almost as if they were father and son.

And as the silhouette of his brother got smaller, James asked the Lord God to watch over Jesus and bless all of his efforts in the coming months and years.

CHAPTER 21

JESUS TRAVELED TO CAPERNAUM, leaving his unpleasant experience in Nazareth behind. During the trip, he reflected on his situation, wondering how to penetrate the barriers that kept people from understanding his teachings and believing in him.

Now with John the Baptist in prison, Jesus knew it would be difficult to win over the people. God's truth was a powerful force, but Jesus realized that words alone were not enough to win the people's support. So after hours of deep thought, Jesus came to the conclusion that special spiritual forces had to be summoned in order to attract people's attention. It was at this point that Jesus decided to ask God's permission to use his spiritual power on a larger scale.

Days later, on the Sabbath, Jesus went to the local synagogue in Capernaum, where he spoke powerfully to the astonished gathering. Suddenly while he was speaking, a man possessed by a demon rushed into the synagogue. He was raging as he approached Jesus, pointing a finger at him.

"What do you want from us, Jesus of Nazareth?" the man shouted. "Have you come to destroy us? I know you. You are the Holy One of God!"

Jesus knew it was not the man who was talking but rather the evil spirit inside him.

Summoning up his spiritual forces, Jesus ordered the evil spirit to depart from the body of the poor man. Moments later the man seemed to return to normal, a confused look on his face. Seeing what had just happened, the people in the synagogue were bewildered by Jesus' power. Glancing at each other, they wondered aloud who this man could be. Some of them ran out of the synagogue, recounting to the people in the streets what had just witnessed.

Jesus left the synagogue in the company of the two brothers James and John, who were in town for business. While the three of them walked toward the house of Simon and Andrew, the brothers listened intently as Jesus explained how evil spirits influence people to commit sinful actions.

Upon reaching their destination, Simon and Andrew gave a warm welcome to the small group, inviting them inside.

After everyone made themselves comfortable on floor cushions, Jesus smiled at Simon's wife as she entered the room. "We appreciate your hospitality," he said to her.

She didn't respond, giving him a look of annoyance before hurrying outside without serving them any water or food.

"Forgive my wife's attitude," said Simon, visibly embarrassed. "She's quite disturbed that I might interrupt work activities and shirk family duties to spend time with you. Also, my mother-in-law is quite sick. My wife hasn't gotten much rest the past few weeks."

"What is ailing your mother-in-law?" inquired Jesus, his eyes full of concern.

Simon replied, "She is confined to bed and is very weak, with fever."

"Well, let's offer God's love to her," said Jesus, rising to his feet.

As Jesus followed Simon into the dimly lit room, he saw a frail, elderly woman laid up in bed. Moaning in agony, she raised her head slightly and stared at the two men, her small eyes set deep in her swollen face. "Who are you?" she asked faintly.

Simon said rather loudly, "Mother, you have a special visitor. Jesus' a rabbi from Nazareth."

"Have you been sick long?" asked Jesus, moving to her side.

"Yes, Rabbi. I cannot breathe well, and my skin feels like it's on fire," said the woman, barely finding the strength to talk.

Kneeling next to the bed, Jesus held her hand with a loving look on his face.

"Pray for me, Rabbi," the woman implored him.

"Don't worry. Soon the sickness will leave you." Glancing at the doorway, Jesus saw that Simon's wife had returned, and she was glaring at him.

He gave her a reassuring smile, then set his hands on her mother's head, just above the temples. Then closing his eyes, he spoke in a commanding tone, "Fever! I order you to leave this woman!"

Almost immediately, the woman's body went slack, and an invisible power entered her and spread throughout every part of her body.

"Rabbi, what is this sensation inside of me?" she said, puzzled. "The fever is vanishing!" She looked at her daughter, who was moving closer to the bed.

"Mother, how do you feel?" she asked, her eyes wide with wonder.

"It is a miracle!" she exclaimed. "I feel fresh and rejuvenated." She put her hands out. "Help me to get dressed," she said, beaming. "I want to serve these men!"

Simon and Jesus returned to the front room, talking and laughing with the others. Minutes later, Simon's mother-in-law stepped into view with clear eyes and a grateful smile. "Oh, Rabbi!" she said, at a loss as to how to thank him.

"Your bright spirit is gratitude enough," Jesus said, pleased to see her looking healthy again. Soon the food and drink were on the table, and Jesus gave thanks to the Lord God for the nourishment and warm friendship of Simon's family.

Simon's wife was still quiet and a bit standoffish with Jesus. Though she was thankful for the healing power of his prayers, she remained firm in her desire for Simon to remain in Capernaum to care for his family, and not to wander about the land with Jesus and the others.

Late that afternoon, small groups of people from the area started coming to Simon's house, for they had heard rumors about Jesus' actions at the synagogue earlier in the day.

They brought with them all kinds of sick people, requesting that Jesus heal them. Laying his hands on their heads, he prayed strongly and, by the power of his faith, expelled the evil spirits who possessed those men, women, and children.

Jesus slept at Simon's house that night as a half-moon journeyed across the starlit sky above Capernaum. About an hour before dawn, Jesus awoke abruptly and left the house, searching for a solitary place to pray. That was how he began each day ever since he had pledged to God to assume his responsibility as the Messiah. In fact, early morning prayer had become such a part of his life that he couldn't imagine starting his day without it.

About mid-morning, Simon, Andrew, James, and John went to look for Jesus. They found him by the lake, gazing at the sunbeams dancing upon the ripples of the water.

"Teacher!" Simon called out. "There are people at my house who are asking for you."

Jesus gave no answer, his eyes fixed on the boats on the water.

"Is something wrong?" Simon said worriedly.

Jesus turned his face toward the men. "You will understand God only if you learn to love Him," he whispered, moving his eyes back to the lake.

He lapsed into silence again for a minute, then looked at the four men. "You have seen what God allows me to do. However, I don't heal people so they can continue to live a sinful life, ignorant about God. The power you have witnessed has no meaning if my deeds are not followed by a deep understanding of God's truth. I heal people so they and others can make a connection to me and listen closely to what I teach."

His eyes searched their faces. "Do not take my words lightly. People have to understand my teachings in order to change their bad habits and replace them with new ones in accordance with their divine human nature."

Simon and the other three stood motionless, afraid to speak as Jesus stared at them with piercing eyes. "Simon, why do you want me to come with you?" he snapped in irritation. "The people shut their ears to me. They aren't interested in me as a man of God. All they want from me is to cure infirmities and liberate them from evil spirits!"

After a long moment of silence, John spoke up in a respectful tone. "Master, we follow you not to receive favors but to receive God's love and truth."

Andrew nodded in agreement. "We believe your words come from God. I heard John the Baptist testify so. I listen to your teachings so I can better understand who you are and what you hope to accomplish."

Simon looked at his brother disapprovingly, then turned his gaze on Jesus. "What do you actually want from us?" he said in a confrontational tone. "Do you want us to leave our families and follow you blindly around Israel from one poor village to another?"

Not surprised by Simon's outburst, Jesus listened quietly, and then Simon added in a brusque tone, "How can we do it? Who will take care of our families?" His voice rose in anger. "You want us to leave our hometowns merely to watch you cast out demons and cure people of disease? I will not accept such a life, and neither will Andrew, James, or John." He shot his brother a threatening look. "You have to remain here and help with our fishing!"

Andrew began to object, but Simon held up a quick hand and added curtly, "Jesus, you know what I think? Those people weren't really sick but weak in their minds, and you somehow convinced them of your *miraculous* healing powers, which made them feel better, maybe just for the moment."

Although Jesus was smiling, he spoke in a sad, weary tone. "Simon, why do you have such little faith? You have heard my words, and yesterday

you witnessed how I cured your mother-in-law, along with many others."
Shielding his eyes from the sun, he added flatly, "Since you are the oldest
here, you like to exert your authority and control Andrew and the other
two brothers, eh?"

Making no comment, Simon wilted a little as the others stared at him.

"Why are you so stubborn?" Jesus continued sternly, yet there was
no judgment in his voice. "You know you have power and prestige in this
area. So you don't wish to humble yourself before me or the other men
here."

Simon lowered his gaze under the watchful eyes of Andrew, James,
and John.

Putting a firm hand on his broad shoulders, Jesus added in a lighter
tone, "Why do you continue to look down upon me? Simon, don't let my
appearance cloud your judgment. You and most others are expecting the
Messiah to come in a glorious form. But here I am in humble clothes, an
unknown man, with no wealth or social position."

Pausing, Jesus studied the faces of the four men with a sudden intensity they had never seen. "When Moses led the Israelites out of Egypt and
toward the Promised Land, was he attired in fine raiment? He was draped
in God's love and armed with God's truth and power! It is no different
now. The Lord is my Heavenly Father and provides everything for me."

Finding his voice, Simon said in a subdued manner, "Rabbi, I have
no doubts that you are a special man with high knowledge and strong
willpower. But we are just ordinary fishermen with no religious training.
How can we be certain that listening to you and following you is what the
Almighty wants us to do?"

Simon paused, looking at the others. "With our limited education
and experience, how can we make the right decision? The Pharisees and
scribes are the ones best prepared to decide the matter."

Andrew and the others didn't respond, but turned to Jesus to hear his
thoughts.

After short contemplation, he said with a look of concern, "Simon,
just as the Lord God cannot force humankind to have faith in Him, I
cannot force you or others to have faith in me." He scanned their faces for
some support. "If you are unwilling to follow me at this time, then I will
not push you ..." His voice trailed off. "May God be with all of you," he
said in parting, then walked off in the direction of Bethsaida.

During the next few weeks, Jesus traveled to nearby villages and
towns. He spoke to various groups of people, always stressing God's

profound love for His lost children who had come under Satan's dominion. He would speak about the purpose of the Messiah's coming, but he never revealed his true identity and his ultimate mission, as he had done with the four fishermen.

Many people came to hear Jesus out of curiosity, but they cared little about the spiritual richness of his teachings. Very few gave much thought to whether God's divine nature was a part of their own nature, nor did they give serious consideration to the presence of evil in their lives, for they doubted the existence of Satan and evil spirits who could manipulate human affairs.

Although Jesus felt lonely and frustrated at times, he met many generous individuals who welcomed him into their homes. Sometimes members of an entire family would receive him with open hearts, thirsting to hear his words. But how much, he wondered, did they really understand about his teachings and about his nature?

About three weeks later, Jesus returned to Capernaum. How he longed to find loyal followers who could understand the depths of his heart!

The day after his arrival, he went in search of the four fishermen, walking toward the area of the lake where they usually kept their boats. He knew that if he could convince Simon to follow him, then the other three men would give themselves without hesitation, and Philip and Bartholomew would follow as well. Since this group of six men were the best Jesus had found so far, his hopes rested on them quickly joining him in his effort to bring the people of Israel to a deeper understanding of God's will to establish the heavenly kingdom on earth through him.

As he approached the muddy shore of the lake, Jesus found Andrew on his anchored boat, bending over and muttering angrily to himself as he separated a rope that had become entangled with some nets. Since Andrew didn't notice him, Jesus kept silent and prayed for him and the others, hoping he could touch the depths of their souls before his departure.

When Andrew straightened up to wipe the sweat off his brow, he noticed Jesus on the shoreline, staring at him with a humorous expression.

"Good day, teacher!" he said, waving to him. "Do you find my labors amusing?"

"Amusing and inspiring!" he replied with a chuckle. "Where are the others?"

"James and John are fishing. They won't return until later this afternoon."

Jesus stepped onto the cluttered deck of the boat and stood next to Andrew, draping an arm over his shoulder. "During my recent travels, I thought about you and your brother often. By the way, where is Simon?"

"In the city, selling yesterday's catch."

Sitting on a barrel of hooks, Jesus began to help untangle the rope and nets.

After a few minutes, he said offhandedly, "Is Simon still skeptical?"

"Yes, he has severe doubts. If he weren't so busy with worldly tasks, he could perhaps take the time to consider the matter more seriously."

Jesus said nothing as he concentrated on what he was doing, his thick fingers surprisingly adept at sliding the rope through the tiny holes of the nets.

After a short while, Andrew said reflectively, "I think my brother is hiding his true feelings behind his work and family. He also still wants to believe that the Messiah will come in a grand and dignified manner."

"What about you?" said Jesus, glancing at him. "Initially you and John showed great interest in following me."

Looking downcast, Andrew said, "You know that I want to come with you. But Simon has the final word." A regretful note entered his voice. "He already let me spend a few months with John the Baptist. And what good did that do?"

Jesus looked up from the nets. "Your experience with John led you to me."

"True," said Andrew, smiling at him.

"Will you and Simon be fishing in this area tomorrow?"

He shook his head. "For several days we're going to fish the waters near Gennesaret. James and John will fish alongside us. Whatever we catch will be sold there."

"Very well then," said Jesus, as he finished untangling the rope and nets. He rose to his feet.

The next day after his early morning prayers, Jesus took the road toward the fishing town of Gennesaret. Upon his arrival, he stood in the center of the town and began preaching in a deep, sonorous voice. Within minutes, people gathered around him, listening closely to his words.

About noontime the following day, Jesus was preaching to an even larger number of people who were eager to hear his words. Many couldn't see him or hear him well due to the great number of people who pushed their way closer to him.

Realizing the situation was getting out of hand, Jesus moved backward from the crowd. Turning, he was relieved to see James and Simon's boats near the shoreline, with Andrew, James, Simon, and John ashore cleaning their nets.

Coming up to the four men, he admonished them, "Why are you sitting here? You should support me during my sermon." Focusing on Andrew's drawn face, he said in a hurt tone, "Didn't you know it was I, your teacher, who was surrounded by the multitude?"

Feeling an onrush of shame, Andrew kept his eyes lowered as Simon spoke up in a dull tone. "Sorry, Jesus, but since we caught few fish this morning, we plan to go out again tonight. We have to finish mending and cleaning our nets."

"Simon, do you really believe that cleaning your nets is more important than cleaning your souls?" He turned back to the other men, sensing the repentance in their hearts. Somewhat mollified, he glanced at the boats and said in a milder voice, "Let me stand on your boat so the people can see me better."

Simon nodded silently, getting to his feet. In silence, he and Jesus stepped onto the fishing boat and braced themselves as the other men pushed it away from the shore into the calm waters of the lake.

A minute later the boat was anchored about fifteen meters offshore, with Jesus standing erect upon the bow while surveying a crowd of over five hundred people, which included a number of local rabbis and other religious authorities.

After gathering his thoughts, Jesus started to preach to the people, Simon occasionally rowing back and forth to keep the bow facing the shoreline. For the next thirty minutes, Jesus gave a powerful talk about the sorrowful, anguished heart of the Lord God, who had lost His children to the Evil One. Although James, John, and Andrew continued working on their nets, all three listened to Jesus as he explained how God had been working day and night for thousands of years to save mankind, preparing Israel for the Messiah, the Second Adam. Many people in the crowd were brought to tears by Jesus' profound explanation of things. When he finished speaking, most of the crowd dispersed and returned to their homes. But a small number of men and women lingered in the area, hoping to get a closer look at this Jesus, who was very different from other rabbis.

As Simon began to pull up the anchor, Jesus stepped over to him. "The winds have changed," he said, surveying the open expanse of the waters. "Simon, these are perfect conditions to catch a great number of fish."

Giving him a skeptical look, Simon laughed gruffly. "So now you are an expert fisherman, as well as the Messiah, eh?"

Jesus' lips curled into a smile. "Let's not waste time with idle talk," he said bluntly.

"Listen, we were out all night with no results," Simon continued. "This isn't the right time to fish in this area. After some rest, we'll throw the nets into the water on our way back home. Hopefully we can catch something then."

"Load the nets onto the boats now," insisted Jesus.

"We won't catch anything!"

"Do as I say!" stated Jesus, staring into his eyes.

Throwing up his hands in frustration, Simon rowed the boat to shore and told the others to quickly load the nets and gear onto both boats.

Shortly after, the two boats were well out in the middle of the lake, James and John on their boat, Jesus with Simon and Andrew.

Grasping firmly onto Simon's arm, Jesus said in a low voice, "Why is your faith in me so small? What do I have to do to gain your loyalty?"

Trying not to lose his temper, Simon shook his arm free and looked across the waters, sure there were no fish to be caught on this day.

Jesus leaned closer to him. "I know my humble appearance bothers you. But my grandeur resides in my relationship with the Heavenly Father."

After a while, Simon shouted over the strong winds, "Sorry, I don't mean to be disrespectful. But all I see is a poor carpenter who preaches words different from the law and Scriptures."

"I come with a deeper truth and higher power than Moses and the prophets." Exhaling an immense sigh, he glanced to his left as Andrew stepped closer to them. "Simon, if you do not have faith in my words and healing powers, then I will demonstrate my powers over God's creation!"

With puzzled looks, Simon and Andrew watched silently as Jesus moved to the bow of the boat, his eyes scanning the waters of the lake. Then he held out his right arm and uttered a deep prayer just below his breath.

After a short minute, Jesus turned slightly and said to the two brothers, "Throw your nets into the water!"

Simon shook his head. "It's a lot of work throwing out and pulling in these large nets. We tried fishing all night but came up with nothing!"

"Oh man of little faith," he said, frowning at him then promptly adding in a commanding tone, "Throw out your nets!"

Simon and Andrew gave each other helpless looks, then got down to work and tossed the nets into the choppy waters. Within a matter of seconds, they noticed schools of fish swimming just below the surface. Simon felt a surge of excitement when he noticed several big fish flying out of the water near the stern of the boat.

When James and John saw the large schools, they rushed over to their nets and threw them into the waters. Minutes later the nets of both boats were laden with fish, and it took all the strength the men could muster to pull them into the boats.

For the next hour or so, the four men kept throwing their nets into the water, and under the calm eyes of Jesus, each time pulled in greater loads of fish. Soon, the boats were so heavy with the catch that they barely floated atop the rough waters.

When the men had exhausted all their strength, the excitement in Simon's heart turned into shame and remorse. Tears in his eyes, he fell to his knees and looked up at Jesus' placid face. "Rabbi, can you ever forgive me for not having faith in you?"

"Simon, do you believe in me now?" he asked plainly.

He nodded. "Yes, my Lord … I am only an ordinary, slow-witted man. I judged you wrongly. Can you forgive me? I am unworthy to even be in your presence!"

Seeing the tears in his eyes, Jesus looked at him with compassion and helped him to his feet. "It is God's desire for the children of Israel to believe in me through my words. If you had accepted my words and trusted me, this miracle would not have been necessary. Due to your lack of faith, I had no choice but to expend precious spiritual power to convince you."

Simon was motionless, his head bowed contritely. Andrew, James, and John fixed their gaze on Jesus, fully understanding for the first time that he was the Anointed Son of Almighty God. He nodded sheepishly.

"Master, my judgment was wrong." Wiping his reddened eyes, he added with conviction, "The love and power you have shown us testifies that you are the Anointed One whom Israel has been waiting for. I will follow you anywhere! I pledge this in the names of my parents, grandfathers, and their fathers and grandfathers!"

Smiling again, Jesus put his hands on his shoulders. "From now on, your name will be Peter, and you will be a true fisherman of the people!"

"You're changing my name?"

Jesus nodded, glancing at Andrew. "What is your brother's name?"

"Peter!" he said, laughing along with the others.

Jesus said in a hopeful tone, "Andrew, James, and John ... you too will become great fishermen."

"We'll do our best," said James, a smile flooding his face.

Jesus stretched his arms toward the sky, thankful that God had answered his prayers.

"Let's return to the shore," he said to his new disciples. "Then go into the city and sell the fish among the people. Afterward, we can meet by the boats and discuss our future activities."

After such a miraculous catch, Peter and the others committed their lives to Jesus. The four men knew it wouldn't be easy for their families to accept their decision. They worried about their duties as fathers and husbands. The task now was to reconcile the path of faith with those responsibilities. But Jesus had already made plans, deciding to create a community of fishermen that could provide for the needs for its members, while giving economic support for the spiritual mission they were about to embark upon.

Early that evening, Jesus and his four disciples had a huge feast while discussing various plans for the coming months. Peter, James, Andrew, and John stayed with Jesus for three more days, then sailed back to Capernaum and returned to their homes, knowing they needed the support of their wives.

Peter was determined to convince his wife about his decision to follow Jesus. When he entered the small courtyard of his house, his wife came rushing out the doorway, an anxious look on her face. "Simon!" she exclaimed with a mixture of relief and anger. "What happened? I've been so worried. The other wives and I thought your boats had sunk!"

"Nothing like that," he replied, entering the front room and dropping wearily in a chair at the table. He reached for some nuts, growing fearful of this small lady who had the temper of a wild boar. "The first night we were unsuccessful. We caught nothing. The next morning we met Jesus while he ..."

"Jesus?" she spat out, dropping into the chair next to him. "What was he doing there?"

"Preaching to a huge crowd," answered Peter. "Though James and I planned to sail back here early that evening, fishing along the way, Jesus advised us to go out immediately." Pausing, a wistful look crossed his face as he recalled Jesus standing at the bow of the boat, his arms outstretched and praying for the Lord to send fish to them.

"Amazing," said Peter, smiling at his wife. "Jesus prayed, then told us to cast our nets into the waters. Moments earlier there were no fish, but suddenly big schools of fish surrounded our boats. We caught so many fish that we almost sank."

"Really?" said his wife, unconvinced.

"We sold the whole catch in a matter of hours and made a big profit!" Taking off his sandals, he added in a casual tone, "On the days that followed, we visited some villages, announcing the imminent coming of God's kingdom."

"You … preaching?" she said with a hollow laugh. "Weren't you worried about your wife and children?" she added in vexation.

"Of course." He took a deep breath. "Dear, I have good news. Andrew, James, John, and I have decided to follow Jesus. We are now his disciples …"

"What?" she snapped, leaning forward.

"We're going. I'm serious," he retorted, clasping his hands. "I and the others are convinced that Jesus is the Messiah."

"Simon, are you possessed?" she demanded. "Only a week ago you told me that this Jesus was a madman!"

"We won't be gone long," he promised. "Don't worry. I'm not going to desert our family. I will go with Jesus occasionally, and only a few days at time. When we aren't fishing, we will be preaching."

"Simon, why did you agree to become his disciple?" she cried out. "Did this Jesus put an evil spell on you?"

"Dear, please calm down. I promise not to neglect my family duties. We will always have this house and plenty to eat. When I'm away with Jesus, I can rent out the boats and also get a portion of the catch."

"Where will this man take you? I cannot understand how he could change your mind so quickly."

"It's amazing what Jesus is capable of doing. Our boats were full of fish! And you saw how he cured your mother?"

"My mother got up because she was feeling better." Scowling, she shook her head slowly. "How could you be so foolish as to get excited over a big catch? That was it? This isn't the first time you and Andrew have caught lots of fish."

Peter was annoyed by his wife's lack of faith. "Now I understand what Jesus meant by having faith in things unseen," he thought aloud. "Dear, I wish you had been on the boat with us."

With a look of annoyance, she said sharply, "Do Andrew and the others actually plan to follow this Nazarene during the coming months?"

"Yes," Peter said, nodding. He patted her hand, looking at her with sudden intensity. "In both my heart and mind, I am certain that Jesus is the Messiah. But I promise, I will not abandon you or our children."

She made no reply, but abruptly stood up and hurried from the house.

Exhaling a long breath, Peter tried to sort out the whirlwind of thoughts and emotions battling within him. His future was with Jesus, no matter how difficult or dangerous the journey would be on the road ahead.

CHAPTER 22

FOR SEVERAL WEEKS John the Baptist had been imprisoned in Machaerus Fortress, about twenty miles southeast of where the Jordan River entered the Dead Sea.

Herod Antipas hadn't planned to keep John there long. His sole purpose was to inflict a hard lesson upon John, to merely frighten him so he would stop accusing Herod of corruption and immoral behavior.

Initially when Herod heard about the teachings of John the Baptist, he had approved of what John was saying. He believed that John was a good man who encouraged others to comply with God's commandments. Since John had known of Herod's tacit support, there was no conflict between the two men. Yet all this changed when John began to openly criticize Herod for having divorced Phasaelis in order to marry his brother's ex-wife, Herodias.

Due to his large following and popularity, John the Baptist had mistakenly thought that Herod wouldn't dare touch him. But Herod, at the insistence of Herodias, finally decided to arrest John.

Herod's intended "temporary" punishment of John the Baptist soon became a prolonged detention. As the weeks passed, John became more discouraged and frustrated with the situation, losing confidence in himself and his mission, and he couldn't help wondering whether God had abandoned him.

It was during one of those days when Jacob Ben-Zarah and some other disciples came to the prison and visited John in his small, dark cell.

"Teacher, are you feeling well?" asked Jacob Ben-Zarah, his eyes adjusting to the darkness.

With a pale, almost lifeless look to his face, John said in a barely audible voice, "As you can see, this isn't a place for a soul to feel well. That evil, bad-tempered Herod has kept me here far too long."

"He's truly an evil man," whispered Jacob Ben-Zarah, not wanting the guard to overhear his words. Spotting a couple of rats in the corner of the cell, he tried to put a note of hope in his voice. "Master, a few priests are putting some pressure on Herod to set you free."

"But so far, Herod has rejected their requests," added the disciple to his left. "It seems he feels that he has not yet made his point."

"People around Herod have convinced him that you are still a threat to his reign," Jacob Ben-Zarah explained, visibly shaken by his master's sorry state.

In a sudden fit of anger, John hit the wall with a clenched fist and shouted, "That damned, sinful son of the devil! Herod's corrupted soul is condemned to the deepest part of hell!"

Shocked by this outburst, the disciples motioned John to be quiet, as they heard the guards muttering angrily in the narrow passageway outside his cell.

After a long minute of tense silence, John spoke in a hushed voice, "How much longer will Herod keep me prisoner?"

His first disciple said in reply, "He has put conditions on your liberation."

With eyebrows arched, John stared at him without a word.

Jacob Ben-Zarah continued, "Herod told the priests that he won't release you unless you swear to cease accusing him of adultery."

After a moment of thought, John shook his head in disapproval.

His first disciple whispered, "Herod wants you to ignore his behavior. He is convinced it's not God's will for you to pass judgment on him."

With a low grunt, John shook his head again. "I will never accept such a condition! My mission is to reveal the corruption in the hearts of all men, both kings and peasants. Nobody can escape God's judgment! Sins and sinful people must be exposed to the harsh sunlight and undergo divine judgment. Sinful people must repent with tears if they wish to be pardoned and avoid the fire of hell."

After another minute of discussion, Jacob Ben-Zarah realized that John's dark, sullen mood had worsened after being told of Herod's conditions. So he and the other disciples bade John a hasty farewell and left the prison, relieved to be out of such a gloomy, miserable place, which indeed was like hell itself.

The days went by slowly, John confined to his prison cell, with few visitors coming to see him. Sadness, confusion, and disillusionment seemed to overwhelm his soul, and he prayed constantly to be set free so he could return to the Jordan River and continue baptizing people. One evening John dropped to his knees in anguish and gave voice to his broken heart.

In the solitude of his cell, a jumble of thoughts passed through his mind. How was it possible that he, the one chosen to prepare the way for the Messiah, now found himself in prison, cut off from his flock? How could he continue his mission for the Lord? Would he ever be released from prison? Was he here because of a mistake or serious blunder in the recent past? If so, what had he done to incur God's severe disapproval? Certainly it was not God's plan for him to be in prison. Or was it? Could this be a test of some kind?

Reflecting on his past, John realized he had received many privileges as the son of the respected priest Zechariah and Elizabeth. And later in the wilderness, he gained recognition for his humble, austere life. Then when he began preaching and baptizing the people, he was admired by large crowds and venerated by his many disciples and followers, who supported him as he spoke out firmly against haughty secular and religious leaders ... But now he found himself confined in Herod's prison ... Why?

Growing more confused and frustrated by the moment, John directed his thoughts to the recent past and began to ponder over the months leading up to his arrest.

As John recollected certain days and events, images of his younger brother kept surfacing in his mind, and suddenly he recalled Jesus' advice on how to best influence Herod so that he would desire to change his immoral way of life.

Sitting on the old wooden stool in his cell, John rubbed his face in anguish and began to wonder whether he should have heeded Jesus' words. And perhaps he should also have done more for Jesus after receiving the revelation from the Holy Spirit. Could this be the reason? Impossible! He was confined to prison because of Herod's lust for power and pleasure!

Several days later, Jacob Ben-Zarah visited John in hopes of cheering him up, and also to keep him informed about certain events happening outside the prison.

John gave a weak smile as his first disciple entered the dark cell and dipped his head in respect. "Teacher, we continue to baptize, as you have instructed," he reported. "People are still responding to the call to repent and be baptized. Many are anxiously expecting your return. They also inquire about the Messiah. They want to know whether the time of his coming has arrived."

John said nothing, just stared blankly at the stone walls of his cell, trying to figure out what he had done to disserve such mistreatment.

Catching John's attention, Jacob Ben-Zarah added softly, "There are some people who even believe the Messiah has already come. Some people are convinced you are the Anointed One. Teacher, they hope to hear you announce that you are the Messiah. If not, the people expect you to lead them to him."

"How long will I be locked up here?" he growled, pulling at his beard. "There is so much to do! Who can benefit from my idling away in this hellish place? Satan wants to keep me from the people. The forces of evil know the time of the Messiah is near."

"Teacher, it is not easy to identify the Messiah. Yet we know he will assume the throne of Israel, and that he comes from the blood lineage of King David."

The disciple waited for a response, but John remained quiet as he rocked back and forth on the edge of the stool.

"What are your instructions?" asked Jacob Ben-Zarah. "Should we look for the Messiah among those men from the royal bloodline?"

"All of us come from the blood of our father Abraham," uttered John. "The Messiah can come from any of the sons of Israel." He hesitated. "I have meditated a lot recently about the Messiah, and the name of Jesus has resounded over and over in my thoughts."

With a sudden frown, the disciple said in protest, "Teacher! How could Jesus be the Messiah? He and his disciples are our rivals. Jesus' teachings often conflict with your beliefs."

John stared at the floor in contemplation. "I should have listened to him," he confessed, his throat tight. "But I didn't take his advice seriously. He warned me it would be pointless trying to change Herod's morality."

Jacob Ben-Zarah stared at him. "Teacher, do you recall Andrew?"

John shook his head, a faraway look in his eyes.

The disciple said, "Last summer Andrew and his friend John were one of us. But now both men and their brothers are disciples of Jesus. I have spoken to Andrew, and he asserts that you indicated that Jesus is the Messiah."

John took a deep breath, his heart searching for the truth.

After a short while, he uttered faintly, "What is Jesus doing now?"

"He is preaching in Galilee," replied the man, wondering why John didn't answer his question. Subduing his fears, he added in a low voice, "We heard that many people are listening to his teachings. But the majority of them have little faith, and they belong to a low social class. However, many people are coming to Jesus' sermons, and the number of his disciples is increasing as quickly as his fame." He paused. "We know that your mother and his mother are cousins."

John nodded. "We come from the same blood," he said, swallowing hard. "Could it be possible that God has chosen the blood of my family lineage for the salvation of Israel?" he thought aloud. "Is it possible the Messiah comes from my family tree?"

Surprised by the question, Jacob Ben-Zarah tried to consider the matter but was too confused to think clearly.

John said half to himself, "Am I open to receive God's word revealed to me through the mouth of Jesus? Is it possible that my very own relative, whom I have always considered insignificant and a source of shame, the living proof of my father's weakness, is in reality the chosen one of God?"

My father's weakness? thought the disciple with growing bewilderment.

"Teacher, how could your cousin be God's Anointed One?"

With sudden energy, John hopped to his feet. "I want you to find Jesus! Ask him if he is the Messiah … or should we wait for another?"

Taken aback by John's sudden interest in his estranged cousin, Jacob Ben-Zarah made no comment as he tried to recall ever hearing Jesus give a sermon of some kind.

"I want a clear answer from Jesus," stated John, sounding like his old self. "I have to remove all doubts from my mind."

Jacob Ben-Zarah gave a reluctant nod. "Very well. I will do as you request."

"You must ask the question directly to Jesus. Do not ask his disciples. I want the answer from Jesus himself. Understand?" John shoved his disciple toward the cell door.

It wasn't difficult to locate Jesus. For the past week he had been preaching along the northwest shore of the lake between Gennesaret and Capernaum.

Jacob Ben-Zarah and four other disciples loyal to John the Baptist traveled straight to the lake shore, where a large number of people had gathered to hear Jesus speak.

Jacob Ben-Zarah and his companions sat silently, glancing about to see what type of people composed the crowd. While he absently listened to Jesus' sermon about God's work of salvation in Israel, he noticed that many people were ill, and many others were relatives of these suffering people. Jacob Ben-Zarah concluded that most of the crowd were here due to illness, rather than to repent for their sins and to be baptized.

A short while later, Jesus took a break in speaking and told the gathering of people to enjoy their midday meal. John's first disciple and his companions quickly got to their feet and weaved their way through the throngs to where Jesus and some of his disciples were standing.

"Teacher! We bring greetings from John the Baptist."

Jesus recognized him and the others, two of whom had treated him rather shabbily when he had been with John at the Jordan River.

Giving the group a warm smile, Jesus said, "What news about my cousin?"

"Sadly, John is still in prison by order of Herod Antipas," replied Jacob Ben-Zarah.

"Would you like me to speak to Herod?"

Not knowing if Jesus was serious or joking, the man said clumsily, "Do you have some influence with Herod?"

"If I had influence with Herod, would I be here now?"

Not knowing what Jesus meant by this, Jacob Ben-Zarah gave a subtle glance at his companions, who looked as confused as he was with the conversation so far.

Sighing inwardly, John's first disciple looked at Jesus and explained, "Herod has made a condition for John's liberation. He wants John to swear that, once outside of prison, he won't speak badly of the king, particularly by accusing Herod of corruption and immoral conduct."

"As I told John before, he alone cannot resolve sin and evil. Only the Messiah can solve these dire problems." Jesus paused, surveying the faces of John's disciples. Then he looked back to Jacob Ben-Zarah again. "John cannot win a confrontation with Herod. In the moral battle to establish God's kingdom in Israel, Herod will be the last to accept the word of God and give up his crown. The crown of Israel belongs to the true king, the envoy of God. Herod is blinded by his desire for power, and he will not relinquish his authority willingly."

One of John's disciples spoke up in a haughty tone. "Everyone knows the Messiah will come from the lineage of King David, so that when he becomes king of Israel, nobody can oppose his authority. Even Herod will bow down."

"No, brothers," said Jesus, shaking his head. "He has come in silence and in humble circumstances. God promised to send the prophet Elijah, who is to prepare the people of Israel to welcome him."

"I have heard that you believe our master to be the returning Elijah. But Elijah will descend directly from heaven!" said Jacob Ben-Zarah.

"How is possible that John is Elijah?"

"I understand your dilemma," Jesus replied, with a look of sympathy. "John is not the prophet Elijah himself. However, in a spiritual sense John, has inherited Elijah's mission. As the angel told his father, he was born in the spirit and power of Elijah to prepare the way for the Messiah."

"Teacher, we know that you and John are cousins …"

Jesus held up a hand. "Actually we are brothers, like Cain and Abel, Shem and Ham, Jacob and Esau …"

"What?" said Jacob Ben-Zarah, looking dumbfounded as he recalled John's utterance in prison. "Jesus, you claim John and you are brothers, of the same father?"

"Yes, we are half-brothers," replied Jesus, noticing that his own disciples were just as surprised as John's followers.

After a long moment, Jacob Ben-Zarah dipped his head in respect.

"Teacher, you speak with authority. John has sent us to ask you a special question. Are you the Messiah, or should we wait for another one?"

Feeling the anger surface in his heart, Jesus stared at him in silence.

An urgent tone entered Jacob Ben-Zarah's voice. "Teacher, we beg you to clearly tell us who you are. If John is to take on the mission of Elijah, he doesn't want to be mistaken when he announces the Messiah."

"My brother knows who I am!" Jesus said. "He received the testimony of the Holy Spirit at the Jordan, and I have already explained my position to him! But he has failed in his duty."

One of John's disciples spoke up. "Apparently John is reconsidering the matter."

"To speak the truth?" Jesus demanded in anger. "The truth is that you and John should be with me now. If John had listened to me, I wouldn't have needed to go into the desert for forty days and then search the land for my own disciples. Precious time has been wasted!"

Surprised by Jesus' tone, John's disciples looked at one another, not sure what to do.

Red in the face, Jesus turned and told Peter and James to find the sick people in the crowd who needed special attention. Then moving his eyes back to Jacob Ben-Zarah, he added, "What is past is past. John and I can still unite, and together we can all build the kingdom of our Heavenly Father. Tell John that I need his support, but he must get out of prison as quickly as possible. He must not waste any more time with Herod. Tell him to simply agree to Herod's demands."

"Teacher," interrupted one of John's disciples, "you have not answered our question."

"My Father has granted me His power. You go and tell John what you have seen and heard. The blind people receive their sight, the disabled walk, the leprous ones are cleaned, the deaf hear, the dead come alive, and the word of God is being spread."

Jesus used the words of the prophet Isaiah to convey the message to his brother, who well knew the Scriptures and would understand the meaning of Jesus' response.

"Blessed are those who don't feel offended by my words," Jesus added.

Hearing this, the disciples of John began to walk away, but stopped when they heard Jesus speak to those around him, "What did you go to see in the desert? Somebody unimportant? Somebody wearing luxurious clothes? No, because people who dress well are in the palaces of kings. Who were you looking for? A prophet? John is more than a prophet. For God has chosen him to meet the Messiah personally, to receive him and assist him with his heavenly mission."

Jesus spoke these words to the astonishment of the various folk who were gathered there listening.

"Although earlier prophets had announced his coming, they did not have the blessing to live alongside the Messiah," continued Jesus. "But John the Baptist has the privilege to testify directly to the Messiah. Yet if he fails his mission, he among the prophets will be the lowest in the kingdom of heaven."

Jesus stood in front of the crowd, aware of the lingering presence of John's disciples. He gathered his thoughts and stepped over to Jacob Ben-Zarah. "There is one way for John to reconnect with God's will. He must openly admit his mistake and be willing to listen me."

When Jesus had finished preaching and healing the lame and the sick, the disciples of John left the area silently. Each man was a bit over-whelmed by the strong impression Jesus had left upon them, and they tried to sort out their clashing thoughts as they undertook their return trip to the prison.

It was about a week later when three disciples of John the Baptist visited the prison to report their encounter with Jesus.

"Teacher," said Jacob Ben-Zarah, feeling sick at heart when he saw John's hollow cheeks and lifeless eyes, "I'd never realized it before, but Jesus has much charisma, especially when speaking in front of large crowds. Though he affects them, I doubt they have a deep understanding of his message. We noticed that when he finished speaking, he was left with only a small group of faithful followers. In fact, even those who a moment before were astonished by his words return to their occupations and their own lives."

Positioned on the wooden stool, John considered this for a moment. "Then why do the people gather around him in such high numbers?"

"I believe most people respond to Jesus because they want to be cured, while others go out of curiosity."

"I agree," remarked another disciple. "While Jesus was speaking, I noticed only a handful of people who were listening intently to his words …" Pausing, he released a dry laugh. "… which according to him come directly from the Lord God on High!"

Though the others laughed, John's face was set in a hard frown as his thoughts drifted back over time. He vaguely recalled segments of conversations with his brother, some in which Jesus had spoken about the divine nature of God, and how humans were meant to inherit His nature and be lords over the entire creation, even the angels.

Expelling a low, sorrowful sigh, John turned his attention back to Jacob Ben-Zarah and the others. "Did you approach Jesus and speak to him?"

"Yes. We asked if he were the One, but he didn't answer directly." At this point, Jacob Ben-Zarah repeated word for word what Jesus had stated.

John the Baptist took a deep breath of the stale air and closed his eyes. When he opened them, his first disciple gestured at the other and added in a faint voice, "Though we cannot be certain, we all agree that Jesus implied that he was the one we are waiting for. Yet, how can we be sure?"

Another disciple chimed in, "Teacher, much of his sermon was difficult to understand, and even harder to accept."

To his left stood an older disciple, who spoke without malice. "Though Jesus is a clever fellow, he's really nothing but a carpenter who has convinced a small group of fishermen that he is some kind of anointed one." A hard note entered his voice. "Jesus talks about God as if He is his actual father. That kind of relationship between him and God is not easy to understand or believe."

Jacob Ben-Zarah added, "Jesus' so-called *Father in Heaven* wants him to share love with all people, even the Gentiles!" With a low grunt, he shook his head. "Jesus spoke about Cain's jealousy of Abel, and then he had the audacity to claim he was your brother."

John had no reaction to his chief disciple's implication that he and Jesus were actually brothers and not cousins.

John stood in silence, and as his mind again searched for memories of past conversations with his younger brother, certain words resounded in his mind. "As you heard with your own ears," uttered John, staring blankly at the cell walls, "Jesus teaches that the best way to understand the Lord is by relating to Him as a loving parent. One time Jesus told me that God is longing for love from His children, just as we long for His parental love."

Perplexed, the disciples glanced at one another, with Jacob Ben-Zarah saying, "How is it possible for the all-powerful God to desire the love of sinful people?"

Sighing again, John asked. "What else did Jesus say?"

"Jesus advises that you consent to Herod's conditions for your freedom."

Looking vexed, John said, "If I decide to unite with Jesus, then I assume he becomes my teacher … and I become his disciple?"

Jacob Ben-Zarah and the others made no reply, but gave limp shrugs as they inched closer to the cell door. "As we entered town this morning," whispered Jacob Ben-Zarah, "I noticed some of Jesus' followers near the marketplace."

John nodded absently and turned away from them as they quietly left the cell and spoke in hushed whispers to the guards.

During the next hour, John the Baptist considered what his disciples had reported to him. While recalling his past discussions with Jesus, he also pondered whether he should follow Jesus' advice and consent to Herod's conditions.

In contemplation, John found the courage to reconsider his thoughts and perceptions about his younger brother. After a long period of prayer and reflection, he finally grasped the magnitude of his terrible mistake and concluded that Jesus, his half-brother from the paternal line, was indeed the Messiah and needed his help to fulfill God's will.

Realizing that he should promptly make peace with Herod, John approached the cell door and called for the guards.

"What is it?" growled a burly guard.

"I need to speak with your superior!"

Minutes later, the head of the guards appeared. "What?"

"I want you to deliver a message to Herod."

"What makes you think Herod wants to hear from you, Baptist?"

"He will. I now see I was wrong," said John, swallowing his pride. "Go to Herod and tell him that I accept his conditions."

"John," said the guard, now in a more kindly voice, "I cannot promise anything, but I'll try to get your message to him."

The following afternoon John was half sleeping when he heard the faint sound of approaching steps on the stone floor of the passageway.

Shaking himself, John got to his feet and focused his blurry vision on the rough face of the head guard. "I've been told that Herod cannot be bothered now with your problems. He's preparing a festivity for his birthday tomorrow. So I was advised to wait a few days to deliver your message."

John began to protest but quickly held his tongue.

The following evening Herod held a huge birthday banquet for himself, attended by many high officials, military and social leaders of Galilee and Perea. Nebat was there, and both he and Herod shared ill feelings for John the Baptist, believing that he represented a constant threat to their various interests throughout the region.

Everyone at the banquet that evening was delighted to know that Herod still had John the Baptist confined to prison. Under pressure from Nebat, many guests had suggested to Herod that he punish John with greater severity. But Herod merely smiled and waved away their requests, for he secretly believed that John was a righteous man, who still had much influence with the common people.

During the festivity, the daughter of Herodias entered the banquet room. Salome was covered with transparent garments, revealing the curves of her naked body underneath. Prompted by Nebat, she danced for Herod and his guests, her seductive movements igniting an intense sexual desire in the king.

When Salome finished, Herod still felt stimulated by her lovely body and the euphoria of the festivity. So he asked her to dance again, promising in front of everyone to give her whatever she asked for afterward. She consented and danced for Herod. Then she scurried over to her mother and inquired what she should request from the king.

Herodias, who despised John the Baptist, advised her daughter to ask for his head. Armed with the wishes of her mother, Salome returned to the chamber. In front of all the guests, she asked Herod to command his soldiers to kill John the Baptist, then cut off his head and bring it to her on a big platter.

Herod was both surprised and appalled by such a vile request, but he knew that he couldn't go back on his promise to Herodias' daughter, especially in front of so many important people at his banquet.

As Herod surveyed the people staring at him in anticipation, he saw the consensus in their eyes. Trapped by his foolish promise, he had no choice but to order his soldiers to go to the prison and do as Salome requested.

It being a moonless night, the soldiers brought torches with them, flooding John's dark cell with harsh light. Confused by the sudden commotion around him, John got to his feet, wide-eyed and terrified as he looked at the soldiers. Seeing the fierce looks on their faces, his heart began pounding inside his chest.

A tall, muscular soldier grabbed John by the hair. "Are you ready?" he jeered gruffly, brandishing a sharp, heavy sword.

Is Herod trying to frighten me? John thought frantically, then pleading with the Lord to spare his life so he could join his brother. John wasn't afraid to die, but he wanted to continue living for the sake of the Messiah.

"Oh, Lord! Please forgive me!" he gasped in anguish, his mouth so dry that he could barely talk. Tears ran down his cheeks as a husky soldier kicked hard at his stomach, knocking him backward onto the stool.

With a dazed look, John struggled to his feet. "Forgive me, God!" he sobbed in despair as the image of Jesus' sorrowful eyes flashed through his mind.

Then John felt one soldier put his hands on his shoulders, bearing down with all his weight and forcing John to his knees. The husky soldier grasped him by his hair, pulling his head forward as the muscular one lifted his heavy sword in the air and swung downward through John's neck, severing his head from the rest of his body. The soldiers laughed as blood splattered on the floor. The husky soldier held John's head up in the air as though it were a trophy.

Within the hour, a large platter with the severed head of John the Baptist was carried into the dining room, amid raucous laughter and horrified gasps.

Sick to his stomach, Herod turned his eyes away from the gruesome sight and ordered his servants to give the tray to Salome, who then took it to Herodias.

When the disciples of John heard about his death, they went to the prison and took what remained of their leader to conduct a proper burial.

My husband, who until then was hoping for his brother to unite with him, found himself alone. Herod had taken away his Elijah.

Once the disciples of John had buried him, they went to inform Jesus about the death of his brother. Upon hearing the news, Jesus went to a silent place and prayed for the spirit of his brother. In his spiritual self, Jesus made a visit to the world beyond, where he met with his brother. With a strong embrace, Jesus expressed his sorrow to John for the violent death that had been inflicted on him. John, knowing that he was physically dead, was astonished to see Jesus communicating with him in the shadowy realm. Three days after his death, when his spiritual body and mind were prepared, John entered the eternal spiritual world.

There was nothing else for Jesus to do but be resigned to the loss of his brother, his Elijah, the one whom he had wanted to be his right hand.

Jesus knew that from now he had to walk with care, for Herod had shown there was no limit to what he would do to protect his position.

Some of John's disciples started to follow Jesus, but Jacob Ben-Zarah, who was still proud of having been John's first disciple, did not. Most of John's disciples returned to their old lives; a few continued baptizing but attracted few worshippers. However, Jesus, flanked by a growing number of disciples and followers, continued preaching while moving about from one area to another.

Local religious authorities growled like dogs, sensing an intruder near their flocks. In their arrogance, these religious leaders thought of themselves as the only conveyors of God's truth. So they decreed that their flocks should listen to only them and avoid Jesus and his followers. Certainly they felt threatened by Jesus, even though they considered him unworthy to teach about God and other spiritual matters.

It was during these days that many people, inspired by his words and healings, joined Jesus' flocks. But the Pharisees tried to dissuade people from following Jesus. When they and other religious authorities couldn't dissuade the new converts, they would put pressure on their relatives, hoping they could pull the converts away from Jesus.

When some of Jesus' followers wouldn't change their minds, the Pharisees would threaten to inform the military authorities. This usually frightened new converts, whose faith was like that of a child's belief in magic. So Jesus often warned his disciples and new followers to be wary of these deceitful practices.

Sadly, due to the death of John the Baptist at the hands of Herod, God's plan for John was thwarted, and now Jesus could not openly announce that he was the Messiah. He had to proceed cautiously and increase his influence and prestige before confronting the religious authorities. Although he continued to do miracles and give God's message, he instructed his disciples not to reveal who he was.

CHAPTER 23

THE CROWD GATHERED AROUND JESUS, most faces marked by the sorrows and hardships of life, their hearts yearning to hear words of hope that could give them the strength to bear their suffering. Jesus continued to convey the words of God to these weak, weary, and disillusioned sheep without a shepherd.

As Jesus stood on a grassy rise and surveyed their faces, he wanted to embrace each person and give God's love to them, inspiring them to live for God and all people. But he had only two legs and one mouth, which limited his ability to give his total attention to every person in the large crowd. He needed loyal followers who could understand his teachings, who could feel the call of God, and who were willing to devote their lives to spreading God's message. "The harvest is plentiful, but the workers are few," Jesus said to the crowd. "Ask the owner of the harvest to send more workers to the field."

Sadly, among Jesus' close followers there were only a few who were prepared to unite with him completely, who were willing to leave everything behind, who could ignore personal desires and obligations and distractions in order to dedicate themselves to a spiritual life, willing to assist him with all their hearts, minds, and bodies.

After the death of his brother, Jesus began to vigorously instruct his close followers. Jesus wanted to give his personal attention to as many of these men as possible, so he traveled about Galilee to meet with them. Since he felt responsible for their spiritual lives, he spoke to them as a father. At the same time, he observed the content of their characters, looking for those among them who displayed a strong desire to receive and understand his words.

To accomplish his mission, Jesus had to find committed followers who would not only spread the message of love in their own villages, but also be willing to travel with him when asked. For this, he had to be careful in selecting each one. One night, he prayed ardently to God for guidance, spending the entire night on his knees, with tears streaming down his cheeks. As the sun rose the next morning, Jesus had twelve men in mind.

His determination set, Jesus traveled from one town to the other to meet with the men, inviting each to travel with him to the next town. About a week later, Jesus and the twelve he had chosen gathered together in Capernaum. They were Simon Peter and his brother Andrew, James (son of Zebedee) and his brother John, Philip, Bartholomew, Matthew, Thomas, James Ben-Alpheus, Simon the Zealot, Judas Ben-James (also called Thaddeus), and Judas Iscariot.

Jesus wanted to build a strong bond among them. So they hiked up a nearby mountain, bringing enough provisions to last for three days. When the group of thirteen reached the upper slopes of the mountain, the air was fresh, with a magnificent view of the lake in the valley below.

"What a spectacular day!" exclaimed the young James Ben-Alphaeus, whose family members were Jesus' followers. "Being atop a mountain makes you feel on top of the world," he said, smiling with satisfaction, probably because he was a man of short stature who was used to looking up at people's faces. He was an intense man of fierce loyalty, and he was prepared to follow Jesus to the ends of the earth.

"Surely the Lord God knows how to please human eyes," remarked Simon, who was called the Zealot due to his past affiliation with the group of the same name, mostly Jewish radicals from Galilee who resorted to violence to drive the Romans out of Israel. Fortunately, since Simon had come to know Jesus, he had undergone a dramatic change of heart, which helped to restrain his fanatic temperament. Jesus had chosen him because he was a man of passion and courage who liked to accomplish a task as quickly as possible. "This is the land in which God has invested His heart," he added, glancing at the man to his left.

"How true," Matthew affirmed with a nod. Before dedicating his life to the calling of God, Matthew was a tax collector despised by most people. Ironically, months earlier he could have been killed by someone like Simon. The Zealots hated tax collectors; they considered them agents of the pagan Romans, traitors at the service of the occupiers.

"Up here, I feel clean and free," Matthew continued, inhaling the fresh air deep into his lungs. Glad he was no longer hounding people for tax payments, he looked at Simon and said dryly, "It's better to be loved than be hated by people who fear you."

He nodded and gazed at the distant horizon of low hills covered by shrubs and trees.

"Let's make camp there," called out Jesus, pointing to several trees bordering a small clearing about thirty meters to the right. Without waiting for the slower ones to catch up, Jesus set off with long strides over rocks and around prickly shrubs.

Thomas followed a few steps behind him. A devoted follower for almost a year, Thomas was a sensitive and compassionate fellow who loved Jesus with all his heart and soul.

After unpacking their food, water, bedrolls, and other supplies, the thirteen men sat in a circle under two fig trees with leafy branches offering pleasant relief from the afternoon sun. After a few minutes of good-natured banter, everyone grew quiet as Jesus offered a prayer of thanksgiving for the food as well as the weather and good health of everyone present. Soon, goatskin bags full of water were passed around, along with fresh loaves of bread, olives, cheese, fruits, and vegetables.

As the men exchanged stories and opinions about various matters, Jesus listened to the timbre of their voices and studied their facial features, trying to imagine what kind of men they would be a year from now. In one sense, the twelve men were quite ordinary, each with his likes and dislikes. Jesus knew, however, that each man had special talents that could help transform them into powerful instruments of God, helping them to become great preachers and spiritual leaders.

After they had each eaten their share of food, their voices gradually became quieter and their moods more serious. Wanting them to know that his heart was full of love for them, Jesus cleared his throat to gain their attention before speaking. "As some of you have guessed by now, I consider you my best and closest disciples. God wants you to be strong and grow spiritually so that you might strengthen others."

The men glanced at one another, with pleased looks on their faces.

"Indeed, it is our honor to be with you," said Thaddeus. He was a man of humility, well liked by the others. "Master, you have patiently taught us about God, the prophets, and the Scriptures, as any learned Jew would have been taught. Yet, you always give us a deeper understanding."

Matthew added quietly, "We all wish to live godly lives based on the morality of your teaching, so that we might be an example to other people."

"This pleases me," replied Jesus, gazing around the circle of men. "God wants to make each one of you a champion of His truth and love."

"Even at the cost of our lives?" remarked Andrew, sitting next to his friend John.

As Peter began to respond to this, Judas waved a fist in the air and said to him, "The real question is whether you are ready to lose your own life in the struggle to free the Holy Land from the Romans."

Judas was the only non-Galilean in the group, he being from Judea. He was also a Zealot like Simon, his old friend and companion in the struggle to drive out the Romans. Judas had come to know Jesus through Simon. But unlike his close friend, Judas' heart was still full of hate and outrage, preventing him from feeling the presence of God's love and direction in his life. Jesus included him as one of the twelve because he thought that if he could change Judas, he could change the world.

"What I see here," added Judas, "is a group of strong, brave men who can do a better service for our people by taking up arms and fighting our enemies."

Frowning at him, Simon said, "We are Jews, and as such we have God, who sustains us in this savage world."

Surprised, Judas fired back, "Simon, how could you betray your past ideas? Our struggle to defeat the Romans is a just and righteous struggle!"

"Judas, my dear brother," interrupted Jesus, his voice mild, "the Lord God will not send a bloodthirsty Messiah to Israel. God's kingdom is a kingdom of love and not of hate … one of kindness and not of cruelty … one of life and not of death."

Hearing this, Judas shook his head in disapproval. "The Anointed One will come in glory, liberating us from the tyranny of our oppressors."

Jesus stared at him. "The oppressors will cease to be oppressors only if they have a change of heart," he said, the others nodding in agreement. "Sometimes it is a long process to change one's mind, and it requires patience and determination to walk along such a path of goodness. In like manner, Israel has to embrace God's heart."

Thomas spoke up. "I believe what Jesus said. God created all humans with a divine nature, receptive to His call to love and serve one another."

Judas' face softened as he lowered his head in silence, considering their remarks.

"The world can be changed," Jesus said, "only when you come to know God's infinitive love and share that eternal love with even your enemies."

Judas lifted his head, a combative look on his face. "Love our enemies?" he scoffed. "Rabbi, we all wait for the Anointed One to help us regain the glory of King Solomon. If you are he, then lead us against our oppressors. Don't be speaking such nonsense as love your enemies."

Breathing slowly, Jesus thought that due to the hardness of Judas' heart, it would be better not to give a direct answer. He looked in Andrew and Peter's direction. "My intention is to lead the chosen people to victory … but not with violence. Goodness will prevail only if we apply God's truth and become instruments of His love."

Somewhat puzzled, Judas asked, "What is the truth?"

Jesus looked at him with kind eyes, searching his thoughts to find the simplest words to explain it. "To understand and relate to God's divine nature, to understand your divine nature and fulfill it, to discover the origin of sin and evil and how to eliminate it from your life, to know why God has created everything including us, and most importantly to come to the realization that to love and to be loved is what makes our lives worth living. This is the truth."

Judas was more perplexed then ever. "Why did you ask me to join you, then?"

"Because you are a child of God, as are the others here." His tone changed. "Give your soul unconditionally to God, and in return He will give you what your heart requires."

"Rabbi, I give myself to God every day. I am ready to die for God."

"No, you are ready to kill for God … and perhaps be killed in the process."

"I want God's holy land free from pagan rule. The Romans can take their heathen gods with them and leave us alone to let us follow the traditions of our fathers."

"That is my intention," Jesus said, smiling briefly. "But it cannot be achieved with spears and swords, only by embodying God's love and manifesting His truth. We are God's children, and sooner or later each child has to respond to His call of love. We then need to spread God's love and truth across the world to all people."

Judas contemplated for a long moment. "So you contend that our struggle for freedom is futile?"

Jesus took a moment to reply. "I will lead you to victory over the Romans. But it will be with the word of God."

"Rabbi, how can you be certain of such nonsense?" Judas said as he glanced around in search of acceptance from the others. But the other men kept silent, their faces expressionless.

"How can I be certain?" repeated Jesus. "Because it is God's way. Our objective is to conquer people's hearts, and for that, words are more powerful than swords, love more powerful than hate, peace more powerful than violence. "

Judas said sharply, "So you believe that your way is God's way? And this is the only chance for our people to attain peace and freedom?"

"Not only Israel, but the entire world. If we deviate from God's way, there is no hope for Israel or any other land throughout the world."

Judas looked angered by this. "Are you saying that we should include the Romans in God's kingdom?"

"We are all children of God."

Bartholomew tried to fight off a frown. "How is it possible to change the Romans?"

Looking at him, Jesus said, "Regardless of our race or culture, we are all children of God, who breathed His spirit into humanity. This includes even the Romans."

"Even the Romans?" echoed Judas, with another gruff laugh. He looked at the men to his left. "Try to convince the Romans that we are all one!"

Jesus made no comment, but simply reached for some nuts and tossed them into his mouth and lifted his eyes to the sky, praising God for such a lovely day.

After a short while, Bartholomew said with a change of expression, "Jesus, so far you have spoken about God's love and what is right and wrong. Are you going to tell us more about God's nature?"

"Of course." As some of the disciples moved closer, he added offhandedly, "There is so much that I haven't told you. We need to understand the nature of God, along with the reason why God created humankind."

Peter said loudly, "Don't forget about original sin. There is no hope for fallen people if we don't understand that."

Jesus nodded, seeing the look of disgust on Judas' face.

"Once we grasp all this," he soon added, "we can then begin to understand why God created Israel."

The twelve remained silent, contemplating his words.

"As I've taught you many times, the Lord God is our Heavenly Parent. He is an eternal Being of divine love, as well as a Being of absolute principles."

Andrew raised a hand. "Are you referring to the fact that all creatures are either male or female?"

"Yes, that's one of God's principles found throughout the creation."

Peter cleared his throat and said, "Before the creation of man, God was talking to someone. God stated that He was going to create man in His image, along with the image of the creature with whom he was talking. Who was God talking to?"

Jesus closed his eyes a moment, searching for the right words. "As Andrew mentioned, when you observe the creation, you become aware of two fundamental aspects among all creatures. In humans there is man and woman, while among animals there is male and female. There is a male-like and female-like quality even in the flowers, plants, and other vegetation that allows for reproduction. To create human beings in His image means that He made man and woman. It was as if God's masculinity was talking to His femininity."

Jesus paused as a flock of birds passed overhead. He and his disciples glanced at them before moving their eyes to the branch of a nearby tree, where two ravens were perched.

Suppressing a worried frown, Jesus added, "In creating humanity, God duplicated from His masculinity and femininity to form man and woman, with the intent of rejoining them upon the perfection of Adam and Eve. Once the first human beings had reached their spiritual perfection as individuals, they could have united as husband and wife with God's blessing. Then, through their conjugal love, they would have given birth to pure children unstained by original sin, and through forming a family truly connected to God's love they would have inherited the parental heart of God Himself. Adam would carry the perfect masculinity of God, and Eve the perfect femininity. Among all creatures, a perfect Adam and a perfect Eve would have been the supreme representative of God, our Original Father and Mother. So would their children after going through years of spiritual growth and building their own families."

As Matthew began to speak, Judas interrupted. "Rabbi, who are you exactly?"

Jesus turned to him as Simon Peter whispered in irritation, "Judas, be patient and listen, please."

After a moment of silence, Matthew said, "Many people don't believe in the total goodness of man."

"I do," challenged Thomas, staring at him. Some in the group nodded in agreement, while others shook their heads in disapproval.

Peter remarked, "They believe that when God said, 'Let's make man in our image and resemblance,' he was talking to Satan. They think it was already decided that Adam and Eve would be born with both a seed of goodness and one of evil."

"They are mistaken," Jesus responded. "God is absolute goodness, so He would never predestine His children to suffer with such a contradiction. It would be cruel if God had made evil a part of human nature."

Thaddeus asked, "But what if evil is an inherent part of our nature?"

"In that case," replied Jesus, "God would never be able to change the sinful behavior of people. Also, there would be no reason for the coming of the Messiah."

The men stared at him with an uncertain look.

"It is Satan who wants people to think that they were predestined to live with evil nature inside their soul. Satan's aim is to discourage every soul from having any hope in changing human thinking and conduct. Satan wants people to accept the existence of evil as an eternal reality. In doing so, they guarantee the perpetuation of evil and Satan's domain."

Glancing at the men to his right, Judas said, "There is only one reason why God sends the Messiah, and that is to lead the chosen people to fight the occupiers. Everyone here knows it. I don't see any reason to fool each other about it."

Most of the men there gave him an irritated look, while Peter patted his knee and gently begged him to keep silent.

Jesus said, "Truly I say to you, God created humans to be totally good and free."

Philip asked, "Free to choose to do either good or evil?"

"No," replied Jesus. "Originally, freedom was not meant to choose between good and evil, but rather to express in your own way kindness, goodness, and love."

Peter and a few others could see that Jesus spoke as a defender, as one who was determined to protect the reputation of someone he loved more than his own life. That was the Lord God, his Heavenly Parent.

A gentle wind swept over the mountain, stirring the branches of the trees. Casting his eyes in the direction of Judas and Simon Peter, Jesus added in a firm tone, "God created human beings to be lords over all things of the creation. It was the responsibility of the first humans to grow spiritually and reach perfection, to rise as the children of God and thus inherit the entire creation. Sadly, the fall of man complicated the original plan of God. Since Adam and Eve yielded to Lucifer's advances, evil nature arose in the physical world. Then after the physical deaths of Adam and Eve, they entered the spiritual world and brought with them their sins and difficulty to harmonize with the Lord God."

Nobody moved or spoke as they reflected over his words.

Then Jesus talked to them about the archangel Lucifer, the Garden of Eden, the serpent, Eve, the fruit, Adam. He explained the events, the feelings, the mistakes that caused the fall of the first human beings. He told them that self-centered desire for power and self-centered desire for sexual pleasure is the core of the original sin. All human beings have inherited these tendencies, though they are more evident in some than in others.

As the sun began to drop behind the mountainside, Jesus concluded his teachings for that day. During the next hour, each man busied himself with various chores before having supper. For late summer, it was an unseasonably chilly night, so the men placed their bedding near the campfire and exchanged stories for a while before drifting off into deep sleep.

CHAPTER 24

I**T WAS STILL RATHER DARK AND CHILLY** when Jesus awoke. Not wanting to awaken the others, he followed the trail up the mountain and found a clearing with a small boulder. Soon, he began praying intensely for each of the twelve men. He also prayed that God would guide his words, and prayed that his followers, particularly Judas Iscariot, would open their hearts and minds to the truth.

As the sun rose, rays of soft yellow light moved across the land, and robins and sparrows raised their voices in joyful song, welcoming the new day. Soon, the twelve men were up and gathering together for a meal of bread, olives, and dried fruits, along with honeyed wheat-flour cakes, and barley water for drink. After eating, they explored the steep slopes above the camp, hiking up to the clearing where Jesus was standing with his eyes fixed on the distant shores of the lake and the low hills beyond.

When they returned to the camp, everyone was sweating as the sun climbed in the morning sky. They washed their faces with cool water and sat in a circle around the charred wood from the campfire that had burned out after midnight.

Jesus' eyes were red with tears after praying for guidance and inspiration. He sat between Peter and Andrew, and as the light chatter around the circle subsided, the twelve men shifted their bodies, their eyes on Jesus and their hearts full of expectation for the words to follow.

Jesus bowed his head in prayer, and although his was not the traditional Jewish way of prayer, the men mimicked him. He thanked God for allowing them to come together in fellowship as brothers, concluding the prayer with "Amen!" which was echoed by everyone in the circle.

After clearing his throat, Jesus began in a casual tone, "God has chosen you because of your deep hearts and strong characters. If you follow my words, then we will win over people's hearts and they will accept us as God's representatives. Then we can help them to rediscover themselves as children of God, and ultimately change the world."

Thaddaeus said playfully, "Can we also change Judas' scruffy beard?"

Jesus laughed along with the others. "That's a matter between you and Judas," he said mildly, glad to see Judas smiling.

After gathering his thoughts, Jesus added in a level voice, "With the support of the people, along with the devotion and obedience of religious leaders, it will be possible for me to ascend to the throne of Israel. The children of Abraham will rejoice in knowing that their generation is the one chosen to welcome the Anointed One."

With a frown, Judas mumbled something to Simon, but Jesus couldn't make out what he had said. After a moment of silence, he continued, "The key to our victory is for religious, social, and political leaders to understand my words and accept me as their spiritual leader. Without a clear understanding, they will brand me a heretic, while Pontius Pilate and the military authorities will consider me a dangerous rebel. If the Romans believe I intend to incite a revolt, they might raise their swords against the people."

Scowling, Judas said, "The Romans are dogs! Why should we allow dogs to approve of our king?"

In a sudden shift of emotion, most of the other men nodded in agreement.

Ignoring this, Jesus said in a light tone, "The Romans will see that my methods are peaceful and constructive. They will not be opposed to the spontaneous and genuine expression of love."

Judas grunted, folding his arms across his chest. "Jesus, how can believe you will usurp the throne from the Herodians? With love?" he asked with a guffaw.

Jesus gave him a confident nod. "The culture of God is a culture of love and unity. When the Romans realize I am a peaceful person, they won't resist the call of God's people to declare me king of Judea first, and then later king of all Israel. Then I will deal directly with the emperor. Rome will help keep peace as the culture of goodness gains more influence in the region."

"How can that be?" said John, glancing at his brother James. "The Romans are our enemy. They are not here to help God, but rather to insult our dignity and oppress our will."

Jesus looked in his direction. "John, don't forget that this world belongs to Satan, at least until we change it. Sometimes we will have to make compromises according to the circumstances of the time. For now, we need to work with the Roman authorities."

Simon's hands flew up in the air. "Even when they treat us like trash?"

Jesus said in reply, "Once there is a nation led by the Messiah, events will move at a swift pace. As I've told you in the past, Satan always tries to destroy what God builds. That is why we need Rome. With the protection of Rome, no enemies would dare to attack us."

Some of the men still had their doubts. Even Peter shook his head and said, disgruntled, "Sorry, but I believe that Rome is the enemy of the Lord God and our sacred land."

Judas spat out, "Ever since invading our land and killing our fathers and brothers, Rome has desecrated our traditions and culture with their false gods and brutal ways."

Jesus responded firmly, "Once the Messiah sits on the throne of Israel, the force of God's love and power will conquer any foe. We will change them! First, however, the chosen people have to accept and unite with the one whom God has sent to accomplish this task. As the chosen people, we have to define our national identity. Our covenant with God has to be brought to a new level of commitment. We have to become a nation of holy people." Pausing, he looked directly at Judas, who was sitting across from him in the small circle. "Violence is not the way to build God's kingdom on earth."

Thomas nodded in approval. "Of course. A person cannot fight with a sword and feel love at the same time. I believe we need to find peace within ourselves if we desire to grow close to God and help others."

Jesus smiled at him. "As children of God, we must look deeply into our souls. In this violent world, however, a nation made of peaceful men and women is vulnerable to attack. Here is where Rome will play its role. The Romans have built an immense empire, and though the military has to put down sporadic rebellions, there is mostly peace in those lands."

"But that peace is brought about by brute force," Judas countered, "with much blood shed by those whom Rome has conquered and enslaved!"

"You're right," replied Jesus. "But now we can spread God's love throughout the Empire …"

"How?" Judas asked in defiance. "Do you really believe the emperor will help you build a world of love and peace, thus sowing the seeds of his own demise?"

"First we have to form governmental institutions in Israel that reflect the culture, the traditions, and the divine laws of God, and in doing so we advance toward our ultimate goal: to become children of God. Israel has to become the model for all other people on earth. Our land will stand as the visible proof of the existence of the God of Abraham, Isaac, and Jacob."

"So what would you have us do, bury our swords?" Judas scoffed. "If you don't have a fighting force, you'll perish."

"Yes, military forces are necessary to defend a peaceful society. After all, there are cruel people ever present. But as spiritual advancement takes place under the guidance of the messianic nation, military forces will gradually disappear."

"But, Lord," exclaimed Peter, "how can we win the support of the Romans? They are brutal and domineering."

"By practicing good diplomacy, proceeding cautiously, employing a meticulous formula combining love, patience, cordiality, and fondness, giving to Caesar what belongs to Caesar as a form of appreciation. With the force of forgiveness and smiles on our lips, we can conquer their hearts. The people of Israel won't be able to ignore me, and neither will the Romans."

"That is ridiculous!" snapped Judas. "That will only encourage them to trample us in the dust!"

"We have already been occupied by the Romans," Jesus reminded him. "You cannot overthrow them with force. They're stronger than we are. We have to deal with Rome politically."

Quite perplexed, Peter said, "Do you actually believe this? What makes you think pagan Gentiles will soften their hearts toward us?"

"Rome has its own problems," responded Jesus. "Though the emperor controls a large empire, Roman society is besieged by persistent problems. Tiberius has no solution to Rome's social problems. There is poverty, corruption, immorality, and lust for power. These troubles have to be resolved. Otherwise, with time, the empire will collapse. The emperor well knows it."

Jesus paused as he moved his eyes to Matthew and Bartholomew. "We Jews will convince Rome that it needs to restructure and modify its institutions so that the culture, traditions, and laws come into harmony with the divine nature of human beings created to be the sons and daughters of God. Israel will stand as a model nation in the Empire.

Arching his eyebrows, Peter asked, "Where do you start?"

Jesus answered, "Evil and sin are manifested in many forms, but sexual lust and greed for power are the most serious sins in Roman culture."

"Roman leaders are killing each other for power," Matthew added.

"They use marriage as a means to gain social status, but are ready to divorce and remarry if that helps advance their objectives for more power. Even though Tiberius loved his wife, he divorced her in order to marry Augustus' daughter."

Frowning, Jesus stated plainly, "Marriage is meant to be an eternal covenant not only between a man and a woman, but between God and each couple."

"Lord!" exclaimed James. "How is it possible to change such a violent people? The Romans are pagans who don't even believe in the One God."

"You see? You agree with me!" said Judas, trying to create discord. "Treating the Romans as brothers will never free us from their evil yoke! Armed revolt is the only way."

Suppressing a sigh, Jesus calmly replied, "Please remember that we all are children of God. Even in the soul of a cruel man, there are aspects of God's nature." He paused for a moment, searching for the right words. "Once the light of God starts shining among people, the light inside each person will shine brightly. Everyone will be attracted to the light. It is like a flame that burns in an oil lamp. This flame will light up many other oil lamps. Likewise, the love in our hearts will ignite many other hearts with divine light."

He paused again, searching the eyes of the men in the circle. "God will continue His providence until each and every person recognizes the truth and attains perfection." Smiling at Judas, he added, "So, we need to forgive our enemies, while also teaching and helping them along their journey to spiritual advancement."

After a short while, Philip said, "Lord, do you really believe the Romans can become children of God?"

"The Romans *are* also children of God, and I am *their* Messiah just as I am for the chosen people."

"I see. So you *are* the Messiah?" said Judas.

Jesus nodded in silence as the other eleven smiled at one another. Yet Judas seemed stunned, his mouth slightly open as he gave him a cold look.

"I am the Anointed One of Israel," declared Jesus. "The Lord God, in His infinite wisdom, has permitted Rome to become a great empire so that the Messiah, in the position of a king, can quickly and efficiently spread his message of love and his teaching to all corners of the empire and the world as well."

"How long will such a plan take?" asked Simon, who up to that moment had listened attentively.

"Clearly the kingdom of God cannot be built in a day, or even in a generation. But I can assure you that once God's nation has been established and guided by my descendants and yours, then no one can stop the expansion."

"Your descendants and ours?" asked John, a puzzled look on his face.

"All life on the earth is transitory. Each human will pass on to the spiritual world, including myself. When I am gone, my son will assume my position, although my wife and I will remain as the first heavenly couple of humankind."

Jesus paused as a sudden gust of wind blew up from the valley below, stirring up the leaves around them.

"Unfortunately," he added, "we lack the support of the chosen people whom God has prepared for this momentous arrival of the Messiah. The children of Abraham should be the first to receive the message and welcome the Anointed Son of God."

Andrew commented in a somber tone, "So far, not many people seem willing to listen, and even fewer to follow. And the religious leaders of each town resist your teachings, and even consider you an enemy."

Some of the men nodded, and Jesus replied, "Such people want things to remain as they have always been. In fact, not everyone will be happy to see God's kingdom arrive. The priests, Pharisees, and scribes pray for the coming of the Messiah, but they will reject both the messenger and his message because it is not what they expected."

"They think you might cause discord among the people," Peter added.

"I know," said Jesus. "This is because they do not know me yet."

Jesus gazed around the circle, looking at each man. "God has called each one of you to participate in this noble cause. Are you willing to offer your lives for the fulfillment of God's will? Or do you prefer to go your own way, and merely be spectators as God's plan unfolds before your very eyes?"

"It is a great task," said Andrew. "It will take much time and effort."

Peter stated in a strong voice, "Lord, I believe I speak for everyone here when I say that we promise to follow and support you in any situation, good or bad!"

"Good!" Jesus replied with a smile, going on to announce, "In a few days, we will travel around the region and speak directly to the religious and social leaders of each area."

Everyone nodded with quiet confidence. Jesus and the twelve started making plans for their upcoming journey, and then each expressed his beliefs concerning the life of faith. For the most part Jesus listened quietly while weighing their words, speaking up only occasionally. Many times their statements were a little confusing. Opinions would be offered, and the others would discuss and debate the issue in loud voices until the matter was settled to the satisfaction of everyone.

"I have to teach in a simple way so that my message can be understood. That's why I sometimes use examples to make the point," said Jesus, glancing at the serious faces of his twelve apostles. "I need to tell you so many secrets that have been hidden from you due to the Fall. Know that God has not created us to live in ignorance, but to live in wisdom. Therefore, between the children and the Father there should be no secrets."

Jesus spoke to them under the dim stars of a calm summer night. He shared with them all the love springing from his heart. He wanted them to understand that God's love was the source of true life, and once a person receives such love he should share it with others. He reminded them to keep in mind the concept of God as both our Father and Mother, and most importantly to understand the nature and mission of the Messiah. Then he announced that he would send them out to preach the coming of the kingdom of God.

"Among the people in the towns, there are those prepared by God to receive my teachings," Jesus told them. "You will find such people, teach them, and invite them to follow the will of God by bringing forward the divine nature within themselves and helping others to do the same."

After Peter offered a closing prayer, the thirteen stretched out in their bed rolls and soon fell asleep while the light of the fire flickered around them then died.

About two weeks later, the twelve apostles, along with some other disciples, started out on their journeys to various towns and villages throughout Galilee to announce the good news. Jesus had instructed them to witness to the people for a month, and then gather together in Capernaum.

They went together in pairs, staying in each area for several days, longer if they were treated warmly. For most of the disciples it was a new and difficult experience. Under sweltering summer conditions, they had to travel on foot over rough terrain and with little food. They slept where they could, usually on the streets or in fields between one town and the other. Some felt like beggars, because they often confronted miserable circumstances, which tested their loyalty to Jesus.

In most towns and villages, the disciples found kind, generous people who gave them food and shelter, and who would listen with interest to their teachings. There were others who were cordial but had no interest in what the disciples had to say. And then there were many who were staunchly opposed to them and their message.

Most of Jesus' disciples maintained their faith, even after discovering how difficult it was to find good people willing to follow them. Though they performed miracles showing extraordinary power, it wasn't enough to convince people to open their minds to what God had revealed to Jesus, change their hearts, and leave the comfort of their homes to follow him.

The difficulty of spreading Jesus' teachings to a mostly indifferent population touched off various emotions in the disciples. They were exhilarated over the miracles that God worked through them, yet they also felt indignation and disappointment over the lack of results. Perhaps the greatest lesson was the stark realization of how superficial and shallow their relationship was with God, and how little they actually understood His plan to gain victory over the pervasive evil of this world. The reality was that as the disciples tried to convert others to God's message given by Jesus, they themselves were not totally convinced, nor did they fully grasp the deep significance of the new age they were now ushering in.

Each disciple was only certain of the fact that he must keep faith in Jesus, by serving and attending him. In the meantime, they could only hope and pray that the chosen people of Israel would soon realize the Messiah was already in Israel, among them. Although their lives were difficult, the disciples found comfort in the thought that glorious days were approaching, which gave them strength and the motivation to overcome any hardships.

Peter, James, Andrew, John, and many others genuinely believed that the walls of apathy and hostility toward Jesus and his teachings would eventually collapse, that people would awaken to the reality that a powerful message was being delivered to their generation.

That burning hope, of course, kept their passion alive and prompted them to visit the villages and town, announcing the good news and trying to love the people, even those who cursed at them. At the same time, Jesus continued preaching his message, traveling from place to place visiting synagogues in the company of some of his followers who had stayed behind.

Whatever town or village Jesus traveled to, his fame preceded him. Most people had heard rumors about his extraordinary powers, his ability to heal the sick and cast away bad spirits from possessed people. By word of mouth, people from all over the region came to listen to his sermons, and see with their own eyes what Jesus was capable of doing.

To the dismay of Peter and other close disciples, most people would gather around Jesus to be cured of their infirmities. Many of them were not Jews but pagans, who showed no interest in God or Jesus' teachings. Yet he held no resentment against such people, for he knew they had no cultural or religious basis to understand the concept of the Messiah or the profundity of his message. "It was for this very reason," Jesus told his disciples, "that God labored so many centuries to prepare the chosen people, so they could receive His son and comprehend his teachings while faithfully serving him."

On their return to Capernaum a month later, all the apostles gathered together with Jesus to report their various experiences and accomplishments.

Jesus noticed their tired faces and lean bodies. They were exhausted physically as much as mentally. Jesus understood their need for rest, as well as their need for spiritual nourishment. After welcoming them back, he expressed his deep appreciation for their sacrifice and diligent efforts that had inspired both him and their Heavenly Father. "Brothers, I will never forget your selfless contributions in helping to build God's kingdom on earth," he told them. "And whoever receives you, it is as if they had received me. Remember this, the person who receives the prophet as a prophet will get the rewards of the prophet. To those who receive a righteous person, the reward of a righteous one will be given. But whoever gives anything to you, even a cup of cool water, they will receive their reward directly from God."

After considering this, Peter thought aloud, "Lord, many people gave us cups of water and plates of food, but they didn't care to hear our words. How can we persuade them?"

"It seems like an almost impossible task," Thaddeus remarked while glancing at the others, some of whom nodded in agreement.

Jesus smiled at them. "If we have faith in God, we will see changes coming quickly."

Some of the disciples smiled and nodded, with hopeful expressions that were nevertheless tinged with the harshness of their recent experience.

Jesus said with a wave of his hand, "Don't worry about poor results. You will see the fruits of your labor in the months to come." Pausing, he turned to James and Matthew. "We must be the model for our children, for our brethren, and for the world, so they all may come to know God through our example. Feel honored to be the chosen ones, the sons and daughters who will help God realize the purpose of His creation."

Despite Jesus' comforting words, the twelve apostles kept their heads down, their hearts struggling with the reality of the situation.

The following morning, Jesus asked the four fishermen, along with Bartholomew and Philip, to come with him. He silently led them down to the shore of the lake, where Peter and James' boats were moored.

A short while later, the seven men got into Peter's boat and sailed away from the shore, heading toward the middle of the lake. Peter and John spoke in hushed voices about Jesus' earlier words, and they both noticed that he had fallen asleep near the bow of the craft. This didn't surprise them, for Jesus was accustomed to sleeping on a boat under all kinds of weather, day or night.

Jesus slept with his head on a cushion, not noticing that a sudden storm came up, causing the waves to crash over the boat and fill it with water.

Thinking the boat was about to sink, the men became terrified and decided to awaken Jesus. "Lord!" shouted James, trembling. "Wake up!"

Bartholomew shook Jesus' shoulders. "The boat is sinking!"

When Jesus opened his eyes and sat up, he was visibly annoyed by the attitude of the men. Then with a strong voice, he shouted out to the wind and the lake. Suddenly the strong winds died down, the rough waves weakened, and the waters were calm.

All six men were astonished, their eyes wide, silently asking who this man could be, when even the waters and wind obeyed him.

Jesus gazed severely at Peter and the others. None of them dared to move or speak, their eyes fixed on him as he said in an irritated voice, "Why are you so afraid? Why are you shivering men of little faith? Don't you know that I made you fishers of men?"

None replied, their heads lowered in shame.

"Be strong!" he roared. "Keep your faith in me, and never be discouraged by burdens or hardships. Always keep in mind that God loves you, and that His rewards are immense." His tone changed. "It isn't easy to spread the word of God."

As his eyes roamed over their faces, he added in a fatherly voice, "I know you put all your heart into spreading the message these past weeks. Yet, despite your good efforts, you were met with yawns, criticisms, and insults. But don't be frightened by those who threaten to kill your body. Rather, be on guard against the forces of evil that desire to kill your will." He paused briefly. "Do not be discouraged if some people mistreat you. Keep in mind that among the doubters, you will find those men and women who are prepared to welcome you. So never lose heart! Never abandon your mission! Never go back to your previous way of thinking!"

Later when the boat reached the other side of the lake, Peter, James, John, and Andrew walked along the shore, talking in whispers about what they had witnessed during the storm. Once again they had seen the miraculous power of God revealed through His chosen Son. The four men also marveled over the fact that Jesus knew their innermost thoughts and feelings so well. Feeling confident again, they returned to their home and slept soundly, then woke up early the next morning and prayed with Jesus on the mountainside.

CHAPTER 25

LIFE MOVED SLOWLY in the village of Bethany, a few miles to the southeast of Jerusalem. When I first moved there with my children, I had hoped the easy flow of life with my sister Martha would wash away my fears and frustrations coming from my chaotic years of family life while in Magdala.

Most of my days in Bethany were serene, yet my heart was unsettled. During that period, I lived only for my children, thinking of their safety and happiness. Even though we were staying at my sister's home on the outskirts of the town, with my brother Lazarus and his family not far away, loneliness and regret ate at me. Since I still felt some bitterness toward Jesus, I had tried to push his image to the most remote regions of my mind.

One morning after a night of light rain, three high priests from Jerusalem and a few other men appeared at the house while I was in the courtyard picking up the pieces of a broken flower pot. A strong breeze had swept the dark clouds away, and the sky was now clear blue, with rays of the sun peeking through the branches of the tree above me. During brief introductions, I learned from their leader, a slender, slightly stooped man called Anath, that he and the others had been sent by Caiaphas, the high priest of the Temple.

When they began to question me more aggressively, I couldn't help reliving the same emotions that had engulfed me in Magdala when the group of thugs had threatened me and my children. I soon realized these men had come with one intention, to harass and frighten me so that I would summon Jesus here for comfort and protection.

"Are you Jesus' wife?" Anath snarled, not trying to hide his dislike for me. "If your husband is a king, then you should be a queen."

"Of course not," I murmured, wishing Martha and her husband were with me.

Another priest said in a mocking tone, "If you are not a queen, how can your husband be a king?" Pausing, he gave me a thin smile. "Who do you think Jesus is?"

"He is my husband and the father of our children."

One man with a scarf around his face spat out, "Do you think he is the Messiah?"

"I think he is a confused person at times who wishes to please the Lord."

"Confused? Your husband is possessed!" he scoffed under the watchful eyes of the quiet priests, who let the man make his nasty remarks.

His words caused my cheeks to burn, and my heart pounded. "Watch what you say!" I blurted out involuntarily.

"If I were you, I would hold my tongue," the man retaliated. "We heard that Jesus and some of his disciples are traveling around Judea on horses. Are you aware of that?"

I nodded, debating whether I should run into the house and bolt the door.

Anath spoke up, his voice milder. "When will Jesus come here?"

"He is too absorbed in his teaching," I uttered faintly.

The other priest said, "Jesus' children are here with you, so he will come soon. We will be in town waiting for him."

Relieved to see them leave the courtyard, I went inside and let the tears flow freely, realizing there was no place to run or hide as long as I was married to Jesus.

To my surprise, two days later Jesus rode into Bethany with some of his followers. As the others continued riding toward the low hills east of town, my husband dismounted his horse. I hurried onto the road to greet him, my steps growing faster and faster. "Jesus!" I called out. Though I was excited to see him, I felt that his life was in great danger.

As Jesus opened his arms to embrace me, he noticed my distress and gave me a warm, comforting hug. "Mary, what is the matter?"

"I want you to live," I said through my tears. "Leave now! You can't be here!"

For some reason he smiled. "I doubt being with you and the children will bring on a deadly disease."

"You don't understand," I countered. "Some high priests from Jerusalem came and spoke harshly to me a few days ago. They are still in the village, spreading lies and turning people against you. Who knows what they will do to you."

"Do not fear," he replied calmly, walking me to the house. He looked exhausted as he dropped onto the soft rug and leaned back against a pillow.

After filling a pitcher with cool water, I returned to the room and sat beside him, handing him a cup of water. "Thank you," he said, smiling and sitting up. "Where are the children?"

"At Lazarus' home," I said, noticing wrinkles at the corners of his eyes. "If those nasty men return, I don't want Isaac and Sara here in harm's way."

"The Lord will protect us," he replied. "As long as we stay united in heart and give God's love and truth to people, then we are safe from harm."

"Oh, Jesus! I will listen no more to your dreams. Other people are more important to you than your own family! Even worse, you have put us into a dangerous situation."

He shook his head slowly. "Though Caiaphas sends men to frighten you, they know you and the children have no direct ties to my activities."

"And we never will," I retorted, standing my ground. "Though I am your wife, I am not obligated to follow you or accept your strange ideas." I reached for his hand. "Dear, please forget this notion of the Messiah. Stay with us."

"I cannot betray our Heavenly Father." He took a sip of water and closed his eyes as if in deep thought. "Why don't the children remain here with your sister's family? And you join with me and my disciples as we spread the message of God's kingdom. The children can join us once we settle down in better circumstances."

"Your understanding of God's word is very different from mine."

Smiling, he patted my hand. "Mary, come with me so I can guide you to fully grasp the meaning of my teachings. While witnessing for the Lord, we can share our hearts and raise our love to greater heights."

"Greater heights?" I said dryly. "I can get more attention from any man in this village than I get from you."

His smile faded. "Be careful, Mary. Remember that I am your husband. So stay pure when I am away."

"I know you are my husband. But don't forget that I am also a mother. I have to see what is best for the children."

"I have a deep concern for our children. As far as those people who oppose me … don't allow them to manipulate your mind. Satan will use such people to drive a wedge between us."

"You put a wedge between us."

As if sensing something bad could happen, he said in a serious tone, "Adultery is like a poison that destroys the trust between husband and wife."

"I am not planning on changing husbands," I said quickly. "I can live without one. When you decide to live a normal life, you know where I am."

Jesus said gravely, "A man can never change the blood that flows in his veins. Most people live in ignorance of God. It is my duty to bring humanity back to their Heavenly Parent. God has asked me to take on this task."

Pausing, he leaned closer to me. "Mary, all I ask of you is to be patient. Within a few years, everything will become clear to you."

I closed my eyes, realizing I still loved the sound of his voice. It stirred up deep emotions within my soul.

After a short while, I looked at him and said with a sense of urgency, "You must leave now. Those evil men …"

"What evil men?" he said quietly, still looking disturbed by my earlier comments. "Do they live in this area?"

"The priests Caiaphas sent from Jerusalem!"

Jesus got to his feet and headed toward the door. "If they are in the village, I'll speak to them."

"Don't go!" I pleaded, grasping at his arm. "They have paid off thugs to kill you!"

Jesus brushed my hand off his arm and walked through the courtyard striding onto the road purposefully.

Catching up to him, I pulled at his arm. "Please stay inside until I get Lazarus. He has many friends in the area who can protect you."

Suddenly, a group of six or seven men well up the road were coming quickly toward us. Leading the way was Anath and two priests, followed by the other men, who were shouting at us and carrying big sticks.

"I can handle this," Jesus said to me, looking unafraid. "Just go inside."

I shook my head, not wanting to leave his side.

With a look of aggravation, he gave me a slight push and said, "I will draw them away from here. When you see it's safe, run to your brother's home."

As I hurried toward the courtyard, I looked over my shoulder and saw the men with the sticks bending over to pick up stones. Then they began running toward Jesus, heaving the stones. All of them fell short of Jesus, as he casually mounted his neighing horse. Then, seeing that I was safely inside the house, Jesus kicked at the horse's flanks and waved at the men as it galloped at an easy pace toward the hills.

The men kept running after him, cursing and throwing stones, but none came close to striking Jesus or the horse, and he had lured the men away from the area.

That night I stayed at my brother's home, with my children snuggled safely in my protective arms. Though I was quite tired, I slept badly, my thoughts going back to my short argument with Jesus. Why had I been such a fool? Instead of comforting him and giving him support, I acted like a selfish child demanding his complete attention.

The next morning, my first thought was of Jesus, and it would be like this every morning during the following months. The love of my sister and brother's families eased some of the tension, yet my heart was still in agony as I raged against Heaven for stealing away the serenity of my peaceful life in Madgala.

My struggles would have been manageable if it weren't for the illness of my brother. Early one morning, Lazarus became quite sick and remained in bed for several days, growing weaker by the minute. Although a doctor examined him, the treatment proved futile and Lazarus' health deteriorated rapidly.

His wife, Huldah, and I soon came to the conclusion that only Jesus' curing power could save him. About a week earlier, we heard that Jesus was along the seacoast near Joppa. So we sent two of Lazarus' friends to fetch him.

A few days later they found Jesus and informed him of the poor health of my brother. Jesus remained in the area. After a couple of days, against the protest of his disciples, Jesus decided to return to Bethany. He chose several men to accompany him, and they journeyed to my brother's home.

Lazarus had already been dead for four days when Jesus reached the outskirts of Bethany. Jesus sent a disciple to my brother's house to quietly announce his arrival. As the messenger walked toward the house, he came across Martha and informed her of Jesus' presence. She walked toward the direction they came from to meet with him, making sure that she was not found out by local religious leaders, or by Anath and other priests who had just arrived from Jerusalem, apparently in hopes of finding Jesus in the area.

"Oh, you are here!" exclaimed Martha, tears in her eyes. "Jesus, I wish you had come earlier. My brother died four days ago."

"Yes, I know," Jesus uttered, giving her a comforting embrace. "Lazarus will be fine. Your brother will rise again."

Martha, who had little knowledge of Jesus' teachings, murmured through her tears, "In the last days, all of us will rise again."

"Martha, I am the resurrection, and my words will waken people's hearts and make their spirit shine brightly. Those who believe in me and lift up their hearts to God, will never die again."

Slowly regaining her composure, Martha looked at him silently as she reflected upon his words. "Do you believe in me, Martha?" he asked.

"Yes, I believe in the spiritual resurrection as you teach it," she said with conviction. "Jesus, I do believe you are the Messiah, the one Israel has been waiting for."

"My child, you will be blessed for your deep faith. Where is Mary?"

"I will let her know you are here," she replied, then turned and hurried back to her home. Without speaking to anyone, Martha went straight to the room where I was lying in bed with my face buried in the pillow. There was a storm inside my heart. My brother was gone. My husband was rarely with me and our children. And now there was an unfriendly feeling toward me among the neighboring families. The security I had built in Bethany had now collapsed with the death of my brother. .

Noticing Martha near the bed, I sat up and wiped the tears from my cheeks.

Although we were alone, she spoke in a hushed voice, "Jesus has arrived. He wants to see you now."

My eyes widened, and my heart pounded with anticipation. "Where is he?" I asked, crawling out of bed.

"He and some disciples are outside of town. Just follow the road."

I washed my face and brushed my hair, then quickly left the house. There were a number of people outside on the road, including Anath and other priests. They all noticed my hasty departure. Out of curiosity they began to follow me.

Not realizing I was being followed, I hurried along the road as my eyes searched for Jesus. When I spotted my husband and several of his disciples, I quickened my pace and practically ran up to him, angry tears burning my eyes.

"My brother is dead! If you had remained and taken care of your family, Lazarus would be alive now!"

Though my words must have stung his heart, Jesus looked at me tenderly as he wrapped his arms around my shoulders. Then he stepped away from me upon noticing the group of people approaching us.

Some of the men began calling out insults and ridiculing Jesus, and Anath said with a scornful laugh, "Jesus, if you are able to give sight to the blind, why can't you give life to the dead?"

Two of Jesus' disciples began arguing with Anath, but Jesus told his men to simply ignore his crude remarks. "Where is Lazarus' tomb?" he asked.

"Come with me," I said, fearing the crowd would start throwing stones at us.

As we began walking toward the tomb, along with Martha and the two grown sons of Lazarus, the small crowd followed us, still making harsh remarks about Jesus' birth and his teachings.

When we arrived at the cave that served as a tomb for Lazarus, I noticed that Jesus was now crying, with an intense, almost painful, look on his face, as though he were battling unseen forces determined to destroy him.

Holding my hand, he gave me a long gaze that penetrated my soul. Then he and his disciples moved over to the large stone that sealed the tomb's entrance.

"Remove the stone," he said to one of them.

"There must be a bad smell inside," said Martha, who was steps away. "My brother has been dead for four days!"

Jesus looked over his shoulder. "Martha, didn't I tell you that if you believe in me, you will be able to see the glory of God?"

Lowering her eyes, she nodded. Then Jesus looked at his disciples and said more forcefully this time. "Move the stone!"

While the men began pushing the rock away from the small entrance, Jesus looked up toward the clear skies. "Dear God in Heaven! I give thanks for Your love and grace, and for this opportunity to show that I am indeed in You and You in me. Let the people who are standing here observe the divine power that You have bestowed upon me, so that they may have a change of heart and believe."

Then with a deep, resonating voice, he commanded, "Rise, Lazarus, and come out into the light of day!"

There was a moment of tense silence as Anath and the other priests looked toward the cave with doubt on their faces.

Martha and I glanced back and forth from Jesus' face to the cave entrance, waiting anxiously to see whether anything would happen. Had Jesus lost his senses, to actually believe he could bring Lazarus back from the dead?

Soon we heard a faint sound, like someone groaning from within. My chest tightened, and my heart started to hammer.

Then, miracle of miracles, Lazarus appeared at the entrance of the cave and a collective cry of amazement arose from the crowd!

Looking weak and dazed, he moved slowly from the dark cave, his hands and feet partially wrapped in strips of burial linen. "Where am I?" he murmured, shielding his eyes from the sunlight. "What happened?"

"Lazarus!" cried out Martha. Hurrying over to him, she and her two sons put their arms around him in support, to keep his body from collapsing to the ground.

Jesus raised his voice, saying, "Death does not linger where it is defeated. Free him from the bindings, then take him home and feed him."

Everyone there, even the priests from Jerusalem, was in a momentary state of shock. After touching Lazarus' legs, arms, and face to make sure he wasn't just a spirit, Anath and the others turned and looked at Jesus, their mouths hanging open but not knowing what to say.

In fact, no one dared to say a word while Martha helped Lazarus out of the burial linens. Then she and her sons helped him walk toward the house, and the rest of the group followed close after them, already beginning to argue loudly over what they had just witnessed.

Jesus and I lagged behind, guarding our thoughts and feelings. His four disciples ahead of us, though, could barely contain their excitement, praising the powers of their master.

Once everyone reached Lazarus' home, the priests from Jerusalem followed Lazarus' family inside, while the others continued down the road, telling everybody they ran into what they had just witnessed. A short while later, the youngest priest stepped outside and told us that Lazarus was himself again and simply needed some food and drink.

After giving some directions to his disciples, Jesus and I went into the house. Several men got to their feet and dipped their heads in respect to my husband, offering their chairs to us. "You have performed the greatest of miracles," one man said in a faint, tremulous voice. "Who are you?"

"I came to do the will of our Father who is in heaven. The Lord's will is that you accept me as the one anointed by Him."

No one dared to contradict Jesus, staring at him in awe as if this were the first time anyone had ever seen him.

Studying his face, another man spoke up in a confidential tone. "Jesus, you should know that there are people in Jerusalem who have talked about doing harm to you and your family."

Upon hearing this, I felt as if my cheeks had been slapped … and all the old feelings of anger and resentment toward my husband suddenly arose again to the surface of my heart as I thought about the safety of my children.

"Tell those evil men not to come here!" I said sharply. "Jesus is leaving today and won't return."

Although Jesus gave me a pointed look, his voice was almost serene. "Mary, do not be afraid. Such men talk big, but never carry out their threats."

"Do not be afraid?" I echoed bitterly. "What about those men who threw stones at you last time? The life you have chosen will no longer permit us to live peacefully."

One man interrupted our conversation, looking straight at me. "I feel that you could become a widow very soon. Many members of the Sanhedrin are quite upset over Jesus' teachings, not to mention the fact that others are claiming he is the Messiah."

"Right," agreed another man. He moved his eyes to Jesus' stoic face. "You are making too much noise to be ignored."

Jesus smiled at this. "My disciples and I are persecuted for our beliefs and practices daily."

As Jesus and the men continued discussing the matter, I became more concerned about my children's lives, and grew angrier with Jesus for putting us all in such a dangerous situation.

Feeling sick to my stomach, I slipped away from the group and peeked into the room where Martha was taking care of Lazarus. He was doing well, if still somewhat miffed, laughing and talking about his four days of "death" and his experiences in the next world with relatives who had died many years before.

I listened for several minutes, still amazed that Lazarus was now alive and looking as healthy as he did. I closed the door and tiptoed quietly through the front room and outside to the courtyard, where I dropped, exhausted, onto the wicker chair.

Closing my eyes and meditating over the situation, I began to consider taking the children back to Magdala. My father was now in poor health, and I could help my mother look after him. Besides, I had other relatives in the area.

"You must be sleepy," said Jesus, sitting in a chair to my right. "You should stay at your sister's home and get a long night's rest."

I opened my eyes and glared at him, "I am tired of living like a nomad, moving from one place to another in fear."

"Mary, it won't always be like this. When the people of Israel unite with me, we'll be able to live together in peace. In fact, our family can then travel to Rome and be the guests of Caesar himself."

I couldn't help laughing at this. "Oh, now Israel isn't big enough for you and your God? You have grand plans to conquer the Roman Empire, too?"

"When Adam and Eve fell, the Lord God lost them and all their descendants to the fallen archangel. So until God can bring every lost soul back to His bosom, He will not be able to rest in peace."

I pondered this, then leered at him. "I have been torn to pieces since coming here. On the one hand, I love you and want to comply with your God. Yet I also love the children and want to protect them from evil people who hate us. Since …" My voice trailed off as Anath and the other priests from Jerusalem stepped into the courtyard.

"Jesus," I said loudly enough for them to hear, "since you haven't won the hearts of the people yet, there will be no peace for me and the children. So I beg you to stay away from us!"

Upon hearing this, Jesus' body stiffened and his face turned pale. Anath gave me a lingering look, then uttered good-bye and hurried down the road with the others.

After a period of silence, Jesus said in a quiet voice, "Mary, I realize the past few years have been difficult. But severing me from your life will not resolve any of our problems. Please be patient until I gain some influence among my following."

"That could take many years," I thought aloud. "I want you to leave today and not return until you get this Messiah obsession out of your head." I rose to my feet and hurried inside, leaving him alone in the courtyard …

When Anath and the other priests reached Jerusalem, they went directly to the house of Caiaphas to give their report.

After a drink of cool water, Anath explained in a reflective, but clearly uncomfortable, tone, "When we arrived at the house of Mary's brother, our information was correct. Lazarus had been dead for four days and was entombed in a cave near the village."

Caiaphas asked, "There was no sign of Jesus or his disciples?"

Anath shook his head. "Mary was in deep mourning for her brother, so upon our arrival we only caught a glimpse of her. Soon, Martha came into the house and hurried past us, without a polite greeting. Then a few minutes later, Mary rushed past us and left the house. Some of the neighbors followed her, thinking she was going to Lazarus' tomb to pray …"

His eyes brightening, Caiaphas said, "She was going to meet with Jesus?"

Anath nodded. "When we caught up with Mary, she was with Jesus."

Another priest spoke up. "With the help of some townspeople, we challenged Jesus about his beliefs, but he didn't respond. He and Mary set off for Lazarus' tomb. When we got there, Jesus told his disciples to move the stone from the entrance. Then he prayed and commanded Lazarus to rise from the dead!"

"What?" uttered Caiaphas, a puzzled look on his beardedface. "What do you mean by that? Lazarus was dead. You said that, right?"

Anath nodded and said, "Upon our arrival in Bethany, the local priest told us that Lazarus had been dead for four days."

Still looking perplexed, Caiaphas straightened up and said with growing curiosity, "So this Jesus fellow must be crazier than we suspected. He actually told the lifeless corpse of Lazarus to rise?"

"It wasn't his corpse," replied Anath. He added in a tone of respect, "The Lord is truly with Jesus. Shortly after he prayed, Lazarus emerged from the cave, still wrapped in burial linens. Though weak, he spoke a bit as his shocked family gathered around him."

Caiaphas scanned the solemn faces of the other men, who were nodding in agreement. "Come now," he said, laughing softly. "You can't be serious. You are claiming this Galilean carpenter resurrected his wife's brother?"

"We were there," stated Anath, picturing the scene in his mind.

Caiaphas eyes narrowed. "You believe this resurrection was authentic?"

A defensive tone entered Anath's voice. "Before returning here, we spoke to the doctor and several village authorities. Each one of them confirmed that Lazarus had died four days ago. They were absolutely certain."

Visibly disturbed by what he believed was Anath's gullibility, Caiaphas said smugly, "Even I can't resurrect my own brother-in-law!"

"But he's still alive," said Anath, with a half-smile.

"That is exactly my point," retorted Caiaphas. "Don't you understand this resurrection was faked? Maybe this Galilean can deceive you with his little schemes, but I won't be fooled."

Anath didn't like being treated like a simpleton, but he and the others kept silent as Caiaphas stroked his beard.

Finally, he said with a sneer, "I sent you to spy on Jesus' family and try to curb his influence, but you were manipulated by his tricks. If he can deceive my most devout priests, then he can easily seduce the common people with his sorcery." He exhaled heavily. "Maybe it's time to silence this charlatan."

After a long pause, the youngest priest asked, "What should we do?"

"I believe it is time to start orchestrating his demise," Caiaphas replied. "But first I need to know more about him."

"We know that he's an expert in not only wood and stone, but also the law. There are many people who are calling him Rabbi and Master."

"What? How did he gain this respect in such a short time?"

Anath found his voice. "Jesus knows the Torah and the words of the prophets thoroughly. And many people now view him as a great leader."

"I see grave trouble coming our way," Caiaphas observed, shaking his head wearily. "If large numbers of discontented people are aroused by Jesus' message, who do you think the Romans are going to blame? If Jesus and his men carried swords, this would be a secular problem. But we know that this Jesus told his closer disciples that he is the Messiah, and he is giving the people false hopes and encouragement. Once the Romans come to know that there is a man declaring to be a messenger of God, they will expect me to do something about it."

Caiaphas stood up and moved anxiously around the small table where Anath and the others were seated. "I am also concerned about the tension between Herod Antipas and Philip. We do not need a third party with a lust for power aggravating the situation. I know the Romans will make us their choice to govern Judea."

Under the quiet gaze of the priests, Caiaphas added, "We have to continue teaching younger generations how to preserve our traditions, our ways as the people of God. I am totally convinced that the power of Rome will pass, but our people and traditions will stay."

He took a deep breath, his eyes anxious. "We just have to survive these difficult times," he said, then stepped behind Anath, setting his hands on his shoulders. "As long as our ancient knowledge is not lost, we will still have our identity as a people. Then the sovereignty of our people in this holy land will be restored by the real Messiah. But this Jesus of Nazareth is undermining the traditions. His words are spreading fast, his popularity growing. We need to silence him as soon as possible."

He took a deep breath. "I can feel the eyes of the Roman governor on my back," he said in frustration.

CHAPTER 26

JESUS AND I HAD BEEN APART for almost a year. But despite all the adversities, I still loved him and thought about him during quiet moments when I was alone. Concerned for his safety, I wondered where he was and whether he still harbored dreams of being the Messiah.

During the lonely nights, I wanted to be held tightly in his arms, and I never lost hope that we would be together again and live happily, as we had during our early years.

As the weeks passed by, I couldn't bare our separation any longer. Conflicting thoughts would pull my will from one side to the other. So many times I decided to make peace with my husband, but then fear and uncertainty made me want to stay away from him. I lived too long with my mind like a battlefield and my heart an arena of dueling emotions.

One afternoon the confusion in my mind was swept aside when exciting news arrived in Bethany regarding Jesus' activities in Capernaum. I was told that he had founded a fishing and boat-building business, and that his group of followers had begun to increase. I was even happier to hear that among his followers were a number of women. So I considered the idea of traveling to Capernaum to see for myself what was actually happening there. After all, I was still his wife and the mother of his two children. My fears gradually subsided as I contemplated the matter. Gradually I become more curious and less afraid of the future.

Driven by the growing desire to be close to Jesus, and encouraged by the news from Capernaum, I began to examine myself in greater depth.

What use are my personal qualities if I cannot adapt them to the character of my husband and his mission? I thought, reproaching myself. Although I had often tried to live in denial of his beliefs, I couldn't help but recall his teachings. His words still rang in my heart, and it became clear how much they had affected me over the years. Suddenly I felt ashamed for having harbored ill feelings toward the man whom I still loved so dearly, and I told myself that it was better to take a risk than to live a faithless life away from my husband.

If I still loved him as my heart professed, then why wasn't I by his side? Angry over my lack of courage, I knew the time had arrived for me to dominate my fears.

During the nights, I heard voices in the wind calling my name, telling me to leave the comforts of home and join my husband. In my dreams, Jesus appeared and affirmed his love for me, promising to protect our family. Often I would awake, my heart burning with the flame of love. "I can only be what I am," I said aloud, and what I am is a woman and the wife of this man. Those sublime spiritual experiences gave me the strength to change. The more I reflected on the past, the more I understood my mistakes, and I realized that I should have supported him and his mission from the beginning.

I felt an urgent desire to make myself available to him, Soon, I even wanted to become a daughter of God. I had never imagined reaching a point where I desired to be no less than a child of God. The day had come to make a major decision in my life, and I came to the conclusion that I was the one who had to change,not my husband. So, more determined than ever before, I cut the tether that had kept me bound to the world of fear and indecision.

After much prayer, I decided to leave my children with Martha, who understood my situation. My brother had heard that several families from Galilee would soon return to their hometowns, which were close to Capernaum. So a few days later I joined their traveling group and waved good-bye to my children as tears filled my eyes, not knowing what the future would bring.

I could see Isaac and Sara weeping as they watched me get smaller and smaller and then disappear in the hills. Though my heart ached terribly, I started my journey toward Capernaum with a deep longing to be reunited with my husband.

It was early afternoon several days later when I arrived in the town of Capernaum. Although I had visited the town with my parents when I was a child, I didn't remember it being so large and busy. After a few minutes, I gathered up my courage and asked an elderly woman where I could find a man called Jesus. To my delight, she broke into a smile and told me to walk northward until I came to an open area with many trees. When I got there, I saw a good number of people sitting on the ground while Jesus stood in front of them preaching. My cheeks turned red and my breathing got heavy as I approached the congregation.

Suddenly I was frightened. What would I say to this man whom I hadn't seen for so long? As I drew closer to the front of the crowd, Jesus noticed me but didn't acknowledge my presence. I felt like a stranger. I drew closer to the group and, in humility, bowed deeply toward him in silence. I wasn't surprised by such indifference. I knew the pain that I had caused in his heart. I wasn't certain, but I thought that he might be waiting for me to give a sign of repentance for my previous words and actions that day in Bethany. Yet, wasn't my being here in Capernaum a clear sign of my desire to be with him again and to follow his direction?

I found a room for rent and had enough money to buy food. But those were very difficult days for both of us, particularly for him.

I would attend his sermons and meetings, hiding my identity under a veil. To others in attendance, I was simply a new follower like many of the other people listening to him.

One day Jesus spoke about the holiness of marriage and the family as the building block of God's kingdom while fixing his gaze on my eyes. I lowered my head, staring at my hands while my face grew hot in shame.

When I found the courage to lift my eyes, Jesus was focusing on various people in the crowd as he continued speaking. When he finished the sermon, he and some disciples spoke to several men and women who had approached them. Then later, as the crowd dispersed, Jesus walked in the direction where I was standing.

I had an overwhelming urge to bury my face in his chest and let the tears flow while releasing all the pain and sadness of the past months. Yet somehow I was able to control my emotions. I knew that I had to take the first step toward our reconciliation, to prove my change of heart and dedication to him and his teaching. But I also realized that he had a good reputation in the town, and he didn't want to lose what he had built.

As Jesus passed near my side, I could tell he was scrutinizing my soul. More than ever before, I felt that I had to give proof of my faith in order to convince him of my sincerity.

Then unexpected news came to my ear. Jesus had been invited to dinner at the house of a merchant named Simon, who had deep respect for Jesus, believing he might be a great prophet. Knowing a little about Jesus' family situation, Simon had told him that a man in his position needed a loyal woman to support him. And since Simon had a sister whose husband had died a year before, people whispered that he hoped that she and Jesus would soon marry.

Feeling as if I had been hit in the face, the world seemed to stop moving. I was disoriented and incapable of speaking. The thought of losing my husband caused an unbearable pain in my heart.

Later I found out where Simon lived. So I went to his house that evening to humiliate myself in front of my husband and everyone else.

I threw myself at Jesus' feet, and with tears streaming down my cheeks I sprinkled his feet with an alabaster full of perfumes. I wiped his feet with my hair and kissed them. I couldn't stop crying and asking for his forgiveness. Sobbing, I told everyone that I was guilty of not believing in my husband. I told Jesus that I loved him very much and that there was no greater blessing than being his wife.

Witnessing this act of faith, Jesus felt touched by the change of heart that had taken place in me.

Suddenly I could see that my presence was welcomed. His eyes beamed with a golden light of excitement. "Mary, your deep heart is incredible. I am so pleased that you are here." Then Jesus forgave me for my attitude, my lack of faith, and said that our relationship had now entered a new phase.

Seeing that I was truly repentant for my past behavior, Jesus gave me such a warm smile that chased away the pain and anguish of the past years.

Suddenly my heart was filled with joy and love, for I realized that Jesus had never abandoned hope that one day I would understand my position and join him. Now his prayers were answered. Now, with his Eve by his side, he could contemplate the substantial fulfillment of his mission.

Naturally displeased with what had just transpired in his home, Simon approached Jesus and asked for an explanation. "Who is this?"

"This woman is Mary, my wife," answered Jesus.

Simon arched a brow and shook his head doubtfully. "Don't you know who this woman is?" he said loudly, glancing around at his guests. "Jesus, how often in the past has she defied you with her temper and lack of respect. She has been absent from your life. She will dishonor your work, bringing only shame on you. She is a menace and is here to destroy your work. A woman who doesn't obey her husband is a source of humiliation."

Pausing, Simon looked at his sister, who stepped closer to us. Then he returned his angry gaze to me. "Woman, you are not fit to be in my house. Get out!"

He filled my heart with bitterness and shame, mocking my earlier joy.

I looked into his eyes and saw a dark soul. "I apologize," I murmured to him.

But Jesus said in a firm tone, "Simon, please let her sit next to me."

He shook his head again. "A woman is not allowed to sit at the table while men are engaged in conversation about God. Women should not participate in such affairs."

"But Mary is my wife," persisted Jesus. "Allow her to stay."

With a snort, Simon muttered, "She can remain in the room, but not at the table." Then frowning at me, he waved at the floor. "Sit there next to the plant."

I was not permitted to talk. I did not dare to. I sat on the floor, keeping silent as the men resumed talking about the prophets, the traditions, and the destiny of the chosen people of God, with Jesus emphasizing that their destiny was to bring a deeper understanding of God.

At the end of the discussion, Jesus stood up and walked over to where I was sitting. He put his hand on my shoulder and asked me to follow him.

We left Simon's house under the silent glare of his followers, and walked along the road for what seemed like a very long time, silence between us.

His humble house was near the outskirts of town. I felt as though we were walking toward our first house after we were married. Jesus opened the door and, with a motion of his hand, invited me in. My eyes scanned the small room and I noticed the well-made furniture. Then I glanced into the other room and saw the bed and a small, round table. "I made everything here," he said offhandedly.

"Of course. You are a skillful carpenter."

"Mary, I thought of you while I was making everything. I even imagined you here, arranging the position of everything to please you."

I stared at him lovingly, overwhelmed by his tenderness.

Once we sat down at the table, Jesus said in a serious tone, "Listen carefully. Over the years, you've heard me say how much God needs me. I am the hope for this dark world. Since the beginning of our relationship, I tried to help you understand how critical my mission is." His voice was calm yet direct. "I am the only person in this world who deeply understands the heart of God. I wasn't born only to be a good husband and father, although both are important. Already before I married to you, my destiny was much more than just living a serene life in Magdala, or anywhere else, in the company of my wife and children."

I nodded in silence, sensing the pain and anguish in his heart.

"Mary, it was wrong to believe that I didn't care about you or the children. I do care very much. You are the primary part of the mosaic of my mission. However, our family has a purpose that is connected to God's work for the salvation of humanity."

His face was as serious as his voice. I kept my eyes on him as a strong breeze rustled the tree outside the window.

"Unfortunately, many people view me as a man of contradictions. How can I teach the importance of the family as the pillar of God's kingdom if I myself do not take care of my own family? That is why people accuse me of being a hypocrite, teaching values that I myself do not adhere to. So, when I came here alone, the people of Nazareth said derisively to me, 'Physician, heal thyself.'"

"I am sorry for judging you wrongly. I simply wanted to live as other wives, and have all your love and attention to ourselves. But you were away from home so often that I was blinded by the fear of our children being harmed by hateful men. I felt your mission was a barrier between us."

"Yes, I understand." He rubbed his jaw. "Mary, I know my mission is dangerous, but I have no choice. I cannot run away from my responsibilities." Gazing into my eyes, he asked frankly, "Is this a visit? Or do you wish to remain with me?"

"I hope to live here with you. If I can help with your mission, perhaps we can grow close again."

He gave me another long look, probably gauging my sincerity.

"Jesus, you are my dear husband, and from now on I will always honor and obey you." I slid out of the chair and bowed before him, touching my head to the floor. "Please forgive me for doubting you and hurting you."

Standing, he bent over and lifted me to my feet. "Mary, I believe you," he murmured, his love filling my heart.

"I am so sorry, Jesus. Sorry for not supporting you as I should have. Many times I went to Nazareth, complaining to your mother and asking her to convince you to return to me and the children. Other times I wept in front of my parents, asking them to speak to you. Everyone came to know my problems. I created so much animosity between our families. I'm so sorry for hurting your reputation."

Grasping my hands, Jesus whispered, "I always understood how you felt. Truly I did. But how could I build God's kingdom if I only dedicated myself to the emotional and physical needs of my family?"

I nodded and said, "You are justified. Men often go to war for the sake of their country, leaving their family behind, and many never come back. Why shouldn't a man of God leave behind his family to fight the forces of darkness with a message of love and forgiveness?"

After pondering my words, Jesus looked at me so intensely that it was as if this were our first time together. With fresh tears soaking my face, I drew closer to him and rested my head on his chest. "I am sorry," I whispered.

He cupped my face in his hands and looked into my eyes. "You can't imagine how much I love you, and how much I need you. I cannot be whole without my Eve. You are my other half. You are very important to my mission as true Adam and father of humanity. God needs you by my side."

In that moment, a fire ignited inside of me. I sensed a strong desire to express my love for him as well as my intention to stay close to him. Suddenly I felt my heart filled with true love. Inside of me something happened that brought a radical change in my soul. I was reborn into a new life, next to my husband.

I looked straight in his eyes. "Jesus, I am sure of my decision. I am determined to follow you wherever you go. I am still your wife and the mother of your children."

Believing that my heart was sincere, Jesus realized the path that I would follow from then on. "Mary, there will be many obstacles in your path of faith. You must find the courage to continue your journey of spiritual growth as the second Eve." He paused an instant. "Life will not be easy. But if you listen to my words, and embody them in your daily life, then you will be able to overcome your limitations and raise your heart up to God."

From that moment on, I lived next to my husband determined more than ever to follow him wherever our destinies carried us. All of the skills that I had developed in Magdala, particularly relating to the fishing business, I put in the service of his mission, our mission now. As a matter of fact, about a week later Jesus asked me to supervise the fishing activities. And so I did.

Later, hearing about our activities, my father was filled with enthusiasm and allowed us to use his boats.

We stood upon a good economic foundation that could help support the families of his loyal followers while also supporting his mission. Of course, I was not the only woman to dedicate so much time to the mission. There were others as well determined to follow and to serve Jesus, accompanying him on trips to nearby towns, where they helped to gather people to hear his sermons.

I felt comforted by all the generations of Jewish women. One night I dreamed of Sara, Rebecca, and Rachel. Their faces were bright with the light of heaven. They smiled at me and clapped their hands joyfully. They danced and sang to the lovely sounds of heavenly music: "We will be reborn through you. Blessed are you, mother of the world. The hands of Heaven are upon you. The great power of Heaven has written your name with the ink of love." And throughout the heavens I saw beacons of lights much brighter than the sun, warming my soul …

The next morning I awoke rejuvenated as a steady rain refreshed the dry land of these hot summer days. Finally I was with my husband, not on my terms but on his terms, which were in harmony with the will of the Lord God.

CHAPTER 27

OUR DAYS IN CAPERNAUM flew by as Jesus and his disciples focused on our fishing business when not traveling to nearby towns to preach and witness. At first, our only boats were those that my father allowed us to use and those belonging to Peter and the two brothers James and John. Yet, as more fishermen joined our group, we used their boats and shared their profits to buy materials to start building more boats for our followers to use.

Those were times when Jesus was working either building boats or consulting with others about developing our business activities. I became quite concerned about Jesus' health. He always worked with ardor and intensity, rarely sleeping more than four hours a night. Only because of his strong spirit and determined mind could he overcome the fatigue. A few months after my arrival, Jesus and some followers who were carpenters finished building three new boats, and we all celebrated when they were launched onto the sea.

For the most part, the women in our group were enthusiastic about our fishing business. Their husbands had steady work and thus could provide for their families. Jesus knew that to get strong and righteous men to follow him, it was necessary to inspire their wives, keeping them happy and free from worries.

During this time, many followers were dividing time between their spiritual and economic activities. As the fish business developed, more people began to join our spiritual group while learning our business activities as well. This allowed Jesus, Peter, James, and other disciples more time for teaching and providing spiritual guidance to those new to the faith, while at the same time sharing what we had with others. Among the followers, there were those who would go fishing, while others would distribute the catch to vendors, who often were followers as well. Though we were a small community, we were well organized and self-sustaining. After a while, most people in the surrounding towns had heard of Jesus.

I have many fond memories of my life in Capernaum. After all, it was where I began my second marriage life with Jesus. This time I was not only his wife, but also a follower of his teachings, determined to be a good example of faith and devotion to his cause.

Our house in Capernaum had become the center of our activities. For our followers, it was a comfortable place to meet and relax, whether Jesus was in the area or away on one of his many journeys around Galilee. People often came to share in fellowship, and when hungry people appeared at the door we would give them food and often offer them temporary shelter.

When Jesus was in Capernaum, there was great joy among all his followers. I truly enjoyed the times when his close disciples and their families came to our home for food and conversation. The smell of fresh bread filled the house, and large pots of stew were prepared so that everyone had plenty to eat. We would spend time together as a big family, where women and men's voices joined together in harmony.

On those occasions, my husband and I often sang duets, and it was as if an aura of invisible light surrounded us. Afterward, each disciple and his wife would stand and sing together, to the delight of everyone. These were moments of great happiness, the air thick with the smells of rich food, fresh flowers, and incense, and our hearts full of joy.

During this period, I had no fears or worries about the future. Jesus was the rock upon which my life stood, and his followers looked upon us as the parents of our growing flock. "Mary, we must teach them a better way of life," Jesus said to me. "We must treat them even better than our own children. Our followers must learn God's way of life."

Jesus gave himself totally to all his followers, loving them and caring for their physical and spiritual needs. If in his presence I neglected to care properly for a person, Jesus would give me a certain look, but the next moment he would flash me a forgiving smile. I never worked harder in my life than I did in Capernaum. Jesus stressed that we were a community of believers. He was a master of creating harmony between men and women. So at times he urged us women to help the men with their various activities, while the men lent a hand with some of our tasks.

Jesus encouraged the wives and husbands to sit next to one another during meals and share with each other as friends. At times, Jesus would ask the men to put their arms around their wives and kiss them publicly. Some of the men disapproved; they were accustomed to the traditions of their fathers and grandfathers.

After so many years of living alone with my children, it was pleasant to be constantly surrounded by people. Somehow, with the help of God, I was strong enough to take care of our home and business activities, along with the various needs of our community of believers. With God's love, I found the courage to become the mother for many people. Later, I realized that I already had such love in my heart. I merely had to expand it and allow God to help me embrace others. As Jesus and I strived to become the parents of our followers, we grew even closer and blossomed as husband and wife.

The weeks and months passed peacefully, my life in Capernaum taking on its own orderly pace, marked by the short journeys taken by Jesus and his most devoted followers. Mornings were usually the busiest time of day. After the morning meal, I handled any matters relating to our fishing activities. Then I joined with several other women, and we walked along the road, talking and laughing while spreading the word of God to other women who came our way. Since we had no time to cook a midday meal, we often brought along loaves of bread, cheese, and fruit. We totally focused on building God's kingdom, so after our light meal we would continue witnessing until the sun grew too hot.

One day during late summer, I was sitting next to Jesus during one of his meetings with his disciples. I soon became uncomfortable, though, because of their dark looks. I knew they believed it was improper for men and women to be together in such a setting. It was on this occasion that Jesus felt the need to talk about the meaning of true love.

Speaking with a lightness in his voice that set everyone at ease, he said to them, "To love and be loved is what makes a person's life worth living. It is out of true love that God has created life. When God gives ..."

Peter interrupted him, asking, "Lord, what is true love, and how can it be recognized?"

"Peter, true love is the love that is given with no reservation, without condition. In the deepest part of your being, you can find the source of that sort of infinite and unconditional love. God is connected to the fountain of love that dwells in each human heart. Love nourishes and gives stimulus to all human relations, as well as the relations between human beings and God. It is a giving and receiving experience. Once you give love, you then open up a space to receive it back from others."

Jesus paused for a moment, smiling at his disciples. "Each type of human relationship calls for a particular type of love. For example, the love shared between husband and wife is different from the love felt by parents toward their children, which is different from the love between brothers and sisters. Nevertheless, all the expressions of love have one common characteristic."

Andrew raised his voice. "What is that?" he asked.

"The willingness to give yourself for the sake of the person you love," explained Jesus. Seeing their puzzled expressions, he added, "In the relationship between husband and wife, there should be no selfish intentions. The man gives happiness to the woman, doing all that is possible to make her happy and help her dreams to be realized. Man should help his wife to realize her potential as a daughter of God, becoming a perfect mother and the lord of the creation."

"The woman has to do the same for the husband," said James, with a wry grin. Several men laughed and nodded in agreement.

"Yes, of course," assured Jesus. "Both man and woman have a role to play. It is also true for the rest of society. Each member of society has to play a part in advancing the welfare of the entire population. We all need to learn how to do our part so that humanity can become better and better. It's a constant process."

"What an unmistakable expression of love!" Matthew exclaimed. "The love of God is expressed in the unselfish love between a man and a woman."

Jesus smiled at him and said, "In the parent–child relationship there is the same dynamic and characteristic. The parents do all they can for the child to become better than themselves. They support the child during his spiritual and physical growth. They assist the child during his intellectual development, so the child's potential can be realized. In the true relationship between parents and their child, there is no antagonism, so the parents delight in seeing their child surpassing their own achievements. It is a divine tendency fostered by God's love. Thanks to such a human heart, humanity can improve from generation to generation."

"But isn't the relation between siblings different?" asked Peter, with a brief frown. "There might be grounds for discord due to feelings of competition."

"It is in the nature of each human being to improve oneself," Jesus explained. "So each person has a desire to be the best. But once you achieve your goal, then as a child of God you should share your accomplishments with your brothers."

Scratching his head, Peter said slowly, "Sometimes, the presence of God makes me want to help others to be better off, to even be better than I am.

"Yes, Peter. True love is wishing that your own child or brother, or anyone else, could be better than yourself and doing what you can to make that happen. In true love, there is no envy or evil thoughts, only goodness shared with one another. People who exercise this type of love are truly children of God. True love comes alive when human relationships follow the divine laws. Those laws allow all types of heavenly relationships to exist and harmonize with the purpose and finality that God has given to each form of life."

We listened eagerly to his words. Then Jesus reminded us that God wants us to share His love with all people. Thus, we should go out and find His children.

About mid-morning three days later, we all departed, carrying food and tents with us. We began the journey by following the road leading to the valleys and hills of the nearby towns of Galilee. Usually we would sing while walking along the road, and sometimes Jesus would hold my hand as he chatted with the others. On this trip the wind came and went in strong gusts, momentarily blinding us with sand. We hadn't walked far before our long robes became very dusty.

We reached the first town early the next afternoon. And that evening my feet ached terribly, and my hands were so stiff I could barely move my fingers, but still I counted myself lucky to be walking in God's presence.

No matter what difficulty came our way, Jesus was always cheerful and seemed to burn with an inner fire. He rarely ate or rested, and he worked harder than anyone when we set up our tents outside the towns. After our morning meal, we went into the towns and talked to people about the imminent coming of God's kingdom. Then at sunset, we returned to the camp. The final day of our journey was memorable. After a long yet satisfying day of witnessing, we approached our camp and were greeted by the aroma of freshly baked bread and roasted lamb, prepared by those who had stayed behind guarding the tents.

After supper, we gathered around the campfire and sang. Then each person gave an account of their day, telling us about the people they had met and guessing at the mood of the populace. When we weren't crying we were laughing at our similar experiences and emotional responses.

When everyone had finished talking about their day, we sang a few more songs, as sparks were flying off the campfire. Then Jesus asked if anyone wished to give a personal testimony. It always took a while for anyone to speak up, and on this night Andrew hopped to his feet and gave a moving account of his life. Encouraged by his story, I hesitantly got to my feet and told the story of my life, opening my heart to everyone there.

After a few others spoke, we began singing again in unison, the high, sweet voices of women merging with the deep male voices, accompanied by the clapping of hands. I was amazed at the beauty and harmony of our voices. The Lord God seemed to be with us, casting an approving eye on His beloved children, who were doing their best to fight the spiritual battle to establish His kingdom on earth.

Throughout the evening some of the men kept the fire alive by adding more wood to it. As we continued singing and sharing our thoughts and feelings, I realized I had found a peace of mind that I had never known before.

When the moon was high in the sky, Jesus took Peter with him to pray and have a deep conversation.

After Jesus prayed, Peter said quietly, "Lord, often you have told us that God has expressed His nature in the creation. Does God have other characteristics that we don't see in the creation?"

"It's possible, Peter. There are truths that can be found only in the deepest parts of your personal relationship with God. Each person has been created with a unique nature. Within this uniqueness a person has a profound and singular relationship with God, inviolable and sacrosanct. It is in this deep intimate dimension that God reveals parts of Himself. In each generation, God puts the mark of uniqueness in each person, and true love is the driving force that binds men to their Creator, qualifying men to be co-creators with God."

Peter took a deep breath. "Knowing this truth, I cannot avoid the feeling of sorrow in seeing how man has degraded himself."

In a hopeful tone, Jesus said, "Nothing is impossible for God, or for men of goodwill. God's truth will open the gates of opportunity for spiritual rebirth to all humanity."

Peter nodded, seemingly more secure in his understanding.

Jesus put a hand on Peter's shoulders, a gesture of pride and affection. A few minutes later, Jesus came to our tent and we fell asleep with the sounds of the night surrounding us.

The next morning, we all emerged from our tents rested and smiling. During the morning meal, I thought about those people we had met in the town, hoping they would keep the light ignited inside their hearts until we could meet them again and share more of God's word.

The tents were dismantled, and we started our journey back to

Capernaum. As my husband had expected, our witnessing actions were noticed by the religious authorities of the region. To Jesus' consternation, news arrived in Nazareth, where his family still misunderstood him and his ministry. They missed no opportunity to let both him and me know how much they disapproved of his beliefs and activities. In fact, most of his relatives were shocked by my conversion to my husband's cause, probably thinking that his disciples and I were all mad fools for following him.

It was the beginning of Tishri, the Day of Atonement, which was a few days away. The sky was clear and a gentle breeze blew off the lake as two of Jesus' brothers approached him, one with a look of worry and the other of anger.

When he noticed them coming his way, Jesus raised a hand in greeting and gave them a warm smile. Although a few months had elapsed since Simon and James had last seen Jesus, they showed little affection as they exchanged greetings. Simon, the elder of the two, was prepared to vent all his frustration over the furor in his hometown caused by Jesus' various activities throughout Galilee.

"You are still causing problems for our family," began Simon. "We can hardly go out anymore without being targeted by the elders of the town, who are mortified by your conduct. They constantly complain about you. Especially to me, since I am my father's first son."

Jesus noticed how Simon emphasized *first*, as if to remind Jesus of his illegitimate birth. Disregarding this, he asked James, "Is it as bad as Simon claims?"

Through a nervous yawn, James uttered, "It comes in waves. People don't bother me much, because they know we are close. But poor mother gets persecuted a lot."

Simon cut in. "They talk to us like we're part of your plan to ruin the reputation of the town. Jerusalem is pressuring the priests in our region, demanding that they silence you. Our rabbis and other leaders are upset because people in other regions think our town is a hotbed of heretical activity. Some people in Nazareth even make threats against us. They are convinced that we support you and approve of your strange ideas."

Jesus gave them a critical look. "You are my family. You and my other brothers and sisters should have been the first to understand my mission and accept me for what I am. But none of you understand my true identity. Though we are brothers, there is an immense difference between us. God has put His hope in me."

"Why must you talk such nonsense?" retorted Simon. "The only difference between us is that you are delusional and we are not! Your teachings are those of a madman! What's this stuff about you being the Son of God, the incarnation of His divine love?"

Jesus made no reply. He noticed a group of young men standing nearby. They were staring at him and his brothers, while chattering excitedly.

Catching Jesus' attention, Simon barked, "What's this about God being a father, and heavenly morality? You live like a Bedouin, leaving your wife and children behind, yet you teach about heavenly morality?"

Jesus looked unfazed by his brother's accusations. "Mary is one of my strongest supporters."

"What choice does she have? You and your crazy followers wander from village to village teaching falsehoods that defile our traditional beliefs! That time in Nazareth when you spoke at the synagogue about the importance of the family in God's kingdom, the men said to you, 'Physician, heal thyself,' for violating your familial duties."

"I didn't abandon my wife and children. I have an important mission, and my family is part of God's plan for the salvation of humanity."

Simon laughed cynically. "Just like the Baptist? Your half-brother saw through your shameful deceptions. Since John was clever enough to avoid your trap, you had to return to Capernaum. Yet you continued teaching the same falsehoods, dragging your family along your foolish path."

"Simon, it is my duty as true Adam to marry and have descendants, and teach the truth of God to the people. My wife plays an important role in God's providence."

Simon shook his head. "And where do you live now? What kind of honest work do you do? Give up this foolish ministry! Return to building furniture and work with stones and become a good father again."

"I wouldn't have had to travel about the land searching for loyal disciples if our family and John's had united and supported me in my mission. But you …"

"Messiah!" grunted Simon. "How can you believe such idiocy?"

"How can you believe the sun rises every morning? Just as you feel the warm rays of the sun, I feel the radiance of my Heavenly Father's love. He wants me to establish His kingdom on earth." He paused, smiling. "Thankfully, my wife now understands her role. The original plan of God was prepared in every detail. But I have been misunderstood by everyone, including you and even our mother, who received visits from Gabriel before she conceived me."

Shaking his head sadly, Jesus added, "Mother should have been actively involved in finding a wife for me among her relatives, as it happened with Isaac and Jacob, who took wives on their maternal side. Mother showed no interest in fulfilling this obligation. So at the Cana wedding, if you remember, I told her, 'Oh, woman, what do you have to do with me?'"

Exhaling a low sigh, Simon said, "Everyone in Galilee knows who you are, so how can you say you are the Son of God? Have you forgotten who your real father is?"

"Simon, I am well aware of my earthly paternal heritage. You and James cannot imagine what I've had to endure since childhood to become what I am now, a spiritually mature Son of God."

"James and I are the sons of our father, while you are the illegitimate son of Zechariah! And he was no God!" Spitting at the ground, Simon threw up his hands in disgust. "The religious authorities in Jerusalem are looking for you. I hope they soon find you. Maybe they can put a stop to your unorthodox teachings once and for all."

"Simon, what do you fear? People don't hate you. They hate me because I teach the truth. You can live your life as you please. As for me, my life … and death … must be carried out in accordance with God's will."

James set a hand on his shoulder. "But our mother worries about you. She hopes you will start a new life. Every day her grief seems to deepen."

"Tell her not to worry. She has to accept the Lord's will for me. I will pray she can find peace of mind."

James couldn't help but laugh. "Don't count on it. Mother will always be Mother."

After another minute of conversation, Jesus bade farewell to his brothers and joined his disciples, who were nearby talking to the group of young men.

CHAPTER 28

NO ONE COULD HAVE IMAGINED, not even I, what thoughts were going through Jesus' mind … the feeling of urgency he felt constantly. "Life is short," he would say, as if each day were the last day of his life. He always felt he had to achieve something important connected with his mission. Each day was so packed with things to do. He was continuously in motion. There were many days in which he moved about from place to place, rarely stopping to eat. In fact, I was very concerned about his health because he often fasted as an offering to Heaven.

Sometimes Jesus would travel during the night without sleeping. Thankfully some of his disciples always accompanied him. Frankly, I just couldn't maintain the same rhythm of life as the Son of God. One of his unique aspects was that he felt responsible for the spiritual life of those around him, as well as everyone else who had heard his message.

As for myself, after my conversion and decision to dedicate myself to my husband's cause, I spent most of my time in Capernaum overseeing our fishing activities. However, whenever we traveled to the area near Magdala, I would spend time with my parents. And whenever we were in Judea, I would always visit our children, who were now in Bethany at my sister's home.

Those were our three major home bases. Sometimes, due to adverse circumstances, Jesus was forced to change his plans so as to avoid confrontation with any opponents who had bad intentions. It was not out of fear, of course. Rather, Jesus didn't want to waste precious time on such encounters, because they offered no benefit to his mission.

On one occasion, however, Jesus was cornered by some Pharisees who directly accused him of violating the Mosaic law. They believed, as did many others, that the Anointed One was not above the Mosaic law, but had to abide by the law.

"Do not think that I came to abolish the laws of the prophets, but to perfect them," he said to the Pharisees, keeping his calm and dignity. "I assure you that until heaven and earth are in perfect harmony with God's love, and men and women in perfect unity with Him, not even the smallest stroke of a pen will disappear from the law. Written laws are necessary for people whose consciences are not in harmony with God's. So until then, the Mosaic law should be taught and adhered to. Those who respect and teach them correctly will be great in the kingdom of heaven. But it must be done with love."

Pausing, Jesus looked at his disciples. "I tell you, if your sense of justice is not greater than that of masters of the law, and that of the Pharisees, you will not enter into the kingdom of heaven."

The Pharisees frowned and looked at one another. Although they felt obligated to do something, they decided not to escalate the confrontation at that moment and moved away.

A few hours later Jesus was sitting alone, deep in contemplation. Hearing footsteps, he lifted his eyes and saw James and his brother John coming his way. Both men seemed perplexed as they stood before him.

"What's the matter?" he said to them. "You look bewildered."

James spoke up. "What do you mean that you came to perfect the law?"

Jesus replied evenly, "God gave the law to Moses at a time when common men had little knowledge of correct moral behavior. Thus, the Mosaic law provides the basic moral guidelines governing human relations among the children of Abraham. And the prophets came to guide the chosen people, encouraging them to respect the law."

John said firmly, "So we must abide by the law, following it to the letter!"

"Naturally," Jesus said, smiling. "Nevertheless, the Mosaic law does not purify the mind and heart. I am here to help men and women to become God's true children, so that their heavenly conscience will be the law." His voice rose. "In the realm of perfection, there is no need for written commandments."

James nodded reflectively. "Teacher, you just stated we have to follow the laws of Moses until heaven and earth achieve harmony with God. What do you mean by heaven and earth?"

Jesus closed his eyes for a moment, searching his mind to find the right words.

"God is our Father," he thought aloud. "He created the physical world and the spiritual world. Since you and I still have our flesh bodies, we live in the physical world. But in the spiritual world, we find the angels and also those human beings who once lived here in the physical world. They, too, have to come to the realization of God's divine presence in them. Both worlds have to be in harmony with God's love, with open communication between people from both dimensions.

"Unfortunately, all humanity is the fruit of the fall of the first parents. Everyone has to be purified from evil. Those who do not know God's love, and whose actions are not in harmony with the universal conscience, still need the law of Moses to guide their thoughts and behavior. Since the Mosaic law was given by God, it should not be distorted or taught incorrectly."

After a moment of thought, James said slowly, "Are you saying our behavior won't be regulated by law once we have pure minds and hearts?"

"Yes," he nodded. "Once your hearts are in harmony with God and you reflect His divine nature, then your conscience becomes the law. God has anointed me with the task of helping you to discover your divine nature."

It was several days later, on the Sabbath, when Jesus and some of his close followers went to a synagogue to preach. His voice was firm and clear as he spoke about the commandments. "You know that one of the commandments says do not kill. Whoever violates that law will be judged. However, it is also a sin to mistreat a person, whether physically or verbally. If you have a problem with a person, try to find a solution and reconcile before you make an offering to God."

Everyone was listening quietly. No one dared interrupt.

"It is also written 'do not commit adultery.' But I say that whoever looks at a woman with lustful desire has already sinned in his heart. Although sexual desire is a natural desire that God gifted to man, it becomes unholy if expressed anywhere except within the relationship between husband and wife."

Jesus often emphasized that adultery is the poison of society because it destroys the basic foundation of human society, which is the family. It is in the family that human beings discover and develop the feeling of love. The parental, as well as the fraternal and the conjugal forms of love.

"As I have said many times," stated Jesus, his eyes roaming across the synagogue, which was by now full of people, "husband and wife becoming one in body is the highest expression of conjugal love. Through such relations new life is created, and a family is built, which is the basis of society. Illicit love scars the divine value of conjugal relations, destroys harmony in the family, and endangers the entire society."

Although some people were noticeably uncomfortable with his speech, no one dared to interrupt his teaching. Everyone listened as Jesus continued with confidence.

"You know it is said to love your neighbors and hate your enemy. But this isn't the correct behavior for a child of God. You should pray for and love those who persecute you. Then you will be known by God as His children. If you love only those who love you, what is the merit in that? Anyone can love those who treat him kindly. And if you greet only your brothers, what is special about this? You have to be perfect as your Heavenly Father is perfect."

As Jesus paused, he saw that more people were trying to gather around him. There was now a multitude in the synagogue, with some men pushing others in an attempt to get closer to the front where Jesus was speaking.

Gazing at the Pharisees in the crowd, Jesus added in a firm voice, "There are many of you in Israel who believe in the law, but follow it only in a self-serving manner. Such men use the law and Scriptures for personal gain. From this viewpoint, there is no difference between the children of Israel and the pagans around us. They place offerings on the altars not with sincerity, but to ask favors. The children of Abraham wish for God to save them from suffering. So they make offerings for the sake of receiving personal blessings. Is this any different from those pagans who approach their gods also hoping for wealth and other favors?"

Stepping to his right, he added forcefully, "Now is the time for all men and women to overcome spiritual death and be reborn as the children of God." Turning slightly, he changed his tone and continued, "Do not give an offering in a pretentious way that can be seen by everyone. Do not seek praise. Offer in silence."

Feeling the press of the crowd, Jesus took a few steps backward. "When you pray, do not be like the hypocrites, who prefer to pray standing up in the synagogue and public roads so that everyone can see them. I say to you, when you want to pray, go to your room, close the door, and pray to your Heavenly Father who sees you intimately. He will reward you. Your Father knows your needs even before you tell Him."

Pausing, Jesus gazed at the men in the front. "You should pray in this way: Our Father, who art in heaven, hallowed be Thy name, Thy kingdom come, Thy will be done, on earth as it is in heaven. Give us this day our daily bread. And forgive us our trespasses as we forgive those who trespass against us. And lead us not into temptation, but deliver us from evil.

For Thine is the kingdom, and the power, and the glory, for ever and ever. Amen."

Now this prayer has become the prayer of those who belong to the Messiah. I knew that by "heaven" Jesus didn't mean the physical sky, which can be seen with human eyes, but rather the purity of the spirit and love of God. And I also knew that he was absolutely convinced that God's will was for His kingdom to be realized both on earth and in the spiritual realm to which we all go one day. Therefore, people who dwell in the spiritual world also have to understand and fulfill God's principles.

CHAPTER 29

JESUS WAS THIRTY-TWO YEARS OLD on that warm, cloudy afternoon when his mother approached the house of the senior rabbi in Nazareth. Earlier in the day, the rabbi's wife had quietly conveyed her husband's request for Mary to visit them. Uncertain why she had been summoned to his home, Mary knocked lightly at the door, hoping he wasn't going to deliver bad news about Jesus.

"Mary, please come in," said the rabbi's wife, her deeply lined face reflecting the passing years.

As Mary stepped through the doorway, her eyes fell upon the aging rabbi, who was sitting at the table, sipping on barley tea from a silver cup. The look of concern on his face was apparent.

She stepped over to him, bowing her head in respect. "Good afternoon, Rabbi."

"I am glad you've come," he replied, smiling kindly. After she sat across from him, he added in a serious tone, "Mary, we need to talk about your eldest son."

Fighting off a frown, she turned to the rabbi's wife, who placed a cup of tea before her and sat down in the empty chair next to her. Setting a hand on Mary's shoulder in a gesture of reassurance, she said, "Don't worry. Nothing ill has befallen Jesus ... not yet, anyway."

Her husband added quietly, "It has come to my ears that Jesus has not stopped creating problems with his false promises. As you know, your son has some unusual teachings. In my opinion, and that of prominent leaders in Jerusalem, his views are blasphemous and dangerous."

Although his voice remained calm, the rabbi's face showed his irritation over the matter. "During the past year or so," he continued, "there have been many instances when Jesus has insinuated that he could be the Messiah." His tone sharpened. "Who does your son think he is?"

Mary said humbly, "Well, here ... everyone knows who he is. Besides, they are only unfounded rumors."

"Your son has no authority to interpret the law and Scriptures. Priests have more education and are better suited than Jesus to teach. He is not qualified to gather people around him to speak about God and other spiritual matters."

Seeing Mary blush, the rabbi's wife said gently, "Dear, you should tell your son that he needs to be careful. In the past, there were those who proclaimed themselves to be prophets or even messiahs. Some died without accomplishing anything, while most others were forced to withdraw their absurd claims, often after being jailed or receiving other harsh punishment."

Mary listened silently, her face now white as milk.

Sighing, the rabbi said to her, "Jesus is no different from those foolish dreamers who have preceded him. Mary, I hope you and your other children can persuade him to stop his subversive preaching, for the good of your family. Everyone in Nazareth is waiting for you to control your son."

"Rabbi, my son is a grown man," she replied in a wavering voice that couldn't hide her emotions. "How can I control him now? I rarely see him." Biting her lip, she added in frustration, "Although you are right, I cannot help feeling responsible for his behavior. He had a hard time growing up."

The rabbi's wife patted her shoulder. "We know you did your best."

Staring blankly at the vase of flowers on the table, Mary murmured, "I was so busy taking care of my other children … and the problems I had with my husband …"

"Yes, we suspected things weren't easy between you and Joseph," uttered the rabbi's wife. "We remember that incident when Jesus was left behind in Jerusalem. He was only a twelve years boy!"

"What incident?" muttered the rabbi with a distant look.

"Don't you recall?" she said to him in a motherly tone. "We were a caravan of about fifty people, mostly from Nazareth." Her eyes moved to Mary's sullen face. "Dear, it shouldn't have taken three days to realize that your son was missing."

"There was tension between Joseph and me during the trip," confessed Mary, recalling the painful experience. "I sobbed over having forgotten Jesus so carelessly, but I was afraid to tell Joseph." She paused a moment. "Joseph's words still resound in my mind. He told me there was no reason to moan, for we knew where Jesus was."

The rabbi's wife nodded, thinking aloud, "My husband had to convince Joseph to go back to look for the boy …"

"Ah, now I recall what took place!" said the rabbi, frowning at the memory.

Mary went on to explain, "We found Jesus in the Temple. When I asked him why he stayed back, he replied, 'I am taking care of my Father's matters.' " Mary's thoughts went back to the day when she revealed to Jesus the identity of his physical father.

The rabbi and his wife's eyes met, certain their suspicions about Jesus' physical father were correct. They remembered that in those days Zechariah was one of the priests on duty in the Temple. But they said nothing as Mary added in a forlorn tone, "Joseph was irritated during the trip back to Nazareth."

"Joseph was a good man," said the rabbi. "I recall that he died about two years after that incident."

Mary nodded, holding back her tears. "Rabbi, I will talk with my other sons," she promised. "In the past, Simon and James have spoken to Jesus about these matters. Perhaps this time they can convince him to quit preaching."

"That would be a wise decision," stated the rabbi. "There is no time to waste. Yesterday I heard that Jesus was north of here, near Sepphoris."

Mary finished the tea, then returned home and summoned her four sons and two daughters who were fathered by Joseph. After telling them about her conversation with the rabbi and his wife, they began discussing how to best handle the matter.

Simon, the eldest son of Joseph, asserted gruffly, "Jesus doesn't listen. I'm not going to go wandering around the countryside again looking for him and his strange followers."

"Mama, this time you need to speak to Jesus yourself," the younger daughter observed.

"I agree," said James. "He might listen to you."

"How can I go alone?" Mary replied, with a helpless look. "Jesus has a strong mind and a clever tongue that I cannot contend with."

Simon stared at her for a moment, considering the choices they had. "Then all of you go!" he barked. "You have to convince him to shut his mouth. He has brought shame to our family, and all Nazareth! People here worry that Nazareth will be known as a place of blasphemy and heretics."

"This is not the Jesus that I hoped he would be," sighed Mary, recalling the prophecy of the archangel Gabriel. "Jesus doesn't act within the limits of our laws and traditions."

Simon continued in frustration, "His interpretation of the Scriptures is totally unacceptable. Everyone in Nazareth knows that he is not the king of Israel, much less the Messiah! Jesus should return to Magdala and lead a normal life like everybody else!"

"Since he was a child, I have known that Jesus is a special person," uttered Mary, half to herself. "He is quite intelligent and knows so much about the Mosaic laws and the teachings of the great prophets. He's also close to nature, and very attuned to people's thoughts and feelings."

"At times it's scary being around him," said the elder sister. "It's as though he can access your innermost feelings."

James nodded and said, "Jesus certainly has more knowledge than all the priests in Galilee. Most people are biased against him because of our humble background."

With a reflective nod, Mary said wistfully, "Jesus has a character and personality like no other person I know. Not even high religious leaders have a pure heart like that of my precious son."

James said with ardor, "Well, if you decide to look for him, I will travel with you."

She smiled gratefully. "Simon, you will accompany us, too."

Simon's face turned red, and he gave a vague nod, keeping his thoughts to himself.

The first daughter said, "If James is going, then I will go also!"

The following morning, Mary and her sons and daughters left Nazareth and traveled along the road leading to Sepphoris, about four miles to the north.

That afternoon they came to an area southeast of Sepphoris, where they saw a large number of people gathered in a field. After speaking to some young men at the edge of the crowd, they discovered that Jesus was close by.

A few minutes later, Jesus noticed his mother, brothers, and sisters coming his way. Yet he didn't stop speaking to the crowd that had gathered around him. When his mother and siblings drew closer, he looked at them as if they were strangers.

One of his disciples, thinking that Jesus hadn't noticed them, gained his attention and told him about the presence of his relatives.

But sensing the reason why they had come, and also sad that his family still didn't understand his mission, Jesus looked at his followers and said, "Who are my mother, my brothers, and sisters? Those who follow me, those who understand my words and my mission, and are willing to do God's will. Those are my true brothers and sisters."

After the crowd had dispersed, Mary and her children spoke to Jesus and tried to convince him to get me and the children and return to Magdala and live a peaceful life there. But their arguments were futile. Mary soon realized it was impossible to persuade her son to abandon his mission. He gave her and his sisters a loving embrace and waved farewell to his brothers, as he and his disciples left the area. Mary and her children spent the night in the area.

The day after, they came to Capernaum to visit me. Mary stayed in town for a week. It was during those days that Mary and I began our friendship and she told me about Jesus' conception, her experience in Bethlehem, and her troubled years with her parents-in-law.

It is the tradition and custom of the chosen people of God that the sons and daughters of Abraham marry. A man and woman become one in flesh, and in so doing they can create new life. However, it is not customary to bestow on a woman the same value as that given to a man. Jesus came to establish new customs and new values, such as that a woman can be considered not only as a mother, but also as a companion of man, having the same worth as he does.

Regarding this, I would like to mention that two weeks after my mother-in-law left Capernaum, Jesus came back in town. He went straight to the synagogue to speak about the task that God had assigned him, my role as wife of the Messiah, and the role of our blood lineage in the process of building world peace with spiritually mature sons and daughters of God.

It was during the time of the harvest of sweet figs. Each family in Capernaum owned at least one fig tree, and the majority had more than one. Although most men were busy harvesting their crops, they still found time to go to the synagogue.

Jesus and his disciples were among those in the large congregation, waiting for the right moment to speak. When the time came, Jesus stood up and moved to the front of the sanctuary. "I am the bread of life," he stated, his eyes scanning the faces of those nearby. "Whoever comes to me will not suffer hunger, and whoever believes in me will not be thirsty. I will never send away a person who approaches me. I have not come from heaven to do my will, rather the will of He who has sent me. It is the will of the One who has sent me that I should not lose anyone given to me. He wants me to raise them up on the last day."

Many men in the congregation leaned forward, intense looks on their faces as they listened closely to Jesus' unusual message.

He added in a level voice, "It is the will of God that whoever sees the Son and believes in him should gain eternal life. Only a person who is one with God comes from Him. I am the living bread that comes down from heaven. Anyone who eats of this will live eternally, and the bread that I give is in truth my flesh. It gives life to the world. If you do not eat the flesh of the Son of man, and do not drink of his blood, you will not have eternal life."

Some of Jesus' disciples frowned upon hearing this, whispering to each other, "What he said is unacceptable. Who could go along with such things?"

Jesus heard their comments. "Does this upset you?" he said to them. "What if you see the Son of man go up to where he was before? The spirit is what gives life. The flesh means nothing. The words that I have spoken are from the spirit."

Many men were outraged at such a declaration, including some of his disciples. A few of them left, not willing to follow him any longer.

Later that day, Peter had many questions troubling him. So he went to Jesus and said humbly, "Rabbi, I am confused by your remarks today."

His face bore no expression. "Peter, you have children, don't you?"

"Yes, Lord. You know how much I love them."

"Your desire is for your children to be better off than you. Also, out of your blood lineage, you hope to have many descendants."

Peter gave a slight nod. "Yes, right."

"The chosen people are from the lineage of Abraham. This means you and I are of the same blood. Isn't it so?"

"Yes, for Abraham is the father of all the children of Israel."

"In other words," said Jesus, "the blood of Abraham continues living within the veins of the chosen people."

Peter nodded again. "We have a unique identity. We have endured four hundred years of enslavement in Egypt. Through such tremendous suffering, God preserved the descendants of Abraham."

"So we have to presume that the common blood lineage, the laws, the prophets, and the Holy Scriptures give an identity to the children of Israel," said Jesus.

"In this way, the children of Abraham grew as a people isolated from others, thereby maintaining their blood connection. From such a blood lineage, God selected the most sacred line to give birth to His Son."

With a thoughtful look, Peter stated, "The Temple in Jerusalem is holy, as is the blood of Abraham, but one part of the Temple is more sacred. So you are saying that there is a particular line in the offspring of Abraham that is more sanctified than the others."

"Peter, I come from such a sanctified blood lineage, which was purified from generation to generation so I could be born without original sin. It was my responsibility to grow strong and true by rejecting the pleasures of this sinful world. I had to make choices and keep growing spiritually. Now I am one with God. Now, since I am His true Son created in His image, I can state that I come from heaven. But at the same time, I am the Son of man, having come from the lineage of Abraham. Adam lost his connection with God, so he wasn't able to attain spiritual maturity and be a perfect reflection of God's spirit. That is why the Messiah comes as a second Adam. And as a second Adam, he needs to restore a second Eve. For this reason I married and had children who are blood of my own blood and flesh of my own flesh. The Messiah comes with the task of becoming the father of humanity to connect all human beings to his blood lineage. This is why I said that people would not live if they didn't eat my flesh and drink my blood."

"Your flesh and blood, which means your blood lineage?" Peter asked, scratching his head as he pondered this. "So if people don't connect with you, they cannot be part of you or be a part of this new identity as children of God?"

"Yes, Peter. As it was for Abraham, so it is with me. My offspring have to develop, and be protected against the forces of evil that want to destroy it. It is God's will for the children of Abraham to connect with my descendants and receive my bread, which are my words, which are the essential nutrients for spiritual growth. All people have to connect to the blood of the second Adam through marriage with his offspring from generation to generation. Initially this marriage blessing will be offered to the children of Abraham, but then later as the blood lineage of the Messiah expands, it will be extended to others. But this process requires time. It will take many generations until the blood of the Messiah spreads to each corner of the world, connecting people to the lineage of the new Adam and new Eve."

With a solemn look, Peter said, "Lord, your words give life. I want to receive your blood and your flesh. I want to eat your bread, so I will never be hungry again. I want to drink your blood, so I never will be thirsty. Let your blood be in my blood. Let my daughter marry your son, for by so doing we become one blood."

"Peter, I am pleased that you understand. Will you keep faith in me even when strong, opposing winds blow in your face? Do not let my opponents put fear in your heart. Have faith, and it will be its own reward."

Saying this, Jesus departed and went to a solitary place to pray.

Feeling lighthearted, Peter went back to join the other disciples who had been in the synagogue that morning. He found them still talking about the content of Jesus' sermon, trying to extract meaning from it. Since Peter now had a better understanding of Jesus' message, he implored the group to be patient and keep their faith strong.

About an hour later, Jesus returned from his prayer. He sensed the spiritual struggle that some of his disciples were undergoing. So he gathered them together to remind them of their position as representatives of the Messiah, and how important their work was to spiritually raise up the people of Israel and save all humanity.

"Brothers, you are the salt of the earth," he said to them. "But if the salt loses its saltiness, it is no longer good for anything and will be thrown out to the street, where people will walk on it. Thus, you need to keep faith in my words and share them with others, so they can be saved through your devotion. A city on a hill cannot be hidden."

As his followers listened with growing expectation, Jesus added, "Let your light shine brightly, so others can see God's love through your good deeds. Then they will glorify your Father in heaven. I came to announce the kingdom of heaven to those who have been prepared by God, our Heavenly Father and Mother. We are all God's children!"

The following day, Jesus and his close disciples traveled to the surrounding area, teaching and healing those who came to listen and repent for their sins. Tirelessly he persisted spreading the word that the kingdom of heaven was at hand. His efforts were not limited to the region of Galilee. His utmost hope was to find dedicated followers from all parts of Israel. So about a week later, he and his disciples set off for Caesarea Philippi, a region under the command of Philip, the half-brother of Herod Antipas.

During their journey, Jesus asked his disciples, "Who do people say that I am?"

James hesitated. "Rabbi, people have no clear idea who you are. Some believe you are the resurrected John the Baptist."

John frowned at his brother then said to Jesus, "How could it be possible, since you were already with us before John was jailed and executed?"

With sad eyes, Jesus replied, "This shows how ignorant some people are about what they don't know or fear. They have small minds that cannot accept the truth." Pausing, he glanced at Andrew. "Those people who say I am John are the very ones who didn't know of me before John's death. These are people who believe only what they see with their own eyes. It is difficult to witness to such an individual with only words. How can you explain the invisible when they are skeptical of even the visible?"

All the disciples nodded in agreement, amazed by this simple truth.

"I am obligated to fulfill the mission that was John's, who was to give full testimony about me. It is one of the reasons that I have had to do miracles and cure sickness. I use this power so people will believe in me. I had to become my own John the Baptist, my own Elijah."

"Right," James interjected. "Some people even say that you are the prophet Elijah."

Jesus stopped walking, a serious look crossing his face. "As you know, Elijah now lives in the spiritual world, so he cannot come personally and testify. It was for this reason that God designated a person with the same responsibility as Elijah, and this was John the Baptist."

As the group continued walking, Thaddeus spoke up. "Some people say you are one of the prophets."

Jesus glanced at him. "Well! Who do you think I am?"

Peter said, "Lord, you are the perfected Adam, made in the image and resemblance of the Creator, the Son of the living God, who manifests Himself through you. We are the fruits of your hard work."

"I am delighted that you understand my identity. Surely, my Father in heaven speaks through your heart. I will give to you what is mine, and united we will continue to spread the word of God. Our blood and flesh will become one." After a slight pause, Jesus added in a worried tone, "During the coming months, do not reveal that I am the Messiah. Lock this knowledge up in your hearts. At this point, it is better for the children of Israel to consider me as a new prophet."

"Why, Lord?" asked Peter.

"The religious elite and the military authorities have more tolerance for a new prophet than for a Galilean who proclaims to be the Messiah. We have to be wary of violent threats against us. But this situation is only temporary until we have the support of the people. When the loyal multitude supports me until their last breath, we will openly announce my real identity loudly and clearly, so Jerusalem can hear."

CHAPTER 30

DESPITE THE MANY DIFFICULT CHALLENGES that Jesus faced daily, he kept in high spirits, ready to give counseling to anyone in need. Neither hunger nor thirst or fatigue slowed down his rhythm in carrying out his mission. Even those few days of rest couldn't be considered as such because he would meditate and pray for the spiritual life of his close disciples and other followers.

After having preached throughout Galilee, Jesus traveled to Jerusalem for the Feast of the Tabernacle, one of the three pilgrim holy days of the year. It took place in the autumn, and the pleasant weather encouraged people throughout the land to come to Jerusalem to celebrate the event.

During his stay in the city, Jesus visited the Bethesda Pool next to the Temple. Most people believed the waters of the pool had miraculous powers. Sick people would often gather around the pool, hoping to be cured of their maladies.

On the Sabbath when Jesus appeared there, he noticed a frail man lying on an old, filthy stretcher, unable to walk. Saddened by the scene, Jesus gave him a warm smile. "How are you, my friend?"

"What can I say?" the man replied with a scowl. "I've been a cripple for almost my entire life. I feel so worthless!"

"God loves you. Do you know that?"

"Hah! God!" the man scoffed. "Where has your God been all these years? I wish God could feel my pain and sorrow!"

Stepping closer to him, Jesus said, "If you believe."

"Believe in what! I just want to walk and be like others." He raised his hands in despair. "No one can do anything for me. Days come and go, but I continue lying here like an old log, unable to enjoy life."

Jesus closed his eyes in deep prayer as the man stared at him, puzzled.

When Jesus opened his eyes, he gave the crippled man a warm look. Then he pressed the palms of his hands against the man's thin legs for a half minute, still softly praying. As he removed his hands, he said mildly,

"You are now cured."

"What?" the man snapped in disbelief. "You say I am cured?"

Jesus nodded. "Move your legs. There should be no more pain."

The man did as he said, staring in amazement as he felt the power returning to his legs. "I can move both legs!" he cried out, trying to grasp what had just happened.

Jesus took the man by the hand and lifted him up from the ground. Like a newborn baby horse, the man took a few wobbly steps.

Jesus smiled at him. "Take your stretcher and walk from here, and offer praise to the Lord God for pouring His blessings on you."

Joyfully thanking God, the man gave Jesus a long embrace with tears streaming down his face. Then he slowly walked away, taking the worn-out stretcher with him.

Since the man had never met Jesus before, he had no idea who had cured him. While exuberantly walking along the road, he came upon some Pharisees, who saw him carrying the stretcher. They thought he had been commissioned to deliver the stretcher in return for pay, so they castigated him because it was the Sabbath, a day when people were not to perform any physical work, not even carry a stretcher.

But the man did not even try to explain himself, only exclaiming instead, "Now I can walk! It's a miracle!"

"Do you take us for fools?" said one of the Pharisees. "You will be punished!"

"I speak the truth!" he said in fear. "I was crippled for years, but today a man healed me and told me to take my stretcher and leave. And I don't even know his name."

Later that day, Jesus was climbing the steep road leading to the Gate of Benjamin, which opened into the Temple courtyard. He lingered in the courtyard for a while, recalling earlier visits when he was a child, and then he assumed a prayerful heart and stepped into the Temple. He weaved his way through the crowd, admiring the majestic structure built by King Herod the Great, the father of Herod Antipas.

The frail man who had been a cripple spotted Jesus and hurried over to him with a grateful smile. "Thank you for healing my legs," he uttered, kissing his hand.

Jesus set a hand on the man's shoulder. "Now that you are cured, you can begin doing the will of God."

"The will of God?" the man asked, puzzled.

"Yes," Jesus said sharply. "Do you believe you were cured so you could live a life of sin? God wants you to love and serve Him with all your heart and soul."

"I will," the man promised. "Even as a cripple, I came here almost every day. What more could I do?"

"Accept God in your heart. He wants you to listen to my teachings. Follow me and do not commit sins. Use your legs to walk the path of spiritual perfection. The journey may be difficult, but you can do it if you devote your life to it."

Lowering his eyes, the man tried to understand what Jesus meant. After all, he had always thought God was there to do things for him, not the other way around. Suddenly the man turned and disappeared into the noisy crowd. A few minutes later he returned, bringing with him the Pharisees who had berated him on the road for carrying his stretcher. "This is the man who cured me," he said to them, pointing a finger at Jesus.

They stared at him with hard faces. "Who are you?" said the elder of the group. "And who authorized you to cure this man on the Sabbath?"

"My Father who is in heaven has authorized me to liberate the oppressed," he answered with a calm expression.

"It's the Sabbath!" snarled another one.

"Love is always present in the human heart, even on the Sabbath. If one of your children fell and broke his leg, wouldn't you help him? Wouldn't you carry him in your arms to a doctor, even on the Sabbath?"

The Pharisees glanced at one another, each waiting for the other to speak.

Jesus added, his voice rising, "If you have a sheep that has fallen into a hole, would you let it die just because it was the Sabbath? The love of God is not subject to time or location."

The Pharisees muttered angrily among themselves.

"Open your hearts," Jesus said with a look of reproach. "Men have not been created for the Sabbath, but the Sabbath for men!"

The elder Pharisee looked at him askance. "Did you say that God is your Father?"

Jesus gave a silent nod, seeing that a number of men had gathered around them.

"This is blasphemy!"

"I assure you that the Son cannot do nothing by himself unless the Father does it. I can heal people because I see God doing it. Whatever God does, I can do."

"You believe you can do whatever God does?" one said, laughing in condescension. He looked at him as if he were possessed. "Is your mind afflicted with disease?"

"It is not an affliction to be loved by God," stated Jesus. "God loves me, and I love Him. We are one and the same."

The Pharisees glared at him. "What is your name?" asked the elder one.

"I am Jesus of Nazareth."

"Ah hah! We have heard about you. So you are the Galilean who performs so-called miracles!" he said in a mocking tone.

"I am the one who one day in heaven will welcome anyone who believes in me. God wants you to be perfect, so you can enter His kingdom."

"You will welcome me into heaven?" echoed another Pharisee sarcastically. "Since we are children of Abraham, we are already part of His kingdom. God will judge our souls."

"God doesn't judge man. His divine laws guide the existence of life and our relations with the Creator. Those people who violate God's divine laws judge themselves."

"How can you be so certain what you say is truth?" challenged another Pharisee.

"God, our Father, has asked me to show you the correct behavior that is in harmony with His unconditional love.

The elderly Pharisee retorted, "You are only a Galilean, a misguided one who's confusing the people with an immoral doctrine leading people to hellfire!"

"I assure you that whoever practice my words and believes in God will gain eternal life. The Son will raise the descendants of Abraham and all humanity."

"You poor man," said one of the Pharisees. "You have exalted yourself over your merits."

"God has called me so that it can be realized."

"You are disturbed, and what you say is pure madness."

"You keep your hearts closed, unable to recognize the sign that John the Baptist showed to you. You sent an emissary to John and he testified about me, although with little conviction."

One of the Pharisees said, "Yes, I know that Caiaphas sent representatives to the Jordan River to speak to John about his mission. At the time, John gave testimony about you. We sensed that John wasn't convinced of what he was saying."

Another Pharisee pointed a finger at Jesus. "If you are the Messiah, why didn't John follow you and become a disciple?" He quickly added, "Everyone knows that before the Messiah arrives, the prophet Elijah will come and announce him. So where is he? John clearly stated that he wasn't Elijah."

Hiding his frustration, Jesus said, "The spirit of Elijah was with John, but he couldn't overcome his narrow-minded thinking."

"Are you saying that John was wrong?"

Jesus nodded in silence, his bitter feelings toward John surfacing in his heart.

The elder Pharisee stated, "The only mistake John the Baptist made was giving Herod an excuse to arrest him. If John were alive today, he would still keep his distance from you!" Glancing at the crowd listening to the discussion, he added in a damning tone, "Jesus, even though John was temporarily deceived by the Evil One, he soon separated himself from you, realizing that you are a blasphemer whose words confuse the people! How dare you claim to be the divine Son of God who can do whatever God does!"

"I do what I do and say what I say so you can understand that God is in you, too, so you can come to the realization that you are sons of God. John gave testimony of me."

The elder Pharisee retorted, "Jesus, you are not the Messiah. When he arrives, the chosen people will bow down to him as the rightful king."

Ignoring the Pharisees, Jesus decided to speak directly to the crowd. "There is no doubt that John should have done more. Yet my testimony is even greater than his. It is the work that my Father has delegated to me. I have performed great miracles that give testimony to the presence of God, our Father, within me."

The elder Pharisee waved away this pronouncement as if it were an annoying gnat. "Jesus, there are others who also conjure up such magical charms." He shook a finger at him. "What is so special about you?"

"You do not know what I know," responded Jesus. "You do not know the invisible world as I do. You do not understand the origin of evil, nor do you understand the original nature that dwells in you. Such nature makes us children of God."

The Pharisees gazed at Jesus, taken aback by his audacity. Before one of them could respond, he added in a scornful tone, "The Scriptures testify to me."

"Who gave you the authority to say such things?" asked a Pharisee, visibly upset. "God has given you no authority. You do what you do out of lust for power over the people."

Jesus said, "I am not looking for personal power or human praise. I presented myself to you to perform good deeds, to spread His love, and to bring peace to the world, but you will not accept me. If another person would come in his own name, having no deep relationship with God, then you would accept him."

"There is no need for more. We have the laws, the traditions, the prophets, and the Scriptures," retorted the elder Pharisee. "The Messiah will liberate us from oppression, from foreign occupation. You are trying to gain power with sorcery from the Evil One."

"You are mistaken," stated Jesus. "Have you forgotten that the chosen people asked God to elect a king?"

Pausing, Jesus turned to the crowd again. "After hearing the cries of the people, the Lord God instructed Samuel to choose Saul as the first king of Israel. It is God who elects the eternal king, not men. And it is the king who selects his helpers, choosing them from among those who obey God's direction with humility. How can you believe if you are interested only in honor among men, without looking for the legacy that comes from following God's heart?"

"What do you accuse us of?" demanded the elder Pharisee. "We are not hypocrites. We do the will of God."

Jesus shook his head. "I am not the one who accuses you. If you believe in Moses, you should believe in me, because he wrote about me." Jesus looked around, pointing to the majestic structures of the Temple. "Don't you know that the God of Abraham, Isaac, and Jacob promised to give them descendents? The chosen people have been elected to teach that there is one God and that from the bloodline of Abraham would be born a Messiah as Son of God, who brings salvation to all humanity. But when he does come, you reject him and even chastise him. You incredulous leaders of this generation!"

Fuming with indignation, the elder Pharisee shouted, "You blasphemous serpent! How dare you call yourself the Son of God! We all are God's servants. You have the Evil One inside of you!"

Without consultation, the elder Pharisee called for the guards of the Temple. Realizing the situation had become unsafe, Jesus quietly stepped into the crowd to his left. A few men who admired him opened a way for him to escape into the courtyard as the guards arrived to apprehend him. Once outside the Temple, Jesus disappeared among the multitude.

Jesus was keenly aware that performing great miracles and healings was not enough to change people's hearts. His primary focus had to be on finding those men and women who could understand his message of truth and love and who could join him in his mission to transform the society, the nation of Israel, Rome, and the world.

CHAPTER 31

SHORTLY AFTER JESUS TURNED THIRTY-THREE, the challenges and struggles became more intense and arduous for him and his followers.

The twelve apostles were his closest followers, of course, but among them Peter, James, and John were the most faithful. One day Jesus called the three men and took them with him to the mountain bordering Galilee and Judea. The path was rocky and the terrain dry as gusts of wind blew dust in their faces. Yet the four men moved steadily toward the top in what felt like an endless effort.

Like the other apostles, James was panting heavily as he tried to keep pace. "Lord, do we have to climb to the top of the mountain?"

"Yes, James. We have to be away from people."

"Why did we come to this mountain?" asked John, raising his voice above the wind.

Jesus glanced at him. "To pray and converse with some important people."

Peter asked, "Lord, who are we going to speak with?"

"You will see. ... Not with your physical eyes, but rather with your spiritual eyes."

Jesus' response was perplexing to Peter, but he said nothing as they continued hiking up the mountain trail. When they finally reached the summit, everyone was tired and gasping for air. After resting a few minutes and enjoying the view, Jesus moved a few steps away and began praying deeply in a strong voice, with tears in his eyes. Then he asked the three men to join him. Peter, James, and John stepped closer and bowed their heads, listening closely to his words. After a short while, their eyes became heavy and they lowered their bodies to the ground, their backs resting against a huge boulder as they drifted off to sleep.

The three were in a semi-conscious state of mind when the appearance of Jesus' countenance changed. His face began to shine like the sun and his garments were resplendent with heavenly white light that emanated from his spiritual body. Then there appeared two figures in glorious splendor, their faces dazzlingly bright. The three men heard Jesus calling them Moses and Elijah.

At the same moment, the spiritual bodies of Peter, James, and John left their physical bodies as well, and the six flew through a tunnel of light.

The apostles' eyes darted about the enchanting surroundings, taking in all the vivid sights and sounds. Every color, every sound, every feeling, surpassed anything they had ever experienced on earth. And they were totally conscious of what was happening to them!

Turning to Jesus, the three men were struck by his confidence and serenity. For him, the situation was entirely natural, because he was so totally accustomed to the spiritual dimension. Each man felt heavenly light permeating every part of his being. Their senses were totally engaged in this extraordinary experience, with radiant light surrounding them. Their minds and hearts were filled with such a powerful, intense love that when Peter recounted the experience to me later, words often failed him.

As they stood in front of an immense, brightly colored gate guarded by two angels, they noticed a group of people gathered just outside the gate. Their faces were familiar to Jesus. The apostles came to realize that these men were the prophets of Israel, whom God had called at different times to serve Him by guiding Israel. It seemed that they knew each other, although they had lived centuries apart on earth.

Peter, James, and John stared at the beaming faces of Moses, Elijah, and the other prophets, who were all shining in luminous light as they greeted Jesus. Yet the Son of God shone with even greater brilliance.

Peter later told me that he, James, and John had witnessed the greatest expression of human affection and friendliness that they had ever felt in their lives. Everyone was as real as any person on earth. It felt like a family reunion.

Jesus broke the silence. "Brothers, I have brought three of my most faithful disciples with me."

Moses spoke in a worried tone. "The religious leaders, particularly those in Jerusalem, are maliciously opposing you. How can we help them realize there is a greater truth that can lead them closer to God as their Parent, and help them find rebirth as children of God?"

"They have hardened their hearts," Jesus conceded. "They do not want to listen, and those in power are doing everything possible to block the path for others to come to me. Many good men and women are intimidated by these threats."

Jesus looked at the prophet Elijah. "Beloved brother, Elijah! What do you think?"

"The truth is that most people are not spiritually prepared to understand the significance of your words. I am very sorry, Jesus. You have suffered a great deal. How many silent tears you have shed! All of us prophets have great respect for you and accept you as the true Messiah and second Adam. How we wish we could do more to help you!"

"I am grateful for your support," replied Jesus. "Don't feel guilty for John's lack of faith. I know how hard you tried to influence him."

Elijah gave him a warm smile of appreciation.

Jesus added, "As it was predicted, the forces of evil are working among the children of Israel to hide the truth from them, and to distance them from me. All of you sacrificed your lives for the coming of the Messiah. Many good people have suffered for the arrival of this day!"

Moses set a hand on Jesus' shoulder. "You are doing everything you can. All of your deeds are an expression of goodness and love, but many people only see them as works of the devil."

Jesus nodded. "Yes, it's difficult to break the hold that Satan has on their hearts, creating divisions and enmity. But although most people oppose me, I have determined to continue my mission until my last breath."

With a somber expression, Elijah uttered, "Sadly, those of us who live here in the spirit world cannot give higher positive energy than we already have. A new spiritual level needs to be opened where the light of God is stronger. Then we can revitalize ourselves with greater energy and inspire generations to discover the richness and beauty of their souls. Then they will be able to understand your words."

Of course, Jesus was already aware of this. Yet he was grateful that Moses and Elijah were here affirming it.

Jesus thought aloud, "Unfortunately, the evil that exists in the lower realms of the spiritual world blocks the high spiritual energy from reaching the people on earth."

They all nodded in agreement, and Moses remarked, "It is like rays of the sun that are blocked by dark clouds. Yes, occasionally the light can shine through. But it isn't the same as having the sky clear blue at all times."

After a moment, Jesus stated, "It is necessary to educate those poor men and women who are trapped in the lower parts of the spiritual world who lived a life of sin on earth. They influence people negatively. If we can clear up those lower realms successfully, then the light that illuminates the mind and spirit can penetrate to the earth and prove more influential."

Elijah said in a serious tone, "Lord, this higher spiritual level has to be opened as soon as possible."

Moses nodded, with his eyes on Jesus. "As a perfect Adam, you are the only one who can ascend to this new level."

"None of us have succeeded in our attempts," Elijah confessed. "Lord, before you appeared on earth, no one had ever attained the spiritual richness and understanding of God that you have."

With a sense of urgency, Moses said gravely, "But faithlessness is prevalent among the religious leaders, and your mission has become extremely dangerous."

"Also there is a risk that your few loyal followers might lose heart and leave you," said Elijiah, a look of concern crossing his face.

Moses added, "Lord, how long can your closest followers contend with the frustration and discouragement brought on by the continued rejection of your teachings?" He paused, then continued, "Before your disciples lose their faith and abandon you, it might be wise to restart your mission in the spiritual world."

"The faithlessness of this generation causes great feelings of sadness among us. It shouldn't have happened this way," lamented Elijah.

In a burst of anger, Moses cried out, "O generation of disbelievers! How much suffering will God and humanity have to endure because of you?"

"Lord, we must apologize to you," Elijah confessed, his face downcast. "There is a possibility that you might have to die. Before your birth, we knew there was a possibility that the Messiah would be rejected. Thus, the prophet Isaiah prophesied two distinct possibilities: one, that the lord would come in glory, in the case of absolute acceptance, and the other, that he would come and suffer and die, in the case of rejection. It is with heartfelt pain that we have concluded that due to the present circumstances, the only path that remains is one of suffering."

Jesus nodded. "Yes, I have also reflected on this possibility. A few days ago, I told some of my followers about my imminent suffering and death at the hands of my opponents." After a pause, he added, "They will soon find a way to kill me. If my twelve most faithful and other disciples abandon me, nothing of me or my teachings will survive. Without them, even if I die, all will be for nothing."

After a long moment of contemplation, Moses said to him, "It is better that you die at a specific meaningful moment. We will assist you during the phase of the delicate transition from the physical world to the spiritual world. You will have to pass through the lower levels, where the forces of Satan are more powerful, but we will be with you until you reach the level of paradise. We will enter into the new spiritual dimension with you."

Looking into Jesus' eyes, Elijah said, "Yes, we will enter with you into paradise. When our spirits resurrect to the new level, a more brilliant light of God will strengthen us and we will be able to give greater spiritual support and energy to those who do His will on earth."

Meanwhile, the three most faithful, in a state of ecstasy, were gazing at the gate. They took a few steps toward it, and each time they stepped forward, the light grew more intense. Their hearts were gleaming with joy and excitement. But Jesus promptly called them back, so they stopped and walked back to Jesus and the others.

Moses, Elijah, and the others gave the three men warm hugs, then walked away, returning through the gate.

Suddenly Peter said, "Lord, how wonderful this is! Why don't we stay here with Moses and Elijah?"

"Peter, that you ask makes me fear you do not yet understand." His tone changed. "I wanted you to experience the reality of the spiritual world, to know of its existence and be conscious of the beauty of its surroundings. You among all the children of Israel have been chosen to see this. May the memory of this experience give you strength and motivation to keep your faith alive."

James asked, "Lord, what is beyond the gate?"

Jesus smiled. "A simple community of believers and a brilliant light that nourishes the spiritual body of those who live there. The colors of the flowers are more brilliant and the water crystal clear, while the majesty of the mountains and the vast plains are of such beauty that those in the physical world pale in comparison."

Under the enchanted gaze of the three, Jesus added, "There are places in the spiritual world even higher than this, where the colors are more brilliant and the love of God even more intense. There are places where no one has lived before. There are three distinct levels in the spiritual world, and each has various mansions. The highest level is the perfect dwelling place, and it is reserved for beings with the deepest and purest hearts. It is the eternal destination. That really is the residence of the children of God who, during their life in the physical world, completed their spiritual growth, becoming the image and likeness of God, beings of divine love and conscience."

Peter, James, and John looked about, contemplating the beauty of their surroundings. They never dreamed they would experience such grace and joy of heaven with its luminous radiant light.

"As I have told you before," added Jesus, "there are different levels in the spiritual world, and in each level there are angels whose responsability is to assist men and women according to their needs during the process of growth toward perfection. Likewise on earth, humans follow three stages: the first, within the maternal womb; the second, from birth to physical death; and the third, life in the spiritual world. In each phase there is an inner evolution appropriate to that stage of growth. God is present in each stage from the beginning of life through its development." He said all this in that blissful place where everything around glows with dazzling intensity and where time has no meaning.

The three seemed puzzled, though, unsure whether they understood.

Jesus added, "In the journey of life, the soul of a human being grows in accordance with its needs, and the needs are suited to its particular state of being."

"Even inside the mother's womb?" Peter asked.

Jesus nodded. "It is a gradual spiritual formation. It is as if there were a particular spiritual identity for each stage in the process of the formation of human essence. Of course, its spiritual identity will evolve as the journey of life moves forward."

"In other words," said Peter, "there is the presence of the spiritual essence since the very moment of conception."

"Yes," replied Jesus. "This spiritual essence, this spiritual body in its primordial stage, evolves along with the formation of the human being."

"So the spirit of the person comes into existence in the very moment of conception, then goes through its gradual evolution."

Jesus nodded. "Remember wherever there is life, there is spirit. Of course, the spirit suits the kind of life form it inhabits."

Peter, greatly enthused by the way he was now developing insights on his own, added, "Most people have their own particular viewpoint, believing only in what they see. For instance, for them, life begins at the moment of birth. Thus, they don't realize the significance of the moment of conception or the development of life within the mother's womb. It is difficult for them to believe that life in the womb is as important as life outside the womb."

"Men have lost contact with God," Jesus said. "They are not in harmony with the conscience of God, so they lack divine sensibility. The greatest respect for life dwells in the deepest recesses of the soul."

John asked, "Then life begins at the moment of conception?"

"Exactly. This is where life begins. Then later, through its physical and spiritual development, it reaches perfection and becomes the image and likeness of its Creator."

"Lord, your words give life," Peter said. "The more you speak, the more I know how much I need you. Without you I would have nowhere to go. Forgive me for my previous lack of faith and for not understanding the immense value of your life. You are the Son of God, my older brother, and the brother of all humanity. Abraham, Isaac, Jacob, Moses, and the prophets will be known by all the people on earth because of you. You are the incarnation of the truth of God, and because of your grace, we can live," he concluded while James and John nodded.

Looking pleased, Jesus smiled. "My friends, it is time for you to return to your physical bodies."

"Lord, why can't we stay here longer?" asked John, gazing through the gate, beyond which in the distance a majestic mountain rose up surrounded by golden sunlight.

"No, we cannot remain outside the physical body for too long. We still belong to the world of flesh."

James said, "Lord, I want to have more experiences like this. I want to become a man of absolute goodness and able to love."

"James, your desire comes from deep in your soul. This is the desire of men who want to become trees of life, perfect beings in the image of our Heavenly Father. Within each man there is the desire to go beyond his own spiritual and intellectual limitations, to love and to be loved, and to be free of worries and suffering."

"Oh Lord!" Peter exclaimed. "How I wish that evil did not exist! It would have been better for Lucifer to follow the laws of God and never to have become Satan. But what is done is done. In the meantime, man continues to live in complete ignorance."

"And do evil and be the primary enemy of himself," added James.

Jesus nodded. "The Messiah can lead humanity to perfection. For this reason, God has created the children of Abraham. Under the guidance of the Messiah, they can convey goodness and peace, express the love of God, and be the light that creates a path on the earth that leads toward Him."

"Lord, truly you are God's Son," said Peter, beaming brightly. "Tell me, how can we have a personal relationship with God in the deepest sense?"

"By maturing physically and also spiritually. Our good essential human traits came from the traits within God Himself. He gave them to us so that we could relate to Him. God has the heart of a Parent, so His love for us is infinite and unconditional, just like our love for our own children. And we must love the rest of humanity with the same parental heart."

Then John asked unexpectedly, "Lord, which is the highest achievement a human being can reach?"

"The highest expression of perfection is to create, just as God created, and to become the managers of the creation in partnership with Him. Then we will be children, friends, and eternal companions of God, having infinite possibilities."

Then a luminous cloud covered Peter, James, and John, and the voice of God said that Jesus was His beloved Son and that they should listen to him. Suddenly they fell asleep while the cloud guided them through the lower levels, protecting them from the attacks of evil spirits. It guided them until they re-entered their physical bodies.

Jesus remained a little longer in the spiritual world. Then he, too, returned to his physical body, and touching the three apostles, he awakened them. It had been an incredible spiritual experience for them, especially Peter. Such an unusual spiritual phenomenon left them a little shaken. But Jesus told them not to be afraid. They looked up at him and realized that they were no longer in the spirit world and that there was no one with them but Jesus.

A few minutes later they started descending the mountain. Jesus asked them not to speak to anyone about this experience.

CHAPTER 32

AFTER DESCENDING THE MOUNTAIN, the four men went into the town which stood at the foot of the mountain to look for the rest of the disciples. At the center of town, they found some of the disciples surrounded by a small crowd of people. Among them were a few religious scholars of the law. When people in the crowd saw Jesus, they became quiet as his followers greeted him. Jesus asked them what they were discussing, but they remained silent.

Suddenly a man from the crowd grasped Jesus by the arm. He had heard that Jesus' disciples were in town, so he had brought his sick son to be cured. Kneeling before Jesus, he implored him to help his son, who had an evil spirit inside his body.

Jesus said sharply, "Do I still have to do miracles and healings to convince you to take my words seriously! People of little faith! Why can't you come to me for the sole purpose of listening to my teachings?"

"But you are a powerful healer," retorted the man, a sorrowful look now on his face.

Jesus stared at him in frustration. "What good is there if you do not believe in my words? My true mission is to care for your spiritual growth and to help you discover the origin of your divine nature." He gazed at the faces in the crowd, and spoke to them as though they were inept students. "My mission is to explain the origins of the evil nature in the rebellious angels, which was transmitted from generation to generation to this very faithless generation."

Pausing, Jesus looked down at the boy's father, who was still on his knees. He grasped the man's upper arm and pulled him to his feet. Then looking at the crowd, he added, "How can you go from being dominated by evil to becoming God's true children if you don't receive my teachings?" Turning back to the father, he said shortly, "Why do you only consider me a healer of disease? How long will I have to endure the humiliation of being misunderstood?"

The man stared at Jesus, not knowing how to reply.

Frowning, he pointed at his disciples. "Not even my own disciples have enough faith. They do not fully give their hearts to God, nor do they make a serious effort to fast and pray frequently." With a low sigh, he said to the religious scholars scowling at him, "Once again, you will be witnesses to the power that God has given me."

He looked into the father's eyes. "Bring your son to me."

Some men brought the possessed boy. As soon as the spirit saw Jesus, it contorted the boy violently. He fell to the ground and rolled back and forth, foaming at the mouth.

Then Jesus asked the father, "How long has this been happening?"

"Since childhood. Many times this spirit tries to kill him, throwing him into a fire or deep water."

Jesus gave the father a steady look. "A spirit also entered me during my infancy and childhood. But it was the spirit of love and truth."

The father said, "But why does this spirit want to kill him with fire and water?"

"Because there is a struggle between good and evil within each human. The good side wants to repent and be purified, but the evil side wants to sin and do evil."

Hearing this, the father shrugged, an uncertain look on his face. Then he glanced at his son, who was being held down by a few strong men from the crowd.

The father asked, "But what does the spirit want?"

Glancing at the faces in the crowd, Jesus said, "Those angels who rebelled against God were originally created to be good. There is a struggle between good and evil, even within the mind of a fallen angel. Though this spirit wants to return to God, it is still inclined to do evil." Jesus paused, giving the boy's father a hard look. "You and your parents have committed many sins through a life distant from God."

"I am so sorry," uttered the father. "Please have compassion on us."

"You have to repent for your sins and live according to the will of God by loving your enemies and living for the sake of others. For this reason, everything is possible for him who believes in the Lord."

"Oh, I believe! Help me to have deeper faith."

"What is faith for you? To have faith is not only to ask for God when you need help, but to seek with complete sincerity the company of His spirit. Maintain a humble and pure heart, and genuinely seek to understand God's words so you might live your daily life according to His will."

The man nodded, his heart anxiously waiting for a miracle. But Jesus went on in a firm voice, "All sinners need to repent and be determined not to commit any more impure acts. But this can only occur if they hear the truth, which carefully exposes sin. Without a clear knowledge of the nature of evil, people cannot understand the need for repentance. For this I have come, to teach you the truth. Have you come to gain eternal life? No! You are here for the flesh, not for the spirit. And what will you do after receiving my help? Continue a life without any spiritual significance?"

Jesus took a deep breath, his eyes darting around the eyes of the men in the crowd. "In a decade or two, your physical lives will be over without your achieving spiritual progress. Without my words and my family, you will go through your physical life without spiritual growth, unable to free yourselves from the control that Satan has over you."

While Jesus spoke, more people came to listen. Then, standing over the sick boy, he ordered the filthy spirit out of his body once and for all, and to never return. Immediately the evil spirit left the boy, but not without first violently contorting him on the ground, leaving him motionless.

Those present thought the boy was dead. But Jesus took his hand and helped him to rise, and the boy was able to stand on his own.

All the disciples approached Jesus, their eyes on his stern face. After a short while, Thomas broke the silence. "Why could we not cast out this spirit?"

"Such spirits can only be cast out with prayer and fasting."

That evening a strong breeze blew through the valley when Jesus called Peter to his side.

"Peter, when I was speaking to Thomas, did you understand what I meant by prayer and fasting?"

"Well, I believe you wish for us to pray and fast more to receive greater spiritual strength, so that we are capable of confronting all types of evil spirits."

"A person has to achieve a level of internal growth to communicate fully with God. Then he will receive such authority," explained Jesus. "There are divine laws that regulate the power of the children of God. These powers are given only to those people who are spiritually mature, who have achieved a level of growth and understanding of the divine laws. Without being one with God, without being in complete harmony with His love and His conscience, you cannot comprehend the revelation about His divine laws. As a rule, it is not permitted for immature men to receive or use the power of God. First, you have to be a responsible and trusted son in the eyes of God. Then He will give you greater power and more authority to cast out evil spirits. For this reason I say that you need to pray, fast, meditate on the significance of my words, and practice them daily. Then you will grow internally."

"Lord, can I achieve spiritual perfection one day and become a true child of God?"

"This depends on you, Peter. The path to perfection begins with repentance. Then you have to cleanse yourself from all traces of impurities. At the same time, you must elevate your internal nature coming from God. This requires great effort on your part, to choose always what is from God and to be willing to renounce what is of evil. You need me because without me you cannot come to life."

"Lord, you know I love you. I have no doubts you are the Messiah. I want to understand your words in all of their depth. I want to be like you."

"Peter, you must conquer fear. Always be ready to give your life for the sake of God. Be careful that the temptations of the flesh and the words of my opponents don't weaken your faith."

"Lord, there is no doctrine or temptation that can discourage me from following you."

"What about the fear of losing your life?"

Peter hesitated. "Until now I have never had to choose between you and my life."

"You need to strengthen your heart."

The moon was already high in the sky when Jesus called his other disciples in the area to join with him and Peter.

After Jesus offered a spontaneous prayer from the deepest part of his heart, Judas began telling him about his confrontation with the scholars of the law.

Jesus gazed at him. "When I returned from the mountain, I saw you and Simon with these so-called scholars. But as soon as you saw me, you both quickly stepped away, as if you didn't want me to see you with such men."

"Forgive us, Master," uttered Simon the Zealot.

Jesus gave a little nod and turned back to Judas. "The scholars of the law and the religious authorities would rather see me dead than preaching the way of heaven."

"Are you he?" asked Judas roughly.

Jesus nodded. He sensed that even his longtime followers were losing faith in him. Whatever Jesus did or said produced a negative reaction by his opponents, which in turn slowly discouraged his disciples.

After having spoken with Moses and Elijah on the mountaintop, Jesus began to prepare himself for the possibility of giving up his life, in case his opponents continued obstructing his ministry.

The following morning, Jesus gathered his disciples again. He informed them that soon he would go to Jerusalem and suffer greatly at the hands of his opponents and be killed. He also told them that on the third day of his physical death he would resurrect in the spirit.

The disciples were shocked! They begged to know what he meant by all this, but Jesus did not wish to give further details.

Later that day, while Jesus was resting a short distance from his followers, Peter approached him and said, "Lord! Have you not said the final goal is the throne of Israel, and that the Romans will welcome you when you attain the support of the religious leaders?"

"Yes, you know my words very well. But they are rejecting me."

"They are wrong! If they knew you as we do, they would quickly change their opinion about you."

"But they do not understand, nor do they want to understand. And now, because of lack of faith it is necessary for me to leave this world. Peter, I may have no other choice but to offer my life now and pass on to the spiritual world."

"You might die? But you taught us that our mission is to convince this generation that you are the Messiah and that the kingdom of God is at hand." His voice rose anxiously. "Lord, how can this nation become a model nation and testify to God's presence among men if you die?"

"I know, Peter. But for me the path is of suffering."

"Lord, what about our blood? If you die now, what will happen to my dreams, to all of the plans for you to become the king of Israel, and to me, your most faithful subject?"

Fully aware of the spirit lurking behind Peter's self-concern, Jesus rebuked him, shouting, "Get away from me, Satan! Your feelings are not of God, but of men!"

After a long moment of tense silence, Jesus spoke in a milder voice. "Peter, you know that I have tried to convince this faithless generation to change their opinion of me. The harder I try, the more they oppose me. So it has become necessary to end my ministry in this world and continue it in the spiritual world."

Peter stared at him in silence, unsure whether there was a deeper meaning in his words.

Jesus added, "Soon I will open a new mansion in the spiritual world. From there humanity can receive new inspiration, and you and my other followers will receive stronger spiritual energy to continue your mission. Together, with the help of the Holy Spirit, we will inspire people to understand the deep significance of my words."

Peter was speechless as he continued staring at Jesus, hoping this was all a dream. His face expressed the sorrow in his heart.

"Now, Peter, do you understand why I scolded you just now? Of course my Heavenly Father does not desire an early death for me. Yet over the centuries, God has seen how the prophets were badly treated, so He is aware this could also happen to His Son. For this reason, Isaiah spoke of two prophecies. In the case of absolute rejection, there is no other alternative but for me to sacrifice my physical body."

Still not convinced about this, Peter said in a low voice, "Lord, all of us disciples will support you no matter what. Well … almost all. We are worried about Judas' attitude. He acts as though he is not part of us."

Jesus nodded reflectively, then said with finality, "I will speak to him."

About an hour later, Jesus and Judas were walking just outside of town along a road bordered by a low stone wall and wild bushes.

"You still don't believe that I am the Messiah, do you?"

Judas gave a vague shrug, a crooked smile on his face.

Jesus was silent for a while before saying, "The Lord God wants you to conform to the new path of freedom. Are you willing to give up the old ways of violence and lay down your sword?"

Judas remained quiet as he stared at the road ahead.

"Are you willing to make space in your heart for God and make yourself new?" asked Jesus.

"What for?" Judas asked, his voice faint.

"Recently you've met with your Zealot friends, haven't you?"

Judas gave a half-nod, wondering who had told Jesus about it.

"I know how much you detest the Romans," added Jesus, with a note of concern. "But if you do not transform your hate into love, and your malevolence into peace of mind, then you won't be able to hear God's call. Without heavenly guidance, you will be unable to follow the true spiritual path that can lead you to become a perfect child of God."

"Perfect child of God?" echoed Judas, with a gruff laugh.

Stopping where the road forked to the north and west, Jesus said quietly, "Judas, I cannot interfere with your decisions. You have to answer to God's call by your own will."

"God gave this land to us Jews, just as His promises are for us! I cannot accept the idea of sharing God's covenant with those not coming from Abraham's blood."

Jesus shook his head sadly as they began walking back to town.

"Violence and hatred have never brought man closer to God."

"But Kind David fought his battles with swords."

"Those were different times and circumstances. Now is the time for people to open their hearts to God's unchanging love and their minds to His eternal values."

"Your way is the cowardly way."

"Judas, it isn't my intention to submit to the will of Rome and her pagan gods and rituals. Don't make little of the power of God's love and the truth. Trust in me. I am the vessel of His love and truth. It is His will that you follow me."

Judas shook his head in disapproval. "You've told me to be patient and wait. Wait for what? I plan to do great things for God. It is difficult for me to just sit and listen and wait for your great miracle to happen."

"But Judas, you do have to be patient and learn to control your heart."

"In a certain way, I admire Peter and your other disciples. But I feel like an outsider when I am among them."

"Well, they feel uneasy with your hostile disposition."

"I know. They make their feelings known to me."

"They worry you might bring danger to them and their families due to your affiliation with the Zealots. They don't want to be mistakenly labeled as rebels by the authorities."

The two men walked in silence for a couple minutes. Then as they reached the outskirts of town, Judas said abruptly, "I don't care about your teaching." His voice was a tense whisper.

Not showing any surprise, Jesus nodded slightly.

Feeling as if his heart were being pulled in opposite directions, Judas muttered good-bye and quickly walked up the road into town.

CHAPTER 33

It HAD ALREADY BEEN DECIDED for Jesus to venture into Judea to offer himself on the altar of sacrifice. So the next morning he met with his close disciples and asked them to accompany him to Jerusalem. One of his followers asked if first he could return home to bury his father, who had just died. Jesus told him it was better to go to Jerusalem now and announce the word of God, and let those who are spiritually dead bury the dead.

Another disciple asked Jesus if he could go home and say good-bye to his family before setting off for Judea. Jesus knew this person had no intentions of following him to Jerusalem, wanting instead to return to his ordinary life. So Jesus answered that whoever put his hand to the plough and looked back was not fit for the kingdom of heaven. Although some of his followers drifted away, the twelve apostles and a number of disciples traveled with Jesus toward the capital of Judea.

During their journey, they would stop in towns to preach to the people. He was still intent on giving spiritual life to those humble men and women who had a deep thirst in their souls for God's love and for freedom from affliction. Yet, as they drew closer to Jerusalem, Jesus knew that all his efforts had to be directed toward his early physical death. Up to that point, only his closest followers knew of such a turn of events.

Not even I was aware of my husband's decision to leave this world. Jesus thought it was better that I didn't know. Though he still hoped to find support among influential Judeans, he realized that after the failure of John the Baptist, he would be fighting an uphill battle. Now many of his own followers were losing faith.

In reality, until reaching the gates of Jerusalem, there were few men who had actually given up everything to follow Jesus. Many of those who surrounded him were only passive spectators who never had deep faith. Jesus had tried to win support in Capernaum, Corozan, and Bethsaida, hoping that people living in those towns would listen and respond to him.

On one occasion, Peter reminded Jesus that the twelve and some other disciples had left their old lives behind to follow him. Jesus expressed his gratitude for such faith, saying that those who followed him and left behind their parents, siblings, wives, and children would receive great rewards.

It was during this time that a wealthy man approached Jesus and asked what he must do to gain eternal life. Jesus told him that he should sell all his belongings and give the money to the poor and then follow him.

Upon hearing this, the man walked away sadly, not willing to renounce his comfortable life. Jesus looked at his disciples and stated that the rich and powerful rarely enter God's kingdom, because of their attachment to earthly things. He concluded by saying that it was easier for a camel to go through the eye of a needle than for a rich man to enter God's kingdom.

During the journey to Jerusalem, Jesus announced his death and the dangerous situation his followers would encounter upon entering Jerusalem. Those religious leaders and other vocal opponents who were critical of his ministry would be on the lookout and arrest him. Jesus explained to his disciples the prophecies would come to pass regarding events that might take place if the Messiah were rejected. He told them that after his physical death, he would go to the spiritual world and open up a new mansion where he would be a spiritual leader.

Astonished by this, James and his brother John approached Jesus to ask a favor.

James said imploringly, "If possible, we hope that in the kingdom of God one of us will sit on your right and the other on your left, so we can share the glory with you."

Jesus gave them a solemn look. "You don't know what you ask. From this moment on, the kingdom of God will be built slowly with the blood and sweat of the martyrs." He focused on John. "Are you willing to suffer and be persecuted for my sake?"

"Yes, Lord. We are ready."

"I appreciate your strong faith. Beware, for you will suffer due to your loyalty. My foes will mistreat and persecute you. But it is not on me to decide who will sit on my right and my left." After a brief pause, Jesus added, "Abraham, Isaac, Jacob, Moses, Elijah, and all the prophets who preceded us will rise with me in paradise. Their places have been reserved."

The others disciples, on hearing the petition of the two brothers, expressed their disappointment because each one of them hoped to be closest to Jesus in his kingdom, to sit at the right hand of the Messiah.

Jesus, who knew that Lucifer's prideful desire to seek after power and honor was embedded in the minds of men, called his disciples around him and said, "The thirst for power is not part of God's nature, nor is it part of the original nature of man. It is a fallen aspect of Lucifer, who didn't want to relinquish power to the children of God."

By telling this to his faithful followers, Jesus wanted them to understand that men have the responsibility to rid themselves of their fallen nature inherited from Lucifer.

Jesus added, "You know that kings, emperors, and military leaders of the world like to impose their will on people, often suppressing their liberties and stripping them of their dignity. So when you are trapped by a desire for power, the best thing to do is to choose the humble way instead by serving others. Therefore, if any among you wish to be more important than others, you should instead become their servant.

He told them to maintain trust in both God and him. For in the house of his Father, there is ample room for everyone. Although Jesus had spoken about this before, some of the disciples were uncertain what he was talking about.

With a puzzled look, Thomas asked, "Lord, how can we understand the path to get there if we have no idea where you are about to go?"

Jesus explained that they indeed knew the way. "Simply trust me. Believe that I am the Messiah. And put my teachings into practice."

A few days later, scholars of the law, as well as the Pharisees and the Sadducees, attempted to ridicule Jesus and make him look ignorant. They confronted him, trying to humiliate him in front of the people. One Pharisee asked when the kingdom of heaven would come. Jesus replied that the kingdom would not come in a spectacular way or be announced with the sound of trumpets, but rather by the spiritual growth of individuals, since God resides inside each person. "The kingdom is in the deepest part of each one of us," he said to them.

Another Pharisee asked Jesus which was the most important commandment. He answered that the first commandment is to love God with all your heart, all your soul, and all your strength. Then he added that the second commandment is to love your neighbor as yourself. He told the Pharisees there were no higher commandments than these two.

Jesus wanted to instill these commandments into the hearts of his disciples, teaching them that God's children should love Him and others as well, and also to love and respect the world of God's creation. These commandments form the basis of goodness, connecting God's heart of love with the hearts of all human beings.

Through his interaction with the Pharisees, Jesus observed that among them there were some who were prepared to receive his teachings. Unfortunately, they couldn't perceive Jesus as anything other than a simple messenger. It was almost impossible for them to even consider that Jesus was from the blood lineage of King David, especially since most Judeans had a low opinion of those men and women from Galilee, a region known to be full of pagans.

At this point in Jesus' ministry, Peter was the one who had the closest relationship with him. For over a week Peter had been pondering many matters, one of which was the miracle performed by Jesus in Bethany.

With several questions on his mind, Peter approached Jesus as he stood alone near an orchard of fig and pomegranate trees. Peter couldn't remember a more perfect day than this one. The air was filled with the scent of early spring, flowers adorning the bushes and trees. They were only a few miles north of Jerusalem, so Jesus' prayers had become even more serious, begging God to show him a way to continue his mission on earth.

Seeing Peter walking toward him, Jesus wiped the tears from his cheeks and greeted him with a strained smile.

"Lord, may I have a short talk with you?"

Jesus nodded and stepped over to the low stone wall bordering the orchard. They sat on the top stones, which had been leveled off, and looked at one another for a long moment, both realizing this could be their last time together like this.

"Lord, I have a question about the resurrection of your wife's brother. You knew you were going to resurrect him, didn't you?"

Jesus answered with a smile, "Yes."

"If you knew you were about to resurrect him, why were you crying?"

"Peter, the truth is that Lazarus was not dead. In reality, his spiritual body was not detached from his physical body. It was the same for the other people I had resurrected. In the case of Lazarus, with a little help it was possible to bring the floating spiritual body back inside the physical body again. All I had to do was to direct Lazarus' spirit into his body."

He paused. "I knew that God had prepared such an event so that I could intervene to give witness to the fact that God had sent me." Jesus concluded without answering Peter's question.

"Lord, is that why when you were informed of his death, you said that the infirmity was not of a dead man but rather an opportunity to show the power of God and the glory of the Son of God?"

"Yes."

Peter met Jesus' gaze. "Miracles inspire the believers and help them to maintain strong faith."

"Right," said Jesus. "But miracles are necessary for those whose faith is unstable, who are not strong spiritually and whose relation with God is not deep enough. For those who have a strong faith in God, whose hearts are connected to God's love, there is no need for miracles."

"Yes, Lord. But why did you cry?"

Jesus hesitated, searching for an appropriate response. "I told you that the Messiah comes as a second Adam to repair the damages made by the first Adam, because the sin of the first man became the sin of all men."

"Yes," said Peter, nodding.

"So if there's a second Adam, then there has to be a woman in the position of a second Eve. Right?"

"Yes, Lord. This is what you have taught us."

Patting Peter's shoulder, Jesus added, "You understand it well. I am the incarnation of God's masculinity. Yet I'm not complete without my complementary part, a woman. She is the femininity of God, His daughter, and the second Eve."

Peter nodded as he caught sight of Thomas and James, who were on the road and helping an old couple unload some baggage off a donkey cart.

Jesus cleared his throat. "The Messiah comes as the father of humanity. I need my Eve to be able to realize my mission. I have not come only to teach words. I must also set the path for family life. It is very important that human beings become related by flesh and blood with the parents of humanity so that everyone becomes connected substantially with God's eternal family."

"Now I understand your sermon in the Capernaum synagogue when you talked about your blood and flesh," said Peter, with a half-smile. "Is this the meaning of your being the true olive tree? Didn't you say that we are the branches of the tree, and you are the roots?"

After a moment of reflection, Jesus answered, "I stated that I am the good olive tree, and fallen humanity is like a wild olive tree. In order for you to become a good tree, you need to graft onto me. Fallen men, imprisoned by the original sin, are unable to generate children without original sin. As I explained to you more than once, it is necessary to be connected to the Messiah in spirit and in flesh. The children of the Messiah will create new lives which will intermingle with people by marriage, which in time will generate more blood and flesh of the Messiah. It is like an immense tree whose branches generate more branches. The flesh and blood of the Messiah would extend from generation to generation until everyone in the world is connected with him not only spiritually but also in flesh. Then the world will be one big family."

Peter's eyes opened wide. "Lord, now I understand why you cried in Bethany. It was not for Lazarus, but for the lack of faith of your wife and of the chosen people. You were concerned about your lineage! The risk of not being able to leave a family structure well rooted in the earth."

Jesus nodded. "Truly in my heart there was no greater pain than that of knowing how important my family was in God's plan and not being able to fulfill it successfully according to His plan. There was no stronger desire in my heart than that of having my wife and children live in harmony with God's plan."

A sad look crossed Peter's face. "Lord, why must you shed so many tears?"

"No one is forcing me to sacrifice my life. I could renounce my mission and live peacefully. But I know the Father, and how much He suffers from having lost His children to evil. I know how much God needs me to establish the world that He had planned for Adam and Eve ..."

A few days later Jesus and many of his close disciples arrived at last to the walled city of Jerusalem, which teemed with activity on the day before the Sabbath. Peter had more questions to ask, so he pressed Jesus to meet with him. Jesus agreed and led Peter along a path bordered by olive trees toward the upper slope of the Mount of Olives.

The two walked in silence uphill under the warm rays of the sun on a pleasant spring day. As the noises of the massive city gradually faded, Peter recalled his wonderful spiritual experience when Moses and Elijah had appeared to Jesus. The event was still vivid in his mind, filling his head with puzzling questions.

Jesus stopped walking and lowered his body onto a large rock near the gnarled, bent trunk of an ancient olive tree, its branches of green leaves providing them with shade.

For several moments, Peter gazed at the upper section of the Temple far below. Worried about what might take place during the coming days, Peter suppressed a sigh as he sat cross-legged on the grassy ground in front of Jesus.

"Lord, since coming to know you, I've learned so much about the prophets and the Scriptures. But I still have more questions than answers in my head."

Jesus made no comment, only a slight nod, his reddened eyes roaming across the city below.

Breaking the silence, Peter said, "Can a husband and wife have children in the spiritual world?"

"Despite the fact that life in the spiritual world is active, centered upon the family, there is no procreation." After a pause, Jesus added, "Children can only be born from the physical body."

Peter thought aloud, "So people can become parents only in the physical world?"

"Yes. Also you need to know that until the true Adam and true Eve go to the spiritual world as a perfected couple, the men and women already living there cannot come together as husbands and wives. This is why I said that when men and women go to the spiritual world, they will live as do the angels, apart from each other. Since the creation is in a state of imperfection, the masculine and feminine genders have to stay separate." A frown crossed his face. "Do you recall when one of the Pharisees tried to trick me with a question regarding life in the next world?"

"Yes, Lord. It was about a woman who got married seven times with seven different brothers. She married the first, but he died without ever giving her a child. According to the law of Moses, the next eldest brother had to marry his sister-in-law. But he also died, leaving no descendants. So she married the third. The same fate happened to all the remaining brothers. None of them left descendants. In the end, she died as well and went to the spiritual world. So the Pharisee asked you which of the seven brothers she would stay with in the other life."

"Yes, and I answered that at this point it is useless to ponder such matters, for in the next world men and women live as the angels in heaven. In other words, they will not live as pairs. There is an invisible barrier separating males from females. As I said, it is because true Adam, the perfected son of God, and true Eve, the perfected daughter of God, have not yet appeared in the spiritual world. However, when the true son and daughter of God arrive there and take on the roles of perfected parents and lords of the creation, then the gates of heaven will open for every-one. On that day, the kingdom of God will be proclaimed, celebrating the unity between men and women. Those will be the last days of the existence of evil. Only goodness will prevail."

Peter nodded reflectively, thankful to be hearing Jesus openly talking of mysteries that until then the Lord had shared only with me.

CHAPTER 34

DURING THEIR JOURNEY TOWARD JERUSALEM, Jesus and his closer followers were accompanied by a number of lesser disciples, me and several other women supporters. Since Bethany was only a short distance from the restless capital of Israel, I decided to visit my sister Martha.

On my third morning there, Jesus came to Bethany. Even though only a few days had passed since I was last with him, my heart longed for his presence. I had thought we would be separated for a couple of weeks. So when I heard that he was on the road leading to the house, I ran outside to greet him. In my haste I forgot to put on my sandals. But my emotions were so high that I didn't feel any pain as the tiny stones pressed against my bare feet.

Only a few carts being pulled by oxen and mules were moving along the road. There was also a small flock of sheep being guided by a shepherd and two barking dogs. When I saw Jesus drawing closer, I called out his name and hurried toward him. In our culture, married couples seldom display affection out in public. But since Jesus was unlike other men, he opened his arms as I moved closer to him, resting my head against his chest.

"I missed you so much," I whispered. Soon I noticed everyone staring at us, so I stepped away. An elderly lady was scowling at me, while the shepherd gave Jesus a welcoming smile. "Rabbi! One day come to my home for a meal."

Jesus nodded and greeted several other people who were crowding around us.

Some of Jesus' followers living nearby heard he was in Judea. They came to town, hoping to see him. Many of them had met Jesus at the beginning of his ministry in Judea. But he hadn't seen most of them since the imprisonment of John the Baptist, when he had to flee and return to Galilee. Unfortunately, there were also many opponents of Jesus, whose faces were visibly irritated.

Before reaching Martha's home, I said to him, "Some of my brother's acquaintances from Jerusalem are inside. They are trying to convince Lazarus and Martha that you are a blasphemous devil and a grave danger to Israel. They also want me to separate myself from you."

Jesus gave me a sad smile. "You haven't fallen into their trap, have you?"

"I am the wife of the Messiah," I said with confidence. "No force in this world can pull me away from you. You are my Lord, my Adam, the father of my children."

Jesus had a complacent look as he reached for my hand and kissed it. I suppose he now knew with certainty that he could count on me under any circumstances.

I murmured, "Dear, thank you for never losing hope in me. You saw things in me that I was unable to see. Forgive me for disappointing you in the past. I should've listened to you from the very beginning."

He looked at me with a serene smile. "I felt you were an exceptional woman, someone ready to be educated and to be elevated to the position of Eve."

"I am sorry for causing so much trouble for you, Jesus."

He gazed at me, his eyes full of love. "Mary, those were days of uncertainty when you weren't able to overcome the difficult situations. Not only were you distracted by your daily chores, but your parents and neighbors kept criticizing me for being away from home so often."

I remembered the time when my father warned me that my marriage with Jesus was in serious trouble, due to his frequent absences. Several days later when Jesus left again, I finally relented to my father's pressure and decided to separate from my husband.

Jesus must have felt my anxiety, for he uttered in a warm voice, "Mary, you fill up my heart, making me feel less alone in the world."

This was my husband's nature. He was the perfect incarnation of God's love.

I looked at him with wet eyes, allowing my thoughts to drift back to the time when I cursed anyone who came to our home to discuss religious matters with him.

That day in Bethany, my heart was still crying when I noticed Jesus looking at me with compassion, as if he knew what I was thinking. He put the palms of his hands on my cheeks and kissed my forehead.

"Forgive me for not being a better wife during our early years together. I didn't want to abandon the security of the house, and I was irritated by the presence of so many people. Our house was almost like a synagogue, with men debating with you all the time. I was unable to recognize the importance of your mission, your loyalty to God. I resented you spending time with others, instead of me and the children. It was as if I were possessed by evil spirits!"

After catching my breath, I added, "I should have controlled my emotions better. There are no excuses for my behavior. I knew you were a very special person. Despite that, I didn't take you seriously. But now I have no greater desire than to ease your suffering. I want to do all I can to please you, and to help you to accomplish your mission."

"I know, Mary." He hesitated, then spoke in a low voice. "I might not be able to fulfill my mission in this world. So my physical life could be drawing to a close."

I saw the serious look in his eyes. "What?" I asked, my hands trembling noticeably.

"I have almost no support," he said, his voice tense. "All the important religious and social leaders who should have lifted me up ... well, they are the ones who have turned against me. Even my closest disciples look at me differently now."

In the past I had heard Jesus make similar comments, but now his words had a bitter tone, foreboding an unavoidable tragedy.

"Forgive me," I whispered again, with an imploring look.

"Mary, there seems to be no alternative other than to offer my life for the sake of God's providence. Unless some powerful men suddenly come to my side, my opponents will have me killed one dark evening. Also, your life and the life of our children will be in grave danger."

My heart was breaking into a thousand pieces. "Jesus, don't say such things," I uttered, tears on my cheeks. "I will always be nearby and serve you as my king."

"Mary, if it's necessary to sacrifice my life on the altar of the world, then I must go down that lonely path. My followers cannot keep their faith in me unless they get special spiritual help. Energized by it, my followers will overcome adverse circumstances. It is my hope that through their voices and deeds, the chosen people will open their eyes and recognize that I am their Messiah."

"How can I live without you?" I asked in despair.

"Mary, I will go to the spiritual world first, and you will follow later. But you need to understand that in the spiritual world we will not be able to live together."

I realized that I had wasted precious time during those unfaithful years, when instead I should have given my heart fully to him and grow spiritually.

How many years were wasted! So many opportunities thrown away!

Trying to be optimistic, I looked at Jesus with a forced smile. I told him that whatever decision he came to, I would be there, willing to give all of my heart for the success of his mission.

He looked at me, his gaze filled with warmth. "Mary, I've waited so long for the day when you would understand your mistakes. And in so doing, you have joined with me in my endeavor to bring God's love to humanity. By your own will, you've come to me with the desire to make changes in your life. You have asked me to help you free yourself from doubts and the pressure from those who are hostile to me."

I kissed his cheek. "Thank you for helping me. I feel like I've been liberated from negative spirits."

Jesus looked toward the sky and raised his hands, his expression imploring. "Ah, if the chosen people would only listen to me! Then my mission on earth would continue and my family could become the visible model for humanity."

We were about to enter the courtyard of my sister's house when Jesus noticed some of his Judean followers coming up the road with big smiles on their faces.

Jesus greeted each one of them fondly. We all sat in the courtyard and sipped tea brought to us by my sister. Jesus and I listened with interest as these warmhearted men and women spoke about their families and their faith in him.

After an hour of light-hearted sharing, Jesus offered a farewell and reached for my hand and led me from the courtyard. Saying little, we took a walk along a path bordering the furrowed fields just outside of town, simply content with being alone together.

When we returned to Martha's house and stepped into the front room, I was surprised to see so many people. To Jesus' delight, Judas and some other close followers had come to pay their respects to my sister's family. Lazarus' friends from Jerusalem were still there, and they began questioning Jesus about his teachings in a harsh tone. Yet after a half-hour, Jesus seemed to touch their hearts, speaking eloquently about the importance of being good parents, and emphasizing the love between husband and wife, as well as between parents and children, and brothers and sisters. "Healthy families are the key to building God's kingdom on earth," he concluded, pleased to see agreeable smiles on their faces.

After Lazarus left with his friends, Martha and I joined Jesus and his disciples for the evening meal. I was seated next to my husband, listening quietly as they spoke about a variety of matters. Soon, I stood and got an alabaster vase of perfume made of pure nard. I broke the vase and poured the perfume on Jesus' head. In my heart was the desire to anoint him in the position of a father, for I was the one who made him a father by giving him descendants. In Capernaum, I had anointed Jesus' feet as though I were a stranger. But in Bethany I anointed his head in my position as wife of the Messiah. It was through my womb that he had assured himself of a descendant.

Upset by my use of expensive perfume, Judas suddenly stood up and expressed his disapproval over what he considered was a waste of money. There was much anger in his heart, so Jesus called him from the table to have a serious talk.

As they stepped into the courtyard, Jesus said to him, "Would you like to sit, or take a walk?"

"Let's walk," uttered Judas, regretting his flair-up at the supper table.

Jesus remarked, "Judas, I see much hate and bitterness in your eyes."

"Jesus, you are a powerful man. I've never seen anyone with such amazing abilities. God has given you supernatural power! I am convinced that God wants you to use this power to battle the enemy, to testify to His greatness against the pagan gods of Rome."

"Judas, you have great expectations of me. Sadly they are not spiritually motivated."

"I am a Zealot. I do believe in His kingship, in God's sovereignty in our land."

"I haven't come to curse or kill, but to give love and life to all people."

"Jesus, you are a good man. But you aren't the kind of Messiah who can lead us to victory. You are too conciliatory. Such traits are useless against the Roman military. What we need is a strong hand, and that's why you aren't the leader we seek."

"Judas, not long ago I asked you to follow the example of my other disciples. They have offered their lives to my ministry, earnestly trying to understand my teachings while loving others with all their hearts."

"And what does that achieve?" retorted Judas. A note of arrogance had entered his voice. "Most of your followers are ignorant fools mesmerized by your magic powers."

Jesus narrowed his eyes. "You have neither repented for your sins nor responded to the call of God's love.

Taken aback by Jesus' words, Judas said defensively, "I don't hate you or the others. I just think you should be more aggressive."

"At this point, you know where I stand. And though you are familiar with my beliefs, you have decided to ignore them and insist upon your shortsighted views."

"No, Rabbi, believe me I have wanted to have faith in you. I have been waiting for you to make the ultimate decision to start a revolt. There are many others like me who are prepared to take up arms against the enemy. Be the leader we know you can be!"

"Judas, a violent revolt won't subdue the Romans. Only a revolution of …"

"Yeah, I know," interrupted Judas. "A revolution of the heart. You keep saying that, but everyone knows that won't be enough to chase the enemy away!"

"God doesn't want to chase them away, but to help them to become truer human beings. If you would only listen to me! Love and truth have the power to change a person's heart."

"But the Romans have no use for your kind of love and truth. They are content with their own gods and way of living."

"Judas, have faith in me, and apply God's words to your daily life. Soon you will see a change of heart in yourself."

"It is you who needs to see the truth." Judas gave him a twisted smile. "Sorry, but I am disillusioned with your naive ways. I was a fool to have thought you could be the Messiah."

"Surrender your heart to God, and be guided by His spirit."

Scowling, Judas blurted out, "Maybe it's better to put an end to your childish mystical message before more people really begin to think you are the Messiah. We believe the real Messiah could arrive anytime now. So it's in the interest of our nation to save people who are being manipulated by naive Messiahs giving false hope." He made an angry gesture. "We want to be ready when the battle starts. We are people of action. We have spent our lives in preparation for this day!"

Jesus was silent a long moment. "What are you planning against me, Judas?"

"Nothing. I will not raise a hand against you. You're a good man, but you are giving people false hope and distracting them from their real duties. We have to focus on the real promise of building a strong Israel."

Jesus' voice was low and stricken. "Judas, don't let misguided passions sweep you away into thoughtless actions."

"It is your misguided passions that are the real danger. Surely we don't want people divided into groups, each one following their own Messiah. We need to answer in unison to the real Messiah's call and be ready to fight until death if necessary."

"Judas, don't sentence yourself to spiritual death. Follow the bright light of God's eternal love and truth."

"I am ready to give my life to God. I will fight for God, and I'm even willing to die for the glory of God!"

"Open your heart."

"Bah!" Judas said, throwing up his hands and walking quickly away toward the center of town …

The Feast of the Passover was approaching, and the population of Jerusalem was preparing for the large influx of people from the surrounding countryside, as well as those from towns and villages throughout Galilee, Perea, and Samaria. Pilgrims flocked into the walled city, hoping to find places to lodge. The religious authorities of the Temple were also busy as they made arrangements for the presence for additional priests who would provide support and assistance with the offerings. Extra stalls had been added to the various markets around the city. Mules and carts loaded with a variety of vegetables, fruits, and other goods were on their way to the city, while vendors put out merchandise when not dealing with customers.

Once more, the children of Abraham would celebrate the annual events that commemorated the exodus of the Hebrews from Egypt after four hundred years of slavery. By all appearances, it seemed this year would be no different from previous ones. No one had any idea of the tragedy that was about to unfold that would change the destiny of an entire people. Only those who had been plotting knew of the drama they were about to play.

Presently at the Temple, the high priest was sitting at a table in a small meeting room near his office, studying the face of the man across from him. Judas Iscariot was staring back at Caiaphas, trying to penetrate his enigmatic look.

For the past minute or so, neither one had spoken a word. They quietly sipped water and tried to read each other's thoughts. Finally, Caiaphas said in a low voice, "If we detain Jesus for a lengthy period, it will be done in a discreet manner."

"There is no need for a long detention," replied Judas. "It's only a simple matter of convincing Jesus to renounce his senseless methods."

Caiaphas shrugged. "We just want to talk to him. I am sure he can be reasoned with."

Judas wondered just how much the high priest knew about Jesus' teachings and the sincerity of his heart. "Remember, I will help you only if you promise that no harm will come to him and his family."

"We have no plans to punish him. For every false prophet that is punished, it seems fifteen more rise up to take his place."

"Just convince him to return to his senses. That is our understanding. Correct?"

The high priest raised his eyebrows. "Are you with us, or not?" he said sharply.

Judas hesitated, his lips pressed together. "I am with those patriots who long for the coming of the Anointed One, who will fight shoulder to shoulder with us as we drive all heathens from our lands and regain our former glory!"

Caiaphas failed to hide a grimace as he looked at Judas silently. "We have no intention of seeing one more Jew killed," he said. "But you must remember these are restless times. Sometimes harsh means are necessary to keep the peace."

Judas' throat tightened. "Jesus has a strong mind, full of convictions. It might not be easy to convince him. But he has a good heart and a generous nature."

Caiaphas drew a breath, looking at him suspiciously. "Tell me, Judas. Why are you betraying your Messiah?"

"He is not my Messiah!" Judas said with a flash of anger. "But I know him to be a righteous man who loves the Lord. I disagree with his ideas of sharing our destiny with the Romans and other pagans. He wants to share God's blessings with all Gentiles, as if they and others came from Abraham's blood." His tone changed. "Some of his beliefs are pure madness, and his judgment of human nature is naive and foolish."

Rubbing his temples, Caiaphas uttered, "This Jesus sounds like a dangerous man. Under his message of love hides personal greed and lust for power. His eyes are now on Judea. Certainly he is scheming to sit on the throne of this holy land."

Judas nodded absently. "Jesus hopes to become king of Israel, then march to Rome and conquer Caesar with love and truth ... Pure madness!"

Caiaphas folded his hands and rested them on the table. "Judas, we need to be very careful in the days to come. Caesar keeps our nation divided for practical reasons. He knows we are a strong people willing to die for our sacred beliefs."

"And willing to kill to regain our former glory. All we need is a great leader!"

Caiaphas nodded. He sipped the water, then returned his gaze to Judas' somber face. "If the common people clamor for this Nazarene to be king, the Romans will think we here at the Temple are behind it. Then the military will convey their disapproval by inflicting pain and suffering upon us all."

Judas shook a fist in the air. "If they try, we will be ready to respond!"

Caiaphas smiled without humor. "People like you and the Romans use swords to gain power, but this Jesus is clever. He relies on the hopes and expectations of our people. He plays with their dreams to gain his objectives." A note of irritation entered his voice. "I am the liaison between the Romans and the religious leaders. The eyes of the Roman governor are always on me. Pilate watches my every move like a cat toying with a mouse."

"Stand up to him," insisted Judas. "Don't be intimidated by his bullying!"

"No one intimidates me," Caiaphas remarked in an undertone. He paused, closing his eyes as he came to a decision. "Jesus must be stopped before it's too late," he said suddenly. "I know what I must do."

"Do you plan to imprison him during Passover?"

"I will do what I have to do to convince this Nazarene to stop making trouble for us." Turning slightly, he signaled his assistant standing near the doorway. "Pay this man," he said dully, and watched as Judas accepted the pouch of coins.

Caiaphas added offhandedly, "When you are ready, contact the head of the Temple guards. Then quietly lead them to your master. Is this clear?"

Judas nodded, quickly counting the thirty pieces of silver.

"Do not come here again," Caiaphas uttered, before dismissing Judas with a wave of the hand.

Judas got to his feet and moved to the doorway. Suddenly he detested Caiaphas for making deals with the Romans, but he despised even more what he thought was Jesus' naivety.

CHAPTER 35

ALTHOUGH CAIAPHAS WORE A PLACID EXPRESSION, his insides were churning as he hurried through the Tyropoeon Valley leading to the Antonia Fortress, the military barracks built about seven decades earlier by Herod the Great. The fortress, with its four towers, stood atop a 150-foot-high rock escarpment in the northwest corner of the Temple Mount, overlooking Jerusalem. The Romans had chosen the fortress as their main military post for its strategic location because from its towers soldiers could watch any suspicious activities in the Temple courtyards and around its colonnades. The structures were connected by two colonnades with a narrow walkway between them. Although the Antonia Fortress was used by the Romans as a garrison and observation post, it also contained many luxury apartments and baths for its commanders and soldiers.

The Roman officer in charge of the guards that afternoon recognized the high priest and signaled the soldiers down below to open the gate.

Holding his head high, Caiaphas walked through the gateway and assumed a dignified manner as a Roman officer escorted him through torch-lit corridors that led to a large chamber used by the Roman procurator when he was in Jerusalem. The stale, dank air of the foreboding fortress always left Caiaphas feeling frantic, as if he were visiting the bowels of hell. He was made to wait in the corridor as the officer went into the chamber, and then a few minutes later the heavy oak door opened, with the officer waving the high priest to step inside.

"Good afternoon, Illustrious Procurator," greeted Caiaphas as the door shut behind him.

Since the Roman procurator was discussing some matter with his secretary, Caiaphas remained standing while deciding what tactic to use in the pending discussion.

Pontius Pilate glanced at Caiaphas from his chair without much interest, then spoke softly to his secretary to his right. On the stone wall behind them hung the symbol of Rome's power, the iron eagle with its wings spread open. Pilate's eyes were focused upon a parchment that his secretary had given him that morning. After reading the document again and getting sufficient answers to his questions, Pilate pressed the seal of his ring on the bottom of it, marking his approval of its content. The secretary rolled up the parchment and left the chamber as Pilate gestured the high priest to come forward and sit in the chair across from him.

Almost seven years had passed since Pontius Pilate had become the governor of Judea and Samaria. Appointed by Emperor Tiberius, Pontius Pilate had authority to tame the unruly provinces with an iron hand.

Being from the upper class of Roman citizenry, Pilate looked down upon other lands and cultures, believing the Jews were inferior and less civilized than the Romans. Pilate and his family resided in the pleasant harbor town of Caesarea, just south of Mount Carmel. But several times a year Pilate had to travel to Jerusalem to conduct official business. Although Pilate disdained the various Jewish festivals, this year he couldn't avoid attending the Feast of the Passover. For political reasons, he would put on a good face to appease the social and religious leaders.

Gathering his thoughts, Pilate lifted his tired eyes to Caiaphas' bearded face.

"What troubles are you bringing today?" Pilate asked in a clipped tone, suggesting he had already heard too many complaints for one day.

"Your Honor, I want to talk about some disturbing events in recent months." He minced his words. "Though your spies keep you well informed, I thought you should hear from me before this reaches your ears from another mouth."

Pilate allowed himself a smile. "Keep it brief. These Jewish holy days besiege me with constant headaches."

"What a pity," he remarked, feigning a look of concern. "Your Honor, now you know how I feel when I walk by one of your statues of god Caesar."

"Caiaphas, your shrewd tongue is one reason why I seldom visit this tumultuous city. I am no match for you and other aged priests who beg to be sold into slavery."

Frowning, Caiaphas shifted slightly in the uncomfortable wooden chair. "Earlier today a Nazarene madman stormed into the courts of the Temple and harassed the crowds. He drove off the money changers and turned over tables belonging to merchants. We would have arrested him, but many in the crowd seemed to admire his actions."

Pilate looked irritated. "You steal my time over that? What happens at the Temple is of no concern to Rome. Unless, of course, you priests are plotting against Caesar."

"Sleep well tonight. There are no plans in the making to overthrow Rome's power."

Pilate looked at him questioningly. "Then what? Have you come only to speak about this Nazarene who upsets your money-making schemes?"

"There are many troubling things about this man. You should be aware of his religious teachings before he creates a misunderstanding between us."

"Misunderstanding?" echoed Pilate. "I understand you stubborn fools quite well."

Caiaphas ignored the remark. "As you and god Caesar know, we are a people who have been long awaiting the advent of the Messiah."

"Ah, the Messiah! You mean the almighty warrior who will restore the glory of your ancient kingdoms." He stood and stretched his arms. "Even if David and Solomon both return with your Messiah, you Jews will never defeat us. If you incite a revolt, it will be the end of you and your Temple."

Stepping over to a side table, he reached for a carafe of Tuscany wine and filled a large silver cup about half way. Not bothering to offer any to the high priest, he returned to his chair and dropped into it, heaving a weary sigh.

After taking a gulp of wine, Pilate gave Caiaphas a look of disgust. "You Jews should stop clinging to the idea of a mystical savior. Rome is your savior. When you cast off your archaic beliefs and useless traditions, then your people can join us as we build a great civilization, spreading beyond the lands Alexander conquered."

Although Pilate's remarks angered Caiaphas, he suppressed his emotions and spoke in a calm manner. "Our expectations for a Messiah are part of our religious traditions. Like you Romans, we have our identity as a people that we will never relinquish, even at the point of your spears."

"Yes, Tiberius knows about your stubbornness. You Jews are ready to die for what is sacred to you. Ready to sacrifice your lives in the name of your One God."

"You do understand that our people will not be deprived of their hopes, of their faith."

Groaning, Pilate gulped some more wine. "Tell me, how many generations of Jews foolishly believed the Messiah would appear in their day?

This generation is no different. But if your so-called Anointed One falls from the clouds tomorrow and lands in the courts of the Temple, he will have the misfortune of facing the swords of Rome's legions."

Pilate laughed again, scooting his chair back and propping his feet upon the table.

"Tell me this, Caiaphas. How many messiahs have roamed about Judea since you were a boy? Even now there are twenty madmen wandering about the countryside, stirring up farmers and smiths with their false promises."

Caiaphas lowered his head for a moment. "Yes," he admitted, "over the centuries there have been men claiming to be messiahs. But most never traveled far from their own towns and villages. And those that did were soon unmasked as pretenders. Besides, there can be no Messiah before the return of the prophet."

"Oh, are you talking about Elijah?" said Pilate, leaning forward now.

Caiaphas raised his brows in surprise. "You know about the prophet Elijah?"

Pilate laughed again, this time without rancor. "Caiaphas, I know you think of me as a crass pagan. But the morning after I received this appointment from Caesar, I visited a district in Rome where many Jewish merchants conduct business. I chose three of the smartest ones, and over the next few weeks they came to my residence to tutor me about this land and your religion."

"Then you know these false messiahs seldom cause trouble." His tone changed. "But this Nazarene is different. He has strange powers and seems to grow stronger by the day, with more people gathering behind him. They listen to his dangerous teachings with interest and hope."

Pilate's expression grew serious. He removed his feet from the table and sat erect, his eyes focused on Caiaphas' concerned expression.

"This Nazarene is the same man you mentioned earlier, the one with courage enough to drive out the greedy swine from the Temple grounds?"

Caiaphas nodded and said, "I and other members of the Sanhedrin do not endorse his teachings. Jesus acts on his own accord, and roams the land with a group of disciples."

Pilate thought a moment. "If this Jesus is a thorn in your side, then imprison him and throw away the key."

"If we did, his popularity might grow. I know Rome doesn't want to see large crowds of unruly people in the streets of Jerusalem. Already there is much tension. The Zealots are spreading discontent everywhere."

Pilate looked at the high priest disapprovingly. "Though you deny it, such riots would make you smile. Anything that gives me a headache pleases you, eh?"

"On the contrary, my desire is to keep my Jewish brethren safe."

"All Jews, that is, except Jesus and others like him who threaten your power."

Before Caiaphas could respond, Pilate added churlishly, "This is your problem, not mine. Do away with him if it serves your purpose."

"During the past two years they attempted to arrest Jesus. But I heard he is a clever one always a few steps ahead of the guards. Jesus is protected by his disciples, rough laborers and fishermen. So there would be too much commotion. None of us will risk going against Rome's ordinance so publicly."

Pilate let out a long, slow breath. "You Jews and your Messiah," he muttered sourly. "Could this man be plotting against Rome?"

"No sane Jew would plot against Rome," he said innocently. "We are a peaceful people. We hope to live in peace while practicing our beliefs and traditions in the service of the Lord God."

Pilate said flatly, "Rome allows you to worship your One God."

"Yes, but we prefer to worship the Lord without fear of retaliation from your military. We prefer to walk the streets and meet in private without being scrutinized by foreign occupiers who might invent plots when no plots exist." Frowning, he spread his hands and added, "Misunderstandings could take place, and mistakes could be made that cause innocent men and women to lose their lives."

Pilate nodded in agreement. "And that's exactly why you and I meet. We shall keep our lines of communication open so that misunderstandings can be clarified." He smiled wryly. "In return, we give you our protection."

"Protection, you say? Are we helpless children who cannot protect ourselves?"

"Apparently. If Rome's legions hadn't conquered you, then another foreign power would be dominating you now. At least Tiberius tolerates your religion."

"How generous of your emperor," Caiaphas stated with a bow of his head. "If Tiberius is so tolerant, perhaps he would grant more concessions."

Pilate regarded him in silence. "What sort of concessions?"

"Relaxing some restrictions that are decided locally. The high priest should not have to come to you asking for the release of holy robes used to access the most holy place in the Temple during the celebrations of Passover, Shavuot, and the Succot."

Pilate shook his head. "As far as I am concerned, Rome is already too lenient. The Jews enjoy civic and religious liberties forbidden in most other provinces throughout the empire."

"But Rome uses the resources of the provinces to support her military campaigns."

Pilate gave him a hard look. "Rome listens to her subjects and cares about them."

"If Tiberius would listen carefully to the voice of Israel, perhaps he would be more popular among the Jews."

"Believe me, Caesar keeps a close eye on the affairs here." Pilate drifted off as he finished the wine. "Did you know that Tiberius did not want to be chosen emperor? After the death of Augustus, the people had to beg him to assume the position. When he was proclaimed emperor, his first words were to assert that the empire is a brutal beast, and that he would rather let someone else rule."

"Yes, I heard that Tiberius delegates many of his daily tasks, and that he now lives in isolation on the small island of Capri."

"Not total isolation, I assure you." Pilate grew silent again, then looked at the high priest, relaxed. "Initially Tiberius delegated much of his authority to Sejanus, the head of the Praetorian Guards. But about two years ago, Tiberius ordered his arrest and executed him for treason."

"What a pity," murmured Caiaphas. "Perhaps a religious culture such as ours would be more pleasing to your emperor."

Pilate laughed dryly. "So should Caesar take advice from the Jews on how to run his empire?"

"Why not? I hear that Roman society is rife with conflict and immorality. You and other lands could benefit from our just laws, our morality, and our family structure."

After glancing at a mouse scurrying near his chair, Pilate said offhandedly, "Days before ordering the execution of Sejanus and his conspirators, Tiberius mused that he might look to the provinces to find someone worthy to assist him in governing the empire. But later everyone decided that Tiberius was merely joking."

Caiaphas was quiet for a moment. "It appears there are problems affecting Romans that no one in Rome knows how to resolve." In his mind, he added, *You Romans kill each other for power and use marriage as a means for political advancement. You can definitely learn from us.*

Pilate gave him a look of annoyance. "Caiaphas, don't worry about Rome's problems. You Jews have enough problems of your own. Your own history is replete with political intrigues and religious divisions. And you want to teach morality to a Roman? You yourself married the daughter of the former high priest to attain power and social status!"

Though angered by this, Caiaphas kept his voice level. "She is still my wife, and I have no intention to replace her." He paused to clear his throat. "According to our Mosaic laws," he went on, "divorce is acceptable only under certain circumstances, and adultery is a crime punished by death."

Realizing it was useless to argue with the narrow-minded priest, Pilate folded his hands together and rested his elbows on the table. "Tell me this, who in Israel should Tiberius listen to? You Jews cannot even give a recommendation for a worthy man to replace the deposed tetrarch of Judea and Samaria," Pilate added in a vexed tone, referring to Herod Archelaus, the brother of Herod Antipas. Caesar Augustus had removed Archelaus because of his cruelty against his own people. Twenty-seven years had passed since then, and Rome had not replaced him, choosing instead to rule the provinces from afar.

Caiaphas found the political vacuum in Judea and Samaria advantageous. As the high priest of the Temple, he was now the most powerful among Jewish leaders, which allowed him the opportunity to meet directly with the Roman procurator.

Pilate rose again from his chair and walked about the room, his eyes fixed on the stone floor in contemplation. He stopped near Caiaphas' chair and uttered in a low, menacing voice, "So where is this Messiah of yours?"

Caiaphas tilted his head back and looked into Pilate's eyes, dark and unreadable.

Not wanting to antagonize him any further, Caiaphas lowered his eyes and gave a vague shrug. "Our Savior will come when the Lord God deems it necessary."

Pilate returned to his chair. "I say one thing for the One God, he has more patience than you Jews." With a weary look, he added, "Caiaphas, I wish your Messiah would come today and take over Judea for me."

"Illustrious Procurator, unfortunately you and I have to deal with the reality of the times."

"That's something we can agree upon. Unless I am mistaken, the reason for this visit is your concern over the Nazarene who caused trouble in the Temple courts."

"Jesus has been causing trouble for everyone these past years. He preaches that God's kingdom is at hand, and his disciples proclaim he is the one who will build it."

Pilate yawned softly. "So there are many who believe this Jesus is the Messiah you have been waiting for?"

Caiaphas frowned. "Believe me, Jesus is not the kind of Messiah that the Lord God will send to us. This Nazarene carpenter is an uneducated, insolent commoner who suffers from supreme arrogance to proclaim himself as the Son of God."

"This Nazarene believes he's the son of your One God? In that case, this Nazarene could very well become the next emperor of Rome!" he said sarcastically.

"Your Honor, this is a serious matter. Wherever Jesus goes, he causes intense emotions among the people. Those who support him often clash with his detractors. That's why I have come see you. I don't want you to mistakenly think that I and other priests approve of this madman."

At hearing this, Pilate's eyes fixed on him intently. "Caiaphas, do you take me for a fool? As far as I know, you could be supporting this so-called madman." Pausing, he pointed a finger at him. "I warn you, if I discover that you and other religious leaders are backing Jesus, I will take over Temple affairs and throw you onto the street for the dogs to feed on."

Knowing that Pilate was a man not to be taken lightly, Caiaphas nodded and silently cursed Jesus and other fanatics who created havoc within his sphere of authority, jeopardizing the safety of all Jews.

Pilate then added with a tone of finality, "Now, you and the Sanhedrin handle this matter. But if you feel this Nazarene is going to outwit you, then send him my way. My military commanders have special means to persuade him to give up on this Messiah madness."

Caiaphas gave a grateful nod. "Your Honor, since Rome has more experience dealing with rebels, I am certain your advice will solve our problem."

Pilate grunted and with a quick gesture dismissed the high priest, then glanced into his empty cup as he reached for the rolled parchment on the table.

Caiaphas rose to his feet and bade farewell to the Roman governor before stepping from the chamber, his head full of worries.

CHAPTER 36

IT WAS THE EVENING OF THE PASSOVER MEAL when Jesus gathered his twelve apostles for what would be their last time together. As Jesus explained to me later, he wanted to initiate a tradition that would remain with his followers for generations to come. He established the ritual of eating the bread as a symbol of his flesh, and drinking the wine as a symbol of his blood. That evening Jesus established a new covenant with his close disciples as a prelude to a new generation of believers that, as we speak, is growing throughout the Mediterranean world.

In the clear night sky shone a full moon, its bright glow casting soft shadows on the roads by various dwellings and buildings of Jerusalem. The pre-Passover meal was about to begin as each person in the group took his place in the circle. Isaac, who was singled out by Peter as Jesus' preferred disciple, was to the right of his father, with Peter and Andrew positioned to his left. A rug had been spread on the floor, and the food had been placed upon a cloth in the center of the circle.

The four ritual cups were placed on the table, together with several oil lamps, roasted lamb, bitter herbs, unleavened bread, vegetables, and salt water.

Jesus began by reading a short prayer of sanctification appropriate for the holy occasion. They all drank the wine of the first cup. After that, they all washed their hands. Then to the surprise of his disciples, Jesus took a towel and one by one began to wash their feet, as a servant might have. The last one whose feet were to be washed was Peter.

In the role of a servant, Jesus knelt before his first disciple. But Peter stopped him, not wanting his master to humiliate himself. "Lord, why do you wash my feet?"

Jesus smiled up at him. "My friend, in the future you will understand."

With a perplexed look, he replied, "But you should never wash my feet."

"Peter, if I do not wash your feet, you have no part in me."

"Then not only my feet, but also my hands and my head," said Peter.

"He who has bathed does not need to wash, except for his feet. Your heart is clean, but not all of you."

After washing Peter's feet, Jesus sat again, at which time he and the others were given bitter herbs and leaves that were dipped in the salt water in memory of the slavery and hardships of the children of Israel in Egypt. They all sang the Psalm and drank the wine of the second cup following the tradition.

After the meal, Jesus broke the remaining unleavened bread and passed it around. He looked quite troubled and told his disciples that one of them was ready to betray him. Startled by this, each man scanned the faces of the others, their eyes and expressions asking a silent but clear question: *Who was it?*

Jesus added nothing more, not even to Peter. Like the others, Peter was very concerned and looked at Isaac. He signaled to Isaac, asking him to get more information from his father. The young Isaac moved closer to his father and asked who the betrayer would be. Jesus looked at his son, the fruit of our conjugal love, and told him it would be the person to whom he gives a piece of bread. Later, Jesus dipped a piece and gave it to Judas Iscariot. Jesus gave Judas a look of disapproval. Judas stood and left the room without saying a word. Jesus drank of the third cup and passed it around. When all had finished drinking it, they sang the Great Hallel Psalm.

The fourth cup, called the cup of consummation, was empty. Under the puzzled gaze of his disciples, Jesus said that he would drink of the fourth cup on the day of the Second Coming, the day of the consummation of God's dispensation. He gave no further explanation of it.

At the end of the meal, Jesus and his disciples stepped outside. To withdraw from people and pray in peace, they walked across the Kidron Valley to the Mount of Olives. While climbing up the slope, Jesus warned the men that tragic events would befall him and that they should keep their hearts strong. He assured them that his spirit would live eternally.

When they arrived at a garden called Gethsemane, Jesus told his followers to stay behind, taking with him only Peter and the brothers James and John farther up the slope. They could see that his heart was heavy with anguish and sorrow. When they reached a tranquil spot, he asked the three men to stay awake and pray with him. Then he moved a little farther away, knelt, and began to pray.

"Dear Father, I am so sorry for not being able to offer You what You envisioned," he said, as if God were standing before him in the flesh. "You prepared the environment so that Your children would grow and become perfect creatures reflecting Your nature and become Your eternal partners of true love. I know the pain You felt when Your first children fell victim to the temptation of Lucifer."

The Mount of Olives had never witnessed such a solemn moment, as Jesus' words came from the deepest parts of his heart.

"Dear Father, it is so difficult to give up," he uttered, his eyes wet. "The thought of knowing that I have to leave this world without first forming a willing nation makes me anguished. Father, if You want, I am determined to go on with my mission, despite the challenges that I have to face daily. I brought with me three of my best disciples. With their faith in me and their support, I can bear the weight of adversities," he said, looking over his shoulder and gazing at the three men.

God must have listened to His son with deep love and gratitude, for Jesus' words sprang from an honest heart. But God answered that it was useless to continue … that Jesus' opponents were determined to kill him, and his few loyal followers were weak in faith.

"Father, let Your will be done, not mine," replied Jesus. He got to his feet and walked over to Peter, James, and John, and found that all three had fallen asleep.

As a light breeze came from the valley below, Jesus shook Peter by the shoulder, rebuking him. "Peter, why are you sleeping? I asked you to pray with me!" Then turning to the two brothers, he said in anger, "Wake up, James and John!"

As the three men opened their eyes and began to stir, Jesus added firmly, "Stay awake and pray with me, so you don't fall into temptation. You know who I am, and how serious this moment is, so please be strong, show that you care."

Their minds hazy, Peter, James, and John looked at Jesus, barely able to keep their eyes open as he added sternly, "Beware! The forces of evil will try to destroy your faith, tempting you. The persecution will be severe. You have to pray to overcome fear, for your flesh is still weak."

His disciples gave vague nods as Jesus stepped away again and returned to his prayers. Even though the ground was hard and stony, he fell to his knees and clasped his hands.

"Dear Father, You had to purify the seed of a man and the womb of a woman so that a baby could be conceived without original sin, a child with all the potential to become Your true son, who would be one with Your will. You called Noah, then Abraham and Sara, his wife. They answered your call, and the seed of Abraham and the womb of Sara became the hope for humanity.

"That is the reason why You asked the children of Abraham to select their wives from the bloodline of Sara. You have been a jealous God. You continued Your project secretly from generation to generation, meticulously selecting the seed from among the children of Abraham and the daughters of Sara to carry on the process of purification. And finally when the process reached its highest stage, in the priest Zechariah and the young maiden Mary from Nazareth You drew them together in order that a purified seed and womb might meet. To the world this seems strange and contrary to the law that You established among our people. But to undo the tragic events which took place in the Garden of Eden, where Eve, under the influence of the Archangel, committed an act of disobedience in order to fulfill a desire for love that took her away from You, You required someone of innocent faith to be willing to risk dying in order to fulfill a desire for love that would bring her closer to You. It was because she was drawn to what she sensed as sacred that my mother felt the impulse to have a relationship with the priest, offering her body obediently. Her motivation was immensely important. It was the key that opened her womb to the Holy Spirit to claim it in the moment of my conception. Truly, You work in mysterious ways. She became the first woman ever to give life to an offspring free from sin.

Jesus continued praying, while tears flooded his face.

"O God, how much hope You have invested in me! Dear Father and Mother, I cannot remain insensitive to the call of Your needs. I came from the children of Abraham and Sara to connect them to a new blood lineage. But as You know, I also came to connect the brothers of the Jews to that blood lineage. Those are the descendants of Abraham and the Egyptian Hagar. Their son, Ishmael, expelled in the desert, is meant to receive this blessing as well.

"Dear Father, my heart is full of sorrow in knowing that I have to leave this world when there is so much to do," Jesus lamented. "If possible, dear Father, let me try one more time to soothe the hearts of this skeptical generation."

Jesus grew silent and listened as God told him that due to the lack of faith among the most powerful in Israel, it was not possible for him to continue his mission in this world.

Jesus rose and returned to Peter, James, and John. Instead of having united with Jesus and praying at this solemn moment as he had requested, the three disciples had fallen asleep again.

Saddened by this, Jesus went back to pray for the third time, more anguished than ever.

"My dear Heavenly Parents, I want to express my gratitude for the life You have given to me, for Your infinitive and unconditional love. You have never lost hope that once men and women receive the truth, they will desire to purify themselves and become Your true sons and daughters. Dear Father and Mother, I can try to gain the confidence of the religious authorities of Jerusalem. If they understand me, all the chosen people of Israel will welcome me as the Messiah and Savior."

But God's decision remained unchanged, for there was no foundation for His Son to continue his mission on earth. Jesus was beside himself with grief over not being able to offer his Father a total victory of goodness over evil in this world. Regrettably, the contradiction that resides within each person would have to remain part of the human condition for years to come, until the Messiah returns to the physical world at the Second Advent to free humanity from its contradiction.

God told Jesus that there was no other alternative but to sacrifice his life to redeem humanity.

"Dear God, let Your will be done and not mine, because I want to be a loyal and obedient son," Jesus concluded.

He stood up and walked toward Peter, James, and John who were still sleeping. Once again he realized how difficult it was for his disciples to follow God's will without special help from Heaven.

Jesus remained silent and prayed in his heart for the three men, giving them time to rest. Minutes later, he heard the sounds of men coming up the side of the mountain. He quickly awakened the three men, and with a sad voice he explained that the time had come for him to be delivered to his opponents.

CHAPTER 37

SUDDENLY IT BECAME DARKER upon the slopes of the mountain, as thick clouds eclipsed the face of the moon. Torches of light drew closer from below, with the cool evening breeze causing the flames to flicker. Silhouettes of men could soon be seen moving up the path. The group of Temple guards and some men sent by the chief priests and Pharisees had become quiet as they carefully climbed up the mountainside, following the lead of Judas Iscariot, whose face was tense with worry and apprehension.

Earlier after the Passover meal, Judas had left his fellow disciples and gone directly to the chief priests and the officer of the Temple guards. Knowing that Jesus often took his disciples to Gethsemane to teach and pray, he led the soldiers and other men to this spot. Since Jesus was ordinary in appearance, the officer had said Judas would need to give some signal to identify his master, so it was decided that Judas would kiss him.

When the group entered the clearing with their swords and clubs, some of the disciples ran off in fear, while the others gathered around Jesus, unsure what to do. Judas walked up to Jesus and kissed him on the cheek, then bowed his head and stepped back into the shadows while the soldiers roughly seized the Savior.

Isaac, who earlier had seen Judas and the soldiers at the foot of the mountain, followed them up to the garden, where he saw them accosting his father. One of the guards noticed the 13-year-old boy and grabbed him by his tunic.

Isaac remembered that recently in Bethany his father had told him how important it was for his blood lineage to survive. So he quickly slipped out of the tunic and ran away naked before he could be apprehended.

The Temple guards bound Jesus and led him away down the mountain, with some of the disciples trailing behind at a safe distance. He was brought to the house of the high priest, where the elders and scribes awaited. The house stood in the affluent upper part of Jerusalem, an area overlooking the Temple's sanctuary and the Mount of Olives. Caiaphas' house was connected by a large garden to the house of Annas, who was his father-in-law and the former high priest. Judas was still with the guards, and he saw that Saul was waiting outside. Saul joined the group as they led Jesus to the house of Annas.

While they advanced through the courtyard, where some officers and servants were warming themselves by a fire, Judas stopped for a moment and glanced over his shoulder. He noticed Peter standing in the distance, an anxious look on his face.

Judas approached Peter, signaling him to come closer. With hesitant steps, Peter drew nearer and asked in a harsh whisper, "Why did you lead the Temple guards to Jesus?"

"He is too naive to be the Messiah," stated Judas, keeping his voice down. "He needs to be stopped before he leads the people astray."

"What will happen to him now? Are they going to imprison him?"

Judas shook his head. "The chief priests want to talk to him. They promised not to harm him. Just to try to change his mind."

"Judas, your behavior is disgraceful!"

Without replying, Judas stepped over to the gatekeeper and convinced him to allow Peter into the courtyard. Then Judas went into the house of Annas, while Peter moved closer to the fire to keep himself warm.

As Jesus was led into a room, his eyes fell upon Annas.

With a vexed look, Annas asked, "Nazarene, what do you teach?"

Jesus stared at him. "I have spoken openly and taught in the synagogues and the Temple where people could listen. I keep no secrets."

The head of the Temple guard struck his face. "Show respect for the high priest!"

Jesus looked at him, his eyes free of resentment. Then he turned back to Annas and said plainly, "What I have taught is the truth. It will save our people, and you should not try to silence me. I have spoken rightly."

"Tell me, how many disciples do you have, and who are they?" Annas inquired in a commanding tone, his heart bitter with jealousy.

Jesus gave no answer, his eyes roaming over the faces of those present.

Annas rebuked him, saying, "Your wild behavior at the Temple is unforgivable! You have insulted God and the faithful!"

Jesus was unruffled. "The way the Temple is used is an insult to God. It has been transformed into a den of thieves. Such activities prey on the good faith of the children of Abraham. You make them pay money for everything."

Red in the face, Annas snapped at him, "But each person must make sacrifices to purify himself and to participate in our rituals."

"The kingdom of God is available to everyone," Jesus replied evenly. "There is no need for elaborate rituals."

Frowning at this, Annas replied, "Everyone has to take part in rituals! Bathing in the pools for purification is necessary, as well as offering animals on the altar of sacrifice."

Indignant, Jesus interrupted him, stating, "The authorities charge unfair fees to those who come with sincere hearts. Your son-in-law and other religious elite take advantage of those who want to express their reverence for the Lord.

"You and the other priests should serve and attend to people's needs," he asserted, "but instead you demand that the faithful serve you!"

Growing incensed over the Nazarene's impudence, Annas turned to the chief officer and ordered, "Keep this heretic under guard until Caiaphas arrives to start the trial."

"Trial?" echoed Judas in surprise. "Why do we need a trial?" he demanded.

With a sudden gesture, Annas said, "This insolent devil is a threat to our faith and traditions!"

Visibly alarmed, Judas countered, nearly shouting, "This isn't what Caiaphas told me would take place. Besides, a trial at night is not in accordance with tradition." Avoiding Jesus' gaze, Judas stepped closer to Annas. "You know well the fate of a man cannot be decided by an unofficial gathering. This matter has to be discussed at an official hearing, with elder members of the Sanhedrin present during the trial."

Annas shook his head. "In an urgent case such as this, it is only necessary for a twenty-three-member panel to convene."

Judas glanced at Jesus, who remained silent as the guards watched him closely.

Raising a hand in protest, Judas said in a combative tone, "But this man has committed no impiety to deserve such harsh treatment."

Annas gestured at Jesus again. "This haughty sinner created a dangerous situation at the Lord's Temple today." Turning, he added snidely, "Judas, you of all men know that any sign of rebellion could ignite a severe response from the Romans."

Judas shook his head in disapproval. "Annas, your only concern is that Pilate will deprive your family of the power and prestige you have enjoyed for so long!"

Annas gave a muffled grunt and walked off. After a moment's hesitation, Judas left and walked through the garden to the home of Caiaphas, where he found a number of elders, scribes, and Pharisees in the middle of animated discussions. The moon was high in the sky when Caiaphas sent a servant to inform the officer of the guards to bring Jesus to them.

Caiaphas led the elders and others to an adjoining room where he conducted public meetings when at home. The room was spacious and well lit, with two big windows allowing the moonlight to filter in and mix with the flickering flames of three hanging lamps. There were also several bronze lamps sitting on a marble floor, which was partially covered by a large blue-and-green woven rug. In the center stood a meeting table, and along the walls low tables with vases of flowers, bowls of fruit, and a silver pitcher and goblets.

All eyes shifted to the doorway as two muscular guards led Jesus into the crowded room. He immediately noticed Judas standing alone in the near corner, waves of regret assaulting him. Jesus scanned the faces of the scribes and Pharisees, many of whom were familiar to him. Some gazed at him with sympathy, but most gave him hostile looks.

Judas felt uneasy, noticing the bitter and hateful looks on their faces. He had no doubt that this gathering was not merely for a discussion of his teachings. In fact, Judas could read the verdict of guilty in the eyes of many who now glared at Jesus intensely. Yet among these religious leaders were some with warm hearts and a strong sense of righteousness.

With a surge of guilt, Judas moved casually to the doorway and slipped away. Most of the men had their eyes on Caiaphas, who was wearing his priestly robes and had his hair and beard neatly combed and oiled. As he approached Jesus, he said in a censorious tone, "Nazarene, on many occasions it has reached our ears that you've been teaching a false doctrine. Also, you have told your inner circle that you are the Messiah ..."

"Let me point out," interrupted Nicodemus, "that these are only rumors, which have grown with the telling." He was a Pharisee and a member of the Sanhedrin who, during one of Jesus' trips to Jerusalem, visited him secretly in the night to hear his teachings. He liked what he had heard and held good feelings toward him.

Looking at Nicodemus, Caiaphas said, "Tonight we will clarify all of this once and for all."

Soon witnesses were brought into the room to testify against Jesus. One by one they made their accusations, but much of their testimonies contradicted each other.

Finally two men were called in by Caiaphas, and they claimed to have heard Jesus state that he would destroy the Temple and rebuild it in three days.

"This is physically impossible," shouted out Joseph of Arimathea. "Such nonsense doesn't meet the legal requirements for a conviction." Extremely wealthy, Joseph was a righteous and honorable counselor who longed for the kingdom of God. He was also another secret sympathizer of Jesus. "This good man deserves a fair trial," he added firmly. "We should wait until after the Passover. All the members of the Sanhedrin need to be present so that we can have a full hearing. We cannot conduct a trial based on rumors."

Caiaphas pushed a smile to his lips. "But these rumors about the Nazarene have been persistent."

"If such rumors are to be believed," remarked one of Joseph's friends, standing beside him, "who here knows how much of this is truly accurate?"

Jesus noticed that a small group of men had gathered around Joseph and Nicodemus, while the majority stood near Caiaphas.

The high priest stared at Jesus. "We want to hear directly from your mouth who you think you are. Are you the Savior that the prophets spoke of, the Anointed One?"

Jesus gave a nod of the head. "Yes, I am the Messiah."

Caiaphas looked at him in disgust. "If so, how come I haven't heard of Elijah announcing your arrival?" Pausing, his eyes roamed about the room. "Have any of you seen Elijah come down from heaven in a chariot of fire, proclaiming this man is the Messiah?" he asked, ridiculing Jesus. Most of those present laughed, shaking their heads in derision, while Joseph, Nicodemus, and a few others remained silent.

Jesus lowered his eyes, thinking back to the period when his brother John failed to make the bold decision to support him.

Suppressing the painful memory, Jesus glanced about the room. "Brothers, how many prophets has God sent to illuminate the dark years of our history so we could see our destiny as a people. So many of our prophets were unjustly killed by those very people whom they came to serve and inspire!"

Meeting the hard eyes of those men ready to cast judgment upon him, Jesus went on, "There have been times when I declared that I was sent by God to complete what He started with Abraham. I can tell you the Lord has inspired me to guide you to the truth so that you might discover your heavenly nature and your destiny as a nation."

There were murmurs of disapproval among the scribes and Pharisees as they glanced at one another, amazed at the arrogance of this pretender.

"The desire of God," Jesus added in a stronger voice, "is for Jerusalem to become the eternal spiritual center of the world. In your hearts you have rejected me without understanding that I am your blessing. But by rejecting me, you are denying yourselves the opportunity to receive the truth that guides you to get in touch with your inner nature and to perfect your soul. You not only deny it to yourself, but also to the rest of the children of Abraham, as well as the children of his son Ishmael."

Caiaphas looked bewildered after hearing this. For a moment there was silence, as if they were all trying to fathom the meaning of Jesus' words. Then came a burst of laughter as Caiaphas gave him a mocking look. "Ah, you have royal blood in your veins! So you are the one we should proclaim king. Would you like us to bow down to you now?"

Fixing his eyes on the high priest, Jesus continued, his voice rising. "If you would only listen and trust in me, then future generations would remember you with admiration and gratitude."

Caiaphas shook his head in disbelief. "Do you really expect us to surrender ourselves to you?" With an ominous look, he added in a brusque tone, "You say we can reform the world? Only God can reform this world, not a scheming demon like you!"

Jesus made no reply, his eyes searching the crowded room for Judas.

"So you are the king of kings!" Caiaphas continued scornfully. "Where is your palace? Who are your subjects? Where are your majestic roots?"

With a sorrowful heart, Jesus said to him, "Even though I was born in humble circumstances and grew up surrounded by adversity, God used this situation so that I would search for His company instead of that of men. Though my life was heartbreaking, the sweetness of God's love was with me during the most bitter of times. The Messiah couldn't have been born inside the walls of a comfortable palace, surrounded by thousands of pleasures to distract him. The spiritual growth of the Messiah is far more important. The solitude and sadness in my heart impelled me to search the deepest part of my soul, where I found God's unconditional love."

Caiaphas retorted, "Rumors have come to my ears that you proclaim God to be your father."

"God your father?" scowled one of the elders. "I have never thought of God as being a father. If God is a father, then who are you?"

"I am the one whom God has commissioned to bring love into this world," replied Jesus with quiet confidence.

Caiaphas' eyes opened wide. "This Nazarene is a blasphemer!" he shouted out, tearing his robes. Each man there was also obliged to tear his outer garment from the neck opening, as the Talmud instructed if they had been witness to an act of blasphemy, and so they did.

Looking about the room with furious eyes, Caiaphas spoke in a loud voice, "Why do we need further witnesses?"

A clamor of excited voices merged as clusters of men began discussing the issue, at times glancing at Jesus' passive face.

After a short while, Caiaphas raised a hand to silence everyone. "Now it is settled!" he declared with an adamant nod. His thoughts went back to his recent meeting with Pilate. "By policy," he added, looking at the Pharisees nearby, "the Roman authorities don't get involved in our religious disputes. But it must be emphasized that they know that the word 'Messiah' refers to a king."

"Jesus is guilty!" exclaimed an elder standing near Joseph. "His claim of being the Messiah is sedition against Rome!"

Many nodded in agreement, and one of the guards spoke with heavy sarcasm, "If this Nazarene is the Son of God, how do we explain to Caesar that he now has a twin brother?" Over the sporadic laughter, he added with a scowl, "To a Roman, there is only one son of God, and that is Caesar, who intends to dominate the entire world."

Catching his attention, Jesus said sternly, "Brother, do not bow to the pressure of those who compromise the destiny of our people. If we make changes in ourselves, we will be able to change Rome. Be strong and bold. If we are united, then the forces of evil will not triumph."

Caiaphas raised a quick hand, as if to strike Jesus. "Nazarene, this is dangerous talk! Rome fears that we may rise again. We could all be arrested if Pilate catches wind of this seditious language in my home."

Jesus smiled benignly at him. "You are the one who brought me here."

Standing next to Nicodemus was Benjamin, an elderly member of the Sanhedrin who stepped closer to Jesus and placed a hand on his shoulder. "Rabbi, you must not utter such things."

Caiaphas gave a little snort and thought aloud, "These days we have enough problems without this Nazarene and his followers adding to our troubles. We have to be careful with such militant rhetoric ..."

At the front of the crowd was a scribe who spoke with a look of anguish. "Jesus, your teachings endanger us! If we can hear your belligerent remarks, then so can Pilate and other Romans!"

"You evildoer!" exclaimed a Pharisee "The Romans will punish us for your words!"

These comments passed from mouth to mouth, casting a shadow of fear over most of the men in the room. Only Nicodemus and Joseph of Arimathea kept silent, their faces sad over the impending fate of this Nazarene.

Suddenly Jesus spoke up. "I have no choice but to speak the truth," he declared, his voice ringing loudly. "If you priests and scribes wish for me speak lies, then on what authority do you do so?"

Frowning, Benjamin said in protest, "But these are dangerous times in which certain truths should never be spoken aloud."

Jesus shook his head and spoke with certitude. "All truths should be proclaimed in each synagogue and even from the top of the Temple. Now is the time to fulfill what God has promised to His people."

"You are mistaken," retorted Benjamin. "If we hope to preserve our traditions and the Mosaic law, then we must refrain from confronting the enemy. If we are patient, Rome will gradually collapse under the pressure of its many burdens. This land will then become ours again as we regain our power and freedoms."

Shaking his head again, Jesus gazed around. "You aren't able to perceive my true spiritual identity. Only God knows who I am. Our people have paid a high price to see this glorious day, but tonight you demean its significance."

Dismayed by this, Benjamin said faintly, "Jesus, you have caused much trouble for yourself." There was a short pause as he glanced at Nicodemus. Then he turned to Jesus and uttered, "Your own follies will lead to your demise."

Benjamin gave Jesus a lingering look, then walked to the doorway. Soon the men around Nicodemus and Joseph left as well.

For the last few minutes Judas had been near the doorway, anxiously observing the proceedings. He noticed that after Benjamin and the others left the room, the anger and resentment of the remaining men grew. It was like an enemy army marching against Jesus, who was standing alone against the same religious elite whom he had originally hoped would support him.

Holding the leather pouch bulging with silver coins that Caiaphas had given him that morning, Judas leaned forward and listened closely to the various arguments taking place in the room. After another minute,

Caiaphas got everyone's attention and announced in a matter-of-fact tone, "Obviously this is a case of sedition against Rome. The only course of action is to turn Jesus over to the Roman procurator. By turning him over, we can convey the unmistakable message that we are not supporting this crazy Nazarene or his subversive activities. Pilate will surely know how to deal with this heretic!"

Judas was shocked, as if the high priest had thrown cold water in his face. Trembling like a leaf, he stared at Jesus with terrified eyes, for he knew well the Roman methods of execution for those found guilty of sedition.

Feeling his legs go limp, Judas leaned against the wall as the magnitude of his betrayal started to unveil in his mind. With waves of regret assaulting him, Judas watched in disbelief as Caiaphas ordered the Temple guards to take Jesus to the Antonia Fortress and hand him over to the soldiers on duty.

The two guards handled Jesus roughly as they led him from the room and into the courtyard, where sparks from the charcoal fire were swirling in the cold night air. The night sky was cloudless again, with a bright moon flooding the courtyard with light.

Jesus quickly spotted Peter, who was still mingling with the servants and soldiers. For a long moment, Peter's and Jesus' eyes met, and precisely at that moment the cock crowed. Almost instantly Peter was short of breath, and his hands and upper body began shaking as he recalled Jesus telling him that before the cock crowed he would deny his Lord three times. Indeed, while he had been in the courtyard waiting for his master, on three separate occasions Peter was recognized by some people as one of Jesus' followers. He had denied it each time … not for lack of faith but rather for a lack of courage.

Peter reproached himself as the soldiers led Jesus from the courtyard.

While some of the servants made disparaging remarks about the Nazarene, Peter's heart was heavy with sorrow, and he burst into uncontrollable tears as he hurried away from Caiaphas' house.

CHAPTER 38

THE TEMPLE GUARDS CHATTED about their young children as they guided Jesus along the quiet streets of the city. When they arrived at the gate of the Antonia Fortress, they spoke to the soldiers there. Soon the gate swung open, and a Roman officer and four soldiers came out. After a brief discussion in which the guards explained the charges against Jesus and that in the morning representatives of the Sanhedrin would come to give more details, the Roman soldiers dragged Jesus by his tunic inside the walls.

Since dawn was hours away, Jesus was taken to a large courtyard lit by burning torches. His arms and hands still bound, he was shoved down to the cold paving stones, where he sat upright while some of the soldiers ridiculed him.

After a while they grew bored, and in need of excitement, one of the young soldiers blindfolded Jesus and made him stand up. Then five soldiers encircled him and began punching at his body, challenging him that if he were really a great Jewish prophet, then he should be able to figure out who had struck him each time.

The cruel game continued off and on until the next shift of soldiers came to relieve them. Having just woken up, this group of soldiers was in no mood for such games. The officer allowed Jesus to sit cross-legged, his back against a pillar not far the charcoal fire that provided some warmth and protection from the cold wind that whipped through the courtyard.

Some time later Jesus was half asleep when he felt someone kicking at his stiff legs. Opening his eyes, he saw a tall centurion in full military garb staring down at him as rays of sunlight streamed across the stone floor.

When the Roman governor stepped from his sleeping quarters, the officer on duty informed him of the presence of some Temple priests in the fortress, as well as a new prisoner called Jesus. *So they caught the troublemaker,* Pilate thought dully.

Frowning, he told the officer to take everyone to the terrace.

After skimming over a document in his meeting chamber, Pilate's assistant informed him of the charges leveled against Jesus by Caiaphas and the Sanhedrin. Realizing the seriousness of the situation, Pilate gathered himself before walking onto the terrace with a clear sense of purpose.

Ignoring the four priests, Pilate nodded at the officer and soldiers before stepping over to the prisoner. After a little yawn, Pilate gave a long, studious look at this Nazarene preacher.

With a passive expression and erect bearing, Jesus stood in front of Pilate and the chief priests, his hands bound and a small bruise on his left cheek where one of the Roman soldiers had punched him rather hard.

Still examining Jesus' strong-featured face, Pilate was struck by the man's clear eyes, which shone with an odd brightness. Yet as the procurator continued studying him, he realized that the toughness, the hard face and body language that are part of a fighter, were not what he was seeing in Jesus. *This Nazarene seems too docile, too submissive, his eyes too tender,* he thought with disappointment, for he had expected to find a rough-looking brute with hate in his eyes and a hunger for violence on his face.

Still, Pilate felt there was something unique about Jesus, something that he could not quite perceive.

Turning slightly, Pilate looked at the military officer, puzzled, his eyes asking, *This is the wild man they are so fearful of?* Then moving his eyes back to Jesus, he couldn't help but wonder whether Caiaphas and the other priests had conjured up a scheme that would give him a severe headache lasting through the day.

"Did they send us the right man?" he uttered to the officer.

The man gave a vague shrug. "The Temple guards brought him during the night, before I came on duty this morning."

Pilate thought about this, then frowned at the priests. "Tell me, why are you bringing such severe charges against this man? He doesn't look threatening."

The elder priest replied, "If this Nazarene were not a dangerous criminal, we would not have handed him over to you."

Pilate stared at Jesus, sensing he was different from other rebels and prisoners he had encountered over the years. "Nazarene, I hear you are the leader of seditionists who plan to drive us Romans from this land. Have you fought using a sword or spear?"

Jesus shook his head silently, his eyes lowered in a humble manner.

"Neither have I," admitted Pilate, chuckling. He motioned at the soldiers. "I let these brave men do the fighting for me. How about you? Do your followers bear arms for you?"

Once again, Jesus shook his head, this time staring directly into Pilate's eyes.

Hesitating, the procurator glanced at the officer. "Other than what these priests claim, what do we know about this man?"

"One of your centurions had dealings with him before. When he arrived this morning with reinforcements, he noticed the prisoner and recognized him."

"Bring him here now," ordered Pilate, turning and stepping closer to the priests.

A few minutes later, the centurion stepped into view and gave Jesus a sympathetic look as he approached Pilate.

"What do you know about this man?" he asked shortly.

The centurion answered in a respectful tone, "About a year ago my best slave was quite ill. No one could find a cure. Yet I was determined to save the man because over the years he has been faithful to my family." He paused to cough, then added in a deep voice, "While serving in Galilee, I heard reports about Jesus … this man … and his miraculous healing powers. So I went to his outdoor gathering and inquired if he could help."

After a moment of thought, Pilate gave a nod. "Go on," he said, momentarily shifting his eyes to Jesus' placid face.

The centurion said, "Jesus wanted to come to the barracks to perform the healing, but I didn't want my fellow officers to see that I had faith in a Jewish healer."

Pilate raised a quick hand. "You had confidence this Nazarene could actually work his … magic … on your slave?"

"At first I had little hope. But after speaking to him, I felt the gods could work through him. So I told him to perform his healing magic from far away, if possible. Without responding, Jesus closed his eyes and prayed in a guttural voice in his language. When he opened his eyes, he smiled and assured me that my slave was healed."

Pilate waited, then threw his arms up in frustration. "So tell us, was he restored to good health?"

The centurion nodded. "Upon my arrival at the barracks, I was astonished to see my slave out of bed and well again. I couldn't believe my eyes."

With a gesture, one of the priests said, "This Nazarene does the work of Beelzebub!"

The centurion bristled at this. "Your Excellency, this here is a good man who has done no harm to anyone."

Pilate made no reply, just waved him toward the doorway and watched in silence as the centurion strode from the terrace, but not before giving Jesus a fleeting smile.

Turning his attention to the priests, Pilate stared at them with growing irritation.

"Why don't you judge this man by your own laws?" he snapped at them.

The elder priest replied in an authoritative manner, "Yesterday evening the Sanhedrin found Jesus guilty of subversion. He opposes paying taxes to Caesar, and also claims to be the Messiah, the king of this land!"

Pilate narrowed his gaze at Jesus. "So, are you the king of the Jews?"

"You have said so," replied Jesus, his voice steady.

Pilate smiled at this, glancing at the military officer and soldiers, who were laughing softly. "This Nazarene is a presumptuous rascal, eh?" With a low sigh, Pilate stepped closer to the prisoner and said sharply, "So tell me, who made you a king, and when?"

Jesus made no reply, but simply lowered his eyes again as the Temple priests whispered among themselves, casting him malicious looks.

Pilate turned to the priests and studied their bearded faces, trying to discern their ulterior motives. *They brought this man here out of envy or to trick me,* he thought in aggravation. "So what other charges have you conjured up against this man?"

The elderly one promptly said, "For several years this devil has been spreading his false teachings throughout Galilee and Judea, stirring up the people against Rome and the peace of this land."

Pilate gave no reaction as his eyes drifted back to Jesus' face. After a few seconds, he gave voice to his thoughts. "Since the prisoner is a Galilean, I will turn the matter over to Herod Antipas. He can deal with it." He looked at the officer. "Take this man to Herod, and tell him that Rome doesn't concern itself with internal disputes."

Minutes later a group of Temple priests and three Roman soldiers led Jesus through the crowded streets of Jerusalem as they made their way to the palace of Herod Antipas, located to the west on a hill overlooking the lower city. During the ten-minute walk, the men were met by curious and suspicious looks from the people, some of whom recognized Jesus as the Nazarene preacher who had created the chaos in the Temple courts.

Although Herod Antipas was in charge of Galilee and Perea, he could often be found in Jerusalem, where he entertained his friends in his luxurious palace. And wherever Herod traveled, he would bring his manicurists and hair curlers, pastry chefs and sauce makers, and bath and bedroom servants to sustain his lavish lifestyle.

On this Feast of the Passover, as on other occasions, Herod surrounded himself with a number of close friends who enjoyed drinking and telling stories at sumptuous parties when they weren't making secret plans to gain more power and wealth.

Among Herod's many guests this Passover was his close friend Nebat. Lounging upon several large pillows, Nebat was admiring a young African servant who was giggling as Herod and the other men encouraged her to sing and dance for them.

Yawning, Herod glanced to his left as a Roman officer entered the expansive room and informed him about Pilate's decision to place Jesus under his custody.

Soon the chief priests, soldiers, and Jesus were escorted into the room. The officer grasped Jesus' arm and pulled him closer to where Herod was sitting.

As Jesus stood before him and the other men, they all had a good laugh over his disheveled appearance.

"Jesus of Nazareth!" exclaimed Herod. "We finally meet."

Nebat got to his feet and stepped over to him. "I and the others have heard so much about your extraordinary powers."

"Give us a demonstration," prompted Herod, chuckling. "Can you heal my toothache, or perhaps cure my wife's grouchy nature?"

This brought on more rounds of laughter from everyone, but Jesus remained silent, his head lowered and his eyes staring blankly at the thick tapestry rug.

After a moment, Herod said to him, "This past year I have received various reports about you. Some people claim you are either Elijah or a new prophet. Some even say you are John the Baptist, raised from the dead."

The captain of Herod's guards said dryly, "If he is John the Baptist, he'd better hang onto his head this time."

Laughter continued to echo throughout the room, but Jesus' body remained motionless, his eyes half open, as if he were in a trance.

Soon Herod blurted out, "Man, don't just stand here like a log! Entertain us with your magical powers!" Growing impatient, he commanded a servant. "Quickly bring us a large jar of water."

He looked at Jesus. "Tell me, how did you get such supernatural powers?"

Jesus said nothing, only staring downward at the rug.

The servant returned with a ceramic jar full of water, setting it on the table.

Pointing at the jar, Herod looked at Jesus and said, "Let me see you repeat one of your great purported miracles. Transform this water into wine."

Jesus made no movement or even seemed to have heard Herod's command.

The senior priest spoke up. "King Herod, apparently this devil has lost all his powers. He cannot even summon the power to speak in his defense. He's a false Messiah who has been turning Galileans against you and your family."

"We all know about his seditious activities," remarked Nebat. With a twisted grin, he placed his fingers under Jesus' chin, forcing him to lift his head. "If you make wine for our king, then he might let you leave here a free man."

All eyes were on Jesus. But he remained motionless, not making a sound.

After a long moment of tense silence, Herod released an angry grunt and scowled at the priests. "What's wrong with this man? Did you cut off his tongue?"

The senior priest replied, "He acts like a mute fool in your presence, but in the villages and towns he feeds people lies and false promises about God's coming kingdom, with him the Anointed One to usher in a new kingdom of love and peace."

"Love and peace, huh?" said Herod, chuckling. "Nazarene, do you have designs on my throne?" he asked in a mocking voice. "I do hope you are a worthy adversary."

Nebat said in vexation, "Jesus, do you know that claiming to be the Messiah is the same as proclaiming yourself as the new king! Aren't you afraid of the consequences?"

Although Jesus remained quiet with a distant look on his face, Herod remarked in a milder tone, "Well, you are certainly no coward." He added with a grunt, "Nazarene, it takes an iron hand to rule over the Jews while also keeping good relations with our Roman masters."

The senior priest spoke up again. "King Herod, you need to deal harshly with this heretic. If given a light sentence, it will encourage others like him to spread their lies throughout the countryside. You saw all the repercussions from John the Baptist. This evil man is even more dangerous to your authority and reputation."

As Herod considered this, Nebat pointed out, "This affair could create an opportunity to foster a friendship between you and Pilate. It would be politically advantageous if you allow Pilate to decide the matter."

Herod nodded in agreement, although the priests and elders murmured strong words of disapproval. Raising a hand to silence them, Herod said to Nebat and his other friends, "If this Nazarene claims to be king, then let's make him look like one!"

Soon Jesus was dressed in fine robes and stood quietly among these shallow men, who mocked and derided him before sending him back to the Roman procurator.

Pontius Pilate and the officials with him broke into laughter when Jesus was led into the chamber wearing the fine purple robe.

The Roman officer announced with a straight face, "Your Excellency, Herod has sent you the new governor of Judea and Samaria, and the future king of all Israel!"

Although there was enmity between Pilate and Herod, the Roman appreciated this clever prank. So he told the officer to convey his greeting to Herod, and invited him for a visit before his return to Galilee.

Realizing he had to make a decision on the matter, Pilate approached Jesus and examined his expressionless face once again. *This man couldn't be as simple and harmless as he appears,* he thought, fighting off his doubts.

Speaking in a low, controlled voice, Pilate said to him, "So Herod tossed you back into my lap. Believe me, I would not enjoy seeing you killed. It is not from personal concern or that you might be a threat to Rome, but I have to take some action to appease your many enemies. Understand?"

Jesus raised his eyes, nodding slightly.

Pilate reached for his toga and wrapped it around his shoulders. "Tell me, what do you teach that stirs up such a wind of controversy among your people?"

Jesus answered softly, "I teach the truth."

"The truth?" echoed Pilate, almost frowning. "What is the truth? Please tell me."

There was a long silence as the two men looked at each other.

Frowning, Jesus wondered how he could explain such a profound truth to a Roman official who lacked the spiritual foundation to receive it.

"The world needs compassion and humility," Jesus replied simply.

Pilate was both surprised and moved by the sincerity with which Jesus spoke these words. Yet still suspicious, he uttered, "Really? I don't know what to make of you. Usually the Jews who end up in here are violent and full of hate for us Romans. So I am very motivated to use harsh means to punish them. But you … you are not like them." His voice trailed off as he turned to the military officer. "Where are the chief priests and scribes?"

"Down in the courtyard with a gathering mob of people. Many are shouting out in rage and demanding the execution of the prisoner."

Hiding his feelings, Pilate said shortly, "Take him onto the terrace."

Cursing the day when he was appointed to serve in this Palestine region, Pilate exhaled a deep breath as they walked along the corridor to the front terrace that overlooked the large courtyard below.

The loud mixture of voices gradually subsided as the restless crowd noticed Pontius Pilate standing on the terrace above them. But as two soldiers led Jesus into view, strident voices mixed with angry shouts and threats made Pilate realize this could quickly escalate into a dangerous situation.

Glad there was a full battalion of troops to disperse the crowd if necessary, Pilate raised his hand to silence everyone. After clearing his throat, he spoke in a full-throated voice. "This morning your chief priests brought this prisoner here. He has been accused of perverting the people with his teachings and with seditious words against Roman authorities. After my interrogation …" He paused to find the right words. "I … I see no evidence that he is guilty of any crimes against Rome. Herod himself found Jesus innocent and sent him back to me."

Startled by Pilate's pronouncement, the chief priests, scribes, and Pharisees began engaging in animated discussions with other members of the crowd.

"Despite his heretical teachings, he is still one of our own," remarked one man. "They might kill him. Do we want a fellow Jew to be killed by the Romans?"

Another man said in reply, "If this Nazarene is set free, he will continue to proclaim himself the Messiah. It would create further chaos!"

A Pharisee interjected, "If there are loud arguments in the streets and synagogues, then Pilate will blame the religious authorities here in Jerusalem …"

"We will be the ones to pay with our lives!" exclaimed an elderly scribe.

The others nodded, with one priest saying, "Pilate is testing us, so we must stick with our decision to have Jesus put to death! Remember that Caiaphas said that it's better for one man to die than for the entire nation to perish."

Turning their attention back to Pilate, one of the Pharisees shouted out in anger, "Don't release the Nazarene! He is a blasphemer and heretic! A rebel against Rome!"

Noticing the inconsistency of people's demands, Pilate stepped closer to his head officer. "If we chastise him severely and they see his bloody flesh, they may feel compassion and leave him alone."

The soldiers took Jesus down to a lower level and stripped him of his clothes, then scourged him violently with a whip. Knowing that hate is not part of God's nature, Jesus forgave them. He closed his eyes, clenching his teeth and tensing every muscle of his body as he chanted to himself, "Pain and humiliation surround me, but I will not allow hatred to fill my heart. Satan, I will never surrender to you! You won't claim my heart and sacrifice! I will maintain my dignity as the true Son of God!" He continued this chant during the agonizing ordeal.

Laughing and mocking him, the soldiers put a scarlet robe on him, and plaited a crown of thorns, which was set upon his head. Then a reed was put in his right hand, and the soldiers knelt before him in mock reverence while hailing him as king of the Jews! Laughing derisively, they took the reed away and began hitting and spitting at him. After having their fun, the scarlet robe was removed from Jesus' torn flesh, and his own tunic was put on him.

The soldiers took the prisoner back to Pontius Pilate, who grew sick to his stomach upon seeing Jesus' horrid condition. His face was bruised and cut, with splotches of blood, and the back of his tunic was soaked in blood from the painful scourging.

For the third time, Pilate decided to test the people of Abraham, hoping to discover whether Caiaphas and the other priests were playing games with him, and whether there was any conspiracy behind it. The Romans had established a practice of pardoning one prisoner during the Passover festivities. Pilate chose a well-known Zealot and murderer called Barabbas to put up for release against Jesus. After all, Pilate concluded, if the people preferred Jesus over the notorious Barabbas, it would show him that they considered Jesus a more important figure in the cause of

Jewish freedom. Convinced this would reveal the situation to him, Pilate decided to bring the issue directly to the people in the crowd outside.

The crowd in the courtyard below the fortress towers had become quite unruly, the mixture of voices and demonstrations of protest growing louder. Part of the crowd consisted of relatives of those prisoners being detained there. Since this was the prisoners' last hope, their relatives were pleading for their release.

In the crowd, there was one group whose members exceeded those of the other groups: the family members who had come to plead for the release of Barabbas. So when Pontius Pilate asked the people which man they wanted to release during the Passover, their voices rose with those of the friends of the Zealot. They yelled in unison, "Release Barabbas! Put the heretic to death!" Their voices eclipsed those of the rest of the people.

Unsure of what to do with Jesus, Pilate asked the crowd, "What should I do with Jesus?"

The same group of people who had asked for the release of Barabbas shouted, "Put him to death! Crucify Jesus, but release Barabbas!"

At this point, Pontius Pilate finally gave up trying to help Jesus. Feeling obligated to comply with the crowd's demands, Pilate ordered his soldiers to release Barabbas, and then he gave instructions for Jesus to be put to death.

CHAPTER 39

IT WAS A SAD DAY FOR HEAVEN when the misguided crowd pressured the Roman governor to crucify the Anointed One. Pontius Pilate released Barabbas and ordered the military to crucify Jesus. The soldiers marched Jesus from the Antonia Fortress, forcing him to bear a heavy wooden cross on his shoulders through the streets, which were lined with tumultuous crowds of people. Many cried out in sorrow, while others yelled insults at the convicted Nazarene.

The Romans had decided to crucify Jesus and two other prisoners on a low hill called Golgotha, meaning "a skull" in Aramaic, not far from the western perimeter of the walled city.

I hurried through the crowds with Isaac and Sara, and we stopped at a place where I knew Jesus would have to pass. Two days before, I had explained to Isaac and Sara that their father might have to offer his physical life for what he believed in. I had told them how important this sacrifice was on the altar of God for the sake of humanity. Of course, it was very difficult for them to accept the idea that their father would have to die soon, and that we couldn't do anything about it. So they had begged me to bring them here so they could express their deep love for him. Early that morning I had warned them that they might see their father in a miserable, painful situation, with people calling him terrible names.

Soon the turmoil of the crowd grew more frenzied as the procession approached. When Jesus finally appeared in the midst of the soldiers, it was a ghastly, heartbreaking sight … far worse than I had expected. I clutched my children to my breast as the three of us cried out in agony. Such brutality! How could he be treated so savagely?

There was my beloved Jesus, bruised and beaten almost beyond recognition, dragging a huge wooden cross through the streets, followed by the jeering men who had demanded his death. Many women were also present, watching in horror and wailing as Jesus stumbled and fell every few steps, the cross pressing hard upon his bleeding shoulders where he had been scourged. Two good men helped Jesus to his feet along the way, even though the soldiers scolded them and lashed them with rawhide whips.

When Jesus regained his balance and began moving forward again, his eyes fell upon our tear-stained faces. We just stood there staring at him, our bodies trembling in shock. Then Isaac and Sara inched forward, their eyes glowing with such love and respect for their father. I conveyed my love and respect with a bow, then tugging at my children's hands, I signaled them to do the same. We wanted Jesus to feel that he was not alone on his path of suffering, that we were there for him, to give our support even if only with our hearts and tears.

Jesus looked at his children, trying to smile. But they could see the pain and exhaustion in his spent body. In a low, hoarse voice he told them to be strong and to love God with all their hearts and souls. Then, shoved by the soldiers, Jesus was forced to move on. Moments later, he disappeared around the corner of the buildings.

As part of the crowd began to disperse, the children and I went up the street to where a few of Jesus' disciples were waiting for us. I told Isaac and Sara to go with them while I followed the procession up to Golgotha. Sara nodded through her sobs, but Isaac insisted that he would remain by my side. So we hurried along with other people and soon caught up with the procession. Jesus was still bearing the cross with great difficulty, sweat and blood mixing on his face. Whenever he hesitated a moment, a soldier lashed him mercilessly. Finally, Jesus collapsed to the ground and another soldier pulled a black man from the crowd and forced him to carry the cross. The man carried it the rest of the way in sorrowful, thinking about the fate of the person for whom he was carrying the cross.

When the group reached the top of the hill, the soldiers told the man to drop the cross to the ground. So he did, then he was asked to leave. They dragged Jesus atop it, then roughly spread his arms out before pounding huge nails through his hands and into the wooden cross. He cried out in anguish as the nails pierced the flesh of his hands and then his feet, the blood spurting onto the ground.

I was close enough to see Jesus gasping heavily and groaning in pain. It appeared that his lungs had collapsed even before the soldiers lifted the cross up and placed the base into a hastily dug hole.

On each side of Jesus were crosses with two thieves nailed to them. To the left of Jesus was a man who mocked him, saying that if he were really the Messiah then he would save himself as well as them. But the thief on the right, who had once heard Jesus preach, rebuked the other and told him to have respect for the Son of God. He said that they had gotten their just punishment, whereas Jesus was a good man who didn't deserve to die. Upon hearing this, Jesus glanced at the man, who then implored him to remember him. Jesus promised they would be together in Paradise that very day. I could feel that Jesus wanted to say more, but just to breathe was such an effort! His tongue was swollen, and he was coughing deeply, almost choking on the blood flooding his mouth.

I was near the cross, along with Isaac and a small group of women who loved Jesus dearly. Among them was Mary, his mother, who had come to Jerusalem with her daughters' families for Passover. When she heard that a man from Galilee proclaiming to be the Son of God was being crucified, she ran to Golgotha, fearing it would be her own son.

Mary fell to her knees and burst into tears as Jesus' body hung upon the cross, which carried an inscription above reading "King of the Jews."

Isaac moved into his grandmother's arms and tried to comfort her as he gazed up at his father in utter disbelief. I put my arms around them. Jesus peered down at his son through half-closed, blood-encrusted eyes that nevertheless conveyed the message that, as his own flesh and blood, Isaac was to carry on his lineage as his representative and replacement. Then his sad eyes fell upon my face and told me to protect our children so that our descendants could be preserved. Struggling to breathe and talk, he looked at Isaac again and told him that he was the man of the family now.

As Jesus' breathing grew more difficult, we could only stare up at him in utter helplessness. There was nothing we could do for him! His mother and I clung to each other as if we were one. The minutes passed slowly, and Jesus' agony increased by the second. Soon I noticed that his upper body was sagging, the nails tearing at his flesh. He struggled to relieve the pain by pushing his body up with his feet, constantly gasping for air.

All the while, Jesus had to bear the nagging curses of the thief on his left and the scoffing of those men passing by who seemed to take pleasure in deriding him, saying, "Nazarene, you who would destroy the Temple and rebuild it in three days, save yourself and come down from the cross!" The chief priests and scribes also mocked him, crying out that if he could save the sick and the dead, then why couldn't he save himself now!

The Roman soldiers soon joined in the chorus, laughing aloud. "If you are really the king of the Jews, then save yourself and the other prisoners!"

The fallen archangel was lurking nearby, of course, playing on the ignorance and cruelty of the people in an attempt to discourage Jesus during his painful ordeal. If Jesus lost faith and hated and cursed those men chastising him, then evil forces could have dwelled in Jesus' heart, making his sacrifice in vane. But Jesus maintained his dignity as the chosen of God and liberator of humanity, forgiving those who harmed and persecuted him. He knew that soon he would have to stand in front of God and open a new mansion in his Father's house, and he couldn't do this unless he presented himself with a clean heart full of unconditional love.

In the sixth hour, a sudden darkness descended, bringing fear and wonder into the souls of everyone present on Golgotha. Soon our hearts leaped with hopeful prayer as we heard Jesus ask God to forgive his enemies. "Oh Father, please forgive those misguided souls who persecuted me and led me to this cross, for they know not the crimes they commit against Heaven."

Suddenly at the end of his ninth hour on the cross, Jesus cried out, "My God, my God, why have You abandoned me?"

Although God was crying in bitter anguish over the cruel treatment of His beloved Son, He had no choice but to let Jesus win the spiritual victory on his own.

Hearing Jesus shout out to God, some of the bystanders said in wonder, "Behold, he is calling Elijah!"

One of the soldiers took a sponge and soaked it with vinegar, then placed it on a reed and raised it up to his mouth. What a despicable act!

Gasping for air, Jesus' breathing became more erratic, and his eyelids grew heavy. During his last moments, I could hear him murmur that his mission on earth was over, and that he was ready to go to the spiritual world and open a new mansion where Abel, Noah, Abraham, and others who had followed God's will would go. Then he cried out in a loud voice, "Father, into Your hands I offer my spirit!" Passing away with the name of God on his lips, the muscles in his upper body went slack and his head fell upon his chest as his spirit began its journey to the other world.

Most people in the same situation would have loathed and cursed those who had brought such suffering upon them. But not Jesus. He didn't allow evil to influence his mind and heart with bitter thoughts and feelings. This was Jesus' great triumph: the victory of good over evil, of light over darkness, the triumph of the Son of God over Satan.

As Jesus transitioned into the spiritual world, Moses and other prophets welcomed him, protecting and attending him during this delicate process of rebirth into a new dimension.

Since it was the eve of Passover, in order to prevent the crucified men from remaining on the cross on the Sabbath, the Jews asked Pilate if their bodies could be taken down. Pilate gave his consent, but not before having the soldiers break the legs of the men still alive. When they saw that Jesus was already dead, they didn't break his legs but instead pierced his side with a spear.

We all wept again when Jesus' lifeless body was removed from the cross and stretched out upon the ground. His mother picked up the body, holding it tightly in her arms, with the blood staining her garments. Isaac and I knelt beside her, and we stroked his face and held his hands, feeling the fading heat of his body.

Joseph of Arimathea, who along with Nicodemus had supported Jesus at Caiaphas' home, tearfully witnessed the crucifixion from a distance. Afterward, Joseph went to Pilate's palace in secret and asked the Roman governor for the body of Jesus. After confirming that Jesus was actually dead, Pilate gave his consent for Joseph to bury the Nazarene.

Joseph hurried back to Golgotha, where Jesus' bruised and bloodied body was still on the hard ground, surrounded by a number of women followers crying and praying fervently for his soul. With the help of Nicodemus and another man, Joseph took the corpse to his own new tomb in his garden nearby. Nicodemus brought myrrh and aloes, and after treating the numerous wounds, they carefully wrapped the body in a clean linen shroud according to the burial custom. During the process, Nicodemus thought back to his various discussions with Jesus, recalling one in particular in which Jesus had told him that he would need the heart of a child to enter into the kingdom of heaven.

Since it was late Friday afternoon, just before the start of the Sabbath, they had no time to properly embalm Jesus' body. So they decided to return on the morning after the Sabbath to perform the ritual, and perhaps move the body to another tomb.

The death of Jesus was an immense tragedy that left a deep scar in my heart. Why did the Messiah's life have to end in such a sorrowful way?

The day after the crucifixion was the Sabbath. I was still heartbroken and so devastated that I had no desire to talk or eat or move about. I couldn't even cry. I had cried so much during the long, dark night that my eyes were burning and my vision had grown blurry. All I could bring myself to do was drink a little water to moisten my dry mouth and throat.

It was early on Sunday morning, right before dawn, the third day after Jesus' death, when I found the strength to walk to Joseph's garden and visit the tomb, hewn on the side of a rocky slope. To my surprise, I saw that the heavy stone covering the entrance had been rolled to one side. With a mixture of fear and concern, I entered the dark cavern and was startled that Jesus' body was nowhere in sight.

Thinking that either the chief priests or the Romans had removed the body, I hurried back into the city to the house where everyone was hiding. I breathlessly told Isaac and Simon Peter that the tomb was empty. At first, Peter offered no reaction. Since Jesus' crucifixion, he had not uttered a single word, his face drawn and his eyes full of pain and misery. So I shook his shoulders hard while repeating that Jesus' body was no longer in the tomb.

Both Simon Peter and Isaac thought I must have been mistaken. Nevertheless, they heeded my pleas and ran with me toward the garden. Isaac, of course, was faster and got to the tomb first. A bit frightened, he remained outside. He looked into the darkness and saw the linen cloth on the floor. When Simon Peter arrived, he entered the tomb with no hesitation. Shocked that the body wasn't there, he noticed that the napkin that had been on Jesus' head was now rolled up and put in a separate place.

My son took a deep breath and went into the tomb. A minute later, he and Simon Peter stepped outside with troubled looks on their faces. After briefly sharing their thoughts with me, they began walking back toward the city gate as the first rays of sunlight spread over the hill where Jesus had suffered on the cross two days before.

Not knowing what to do, I remained outside, near the entrance of the tomb. While I shivered in the morning cold, tears welled up in my eyes as I tried to control my bitter feelings toward the chief priests and Pharisees who had vehemently opposed Jesus.

Soon I heard someone whispering my name. "Mary, there is no need for tears."

Startled, I assumed it was the gardener. I turned around, wiping the tears from my cheeks, and, with the sun in my eyes, said to him, "Did you remove the body from the tomb?"

Thinking he looked familiar, I stepped closer to the man, suddenly feeling short of breath as I recognized my husband's warm smile and loving eyes.

My heart pounded in my chest as I gasped in confusion, "Jesus?" Leaning forward a little, I stammered, "How can it be you?"

In the brilliant, shimmering-white robe he wore, Jesus seemed to be coming directly out of the bright light of the sun. "I am very much alive," he smiled.

"Yes, you are alive!" I thought aloud, with my heart filled with conflicting emotions. But as I began to run into his arms, he held up a hand to stop me.

"Mary, do not touch me," he said firmly. "I have not yet ascended to the kingdom of my Heavenly Father."

He reminded me that the spiritual body and mind had to go through a process of adaptation to the new dimension, focusing on the spiritual and avoiding drifting in the wrong direction by the physical senses.

I stood looking at him, unsure of what I was seeing. As I studied Jesus more closely, I realized that I was seeing his beautiful and pure spiritual body. Thoroughly captivated by his radiant appearance, I uttered with growing emotion, "Oh Jesus, my love! You suffered so much. My heart is full of sorrow for what you had to endure all these years."

His shining eyes fixed on me. "Mary, my physical life has ended. For the next forty days, my spiritual mind and spiritual body have to harmonize with the reality of the spiritual world." Then making a little gesture, he added, "I need your help to reorganize my followers."

I nodded. "Simon Peter, James, John, and the others are hiding out, fearful of being turned over to the Romans,"

"This is a time for them to reflect on their actions," he stated, justifying their behavior. "Hopefully they won't run away. It would bring much sadness to the Lord. Who would spread my teachings and give testimony about me?"

I gave him a reassuring smile. "Don't worry, Dear. I am certain your disciples will never desert you again."

After glancing at the empty tomb, he said to me, "From now on, I will often appear to you in spirit. I will instruct you personally, and you will guide the others to maintain a deep faith and commitment to God's ideals. You are my direct representative."

I thought about this. "But how can I convince your disciples to let me guide them?" I asked, bewildered. "In this world, women are not much heeded."

I wanted to remind him that not even his closest followers were willing to soften their position on that issue. Jesus agreed with me.

"Peter understands it, but he still has his cultural limitations that compel him to reject the notion of a woman leader."

"Be careful, Mary," he warned. "Watch carefully over our children, and don't expose them to danger. Don't fall into the hands of those people who will try to destroy all traces of my existence. The confrontation between God's representative and the evil masters of this world is inevitable. Due to their ignorance, faithless men will succumb to the will of Satan."

Pausing, he grew even more serious. "Mary, you and our children, together with my followers and my teachings, are the most important treasures that I leave in this world. But beware of the evildoers, who will try to destroy it all."

With fear rising in my heart, I uttered faintly, "Jesus, I will do all I can to protect our children. I will be like a tower guarding Isaac and Sara day and night."

"Mary! The path is now wide open for humanity to find the way toward its enlightenment and a better future. All children have to grow up in a more compassionate world where there is love and peace."

The sound of his voice melted my heart. Without thinking, I began to throw myself into his arms again but quickly caught myself and subdued my emotions.

"Jesus, you are the Lord of my existence, and I love you more than my own life."

He smiled at me. "Thanks to you, I have descendants. Soon you and our children, along with our followers, will receive the Holy Spirit. If the chosen people accept me as the resurrected Messiah, I will be able to pass on my spiritual victory to our son. Then in each generation, there will be an Adam who will represent me."

I stared at him in astonishment. "Is that why you told Peter, Andrew, James, and John that this generation will not pass by before they see the coming of the Lord of the Second Advent, the third Adam?"

"Yes," he nodded. "But it will happen only if my followers, strengthened with the Holy Spirit, are able to convince the chosen people that I am the one whose task is to liberate the chosen people and guide them to deepest understanding of our Heavenly Parents' nature."

"Jesus, I am certain that Peter and the others won't disappoint you this time."

"For the glory of God, let's pray that is so." After a short pause, he uttered with a note of regret, "Mary, you need to go now. Announce my resurrection. I will rise to the spiritual world in the company of God, my Father and your Father, my God and your God. Be strong, and keep in mind that you are my beloved spouse, the mother of my children. No one can change that."

Then after saying this, Jesus simply vanished into the air, leaving no trace of his presence except in my heart and mind.

Jesus' words echoed in my mind as I left the garden. Somehow I had to gather all his close disciples and inform them about my spiritual encounter with him. But one question resounded in my mind. Would they believe me?

CHAPTER 40

As soon as I entered the house I could feel the tension in the air. In the front room were gathered some of the disciples, with shame and sorrow written on their faces. Apparently, Simon Peter and Isaac had just finished telling them about the strange disappearance of Jesus' body from Joseph's tomb early that morning.

There were two women in a circle of eleven, so I sat between them as they made space for me on the soft rug. James and John were sit across from me. The brothers were in tears, hitting their chests and reproaching themselves for having abandoned the Lord when he most needed their support and comfort.

Some in the room gave me odd stares when they noticed the peaceful look in my eyes and the smile on my lips. As the room grew quiet unders their stares, Andrew said in a hesitant voice, "Mary, are you feeling ill?"

I shook my head, wishing I could read their thoughts. After a few moments, I couldn't contain myself any longer. In an excited voice, I told them what had happened at the tomb after Isaac and Simon Peter had left. Every detail was still fresh in my mind as I described my wondrous meeting with Jesus. When I finished the account, I noticed the doubtful looks on most of their faces.

After a long moment of tense silence, James said faintly, "You say the man you spoke to didn't look like Jesus?"

"No, but it was definitely him," I answered, wondering how I would feel if I were in their position. "It's difficult to explain," I added, "but the loving and sacrificial heart that Jesus expressed on earth has affected his appearance in the next world. So now Jesus has a lovely, radiant face with a magnificent smile and warm, embracing eyes."

"Praise the Lord," murmured the elderly woman to my right, smiling brightly.

John said to Isaac, "Many times Jesus told us that the appearance of our spiritual bodies reflects how we conducted our lives here on earth."

Andrew said dryly, "In that case, John, there's hope for you."

Everyone laughed at the remark, except for Simon Peter. He was deathly quiet, with a morose look on his face, his eyes red and watery as if he were about to burst into tears.

Suppressing a sigh, I said to them, "Before Jesus departed, he asked me to tell all of you that He has gone to his God and Father, who is also our God and Father."

Although the disciples nodded in approval, I could see they weren't entirely convinced that Jesus had resurrected and then appeared to me at his empty tomb.

Early that evening, most of the disciples were still in the house, for fear that they, too, might be threatened by the chief priests. After a light meal, they began discussing the events of the past four days, as well as debating the veracity of my incredible testimony. Suddenly all talk ceased as they saw Jesus come into the room, smiling warmly at them. Startled, the men jumped to their feet and gazed at him, not quite believing their eyes.

"Peace be with you," he uttered, showing his pierced hands and side. Adding with a level voice, "As the Father has sent me, so I will send you."

"Jesus, my Lord!" exclaimed Simon Peter, falling to his knees. "Truly it is you! Praise be to God the Almighty!"

"Praise be to God," echoed the others, bowing in reverence to the resurrected Lord.

Jesus motioned them to be seated. They sat before him, their eyes wide and their hearts thumping with rising anticipation.

After studying their faces and judging the contents of their hearts, Jesus spoke in a patient tone. "You are now my voice and my arms and legs. As the Father is with me, so I will be with you. Together we will spread God's love to all corners of the world. In the years to come, a new generation of good men and women will emerge who will answer my call to find God in their personal lives and live by my commandments, especially loving their enemies and serving others."

"I will be with you and all God's children until the end of time."

Smiling, the disciples glanced at one another, then moved their eyes to Simon Peter as he threw himself on the floor again. "My Lord," he uttered in a tremulous voice, "I am so sorry for abandoning you."

"Peter, what you did in the past is now forgiven. This is a new beginning! From this day on, you must be strong and set a good example for the others."

"Yes, Lord," said Peter, nodding gratefully. "Will you stay with us?"

Jesus shook his head. "I cannot stay with you, for I no longer have a physical body. I am now subject to the laws of the spiritual world."

His eyes shone with kindness for a lingering moment, and then he vanished right before their eyes.

For a short while the disciples remained silent, in awe at what they had just witnessed. Then abruptly they all began talking at once, with hopeful expressions on their faces.

Thomas had not been present at the time of Jesus' appearance. So later when Thomas returned and joined his fellow disciples, he was told about the miraculous occurrence. Even though the other men swore it was true, Thomas remained skeptical, saying he wouldn't believe it unless he saw Jesus with his own eyes and touched him with his own hands.

Eight days later, when the disciples were in the room and the doors shut, Jesus appeared again. This time Thomas was present. Stunned by the sight of Jesus standing before the group, yet wanting to make certain that his eyes weren't deceiving him, Thomas touched the puncture wounds on Jesus' hands and the wound on his side where he had been pierced by the soldier's spear.

"It is indeed you, my Lord!" said Thomas with his legs trembling.

Jesus said to him, "Do you believe only because your eyes tell you so? Blessed are those people who believe without seeing!"

After few minutes of fellowship, Jesus left in the same mysterious manner he had arrived.

During the following days, some of the disciples from Judea remained together in Jerusalem, doing little else but talking about their spiritual experiences with Jesus.

However, Simon Peter, Andrew, James, John, and other disciples from Galilee decided to return to their homes and families. At my request, Simon Peter took Isaac with him to Capernaum. After all, Peter was Jesus' closest follower, and he deeply understood his teachings. Moreover, he and Isaac had always gotten along well, developing a strong bond like that between father and son.

Two days after arriving in Capernaum, Simon Peter and James planned to take Isaac along when they went fishing. While the two men prepared the nets and ropes, Isaac was carrying food and water onto the boat.

Soon, James noticed Thomas and John approaching, with Philip and Bartholomew a few steps behind, all four waving their hands and calling out to Isaac. "You'd better get your payment in advance!" John said playfully.

"I hope you can swim like a fish," added Thomas, raising his voice. "That boat has more leaks than Peter's head!"

Though laughing inwardly, Simon Peter responded in a gruff voice, "Do you lazy bones plan to babble all night? Or can you join us and do some work?"

"Why else do you think we are here?" replied Bartholomew, swatting him on the back. "We certainly didn't come here to listen to you snore all night!"

Within the hour, the seven of them were on the boat and sailing onto the open waters. But although they were out all night, they weren't able to catch any fish.

The next morning, just after dawn, they were fishing near the shores of Tiberias.

All the men looked frustrated at not having caught any fish though they had labored all night. As John and Thomas were hauling in the empty net, they noticed a man on the shore who was waving his arms over his head.

He shouted out, "Cast your net on the other side of the boat!"

They did as he suggested, and within minutes the net was full of fish. The net was so heavy that John and the others couldn't even haul it into the boat.

Staring at the man on shore, Isaac was the first to recognize him. "It's the Lord," he said excitedly, coming up to Simon Peter. "It is my father!"

Peter, who was wearing only a loincloth, quickly put on his tunic. Since the boat was less than two hundred cubits from the coastline, he dove into the lake and swam toward shore while James steered the boat near him, dragging the net of fish through the water.

Minutes later, Peter stepped from the cool water. Though breathing heavily, he ran up to Jesus, who was standing near a charcoal fire with a thoughtful look on his face.

"Lord, you blessed us again with a great catch!" he said, shaking the water from his clothes.

Jesus glanced at the boat. For several moments, he watched Isaac as he helped the others haul the net of fish ashore.

He turned to Simon Peter and said, "Thank you for taking care of my son."

"He is a fine boy. And he likes to fish, almost as much as you do!"

Jesus smiled faintly, then said in a serious tone, "Peter, I need your help so that my bloodline survives." Pausing, he glanced to his left as Isaac and the other men approached the warm fire. "Everyone is tired and hungry. Bring some fish from your boat."

Simon Peter returned to the boat, along with Bartholomew and Thomas, and the three men brought back a number of large fish. During the next hour, everyone chatted while cooking and eating the fish until their stomachs were full. As the sun rose above the southeastern horizon, James and the other disciples focused their eyes on Jesus' face when he wasn't looking in their direction. Although the face and body in front of them was not identical to that of Jesus', there was no doubt in their hearts that they were in the presence of the Lord.

Suddenly Jesus got to his feet, staring off toward the lake. After a long while, he turned around and gazed down at the men around the fire.

"The Lord God is giving you and humanity a great opportunity," he said. "God's victory on this earth is a fact if we determine it to be so. If you are willing to sacrifice your lives to build God's kingdom, then no force can impede His loving spirit from embracing all men, women, and children."

Jesus spoke for another hour, then asked Peter to come with him. For several minutes they walked in silence along the shore, casually observing the gulls dipping and diving into the calm waters.

"Peter, do you love me more than your own family? More than your house, your boat, and your personal things, even more than your own life?"

"Yes, Lord. I love you more than anything else in this world."

"You need to understand that before my coming, God's providence was centered on the prophets. They were God's representatives. But now God's providence is centered on His Son and the new additional teachings. We have entered a new era of history." He paused a moment. "Peter, why did I have to do another fishing miracle today?"

Peter swallowed hard, bowing his head. "Lord, I am so sorry for my lack of faith."

"My resurrection is real. There is life after death. Even though the Anointed One was put to death, I have risen, and I will bring new life to this earth. Our followers will flourish and overcome all evil."

Peter lifted his eyes to Jesus' face. "Lord, I will never doubt you again."

"Have you forgotten that I made you a fisher of men?" With a little gesture, he added, "There is so much for us to do. Surely you cannot fulfill your task from the comfort of your house, living like you did before coming to know me. Why did you return here to Galilee? Is this the right place for you?"

"Lord, where else could I go? What can I do without you? My life is not the same as when we were together. Without you near me, I feel lost and alone."

After a long moment, Jesus said sternly, "Peter! Do you love me? Do you love me more than your own wife and children?"

"Yes, Lord. You know I do!"

"How can I have grandchildren in common with a man who is only concerned about his own affairs, while ignoring the greater problems of the world?" He promptly added, "We must create an alliance between my lineage and yours. God intends to continue the blood purification of His children to make Israel anew centered on the blood lineage of His Son."

Jesus paused again. "Peter, you need to catch men, not fish!"

"Forgive me, Lord. After your death, I grew confused and frightened, not knowing what to do with my life. At least here, I know who I am, and I can take care of my family and friends while teaching them about your life and goals."

Jesus stopped walking and gave him a long look. "Peter, do you love me?"

Peter stared at him, confused over the Lord asking him the same question three times.

"Lord, you know everything! You know I do!"

"God wants to offer one more chance to the chosen people. Isaac is their chance. But if they continue to reject me, then we must go to other lands to build our base. Until now, you always decided what to do and where to go. But if you want be part of my flesh and blood of my family, then you must do what you don't like to do, and go where you don't want to go. There are people on earth who live in ignorance regarding the existence of our Heavenly Father, and His desire is to save each person."

"Yes, Lord." He nodded as they continued their walk near the shore.

"Peter, the Lord expects much from us. We have to overcome many barriers and endure much persecution." With a steady gaze, he asked firmly, "Are you willing to follow me?"

"Yes, Lord. I will follow you." After a moment of hesitation, he asked quietly, "What about Isaac? He is still so young. Do you want him to come with me as I go among the wolves?"

"Of course not. We cannot allow anything bad to happen to him.

When Isaac and your third daughter are old enough, they will unite in marriage, so our blood can begin to mingle and multiply. Our descendants need to be well rooted and protected from evil forces. As I have told you, God is offering one more chance to the chosen people through the son of the resurrected Messiah. Israel can still be the base of my blood lineage. And God still hopes to use the power of Rome to spread goodness to all people in the world."

Worrying about the future, Simon Peter thought aloud in a faint voice, "But will our descendants survive?"

"Of course. But without the support of Israel, it will be more difficult and painful. Nevertheless, no one can stop the process of enlightenment and growth that will take place from generation to generation."

Jesus fell silent, searching Peter's face for any hint of doubt. "Today I am giving you the responsibility to pastor my sheep. You and my other followers will spread God's love and truth to as many people as possible during your remaining years on earth."

"But won't people fall into Satan's temptations?"

"Yes, that is inevitable. Many will yield to sexual temptations, arrogance, and lust for power. But many others will hear my voice inside their hearts and respond. Let us pray constantly that Israel will listen to the voice of the resurrected Messiah."

Jesus and Simon Peter returned to the fire, where Isaac and the other disciples were waiting patiently. After several minutes of discussion, Jesus prayed fervently and gave his blessings on their future endeavors. Then he smiled lovingly to his son before vanishing again.

CHAPTER 41

AFTER JESUS' TRAGIC DEATH, I returned to my hometown of Magdala with Isaac and Sara. Naturally, my hope was for them to grow up in peaceful surroundings. As the story of Jesus' life spread throughout Israel, the seeds he planted during his ministry began to sprout and blossom as more and more people listened seriously to his teachings. But with this came persecution as well. One of our devoted followers called Stephen was stoned to death, and soon we all felt our lives were in peril. But miraculous conversions were occurring almost daily. Saul of Taurus, who had cruelly persecuted many of our flock, was traveling to Damascus one day when he was suddenly blinded by white light and heard Jesus' voice saying: "Saul, why do you persecute me?" This was a life-changing experience for Saul, and he became one of Jesus' most devout followers. Later on, he came to be known as Paul. Soon Jesus' message spread outside of Israel, and many Gentiles began to believe in the resurrected Messiah.

But as the number of Jesus' followers steadily increased, opposition and persecution seemed to grow more intense. We were often watched when promoting Jesus' message of love in public. Our words and actions were closely scrutinized. The authorities realized a new religious identity was developing within Israel. During those years, Isaac was united in matrimony with Peter's third daughter, as Jesus instructed, and Sara with one of his sons.

Several years after his marriage, Isaac and I quietly visited Jerusalem. It was a few weeks before the start of the olive harvest. We received a warm welcome from the large community of believers there, who embraced us with hope and love. Those were difficult times, particularly for those believers living in Jerusalem. Although the community had grown and was well versed in God's words, there was no change of heart among the Temple priests and Pharisees. For a while they had looked upon our activities with indifference but no longer. Feelings of intolerance surfaced, and persecution increased.

Herod became hostile toward the communities of believers ... to the point that he was obsessed with persecuting us. Seeking to stretch his influence up to Judea, he went after the leaders of the community in Jerusalem. While Isaac and I were there, Herod ordered the arrest of Simon Peter. Thankfully, during the night an angel of the Lord liberated Peter from his chains and guided him to freedom.

Peter cautiously found his way to the house where we were staying. The remainder of the night we spent together in the presence of the Holy Spirit. He and some other leaders loved and respected me, and were concerned about my family's safety, but they fell short of accepting my leadership. Nevertheless, I enjoyed my visits to Jerusalem, where I would give them love and support while conveying spiritual messages. The apostles would inform me about their communities, but rarely did they give much importance to what I had to say. And when they did listen to my suggestions, it was only out of respect for my husband.

Even though they didn't understand that I, as a woman, was essential for the growth of our spiritual communities, I could not help but respect all of Jesus' apostles and other followers. After all, they daily sacrificed their personal desires and families while struggling against many adversaries. Even now, there are many brave men going from town to town, and even visiting lands around the Mediterranean Sea, confronting difficult obstacles along the path of faith as they spread the message of love and hope and spiritual resurrection. I pray constantly for their health and protection. Some nights I'm not even able to sleep, for I worry about their sufferings and tribulations.

The day after Peter escaped from prison, I felt a need to pray and meditate. So I climbed the Mount of Olives to ask God to pour divine blessings upon those faithful followers spreading His word. Although it had been cool and breezy that morning, it was now warm, and I found myself perspiring as I followed the path winding up the side of the mountain. My eyes darted around the rocky ground as if they were looking for the tears that my husband had shed that woeful evening when he was betrayed by Judas and arrested by the Temple guards.

Stopping to catch my breath, I sat on a large rock with a flat top and observed the buildings and rooftops of the city. After a short moment of reflection, I closed my eyes and prayed deeply. Minutes later, with my heart full of love and devotion for my Lord, I felt my entire being permeated by the presence of his spirit.

When I opened my eyes I saw Jesus standing nearby, a loving smile on his face as the afternoon sunlight gave his hair the appearance of shimmering gold.

"Mary, I felt your heart calling out for me."

"Oh, dear Jesus! It's so wonderful to see you!"

Still smiling, he said with a note of concern, "What is wrong?"

Not surprised that he could sense my troubled heart, I replied, "Dear, many of your followers have been struggling and suffering so very much these past few months."

"Yes, I know. But they must endure all hardships with grateful hearts in order to set a spiritual foundation for future generations ..."

"But lately the persecution has grown much worse. Some of your disciples were beaten, and Simon Peter was arrested yesterday by Herod."

Jesus gave a short nod. I realized that he knew about these events well before I did. With rising frustration, I blurted out, "If the high priest and other religious leaders would only humble themselves and listen to your teachings, then we wouldn't have to scurry about in secret like frightened mice!"

"Mary, it's now clear they will keep rejecting me. There is no way to present Isaac as the direct representative of my blood lineage. As a consequence, the Second Coming cannot take place during this generation. It is too dangerous and will fail."

With a sigh of resignation he added, "Since most people don't accept me as the resurrected Anointed One, they certainly won't accept my son. My blood lineage is forced to live in secret for reasons of safety, at least until people are able to understand and accept God's will. At that point, another true Adam will appear and establish God's kingdom on earth."

Jesus paused a long moment, turning his gaze to the Temple beyond the high walls of Jerusalem. "Mary, the time has come for us to increase our effort beyond Israel's borders and start witnessing to the Gentiles. We will spread God's love and truth throughout the Roman Empire in preparation for the Second Coming."

I gave thought to this. "When is the Second Coming?" I asked anxiously.

"When human societies adequately develop and the human heart is prepared to receive God's truth." His tone changed. "Mary, my return will be in spirit, not in flesh. I will come again to guide another, the third Adam, whose mission is to clarify my nature and task, and to continue on with the work I would have done, had I been received well, according to God's desire. He will vindicate me. Then I will be recognized by all humanity as the first perfected Adam. But from now on, all our efforts should focus on spreading my teachings. We should also focus on preparing a nation. This nation will have the responsibility to use its influence to spread God's culture to all corners of the world."

With my arms hugging my knees, I asked curiously, "Lord, what will happen in the days of the Second Coming?"

Jesus glanced at the Temple again, a look of regret crossing his face. He spoke in a solemn tone. "At the Second Coming we might see a repetition of similar events that tormented my ministry during this generation. There may be the same lack of belief, and persecution may arise again from religious and social leaders who resist changing their set ways of thinking and behaving."

Frowning, I thought aloud, "It sounds just like what the priests and Pharisees have done to you by opposing your teachings."

"Yes, Mary. In the future God wants to avoid the same injustices this skeptical and faithless generation of religious leaders has committed against me. Those religious leaders who are 'the columns' that support God's values will crumble, losing their influence. This is what I meant when I once said that the columns of heaven will be trembling."

I closed my eyes, considering his explanation. "So you are saying that powerful people in the future, like those of today, will initially reject God's truth and oppose the Lord of the Second Advent."

Jesus nodded. "Don't forget that lust for power is part of the basis of the original sin. The archangel is well entrenched in his selfish position, and will do whatever it takes to hang on to his power."

With sorrow etched in his face, he continued, "Our Heavenly Parent could quickly resolve all forms of suffering if only everyone were humble enough to recognize that their selfish desires are an impediment to the realization of God's kingdom. That is why I said that not everyone who says 'Lord! Lord!' Will enter in the Kingdom of Heaven. Many will say to me on that day, 'Lord! Lord! Didn't we prophesy in your name? Didn't we drive out demons in your name? Didn't we do miracles in your name?' I will tell them clearly, I never knew you. Get away from me, you who do evil. "

Jesus turned slightly and looked toward the east gate of the city. When he moved his eyes back to my face, I asked, "Who else will oppose the third Adam?"

"Many people place too much emphasis on sexual pleasure. Such people will mock and persecute the third Adam, who will uphold an absolute sexual standard between husband and wife."

"But isn't it a natural feeling given to us by God, causing men and women to be attracted to one another?" I asked with a little smile crossing my face.

"Naturally," he said, smiling as well. "Sexual desire is part of our human nature. But when the fallen archangel poisoned Eve and Adam with his corrupted nature, the human race became obsessed with desire for sexual pleasure, as well as lust for power and wealth and prestige. In reality, selfish sexual desire has kept humans spiritually weak. It is more evident in people who are sexually attracted by the same sex. However, this type of issue can not be dealt with violence or coercion of any kind. Love and persuasion through open dialogue has far more reaching effects than any other means. Sex centered on God's love and principles contributes to wholesome spiritual advancement for everyone."

I reflected on this for several moments. "So as you told me before, it is God's plan to save and restore all people on earth, as well as those in the spiritual world."

"Yes. Otherwise God's efforts to bring an end to human tragedy would have no meaning."

A smile crossed my lips again. "So everyone can become a child of God, huh?"

"Of course. God's kingdom will be realized one day in the future. It's only a matter of time before those glorious days arrive when people discover their God's given nature."

His encouraging words filled my heart with renewed hope, so I questioned him on a matter that I found crucial. "Dear, you often speak of the Holy Spirit. I don't think I understand it fully."

"Mary, the Holy Spirit is a peaceful force that comforts and brings serenity. This energy comes from the feminine aspect of God, the motherly nature, if you will. It gives spiritual rebirth and enduring new life to those who live in a state of spiritual death."

"Lord," I interrupted, "why did you say that whoever offends the Holy Spirit will not be forgiven?"

"Mary, it's not that God doesn't forgive … The fact is that if a person comes to know the truth but consciously leads a life contrary to God's will, then such actions are inexcusable in His sight. And if such people repent after the kingdom of heaven has been realized, then they will not be remembered by future generations as those who made a contribution to the fulfillment of God's plan. They will regret not having served God during that unique time in human history when they had the opportunity.

This is what I meant when I said whoever offends the Holy Spirit will not be forgiven."

"My Lord, though I've repented with tears for not supporting you during the early years of our marriage, I still feel pangs of guilt … I feel so ashamed before you and God. If I could only undo all my past mistakes …" My voice trailed off as Jesus stepped closer, offering me a comforting smile.

"Mary, you sincerely repented and made a strong determination to live a good and pure life by serving God and your brothers and sisters. Future generations of believers will be eternally grateful to you, especially since you are helping to build God's kingdom on earth at this time. It was for this reason that I stated that the names of my twelve apostles, as well as the names of all my followers, will be written in the book of God's history. You are the ones who are contributing to the realization of God's kingdom."

Saying this, Jesus gave me a parting smile and disappeared leaving me alone among the olive trees, ripe with fruit that would soon be shaken down and gathered together like God's children, ready to be harvested …

EPILOGUE

FOR THREE DAYS MARY HAD BEEN SPEAKING to the small group of men and women on the island of Patmos. They had listened to her story with great interest, taking breaks only for meals and evening rest. It was now late afternoon of the third day, and as the sun began its descent toward the horizon, Mary's testimony drew to a close, her voice growing emotional and her eyes large with intensity.

"It was twelve years after Jesus' death when the persecution against us in Israel became more intense than ever. Since we had promised to preserve Jesus' lineage, his close disciples and I discussed the matter and concluded it would be better for my family to move to a location outside of Israel."

Pausing, Mary searched her memory. Soon she said, "Isaac, who was already a grown man, and Sara agreed with my decision for us to move to the city of Ephesus in Asia Minor. To avoid possible danger, during our trip, Isaac changed his name to Mark, and then later, once we settled in Ephesus, he changed it again. Now he is known as John.

"We all spent many years in Ephesus hiding our true identities but without concealing the fact that we were followers of the resurrected Messiah, like the other disciples. In the eyes of others, we were simply ordinary people who loved and followed Jesus. However, in God's eyes we were the blood of His beloved Son. During those years in Ephesus, Isaac and his wife had children, as did Sara and her husband.

"With the passing of time, hostilities arose in Ephesus as well. Isaac, who now goes by the name of John and has always been actively involved in spreading his father's message, was forced into exile. Even today it continues to be that way. Only recently did I come and stay with him here on this peaceful island. Thankfully, his family is here as well. Oh how much I pray for the branches of our blood lineage to grow eternally, unchanged and undisturbed, protected by the waves of the sea while I patiently wait for the day when my eyes close forever.

"My son Isaac decided to take the name of John, the same name as his uncle to atone for John the Baptist's mistake of not properly proclaiming Jesus as the Messiah, boldly, loudly, and continuously, as God intended. And he has been writing the history of Jesus' life, that for generations to come, in all parts of the world, people might know the nature and compassionate love of his father. Jesus' heart and Isaac's heart have merged into glorious oneness.

"The day after Isaac's first child was born, we were on the terrace enjoying the cool evening breeze. Suddenly he said to me, 'Mother, we are the new Israel, the new world, the beginning of a new chapter in the history of humankind.'

"I almost fainted upon hearing these words from Isaac's lips, for he spoke in the same manner as his father. The timbre of their voices were so similar!

"Isaac is well aware of being the son and preferred disciple of Jesus. From the time he was a toddler Isaac had been very close to his father. 'Only true love can open the gates to heaven, capturing the intimate relationship with the Creator,' he said to me one time. He often talks about God's love and warm embrace as though his father were speaking through him."

Mary paused a moment, admiring the distant sea as more memories began to surface in her heart. Then looking at the men and women sitting to her left, a serene expression crossed her face. "I clearly remember one summer day in Capernaum when Jesus spoke to me of God's love and of the personal relationship that each person needs to develop with his Creator. At the time, we were sitting on a rise of land near the shore of the lake, where several boys were playfully splashing in the water.

" 'Mary,' he said, 'in the state of perfection, all of us, as children of God, will be connected by way of God's spirit. We will feel, we will perceive, we will know each other, as our hearts become one with God's heart. And we will share the same conscience, we will respect each other. And all of this will be in the presence of God. Each one of us will be in perfect unity in the presence of His spirit and love, in a perfect circle.'

" 'In a perfect circle?' I responded, perplexed.

" 'It is difficult to find the appropriate words to express the intimate, personal, and unique relationship that each one of us will have with God. Due to each person's own uniqueness, it is a wholly personal relationship, and thus, each of us has to experience it for ourselves,' he patiently explained. 'For example, imagine that the spirit of God is a great sphere, and that His heart occupies the center within the sphere. You can walk around the circumference of the sphere without moving away from the center. So from your perspective, you will be near the center of His love, and it won't matter where you move, to the left or right, forward or backward, because from the intimate, unique, and personal relationship you have with God, you will always find yourself connected with the center. Because of this type of intimate relationship that God will have with you, He will be permanently present at the center of your life.

" 'All of humanity is the surface of the sphere, and each individual, in relationship with God, is at the center. So one person's experience of love will be the experience of everyone, and that which God feels will be felt by everyone, and God's sentiments will be everyone's sentiments. The emotions of the children of God are very strong. Of course, as children of God we cannot be numb to the suffering of another person, so if we realize that one person is suffering, then we will all suffer. All of us have been created to share in the joys and sorrows of God.

" 'If one person cries from hunger, God's children, because of their divine nature, will respond in a spontaneous way and feed him. The conscience of God's children is the same as the conscience of the Father, and thus, what the Father feels the children will feel, what the Father loves the children will love, and what the Father knows about creation the children know as well,' he concluded.

"What a man my husband was!" Mary exclaimed, returning the smiles of those warmhearted people who had come to hear her testimony. "How often I wish we had been together all these years. At this advanced age of my life, how good it would be to have Jesus near my side, holding my hand as we watched our grandchildren play.

"Often I feel his presence nearby, inspiring me with heavenly guidance and comforting me with his deep love. When he appears to me spiritually, he floods me with a warm, healing light. His image looks the same as when he first appeared to me. It is as if time has stood still all these years. I recall one of our early meetings when I inquired how such a thing was possible. I was still living in Magdala, and Isaac was traveling in the company of some disciples. My father was resting, and Sara was helping my mother prepare dinner.

"I went outside to the large shed where my father kept his tools. Taking advantage of the last light of day, I stepped into the shed and gazed at the various tools that Jesus had used to repair boats during the early years of our marriage. Still hanging on the wall were the same axe, chisel, and saw that he had brought with him when he came to Magdala.

"I ran my hands across the surface of his tools, as if by touching them I was caressing his face. My mind recalled vivid images of our first meeting, and the following months when we revealed our hopes and inner thoughts to one another. I was on the verge of tears when a bright, radiant light suddenly flashed near the doorway of the shed, startling me.

"I took a deep breath, knowing it was Jesus. I closed my eyes for several moments and silently let the energy of his presence flow into my heart. Then I opened my eyes and turned slowly toward him, not to disrupt the sacred feeling. He gave me a broad smile while I looked at him in wonder, still amazed that he was able to appear and vanish at will. 'Dear, you seem to appear when I least expect you,' I uttered, stepping closer.

"He laughed softly. 'Mary, though I may be busy elsewhere, our Heavenly Father is always nearby, watching over all of you.'

"I nodded and told him about Sara and Isaac's recent activities. Jesus remained silent, a pleased look on his face. But when I told him how Peter and other disciples could not accept me, a woman, as any kind of spiritual leader, his eyes narrowed and his lips tightened into a thin line. But he made no comment or asked any questions. So I assumed he already knew about the situation and felt no need to discuss the matter. After a short while of silence, my curiosity got the better of me, and I inquired how he was able to travel so easily from one world to the other.

"Almost as if he had expected the question, he replied smoothly, 'Only divine spirits have such ability. However, there are divine laws that regulate the relationship between the two worlds, and I move according to those laws.'

"I remained absolutely silent, giving him my complete attention, while through the open window I felt a nightly wind that swayed the branches of the trees. At that moment, no other reality existed but the two of us.

"After finishing, Jesus gave me an affectionate good-bye and vanished, but not before asking me to continue loving his disciples as much as I loved our own children."

Mary paused, gaining control of her soaring emotions. Breathing deeply, she studied the kind faces of the people sitting in front of her.

Gathering her thoughts, she went on, "Jesus often appears in my dreams, explaining how best to spread his teachings and protect our lineage.

"During those spiritual encounters, I wanted nothing more than to listen to his teaching and make sure I would have a clear understanding of it. His words are like a cool breeze on a hot afternoon."

"On one occasion when he appeared to me, I asked, 'So each time that you reach a new spiritual level, it's like a small resurrection has taken place, isn't it?'

"Jesus nodded. Moreover, I realized that once the physical body has fulfilled its purpose, it dies and returns to the earth forever, while the spirit returns to God eternally. For that reason, I understood that there would be no physical resurrection in the Last Days, only a spiritual one. People need to understand that the spiritual world exists in reality, not just in our imagination. There is actual life there, and it's quite active. The possibility of internal growth is enormous in both worlds.

"How many precious memories I have of my husband! Even though the years have consumed my youth, they have not erased the memory of his words, of his gleaming eyes and friendly smile. On top of this island, there is a soft breeze. It is here that I take refuge during the morning hours in the company of my memories. I let its faint wind caress my face. Awed by its beauty and by the peace that emanates all around, I smell the sea while observing the fishing boats that slowly disappear over the horizon. I think about the life that could have been. I think about Jesus constantly, wishing that the winds passing across the island would capture my thoughts and my love and carry them to the top of the sky so he could feel them. My mind goes back to that summer night when we were in bed in a warm embrace. I felt so completely cared for by Heaven, with my head on his chest and his hand on my head.

"Stroking my hair, he reminded me, 'Always keep in mind that supreme perfection is not only of the individual but also of the couple. In truth, the pathway to perfection goes through the relationship between husband and wife, as they perfect their heart and character together centered on God's divine love and finally become perfected parents as God is.'

"I understood that woman is the complementary part of man, who completes him just as he completes her, and it is in that unity that God is reflected.

"Oh, Israel! Why didn't you listen to my husband? Are you still looking for a king from the lineage of David? God gave you His Son, the Messiah, the Savior, and the king of your house."

Mary wrestled with her frustration for a moment, then heaved a big sigh and let it go, in an effort to regain her composure. Seeing that the hour was late and she had reached the point of closure, she asked everyone to bow their heads as she ended in prayer.

"My dear Heavenly Parents. You made him, and he was born as the Son of man after a profound and careful process of purification. You let him grow as a tree of life, and You patiently taught him about the great importance of the Messiah's mission, the task of bringing a clear understanding of Your nature and the divine nature that dwells in each human being to the chosen people, to the pagans of Rome, to the children of Ishmael, and ultimately to all humanity. With the help of his brother John the Baptist, he could have gained the confidence of the chosen people, presenting himself as the true Adam, with true Eve at his side so that we could have been welcomed as the new parents of humanity.

"With the help of the people and the religious authorities of Jerusalem, Jesus could have become king of Judea and Samaria, then later the legitimate king of all Israel. Then he could have ensured the survival of our family and our descendants. His task was to remodel the government and all institutions, to give life to new traditions, customs, and laws, and also to shape the character of the entire nation in such a way that Israel could have reflected Your nature and divine laws, as well as the true nature of human beings. In just a few generations, all the footprints of evil would have been erased from the face of the earth and of the spiritual world, as a new earth and new heaven were born, populated by perfected men and women, the children of God who could live eternally in the company of Your glorious spirit.

"But tragically, Jesus found no faith in the hearts of those leaders who should have rejoiced to see him. Due to the adverse circumstances, he was pressed to give his life in order to preserve the covenant that You had established with those whom he loved so much. Through his victory on the cross, You, dear God, offered one more possibility to the chosen people. These have been years of great expectations, particularly for the church in Jerusalem. With the death of Jesus, Your desire was for the children of Abraham to accept Your resurrected Son, and to help expand his blood lineage. Then Isaac would have replaced his father in all his glory in the position of the third Adam, fulfilling Jesus' promises to his disciples that they would witness the Second Coming of the Lord before they left this world. But all hope faded with the increase of persecution and hostilities toward my husband's followers. Even that possibility has now been lost.

"How many years will pass until humanity sees the third Adam and Eve appear, so they can fulfill those goals that have not been accomplished during our precious time?

"Dear Lord, will You be choosing him from the lineage of Abraham, or will you look for Your champion from distant lands?

"Will the Lord of the Second Advent find faith in this world, or will he be rejected again and suffer at the hands of those who should be the first to recognize him?

"My dear Heavenly Father and Mother, I pray that we may always be humble before You, that Your kingdom of true love and peace might come quickly to us all. Amen!"

INSPIRATION FOR

JESUS THE SECOND ADAM

In *Jesus the Second Adam* I endeavor to address the important dimensions of the life of Jesus, from the mysterious circumstances of his conception to his decidedly short public ministry with the apostles, from his possible intimate relationship with Mary Magdalene to his tragic death and resurrection. The book underlines the responsibilities of those figures that in one way or another were vitally connected with the critical moments of his life. In it I seek to bring to life the delicate interplay of the sacred and the mundane through the possible interactions between these various personages.

According to the Gospels, Jesus was conceived by the Holy Spirit, but was it only the Holy Spirit as a spiritual entity that caused Mary to become pregnant? Christians accept the identity of Jesus as the Son of God, but many have started to question the official view of the Church concerning his conception. Many consider the possibility that Jesus had a biological father. If he did, then who among the characters mentioned in the story of the nativity could be the one?

Obviously, in the eyes of Joseph's relatives Jesus was an illegitimate son. We have to take into account that not everyone had received a spiritual revelation about his conception. How did the attitude of Joseph's family and the neighbors affect Jesus during the early years of his life? It is possible that at a certain point people knew that Joseph was not the real father of Jesus.

The Gospels do not present a complete and detailed description of Jesus' relationship with his extended family either. For example, traditional belief holds that John met Jesus for the first time at the Jordan River, just at the moment when Jesus asked to be baptized. But is it not possible that they had met earlier? After all, they were close relative. What was the real link between them? Why, after testifying that Jesus was the Messiah, did John assume the role of a passive spectator instead of becoming an active disciple? Why, during his stay in prison, did John send his disciples to ask Jesus whether he were indeed the Messiah, or whether they should wait for another? What made John doubt? Was it necessary for John to die prematurely, as Jesus did? What were the human and spiritual circumstances that brought about such tragedies?

In the book I also explore the possibility that Jesus was married. That may sound blasphemous, but in the Jewish tradition a man is not a man if he does not marry and procreate. Perhaps his marriage did not work out, but most Jews got married early in life.

It is clear that the Gospels do not offer a full and detailed picture of Jesus, including the meaning of his words and his mission. I think that this is why there are so many denominations with various interpretations.

Jesus, according to the Christian belief and my own, was the Messiah. He came to free men from slavery to sin and to guide each human being to discover the inner beauty of his or her soul. His main mission was to help each one of us to become human beings in the image of God, as he was. But given that the world is still in such chaos, I think we can agree that neither his mission nor our responsibility has yet been completed.

What happened to the promises God made to Abraham and his descendants? What happened to the Christian doctrine? Who is Jesus? Is he truly God? Could it be that he had a wife? Can we be sure that the premature death of Jesus was the one and only way of obtaining salvation for humanity? Was the crucifixion the original will of God, or the result of misunderstanding by those who were prepared to receive him? Is it possible that, despite the huge sacrifice of the early Christians, Christianity began with the wrong understanding?

Through this book, I put forward a line of thought that leads the reader to reflect on Jesus from a perspective that is different from the traditional one.

Although I do believe that some aspects of this novel are true, others are purely fictional. Therefore, I would like to remind the reader to keep an open mind and to know that what is in this book is not meant to be a new Bible. In fact, it is not my intention to present the content of this novel as absolute truth.

Finally, I want to underscore the point that my purpose is not to offend anyone's cherished beliefs but rather to invite the third-millennium reader to consider, *Perhaps ...maybe ...it could have been that ...*

ACKNOWLEDGMENTS

I would like to thank Suna Senman-Lane for helping me shape the first chapter and Burton Leavitt for his enthusiasm and support in editing the book. I also would like to thank Don Druker, Melvin Haft and Stephen Osmond for reading the manuscript and giving me feed back.

ABOUT THE AUTHOR

PIETRO MARCHITELLI continuous search for understanding God has brought him to appreciate the richness that each faith can offer to humanity.

Pietro is a dreamer. He dreams that one day we will live in a world free of violence where there will be love and unselfishness. He believes that world peace can come only if man resolves the turmoil within himself becoming a vessel of goodness. After all, the world is the reflection of oneself state of mind.

A foreign language teacher, Pietro has a Master degree in Religious Education and one in Spanish Language.

Author website for more information and to order books:
www.JesustheSecondAdam.com